D0385867

THE CROWN AND THE SHADOW

BY PAMELA HILL

The King's Vixen
The Crown and the Shadow

PAMELA HILL

THE CROWN

AND THE

SHADOW

THE STORY OF FRANÇOISE D'AUBIGNÉ

MARQUISE DE MAINTENON

G. P. Putnam's Sons   *New York*

Library of Congress Catalog Card Number: 55-5667

MANUFACTURED IN THE UNITED STATES OF AMERICA

Contents

To J. AND M. C.

PROLOGUE

Saint-Cyr, 1717

CZAR PETER ALEXIEVITCH lay back in his carriage and twisted together in his fingers a complicated knot of yellow silk. The exercise of this ingenuity he found allowed his thoughts free play; his mind was disturbed when his fingers had nothing to do. Now, conscious of the gliding silk assembling itself under his hands' touch, he also felt, in their proper perspective, the comfort of the cushions on which he lolled; and saw the coach, ornate and gilded and of a shape too high-swung to be employed in his native Russia, bowling along the flat dust-colored roads that the late King Louis had made.

He had left Versailles behind, and that vast unfinished monument to the precision of dead royalty had failed to impress him, as the bowing and scraping of the ornate, dissolute new Regent's Court had failed to do. He could have all of that, and more, at home in St. Petersburg; it was not what he had come to Europe to find. There, or in half-Oriental Moscow, they also had gold and silver plate and the intricacies of ritual; a single archimandrite's crown, one massive robe woven of metal threads, could oust the competition of Philippe, my Lord Regent of France, as a parrot outshines a wren. Philippe d'Orléans, with his record of suspected poisonings, his painted lisping men-women and his passion for his own child! Ah, they could all copy the dead King's taste for ceremony, without possessing his innate good taste which had known the borders of ridicule and avoided vice!

The Czar's fierce eyes rolled in his head, as they would do

I

when he was remembering something; he thought now of the great equestrian statue of dead Louis in the courtyard of Versailles. That poised patrician figure looked down the road to Paris, deciding the eligibility of all who might come; ruling, still, over Versailles, as it had done in life. And within, also, one felt the influence strongly. It was still possible to do so in every petty court in Europe, where princelings dined in state off gold instead of attacking a basted bone with their teeth and fingers, as formerly. Had there ever been a man who ruled so in death, as he had influenced every civilized country while living? One included also those on whom he had made war.

The coach sped on; the knot swelled and grew in the long, deft fingers. Peter looked at his own hands curiously, aware of their great strength and of how they could strangle an ox. He had wrought with them once in Deptford docks under the eyes of William the Dutchman, who had made himself King of England but cared little enough for it, and had been astonished to behold the great Czar with nails and tools, soiled and sweating, among the workmen. William was dead now and the English had a German on the throne. The coach rumbled and shook with the Czar's throaty laughter. One had to go into the world to know the world. What things there were to see!

He thought now of the thing he was to see today, listed as an item to be understood in his mind that desired to know everything. With his voracious grasp on life, it was not possible that he should return home now and leave one riddle unsolved, even though the solving of it involved only a visit to a very old woman. The relict of the Grand Monarque, he thought, the widow of King Louis; and such a widow! It was said she had once held all Europe in her hand. The King's will had been her will to such an extent that he had no longer given first thought to his own inclinations. It had been widely known that if one wished to stand well with the King the swiftest way to do so was to obtain the goodwill of Madame de Maintenon.

"They say he wished to have her crowned," he thought, "but she would have none of it." She lived retired now, these last three years, at Saint-Cyr, that foundation she patronized for the relief of penniless girls. She must be almost ninety. An old cadaver, preserved from a bygone age; conveying the image of dead pharaohs, or of the aged tortoise in the gardens of England that had, one understood, been living in the time of Ruric. Impossible to have returned home without seeing her!

"The interview was difficult to arrange," Peter told himself in congratulation. The old lady lived retired and private; the glory of the Czar of all the Russias was no temptation to her. He, though, had been the more tempted by her unwillingness to insist on viewing this phenomenon. A monument to discretion! Such things were strange to him, understanding though he did the capacity of a woman to rule a country from her bed. Russia had many such women, but they were not of the type of Madame. In the end they had prevailed upon the old lady to grant him an audience. His eyes protruded with curiosity. Such things could not happen in Asia, where his word was obeyed without question. But it was his greatest wish to introduce European customs to his country; he must be satisfied then with the personal inconvenience that they might cause him in this instance.

Ushered into the great hall of Saint-Cyr and upstairs, his attendance following, he was aware of the closed, sheltered air. Everywhere, at doors and windows, curtains hung; there was a scent of snuffed candles and of the late burning of incense. Madame was a devout Catholic. He remembered the sneering face of the agnostic Regent; it had become fashionable to deny God since the death of the King. "When she goes out," Philippe d'Orléans had said, "—but of course she has not been out for years—one may behold a catafalque, swathed in black draperies: her sedan chair! She abhors drafts, and even when in the Palace would sit thus in a draped upright coffin lined with plush, or in bed." And Philippe and the Duc de Saint-Simon, who hovered near by, had sniggered. The old lady still, it appeared, aroused considerable hatred. It had been difficult to find out in what

3

way she had injured these gentlemen. "It is as always," the Czar thought, "and they are afraid of power in another."

He flung his great head back on his shoulders and strode into the room. The tramp of his following's high boots vied with the rustling of black skirts; everywhere were these women, dressed as nuns. He had seen the young girls grouped downstairs, brown-clad, rosy-faced above high collars, and with eyes round with awe at sight of the great strange Czar. They wore small coifs of white lawnlike flowers, nodding. It was another world from the Orléans Court, less than ten miles distant.

"Does she ever regret Versailles?" he wondered. A great desire had arisen in him to see her. There had been a portrait, hung in the late King Louis' rooms, of a fine-eyed woman in black satin and rich lace; she held a little girl by the hand. He looked unconsciously for the woman, here in this room. Folly, he told himself; all that had been many years ago.

A great bed stood in one corner of the room; a fire burned in the hearth. The walls were bare and simple, the furnishings not rich enough for the relict of a king. A crucifix— icon, as he called it—hung on the wall, with a prie-dieu near by. A woman stood by it, curtsying to him.

"Madame?" he said, advancing to the woman. She was old, her gray hair covered with black lawn; her face was set in placid lines. He attempted to kiss her hand. "It is a pleasure—"

"Madame will receive the 'Comte du Nord.'" The woman smiled. "I am Marie d'Aumale."

She led him to the bed; the curtains were almost closed and he could not see who, if anyone, lay there. "Madame is not well," she whispered. In the shadows he made out a form; a hand moved. "Who is there?" he heard an old voice say. The firelight made leaping shadows among the drawn curtains.

Mademoiselle d'Aumale answered in a voice that was gentle, as though speaking to a child. "The Czar Peter Alexievitch greatly desires speech with you, *ma mère*, but not if you are not well enough today."

4

Ma mère? he thought, in bewilderment. Had she children, then?

Forthright, he asked of it. The other woman's eyes surveyed him steadily. They were gray, and shone with a clear light.

"Madame has been more to me than any parent could have been. I have the happiness of being her companion."

In the bed the old woman stirred. His eyes grew used to the darkness; she wore, he saw, a white frilled coif.

He bent forward; he was reminded of his own old nurse, a Georgian peasant woman who had lived to be almost a hundred. She had been pleased to see him always and to drink with him a hot bitter beverage made with lemons and the stems of *hakto* leaves. He spoke now as he would have done to the old nurse.

"How is it with you and what ails you, that you are not well?"

A pair of eyes, very bright, surveyed him in the half-dark. "Nothing but a great age," came the reply, and he had the impression that she was smiling. He shifted the near curtain slightly, to obtain light; the calmness of the aged face intrigued him. His full eyes met those of Françoise d'Aubigné, and were held by them; in the end it was the Czar's glance that fell. Always he was to remember the impression he had had in those instants, of the woman of the portrait, grown old through many years in peace.

"I have nothing to say to her," he thought in regret, "I have no ambition beyond this world; her thoughts are fixed on the next."

But she spoke to him with intelligence of his journey, and entertained him courteously. He found her dry, precise knowledge of matters stimulating. As a woman, even an old one, she bewildered him; he had never met anyone like her before. She was cold, he thought, with that air usually found among Englishwomen; but the English were vaguer and more vapid, without the quick-thrusting quality of wit that she possessed. At the end of a few minutes Mademoiselle d'Aumale came again and said that if he wished it they would be glad if he would partake of wine. Peter gazed in

5

astonishment at the delicate glass and tiny cakes they brought him, knowing also that they had been brought to end his interview with the ancient lady, who must be tired.

Seated in his coach again after the visit was over, he found that he could not rid himself of the remembrance of the cold old woman. "Is the mystery solved of her power over King Louis?" he thought. "No, it is not."

He bit his fingers, turning at length to the knotted silk cord again. That old woman at death's gate there—that mummy! How could she still possess the calm assurance of power, when strength no longer remained with her? What had been her secret? "When I lose strength, I will have no more power," he thought, "and I will die."

What did she think of, there all day in the bed, and in the night's dark hours? Of God, and her approaching end?

"It is a different world that I have seen," he thought. He wished now that he had asked her what her thoughts were.

Françoise d'Aubigné lay still after he had gone, her mind active although her body was very tired. About her she heard the rustle of d'Aumale's movements, and once the companion looked in between the curtains to see if she were asleep. She was not, but kept her eyes closed; Marie would be wanting to talk about the Russians, and she knew a desire to be left to herself for a little while. The curtains drew gently again and she felt the warmth and darkness close about her like a wall. A coffin, they said she lay in now; soon she would be in a tomb. She had no notion how soon the summons would come that she had awaited these many years. In the fashion of the very old, she regarded it calmly. They would bury her body here, among the kind hearts she had loved. She had never wanted royal estate, and she did not desire a royal funeral.

She thought of the large-boned, full-eyed Russian who had been here today, with his fantastic whiskered following thrusting in behind him. They had gazed at her, she knew, as though she were some animal; opening the curtains like the door of a cage, the better to stare. She had endured it

6

for a little while, but she was glad they had gone. It might be that the Czar of Russia was her last visitor. She smiled a little. A well-meaning man; a savage, Louis would have called him. An *inconnu*. Louis had had in the last instance an almost unvarying dislike of anything that was not French.

"Yet he loved the little Savoyard," she thought, "who died." A half-remembered pain tore at her heart, remembering how she also had loved that young girl, the wife of Louis' eldest grandson and mother of the present little King. She had died, while they, the old, lived on. There were so many dead to remember.

"It is the penalty," she thought, "of being old." If she had the strength to write she could put many things in her memoirs. While she had been able to compose them there had never been the time. She had written, it was true, many hundreds of letters, but who was to tell whether those would be preserved? No, the only one who could be sure of obtaining a reading by posterity was the little wasp, Saint-Simon, who sat now at the Regent's Court writing his "Secret Memoirs" about what had happened when he was only a small boy. People would believe Saint-Simon because, while seldom accurate, he was invariably picturesque.

"If an added twist makes for greater sensation," she thought, "he will put it in." That had been no crime in the days of Molière, but when one dealt with reputations of living people off-stage, it was different.

She moved a little, in irritation. If only she could write! The thought of Louis de Rouvroy de Saint-Simon scribbling at Versailles, promulgating his twisted truths about her together with his advanced ideas of government by a benevolent aristocracy, was hard to bear. Aristocracy! A parcel of empty-headed fools, caring nothing except for pleasure, frittering away the country's consequence between them, squandering all that Louis had gained!

But she had never taken anything to do with gain, punishment or persecution.

"I was only his wife," she thought. "They find such a thing difficult to credit, in these days when wives and husbands never see each other."

7

If she could write, what would she say? Where would she begin?

The curtains moved a little in the stillness, reawakening her fear of drafts. She raised her head to call for d'Aumale and then, thinking, subsided again. Why, had not the answer to her question been sent to her; where to begin? For surely the commencement of her story began with the cold, the wild wind blowing about the docks at La Rochelle; and a child standing there, her thin skirts whipped about her, and her whole world's belongings clutched in a bundle under her arm?

It had been so cold then, she had thought she would never be warm again. There had been nowhere to go out of the cold, all those years ago; those many years ago!

She stared into the darkness, remembering; no longer seeing through the drawn curtains the comforting glow of the fire.

PART I

The Keeper of Turkeys

I

THE WIND howled and whipped the gray sea into fragments; the frozen rain blew inland. Beyond, the jagged line of the town's roofs was lost in the darkness that had come down. Françoise sheltered her face with her one free hand and tried to see beyond the blowing sleet to where the land-line lay; elsewhere, if one could turn in this wind, there were the ships. They rocked at anchor in the harbor backed by three great towers, from one of which a light shone, picking out the restless water and the lined blocks of rough-hewn stone, jutting brokenly like sharks' teeth out of the sea. The shattered mole had delayed their entry, she had heard, till it was late, and almost dark.

Now that night had come she felt afraid, a little. It was a different fear from that she had felt on the voyage, the day that someone had sighted English ships far out to sea. The English had cut off their own king's head lately and were unlikely to show mercy to foreigners with whom they were at war. But in the end the odd new flat-shaped vessels—frigates, Captain Duparquet called them—had passed out of sight. In any case, as Maman said, they themselves had little enough to tempt pirates, possessing only what they stood up in.

This was France. She said the words over to herself flatly, having done so many times since yesterday's first sight of gray land against the skyline. Repeating the words, she had hoped, would bring belief; "This is France. This is France, and I am home."

That had been when she hoped Tante Arthémise might be waiting on the wharf. At the sight of that tall figure, with its very blue eyes and long-nosed jolly face, the last two

11

years would have receded, she was certain, in a moment. They had been years of heat and fever and poverty, and Maman's harshness and Papa often drunk with wine, and, worse than the dirt and the flies, that feeling, not to be described, of being a poor person, a child of drunkards, beggars, failures. That was what it had been like in Martinique and she would be glad to forget it all, and to go back again to Tante and the cousins at Murcy, where everything was gracious and clean. Day by day on the voyage, with nothing to do but watch the cutting past of the endless sea, she had dreamed of Murcy so often that it began to seem as if she really might go back; that Tante would be waiting, just as if Françoise had never gone away, and that the beginning of it all would be this, the setting of one's small cold feet on a wharf that was empty of everything after all but the wind and the men waiting to unload tobacco-bales.

Françoise shrugged more securely into her thin cloak and glanced, half fearfully, at the group that stood beside her on the wharf. Although they had come all together off the ship and into the little boat, it did not now seem that she was a part of them or they of her. They had withdrawn themselves a little. Maman stood with her cloak about the two boys. In this faint light she looked like a statue; tall, with a lock of gray-brown hair whipping wildly from beneath her close dark hood. So often one had seen Maman stand thus, waiting, not moving; her face, that had lines about the mouth and eyes already, though she was so much younger than Papa, immobile and strange. It was as though she did not feel the rain or cold, any more than she had felt the sun in Martinique. Françoise set her own teeth to still her shivering. Whatever happened, she must make no sign of feeling cold. Perhaps the second boat-load with Papa on board would come soon, and then they would all find shelter.

She looked into the gathering darkness but could make out nothing where the ships lay. Papa would be bidding his farewells in the grand manner that he had learned at the Court of Henri Quatre, toasting the captain in ship's ale that M. Duparquet would have paid for. No doubt that was why he had wished them to go alone in the boat. The child smiled, the shape of her small red mouth curving agreeably while her dark eyes shone. One could not help liking Papa, although it was better to say nothing of that. Presently he would join them, flushed and happy with wine, and would put one arm round Maman and the other about herself and lead them to an inn as though he had not kept them waiting in the cold for more than five minutes.

She thought again of Tante. For many weeks now she had pictured their meeting, experienced with the clear sharp reality of day-dreams. It was so long since she had left Tante and the château and the cousins that it was becoming difficult to remember life at Murcy clearly. In the days when Papa was in prison all the time and Maman stayed with him she had lived at Murcy with Tante Arthémise, but later when Papa was sometimes freed she had had to go to him and Maman in Paris.

She turned her head distastefully, as if to avoid an unpleasantness. Paris had been less disagreeable than Martinique, but at that time she was new to their way of life and, coming fresh from Murcy, had found it hard. Maman had been cross, she remembered, striking her once in church for turning her back when Mass was being celebrated. Later Papa had allowed her to be Huguenot again like Tante Arthémise and himself, as far as he was anything. But always there was the dirt and squalor, and Papa quarreling with Maman because there was no money to buy food, and she and Charles and Constant had been hungry nearly all the time, but Maman would not send her back to Murcy, which she said was a nest of heretics.

So in the end they had all, upon Papa's obtaining an appointment, set sail for Martinique.

Françoise shook a strand of wet dark hair out of her eyes. She felt forlorn without Papa's presence, for, although he was drunk more often than not, he loved her, which Maman did not, and she felt a measure of protection come from him. In this wet and cold which seemed to assemble about her, turning her body to ice, it would be pleasant to hear his

13

laugh and feel his arm about her waist, and his occasional careless caress that smelt of stale wine and the tobacco whose broad, perfumed leaves had hung and dried over the balcony of the little rose-colored house in Le Robert where they had all stayed for nearly two years.

"Françoise d'Aubigné! Do not stand so near the water in this gale."

Maman's voice. In spite of herself she had moved near the edge in looking for Papa, and she might, if she were not careful, have fallen over. She moved back thoughtfully. Although Maman had little love for her, because she had been born in a prison and was a girl and one more mouth to feed, she would take care not to let her fall in the water and drown. That might have happened already on the voyage out, when Françoise had been so ill with sea-sickness that everyone thought she had died, for she did not appear to breathe. But Maman refused to allow them to cast her body over the side and held her in her own cloak, warming her, till she recovered.

"Come here. Do not stand about by yourself or you will be lost. Stand straight and do not fidget. No, you may not sit on the bundles, Charles. I will not have all of you acting like dockmen's children; attend to me. Constant, keep well against my cloak. Ah, can the Mother of God not send that boat soon, or must we wait here till morning?"

That voice, so familiar and yet not well-loved; the voice of a carping woman. The figure in the cloak might have been any age. It was difficult to believe that Maman had ever been young. Tante had said she was bitter with having had much to endure and that Françoise must behave kindly to her. And so she would have done, but Maman made everyone miserable and hard like herself, so that it was difficult to behave well. At Murcy Françoise had never needed chiding, but now Maman chided her all the time; everything she did was wrong, so that although she was freezing with cold here she must not move closer to Maman to creep under her cloak, or she would be told sharply to mind her manners and stand straight in the storm that blew. It had been the same under the hot sun of Martinique, she had had to stand under it for an hour once because Maman had been angry and pulled her hair with a comb. Ah, but she was complaining and grumbling now and she had promised Tante Arthémise that she would not do so, because it was possible to be content inside oneself no matter what was happening in the world outside. . . .

But the world outside was bitterly cold. In spite of herself she could not restrain her teeth from chattering; she was in fear every minute of a sharp word from Maman. If only the boat would come! Even Martinique seemed preferable now, for at least there one had been warm. Here, among the cheerless shapes of distant houses, she recalled it; the warmth and color, by contrast with this inhospitable sky; the heady smell of grown spices, the treed hills fading into the purple distance; the sound of Papa's viola, which he played so well, ascending in the calm air of evening with a wistful quality it would never have had at home. And then Papa, having played tears into his eyes in the facile manner of all drunkards, would weep and talk of France, the land of grace and plenty, which Maman had made him leave to take up a governorship in Marie-Galante. Could she not have found out from her friends who busied themselves with his concerns that Marie-Galante was inhabited only by cannibals, who would have made a meal of herself, her loving husband and her innocent children within an hour of their setting foot on its shores? It was her fault they had come all this way for a chimera, being compelled at last to seek shelter in Martinique, that haunt of failures and second-rates where there was nobody to appreciate his, Constant d'Aubigné's, great qualities as an administrator and governor. Ah, that gallant land of France that he had left, where he had lands and estates in Surimeau, these also having been frittered away and lost through the interference of his meddlesome fool of a wife!

This, then, was France, and she was home. The unloading was all done, and the crop-haired men, roughly clad in faded woolen tunics and dark hose, had finished their task and gone, leaving only wisps of straw blowing where the bales had been. And still Papa did not come.

15

"They are putting the boat out now," said young Constant.

The little group stood on the wharf and watched the small boat come. In the bow a man carried a lantern; every now and again its light would blink and flicker with the force of the storm. Among the great moaning heaving mass of water the little boat was a speck, a straw; a high wave, a fiercer gust of wind than usual, would surely blow it away, overturn it and drown those within.

Jeanne d'Aubigné stood and watched it, with her bitter thoughts. Constant, her husband, on board would be talking in his loud-mouthed way of going now to fight for the Turks. He would never fight, any more than he would ever do anything. All her life she had been hearing of the things he would do.

She stared ahead of her at the dark waves and pictured Constant tossing, with the easy equilibrium which he always brought to everything, sideways and forth upon the sea. Presently he would be here once more and she would have to school herself to endure the sight of his changed face, his thickened voice and unsteady gait and hands. Jeanne loathed and despised her husband as greatly as she had once loved and admired him. There had been too many changes from good to bad, from bad to worse, ever since she had allowed the handsome prisoner in her father's fortress of Château-Trompette to get her with child out of wedlock at the age of sixteen. And that first child had died so that it had all been useless, and she need never have had to marry a man thirty summers her senior and been dragged after him through one debtor's prison into another, from one disgrace to another, all these years.

The boat drew nearer. As it came into focus they could see the men strain hard at the oars against the wind. Constant, who cared for all things relating to ships and sailors, raised his head eagerly in the shelter of her cloak. Jeanne watched him tenderly. He of all her children was the only one who at all resembled her as she had once been; light-haired, clean-limbed, clear of eye and brow, and she loved him. Charles was like his father and the girl resembled no

16

one at all, and those two had come after love was dead and there was nothing left but regret that she had married a sot. But now, seeing her elder boy's pale eager profile raised to the storm, she was reminded of that young girl who had walked in all innocence among the old château's green lawns. Fiercely, while the cold chilled her, she resolved that every sou saved should go to make a man of her son, although God knew how she would ever save anything.

Her mouth set stubbornly. She and the children were hungry; she herself had been for so long accustomed to hunger that she had come to regard it as a natural state and it almost ceased to trouble her. Constant *père* would have dined well enough on the salt pork and red cheese that the ship's stores afforded. When he came she would make him pay for a meal for the children even if he struck her. It did not matter for herself. Then—then—what to do then? It had been the thing that occupied her mind most, all through the long voyage, ever since it had become apparent that they must leave Martinique because Constant *père* would do no good there.

Her husband's sister Arthémise might be persuaded . . . God knew . . . to take some of the children again. Arthémise had been good to her when Françoise was born in Niort prison. She had taken the baby and brought it up as her own, and would have continued willingly, only when one was Catholic it was hard to lose a child to the wrong faith on account of poverty and Jeanne had sent as soon as might be to have Françoise back. Françoise. She had been baptized for her godfather, François de la Rochefoucauld. He and certain other notables had assembled round the font at that shabby christening in Niort church. Jeanne's own kinswoman the Comtesse de Neuillant's child had been the godmother. Perhaps the Comtesse would do something now for Charles. Perhaps . . . ah, the saints aid one, raking through the list of once-familiar great names for a sign, a straw, a vestige of claim on anyone's pity, an offer of help. . . .

"I cannot go on." How often had she said that? At Niort, in labor with that unwanted girl-child in prison. In Paris, living on crusts and filth. In Martinique, where the sun bred flies, and one's husband consorted with native women, and there was still no money for anything but wine. And now again, when after tonight's storm it would be necessary to begin again, somehow, somewhere; with a lecherous drunkard, who might be arrested at any moment again for debt or treason and again might not, but in either case would not keep her in decency; and three children to clothe and feed. Perhaps, if a connection could be worked up, she might take in needlework. She had done that before when Constant was in prison for a while, and before he came out again she had made some headway with it; they said it was incredible how little she could live on. Perhaps, if she could make the arrangements for the children, it might be possible to do so again.

Perhaps—if God willed—unless—perhaps! All her life seemed to have been made up of niggling words; scraping, nagging her husband, alienating the children. The girl Françoise watched her always with her sly dark eyes, thinking as she did that life held nothing better to do but live as a little lady at Murcy. It would give her some satisfaction not to allow Arthémise to have her back.

And yet, what else was she to do? It was useless to hope that Constant would have thought of anything.

Jeanne waited, until presently the boat came and anchored below the wharf. A progression of heads following one another up the ladder revealed among them that of her husband. His form, taller than the other men's and shrouded in a dark cloak, resolved itself out of the night and as Françoise had foreseen he cast an arm about both of them. The light of the single lantern shed itself on his handsome dissolute face and silvered hair.

"Hé! Waiting here, all of you?" said Constant d'Aubigné. "Why did you not go to an inn?"

He smiled foolishly. The drink he had taken blotted out the night and the storm for him, manifesting itself before his eyes in a golden cloud. Resentfully in it he beheld the face of his wife; why was she always there, with her scarecrow's cap, whining at him?

"But *la petite* is here." Amorously he stroked the dark hair

18

of his little girl. It was wet, which he had not expected, and he feared that she might have caught cold coming in. Little Françoise, with her silky dark hair, forced to wait in the night and cold!

He frowned. "It was careless of you, Madame. You could have led her to shelter."

Jeanne d'Aubigné suddenly screamed at him above the noise of the storm. Her face was white and changed like an aged elf's.

"You drunken, selfish fool, you have kept the money! How was I to pay for an inn?"

"Hé, hé," mumbled Constant, taken aback; it was some time since she had screamed at him. He held on, for support of an obscure kind, to his little innocent; following, and not leading the way as he had intended, he plodded after his wife and sons into La Rochelle. Seen through the driving sleet it had a derelict air, without the welcome of many lights or the succor of standing walls.

The child Françoise went with him. At times he would lean heavily on her and she could smell the wine on his breath. The tears on her face were not because of the wet. That Maman should scream thus at Papa was horrible. It had happened many times, but she had never grown used to it.

Perhaps soon they would find an inn. She was so cold that she was beginning to feel ill. She walked on, a blast of frozen hail striking the back of her neck between the blowing strands of her hair.

In the inn a fire blazed and the landlord's wife brought them soup. Françoise edged herself well back on the wooden bench so that her feet dangled above the floor. After a while the moisture started to rise in steam from her cloak and she began to feel drowsed and warm. The shapes of people in the firelit room assumed a vagueness as though she were almost asleep. Dimly she heard the voices of Papa and Maman, talking.

"Françoise." They spoke of herself. What was to become

of her? She heard Murcy mentioned and her heart gave a little turn of gladness. Papa yawned and shifted his position at the fire. Yes, *la petite* could go to Arthémise, they could all go to Arthémise. He would write when he had time.

"But meanwhile how are we to live? And Arthémise may not be willing again to take the children since you and she are no longer friends."

But Papa moved comfortably and stretched and laughed, showing his teeth, that were still white and even in spite of his sixty years, and swore that the children of old Agrippa d'Aubigné could not, in the end, do aught but love each other.

"*Ma bonne sœur Arthémise!* My loving sister Marie!"

He glanced at his wife, knowing he tormented her. Marie's husband had been the cause of the lawsuits over Surimeau whereby the d'Aubigné family had lost such means as it ever possessed. If Jeanne felt anything, she gave no sign.

An old man who had been sitting not far away from the fire rose then and came toward them so that he was outlined by the firelight. Françoise watched the light shine on his dirty white beard and thought how if he were cleaner he might resemble some king. He was very tall and his eyes, pouched like those of a great bird, regarded all of them fiercely from above his jutting nose.

"You are son of Agrippa d'Aubigné? Madame will pardon me."

He made a little bow toward Jeanne d'Aubigné, still looking ahead of her into the fire. The clothes he wore were rough like those of a peasant, but his manner was that of Courts. Looking at him, one knew him for an old Huguenot, that caste brought low by long misfortune, so that great names often tilled the land. He stared now at Constant d'Aubigné with an expression hard to read.

"You will not remember me, Constant. I am Pierre Agneau."

Constant muttered something. He might have known the man and might not, through his haze of wine.

"It is more than a few years now, Constant. Perhaps you have forgotten London, and what befell there."

Françoise beheld the two men suddenly in the silence that had come down. Papa had raised his head, as though he were listening; but there was no sound in the room. What was it that lay between these two? She knew, in a manner she could not describe, that Papa knew very well who Pierre Agneau might be, although he made pretense not to recognize him.

And gradually the silence grew more strange and terrible. Whatever words were said now would be words that would not be forgotten. And although it was not many seconds before the old man spoke again, the heaviness of waiting made it seem like hours.

"Have you walked yet through La Rochelle, which you betrayed, Constant? They have not left us a garden wall standing. They will not let us bury our dead by day."

What did he mean? And Papa, in that stricken and dreadful silence, had half risen from his seat, his face crimson from brow to throat as though he would presently curse in anger. But no words came.

The old man took his stick and began to walk, slowly and deliberately, to the door. As he reached it he turned his head, so that the words, although not loudly spoken, reached them clearly across the still room.

"I see that you have not prospered, which is no doubt God's vengeance upon you. My pity is as much for these about you as for those whom you betrayed. Others may be less merciful than I and forget their pity in their just wrath. For the sake of your children, Monsieur Traitor, I advise you not to show your face in daylight about La Rochelle. There are many who still remember."

He turned then and fumbled with the latch, letting himself out into the storm. The force of it seized his cloak and swirled it about his shoulders. The last she saw of him was in the act of settling his high-crowned hat hard down on his head; the wisps of gray-white hair straggled beneath it childishly. He did not look back again, and Maman's voice reprimanding her sharply made her turn before the door closed between his dark figure and themselves. The flames of the fire guttered deeply with the draft and then rose high again. Papa beat his fist on the table near by and called for more wine. His voice was loud in bluster for having been made to appear a fool.

"Dodderer, bleating old bell-wether ram! Who is he that I should listen to him? No, I swear to you, *mignonne*, I know nobody of the name of Agneau, it is a name not in my recollection. Things have come to a serious pass when a gentleman may be assaulted on his private business by a bleating old ram. . . ."

And then he spoke again of the Turks and how they had need of trained soldiers. "Catholic, Protestant, what is all that to me? I will be an honest Mohammedan and so square my accounts with Allah. Ah, you will all feel the lack of me once I am gone."

Silence. There was nobody else in the room. On the opposite side of the fire the little boys huddled, half asleep. Charles had an adult knowledge in his eyes. Near them was Maman, looking full at her husband. Françoise thought she had never seen such an expression in the eyes of anyone. Later she identified it as contempt.

A blight was about them, emanating like the steam that rose from their damp garments. Perhaps it was to do with that word that the old man had used. Monsieur Traitor. What did such a word mean in connection with Papa?

II

Constant wearied of the company of his wife and children and took himself off as soon as might be; no one knew where he had gone or when he would be seen again. Françoise woke one day to the sound of wailing and angry voices, and found Papa gone and the bill unpaid, and the landlord's wife at loggerheads with Maman, who had no silver. The child listened to the shrill arguments that degenerated into shame. Her face was devoid of expression except for a slight darkening of the eyes. She loathed scenes and anger and raised voices; her mind cried out for calm.

Jeanne d'Aubigné sighed, resigning herself once more to humiliation. It was not easy to ask again for aid when Constant had been so offensive to Arthémise that they had quarreled just before he set sail for Martinique. Constant might, she thought, have written to Arthémise himself; there did not seem to be any humanity in him. She had listened, with no feeling of loyalty and scarcely any of surprise, to the old man's tale about Rochelle. It might have been for that reason and it might not that Constant had so expeditiously vanished. God knew that the greatest blessing of all would be that he might never be heard of by any of them again.

She astonished even herself by the strength of her hate.

Madame de Villette came in her own coach with as much speed as was consonant with propriety, directly on receiving Jeanne's hurried letter. She was not a woman who demanded many explanations. Getting down from the coach door two mornings later they beheld a tall, well-made, competent and rather mannish lady; her broad skirts were of dark stuff, and the laundering of her headgear showed little stress from the road. Françoise ran joyfully out to meet her, petticoats flying so that the hens scattered in the yard.

"Tante! Tante! Tante! Dearest, *dearest* Tante. . . ."

It seemed that she would never be done. Had so much time really passed since they had seen one another? "Tante, you are hardly changed at all. . . . How good it is to see you again!"

Madame de Villette looked down into the small face, its sudden excited color ringed by dark elf-locks. "Calmly, *chérie*," she murmured; her own particular brand of calm seemed to settle on them both, and she returned leading the child by the hand. Jeanne waited in the inn-parlor, ready to scold Françoise for her precipitancy. "Nobody but a hoyden would run out so!" But Tante went swiftly and kissed her, dispelling ill-humor in the warmth of her own greeting.

23

"My dearest Jeanne, in the child's own words, how good to see you!" And in no time at all they were seated about the fire with Tante somehow dominating the group as she did at home in Murcy, with the stiff white cap above the calm face giving her added height and dignity; and the looks and manliness of the two boys having been commented on, and some few inquiries—not too many—being made as regarded their voyage, and the health of Papa, the purpose of Tante's journey was arrived at, without delay or fuss.

Françoise sat watching, adoring her. How thin and withered Maman seemed, compared to Tante's smooth color! Tante's cheeks were like apples, only rather long than round. Her hands were larger than Maman's, white and well-kept. And although her hair was almost silver, by contrast with Maman's which was still quite brown with only a few threads of gray, how much younger Tante seemed in spite of that! How calm she was, arranging everything as of course it should be arranged; deciding one's own future in a few quiet, well-chosen words, so that it now seemed impossible that one should go anywhere else than to Murcy!

Constant and Charles meanwhile were to come too. Maman had hopes, as she said, that Madame de Neuillant would take Charles as her page. Maman was still stiff and queer, as though she did not like Tante greatly. Yet she had returned her kiss warmly enough on her arrival. And Tante was very willing to have Maman also at Murcy. Françoise knew a sinking of shame, realizing that she herself had hoped that Maman would not come.

But it seemed there was no danger. Jeanne's faded lips set in a thin line. "It is already enough that you supply my children with the necessaries of life, as their father refuses to do so," she replied stiffly. "I myself am not incapable of earning my bread, and as soon as I can I will relieve you of the burden which I have placed upon you. Until then, I can only give you my gratitude—and, you may be sure, my prayers."

Suddenly, defiantly, she flung her head up and surveyed the Huguenot woman. That such a one should have charge of her children's souls was abominable, and still more so the conditions that forced her to yield to such a situation.

Françoise watched, fiercely loyal to her Aunt Villette. Why would not Maman be content to leave them in peace?

III

THE Château de Murcy was a homely place of high-pitched gables, thick old walls, flagstone passages, dormers and eight great towers from which one could survey the rolling countryside of Poitou. To Françoise, after she had been home a matter of days—she had always thought of Murcy as "home"—it did not seem as if she had ever been away. The very air breathed peace, banishing the reproach and shabbiness of the past few years into the realm of nightmare; as if she had dreamed it all in the little white-curtained bed in the room she shared with Cousin Marie. Even Constant and Charles, with her at first, seemed different people; calm and cheerful and well-nourished and warmly clad, never at any time a part of that unpleasantness which she strove to forget.

Charles went soon to the household of Madame de Neuillant, that shadowy lady who was her own godmother's mother and dwelt a matter of ten miles distant. Françoise was not too sorry to see him go. He was a sly precocious boy who looked like Papa and would begin soon to act like him, as one could tell already from the way he ogled the servants. At times he could make anyone do anything by being charming. He was lazy and there was some fear that he would not satisfy the Comtesse in the capacity of her page. But as time passed and there was no word of returning him, everyone assumed that Madame was pleased and that Charles' future was assured. It was promised that some day soon he should come and see them.

Françoise was aware of the constraint between households such as the Neuillants', who were Catholic, and the stronghold of her Huguenot aunt. Murcy was very much more Tante's than Uncle Benjamin's, having been given to her by old Agrippa as part of her dowry. She had been his favorite child and he had showered gifts on her, and in the great hall at Murcy his knowing old long-nosed face looked down from its frame. He greatly resembled Henri Quatre, whose friend he had been, even to the short beard and high starched ruff. Sometimes Tante would sit beneath the portrait spinning while Françoise carded her wool, and in that hour of the day when other work was done she would tell the children stories. These varied, but somehow one would always return to the knowing old man above the fireplace, and the tales of him, growing till he had reached giant stature, from the time when he as a little boy had seen the skeletons of Protestants hanging over the walls of Amboise and had been made to swear that all his life he would fight for their cause.

"And riding one day past Meillezais he saw Grand'mère Suzanne de Lezay at her window, and swore that he would win her for his wife. And King Henri was amused and helped him to do so, and danced with the bride at her wedding."

That was Marie, who always warmed to tales of the romantic. Tante frowned a little, held out a firm hand for more carded wool and said gravely, "More important than all that is the learning that made his name live after him. He could read Hebrew and Greek and Latin at the age of eight, and had published his own translation of *Criton* at fourteen." And then she would admonish the children in a few quiet words about something that did not satisfy their tutor, M. le Chevalier de Méré.

Françoise seldom needed admonishing; she loved books and she and M. de Méré brought one another mutual delight. At times she would see him as a figure of fun

26

through Marie's merciless eyes. He was small, stiff, punctilious, and very upright, declaiming in the fashion of a bygone age by means of elaborate little epigrams. To have called him old-fashioned to his face would have been cruel; he fancied himself as an arbiter of the *monde*. He instructed, he told them, families of the upper nobility, the scions of whom would in a year or two, by the will of God, be shining lights of courtesy and social grace at the young court of His Majesty, Louis XIV. That was in the winter; in the summers M. le Chevalier repaired to Poitou, partly because it was his native place and partly, although he would have died rather than mention it, because he needed a spell of rusticity to recover his funds. Living was expensive in Paris.

He lamented the necessity. Who would choose to be here, drumming Virgil and Xenophon and Pibrac into heads too thick to appreciate their fineness? Who would not rather be in Paris, the modern Athens, where everyone of taste and wit was assembled, eager to outshine one another about that honeypot, that spice-tongued lady, that goddess whose beauty had increased rather than diminished with the years, whose arms were as white as those of Venus, whose virtue and piety were unbounded; the Queen Regent of France, Anne of Austria?

But at this point Marie would interrupt him. "That old woman! They call her the *vendeuse des oignons* because she comes from Spain. She is supposed to be married to Cardinal Mazarin, and they say that already she cannot endure him, and her first husband could not endure *her*. She is a Papist, anyway." And then Marie would clap her hands over her mouth and pretend to be very frightened of the Chevalier, while all the time Françoise knew that it was herself she was afraid of having offended. But Marie was too simple to be unkind and one always forgave her for forgetting about Maman.

The Chevalier, though, soon found solace in Françoise herself for all the other thick heads in Poitou. He was in ecstasies over her docility, her attention, her swift intellect, her clear logic that eliminated difficulties as though they had been weeds in a garden. A prodigy had been allotted him, he said; and rhapsodized to such an extent that Tante had to beg him to moderate his enthusiasm in his young pupil's presence lest her head should be turned. But out of it the Chevalier still gave his tongue free rein as well as his pen; the countryside heard of this granddaughter of the Great Agrippa who bid fair to rival Agrippa's own learning, and in Paris silk-clad ladies, not without some amusement, read of this model pupil who absorbed knowledge as though it were sugar and she a bee.

He noted also her grace, which he claimed would, under his tutelage, rival that of any Court lady in the dance. He begged to be allowed to teach her dancing, the etiquette as practiced at the Louvre, the way to hold a fan. But Tante was firm. Her little niece, she said, was not destined for any brilliant future; the best that could be hoped for was to make an obedient, loyal *bourgeoise* of her; needlework and house-keeping were as important to her now as Latin and Greek, but more than any of these it was imperative that she have well-grounded morals, and this Madame de Villette would attend to herself. And so she did, taking the child aside for a time each day to lay in her mind the granite of Calvin's faith. Françoise never forgot these talks, or the matter contained in them.

She found herself in these days expanding in mind like a flower newly placed in the sun.

She grew strong-limbed and rosy; her dark hair shone with health and curled softly and naturally below her cap. The old Marquis de Villette, ambling beyond the range of his dominant wife between his books and garden, found her delightful and often sought her company. The ailing dis-obedient child of Jeanne's Martinique letters was gone, and in her place was this beautiful little creature they called Bignette, for whom life seemed to hold nothing but promise and delight.

But Tante often looked, and wondered what would be-come of her.

*   *   *

Constant was a grave sweet boy whose reserve had prevented anyone from knowing him very well. Charles they saw less of these days since Madame la Comtesse de Neuillant had accepted him as her page. Occasionally they would catch glimpses of him, very sleek and smiling, borne beside Madame in her great coach as it bowled along the Niort road. Once or twice Madame sent him to see them as promised, but never came herself. It was hard work being a page, Charles said. He did not specify the work and looked well fed enough; the serving-maids made a pet of him. He had found no difficulty in being a Catholic to oblige Madame, and Tante was therefore not too pleased to see him.

Françoise and the others forgot him in the round of every day. At night the great drawbridge of Murcy would be closed up, and those within, safe from any chance intrusion, read their Scriptures and sang their psalms in peace. At such times Françoise would see the light shine silver behind Uncle Benjamin's venerable head, and the fire send warm soft shadows among the folds of Tante's gown. Constant would look often at the fire, thinking of no one knew what; Philippe meantime, near by him, carving at model masts. It seemed that there was too much security, too much calm, to be lasting. Already her child's mind was tuned to the violence of change.

It did not come till she had half forgotten it might do so. The order of it she remembered clearly, as if watching figures in a pageant of life and death. Philippe, Marie, Tante and Uncle Benjamin passed before her eyes, not gladly as they were used to do, but fearfully, as though theirs had been the blame for what befell; but how could it have been? How could anyone be blamed for that prank, a "dare" game of boys, that took Philippe and Constant too near a pond?

Memories of that dreadful day would come to her, later, for many a year between waking and sleep; the sound of footsteps, very dull and slow, as they brought back Constant from the place where they had found him among the weeds. Constant's face, pale and curiously peaceful, with one queer smudge of green on his cheek, and his wet-dark hair. The sobbing of someone heard from far away, borne to her knowledge later as the voice of Philippe. And last of all, most terrible of all, the face of Maman, after they had laid away the body of the only child she loved where it would never see the light of day again; Maman who had arrived black-robed, veiled as though she were a widow, although it was not until much later they knew for certain Papa was dead. Maman's eyes, dry and staring at nothing out of her face that was hard and wooden, as though someone had carved it. For Maman did not cry at all, making one feel that there had been something disgraceful and wrong in one's own helpless crying; and hardly spoke at all, or replied to Tante's kind words and solaces in grief. Only once she spoke, and then it would almost have been better if she had not done so; the shock of silence after she had spoken was worse than the gentle whispering while she remained quiet.

"At least," she had said, "he is provided for. It is in the nature of things that it should have to be the one I loved."

IV

Looking back much later to the time that followed Constant's death, she always thought of it as the milestone of change. It was not so much that one day things were thus, and the next day altered; or that she was happy, and then she was not. Only, with the shortened perspective that the years gave, she could see, as it were, all things; and it did seem then that before the death of Constant the world had been bright, whereas afterward it was dun and shadowed as though by the wings of crows.

Yet after the funeral things settled down again to their normal routine. Maman, with her black veils, went back to the employment she had somehow found in Paris. The other guests departed to go their separate ways. One of these was a sour-faced elderly woman in black weeds who was made known to Françoise as Tante Marie. The survey of this aunt's red-rimmed eyes, oddly malevolent, disturbed her; she was reminded, somehow, of a vulture, that bird which came to feast at deaths. With this Tante was her husband, a small ugly bald man of the name of Josué de Caumont d'Addé. The couple did not look at one another or speak, and Françoise wondered if it were her fancy that made her imagine that everyone in the hall, when they were assembled there, drew into little groups and left the Caumonts d'Addé' alone.

Françoise was taken before this aunt, and felt the eyes surveying her. The kiss which she was expected to receive was sharp as a peck and contained no affection. "So this is Constant's girl," said the voice. "Grown, ain't she? It must be an expense to feed and clothe all of 'em. I'd not do it. Eh, Josué?" And the little ugly mean man nodded, neither of them meanwhile looking at the other. Françoise later found that it was these two who had involved Maman in the lawsuit relating to Papa's estates. Tante Arthémise sighed when she asked about it.

"It was all such an involved thing, and the lawyers have made it worse." And she explained, for the child was intelligent enough to understand, the story of Aunt Marie, who had been the ugly elder daughter of old Agrippa and not in the least beloved by him, so that it was only late in her life that he had troubled to arrange a marriage for her, picking Josué de Caumont d'Addé as one who would be unlikely to demand much.

"But he was rich and, when your Papa was short of money, he sold him Surimeau for an annual payment. However, M. d'Addé now says that Surimeau was his by right of Tante Marie's dowry and will not continue to pay; and no one is to say yet that he is wrong, for my father—your grandfather, Agrippa d'Aubigné—in his old age had a change of heart, and wished to make over Surimeau to Marie."

31

"Then he left Papa nothing at all," said Françoise.

She had not framed it as a query, merely taking it for granted that old Agrippa had left nothing at all. Many people were angered with Papa, who had not written. Herself she had almost forgotten him, and was surprised when her aunt flushed in replying.

"My father was—displeased—with my brother Constant. They had not met for many years."

She considered the child before her, ready to change gracefully to some subject less painful for her to hear. There was no need, she thought, to tell Françoise of her father's perfidy to *his* father. No need to tell of Constant as a murderer, traitor—no need to tell of many things. But she had reckoned without the child with bright dark eyes and a mind that would ferret out the truth from mysteries.

"Ma tante, once there was an old man at La Rochelle who addressed my father as Monsieur Traitor. Why was that, if you please? Was it because of that that Grand-père was so displeased?"

Madame de Villette floundered, for once, and paused before replying. She found that he could not meet the child's eyes. How was she to sift out one from Constant's many betrayals? How to say to this child who was in her care, "Your father, *mon enfant,* was the worst traitor, the completest blackguard, the coward most devoid of humanity, the debtor most devoid of shame, who ever walked from Court with roses on his shoes, into disgrace, murder, robbery, seduction, drunkenness, and jail?"

And yet if she did not do so there were those less kind who would make sure that Françoise d'Aubigné one day heard of it.

She looked into the dark eyes. They regarded her steadfastly, the long lids drooping in an adult way as if to cover secrets. She was discreet, little Bignette. One might tell her with safety . . . not like telling Charles, who would blab it about the countryside; not like discussing it with poor Jeanne, who would scarify everyone including herself in the bitterness of her reproach and hate. Arthémise sighed, and prepared to tell; gently and tactfully, glossing over the more sordid places; leaving a doubt where doubt could charitably be left, cutting, with cleanness and decency, roots that were unworthy because decayed. "If thy right eye offend thee, pluck it out, and cast it from thee." As always, she thought, the Book consoled her; there was guidance in its every line.

"*Tu sais,* my little one, the difficulty there is between Catholic and Protestant. You have seen it already in the fact that Madame de Neuillant does not often let Charles come here. You saw also how Maman, although she came to see poor little Constant, did not attend his funeral service, because she is Catholic and claims that by rights all of you should be so too. But I have tried to bring you up in the faith for which your grandfather fought and for which so many have laid down their lives in France, even though we dared not put flowers on little Constant's coffin because the ordinances say that those who will not embrace the State religion may not make use of its forms or symbols."

Françoise saw the elegant lawn kerchief, edged with narrow lace, rise from Tante's dark lap to touch her eyes. She fixed her own on it, saying in a low voice, "Yes, *ma tante,* I am very glad," and waiting for the rest of the tale. In her mind there rose the memory of the time Maman had struck her for turning her back on the Mass in the Rue Saint-Jacques. She felt a little glow on account of that and also because she had never told Tante of it. Tante hated boasting. One thought of it as a very real thing, this faith that manifested itself so clearly at the weekly gatherings, behind the great drawbridge of Murcy, to which dark-clad men and women would come far, often on foot, to join in the service and lift their voices in psalms. Françoise loved the psalms, with their noble words and their memory of the shepherd David. It was difficult to realize that one was fined for singing them in such places as La Rochelle.

But now Tante forgot to whom she talked, immersed in thoughts of the Huguenot wars and the siege of La Rochelle itself. "They held out so long in that last fortress that one would have thought they were more than human. For long they hoped for aid from the English ships, but Richelieu blocked their harbor with the building of his great mole. No food or supplies could come in and the inhabitants of Rochelle almost starved. Many died of hunger; their bodies became like skeletons. They were living on dogs and rats. Still the town did not fall. The Cardinal's men were encamped outside the walls, and every day he and King Louis XIII would walk about the great mole to watch its progress. Then storms came and it was hoped that that would wash the mole away."

Tante sat very still, a girl again, blue eyes shrewd and wistful as they gazed into the shadows. "It was hard for us outside, able to do nothing for them. But think how much harder for those within! Daily they prayed for the mole to break, but always, although lashed by the storm, it grew stronger."

"Like the storm the night we arrived," said Françoise. She remembered the pallid stones of the broken mole.

"This storm sank the ships which would have brought food," said Tante. "Once a party of women, children and old people crept out by night beyond the city walls in search of a few roots and grass. They were unarmed and could have done harm to nobody."

Tante closed her eyes. She had forgotten to whom she was speaking. Françoise saw the pale shapes, faceless, with starved limbs creeping; Huguenot women of La Rochelle in the very early day.

"The children were like little old men with hunger, the women as dead women. It is not wrong for you to hear these things for it will enable you to realize that you are, no matter what befalls, more fortunate than they. However hungry you have been, Bignette, you have not, I think, had to eat grass."

"*Ma tante,* what became of them?"

"They were—killed."

Silence, for a minute. In Paris, in Martinique, one would have prayed for the souls of the poor little children. But Huguenots did not pray for the souls of the dead. Against the impact of horror on her mind, shielding it, was this

34

shifting knowledge. So many things one said were right, the others wrong. The great Cardinal had sat with his armies like a giant cat outside Rochelle and had eaten children. Tante was saying now how three days after the town fell at last a violent storm came and battered down the mole.

"It is almost as though God were on the Cardinal's side."

"Or Satan," said Tante fiercely.

She began to speak rapidly of the things that had befallen the conquered of La Rochelle. The King had been so angered that he would pardon none of them. Whatever other Huguenots he was to pardon, he said, those of La Rochelle must always be excepted. The Royal troops had torn down every standing wall in the town, razed its churches. Other churches had had altars erected so that Protestants would no longer worship in them. "Ah, they did not spare them in the things they made them suffer! There was so much more. . . ."

"What had my father to do with all this?" said Françoise suddenly.

Arthémise answered in the swift cold voice she used for subjects which must be dealt with quickly. "Constant my brother went to a conference in London by which the Protestants met with powerful friends there, in exchange for promised aid revealing their plans. Constant was his father's son and no one there had any suspicion of him. That done, and everything learned, he sailed for France and having landed rode straight to the King and the Cardinal Richelieu, telling them all that the Protestants purposed doing. To him is very largely due the fall of La Rochelle."

Monsieur Traitor. Her lips formed the words soundlessly, but the expression of her face did not change. Presently she said, "Did they—the King and the Cardinal—give my father a rich reward?"

Arthémise shrugged contemptuously. "No, they put him in prison. It did him no good at all, that betrayal. No one ever trusted him again, not even his own family."

And Maman, always, had had for him that glance of contempt. . . .

*   *   *

35

Other crows' wings. Papa was dead at Orange. They had been talking of him as a traitor and all the time, perhaps, he had been lying dead, although no one could be certain whether it had happened lately or some time ago. Poor Papa, whom one remembered less as a traitor, a drunkard, a murderer, than as a loud laugh scented with tobacco and stale wine; a dark weight, leaning heavily on one's shoulder. His hands caressed her still, with the rough careless habit they had had of lingering on her hair. His little innocent, he had called her. He had been fond of her, she thought. The sound of his viola would not come again, from where it lay forgotten in dust with its strings loose and rotting. Poor Papa, dead in loneliness, no one near him. Monsieur Traitor, dead without regret.

It would have been a comfort, she thought, only once to have prayed for his soul. . . .

V

"BIGNETTE!"

A tiny figure, waving and running furiously; Cousin Marie. She held the stick for scaring the turkeys firmly in one hand; it swung as she ran. Françoise laughed, gathered up her own gray skirts and hurried toward her. The wind tugged at her curls and the basket on her arm jolted as she went.

"Careful!" gasped Cousin Marie as they came within speaking distance. "Oh, the cheeses!"

She pounced on the little basket of lunch Tante Arthémise had packed for them. At the foot of the basket, coolly among green leaves, lay small heart-shaped cheeses made of sour cream. The two little girls ate as they walked, leisurely, to where the turkeys were kept beyond the rise. They were both hungry. Marie had guarded the birds all morning and Bignette had remained behind for lessons on the translation of the Fourth Aeneid from M. de Méré.

"How thankful I am that I am stupid!" said Marie. She had no ambition to do anything besides marry someday and have very many children. She loved babies, birds and animals and all the things about the farm. She would in a year or two be pretty, although just now she was too fat. The effort of running to meet Bignette had made her breath shorten and her cheeks turn crimson.

Both girls wore little caps, tied beneath the chin and laundered plainly. The collars and cuffs of their gray gowns were also high and plain. The noise their wooden sabots made sounded less clearly here than in the courtyard; their free hands held their petticoats high to avoid the grasses. Françoise felt her strides strong and high as those of a giant, aided by the loose thick sabots peasant women wore. She gave a little sigh of content; she was happy. Soon she would see the turkeys about the field, long gray necks outstretched and gobbling expectantly. She loved these days of picnicking with Marie, in the sun and air.

Tante had said that they must wear masks to avoid becoming sunburned. Françoise handed Marie hers and watched the concealment of her pink-cheeked countenance behind the long linen snout. Marie's eyes gleamed through the slits, watching her as she did likewise.

"How ugly we are!" said Marie, and giggled. Françoise said that they were like the sailors of Ulysses whom the witch Circe changed into pigs and birds and animals. Marie listened hard and begged to have the whole tale told her. Françoise told it as they went to gather eggs, although Marie must have heard it from her many times before.

The wind tossed away the sound of Marie's laughter, muffled behind the linen. Gathering eggs, carefully so as not to disturb the fierce sitting hens whose gray glance followed her fingers, Françoise applied the story of Ulysses to her own. She also had become changed from the person she had been, although not, as it chanced, into an animal, but something much pleasanter. She even thought of her own name as altered now; Bignette, Aubignette, the little d'Aubigné in the house of Villette. Uncle Benjamin and Tante Arthémise had made her as their own. She could never do enough to show how grateful she was to them. It would not have been easy for everyone to do as much as they had for her, without showing it. And yet Tante on two occasions lately had drawn her toward herself and told her that she was very dear to them, that they loved her and would not part with her, no, not for anyone. . . . And she had been rejoiced, being always a little afraid at the back of her mind that Maman would send for her to come and live in Paris. Then it would have been like the early days, continually dragged from the haven of Murcy to stay with Papa and Maman in some squalid place, in or out of or near to a prison.

Ah, she could be a better person here at Murcy, obedient and natural and calm! Bignette was a younger, gayer person than the waif who had landed from Martinique on that night of storm over a year ago. Bignette could cook and sew. Bignette could argue over any point of theology in a fashion at once profound and sprightly, so that Uncle Benjamin, who took such things very seriously, could not restrain his enjoyment of a tussle, albeit a mock one, with her intelligence and her tongue.

"Supposing, now, Bignette, that I were a Romish priest, and I said to you so and so. . . ."

And then they would argue, and in no time at all she would have reduced the Romish priest and the whole Church of Rome to a cipher, and Uncle would call her to him and bless her, suddenly grave in the midst of his laughter.

"It may be that you will need these arguments, Bignette. I pray the good Lord that it will not be so. But you are a bone of contention, having been baptized in the Romish faith; it may be that they will try to claim you, although God forbid that should happen." And on a warning glance from Tante he had shaken his old silver head, leaving Bignette with the feeling that having been baptized into the Romish faith was a disgrace far deeper than having been born in prison.

Someone who had been at that baptism lived near Murcy and had seen her twice. Since Charles had left her household one heard slightly less of Madame la Comtesse de Neuillant. Charles had not been sorry to go, saying that the old lady was stingy and had given him hardly any money to take with him to the Dragoons but only a pewter medal with Saint Antoine on the back that no self-respecting money-lender would take in exchange. But once when she and Marie had been returning home along the Niort road an old-fashioned coach had met them and stopped, and a woman with a sharp pale face and black hair that must be dyed, worn scooped up over a frame on her head in the manner of Marie de Médicis' time, had leaned out and demanded in a peevish high voice if she might be Constant d'Aubigné's daughter.

Françoise had replied that she was, and Madame had then pulled her sharply to her—all her movements were birdlike and sharp, as if she feared lest something would be snatched away—and given her a swift pecking kiss that brought with it an odor of *sachets de violette* which had grown old and a little stale. And then, while the dust-clouds settled and stilled on the road, Madame had read her a lecture as though she had been an employer talking to a servant, telling her that in spite of what she was being now taught it behooved her to remember that her dear mother was Jeanne de Cardilhac, who through so many bitter misfortunes had never forgotten or betrayed her Catholic faith, even to the extent of braving her husband's wrath in having her children baptized in it. Madame had then fished out of the pocket of her gown a little medal, telling Françoise to wear it about her neck; this she did not do, because Tante would have taken it from her; she kept it in a box.

Then about a week later Madame de Neuillant sent for her to go and visit her at the château.

She had not wanted to go and the Villettes, when they heard of it, had not wanted her to go either. Françoise became conscious of a new awareness in their frightened

39

eyes. Always hitherto she had looked on Tante as a bulwark against the world, and now she and her husband drew close together as if for protection against some far greater power. Françoise felt the old insecurity rise and encircle her, like the tenuous weeds that had drowned Constant. This thing that divided half the families in France had not divided equally . . . one side was weak, the other strong. Madame de Neuillant was Catholic, she was the feudal overlord, if she expressed a wish that Françoise should go to the château there was no real choice but for her to do so. . . .

She had made the journey with a beating heart. The sight of the great towers of Neuillant seemed at first misted, surrounded by a vapor that came from bogs or ponds. There would be damp in the green-gray walls, soaked from the old moat up to the inner chambers. She fancied that she could smell decay in the stagnant water and in the stuffy air of the ancient hall.

Following the servant to where Madame waited, she tried through her fright to recall a vague, familiar sensation in the stuffiness; an odor, a breath. Then she reminded herself; it was incense. Madame's own chapel would be near at hand. She had been familiar with this scent in Martinique, rising from among the flowers and snuffed candles before the altar of the Mother of God, whose statue the Carib women would dress like themselves on gala days, in lace veils and a gown sewn with colored beads. And again in Paris she had noted it, at times like the one when Maman had struck her in church for being a Huguenot of Huguenots, the grandchild of Agrippa d'Aubigné.

She clenched her hands in the gray stuff of her skirts and prepared to make her curtsy to Madame. This place was not a part of her and she would soon be gone.

A vague fright, still felt in her breast, grew calm as she followed the servant upstairs. If Marie were here she would giggle at the haunted castle, where the Sleeping Beauty would certainly not be waiting in an upper room. Undoubtedly Madame de Neuillant was like a witch, and perhaps then Françoise herself was the Beauty, going upstairs to look for her spindle and being made to fall asleep for a hundred years by a prick from a pin. . . . Ah, what a fool to talk so!

Madame de Neuillant was seated in an upper room where the windows were screened by heavy curtains, so that the daylight entered from outside diffused and wan. Her face, as it peered from the chair where she sat, looked less like a witch's than an old child's, interested in a toy. "Come here," she said, and extended a hand.

Françoise advanced, made her curtsy, and kissed the hand, noting that the fingers were loaded with grimy rings. The same odor of stale violets that she had noted before rose strongly. She had a sudden great desire for air.

"Sit by me." All Madame's words were commands. When she had Françoise seated on the edge of a chair she began to question her. How old was she? Was she healthy? Did she have illness often? Was her appetite good? Did she wear out her clothes, her shoes, quickly? Was she tidy, diligent, obedient, industrious? Had her aunt any complaints to make? When her brother Charles had visited Murcy last autumn, had he anything to complain of *her?*

Françoise considered the last question curiously. It was, she felt, almost as though Madame had exposed some weakness in her own armor. Dropping her eyelids to conceal her eyes' sparkling, she reflected that some of the things Charles had said regarding Madame de Neuillant would scarcely bear repeating to that lady herself.

But Madame, mercifully, was off on another tack. "I have daughters," she told Françoise. "All of them perform their share in the day's housework. Suzanne has a spinning task and minds the fowls, Louise cleans the shoes and fetches firewood. There is water to be fetched and wood to be chopped and food to prepare and crockery to clean. Every day a certain measure of oats requires to be made out for the horses."

Françoise, while wondering why Madame vouchsafed this information to her, replied politely that at Murcy also they each one had their tasks. "Marie and I mind the turkeys; I sometimes cook. Then there is work in the dairy—"

Madame listened, nodding perkily like a watchful bird.

When Françoise spoke of the turkeys she interrupted sharply. "Ah! Ah! Then you do not, as I have heard, read Latin and Greek all day? That is as it should be. These things are not for girls to learn. You should be instructed in sewing and cookery and the arts of housekeeping. More than that is unnecessary for you, and is above your station."

"Madame is mistaken," said Françoise. "*Ma tante* encloses every day a little book of verses with the picnic lunch." She added, unable to resist an impish urge, "She maintains that it is not a desirable thing that the mind should remain empty even though the hands are not idle."

She would have gone on to exonerate Tante still further; thinking of the way she had indeed taught her housekeeping; the manner of folding linen with lavender, the way to starch a ruff; the herbs to be picked at certain seasons, either to flavor a sauce or to heal burns and scratches, whichever might be required; and the way to make cool butter even on hot days, and the way to baste a joint of meat so that no matter how old and tough it had been it would emerge tenderly from the oven. But Madame gestured her into silence and began to talk coldly of her daughters once more. This time it was not their household tasks that were put forward, but their social status; in order, Françoise suspected, to impress. Suzanne, her little godmother, besides minding fowls and spinning, was this year to have the honor of becoming maid-in-waiting to Her Majesty, the Regent Queen Anne. Françoise held her peace. It would have been tempting to mention M. de Méré, who reeled off names of the great with so much ease; but as Madame had already asked her, and suspiciously, of the books her tutor made her read (although it was doubtful if she could make much of the names when told), it was probably better to keep silence on the subject. But in the next breath Madame swooped down for more information about the Villette household, and in the course of this the Chevalier's name was disclosed. Françoise was beginning to be cautious now; the Comtesse asked point-blank about their manner of worship. Her uncle had warned her that she might have to answer questions about this and she was ready, parrying deftly and giving away nothing that might injure those who came to the services. In the end Madame accused her of concealment.

"Not so, Madame, but I am grateful to those who have been kind to me."

Madame de Neuillant's face suddenly broke into a smile. It was unfamiliar and almost frightening, engendering many wrinkles and not reaching the eyes. She made a little speech to Françoise in which she stated that she too would be kind to her, and then she rose and made the child follow her into her private chapel, where Françoise's first impression was one of the glitter of gold paillettes which swung and sparkled from the altar-cloths and the robes of statued saints.

This was a very rich place, Françoise thought. However much of a miser Madame might be, there was nothing she seemed to grudge in the beautifying of her chapel. Wherever one looked there was gold and magnificence; the crowns on the head of the Mother of God, and of the Child in her arms, shone with gems.

Madame knelt at a prie-dieu and began to pray fervently, Françoise stood uncertainly behind her, unsure if she was expected to kneel. Presently Madame rose and genuflected deeply, took out a taper from a box and lit it, placing it in a carved rack where many others burned. Turning to go out of the chapel, she fixed Françoise with her eyes, which held no anger but a terrible and determined sweetness. Later she told her that she had lit the candle in a prayer for her soul.

Somehow that sweetness and that candle affected Françoise as though they had been made of death and corruption. Arriving home at the great gate of Murcy at last, she lost no time in flinging herself, sobbing, into Tante's arms. She knew that she was afraid, although she did not yet know of what; and worse than all this she knew that Tante was afraid also.

"What are you thinking about, Bignette?" came Marie's voice.

She remembered where she was with a start, coming back to find herself kneeling by a turkey-nest with hardly any eggs in her basket, and Marie laughing at her.

"See!" said her cousin, displaying her full load. "What *were* you thinking about, Bignette? You have been silent a great deal lately."

Her round blue eyes surveyed the other, curious but not resentful. It was easy and pleasant having Bignette in the family, almost like having another sister. She did not thrust herself forward or boast because she was undoubtedly cleverer than oneself. Nor did it seem to matter that Papa and Maman were so fond of her, almost—Marie had often thought, lately—fonder than they were of herself or Philippe. But then poor little Bignette had had so harsh a life with her sour mother and drunken father that one did not grudge her a little affection to make up for that.

In any case one would never know what Bignette was thinking. She had a way of saying nothing when one asked her such things, only smiling with her little red mouth closed firmly and the long lids drooping over her bird-bright eyes. She would be so pretty, Bignette, when she grew up, with her white skin and her beautiful little hands, and teeth that when she laughed were quite pearly and even, in contrast to Marie's own, which had begun to darken. But she laughed so seldom that one was afraid she was often sad.

Marie suddenly hugged her, scattering the contents of the other basket. "I believe you have been looking at the book!" she said as a little brown volume fell out. "Well, you shall go over to the far stile, and sit there and read in peace, and on the way home you shall explain it all to me so that I shall be able to answer when Maman asks me."

Bignette smiled. "They are verses to learn," she said. "They are quite easy."

"*Eh bien,* then, you shall recite them to me and stuff them into my head on the way home."

The turkeys gobbled indifferently. Bignette went across the field to the place Marie had mentioned and hoisted herself up on the stile. Marie went on looking for eggs. Presently she raised her eyes and observed her cousin's bent head, browsing over Pibrac's *Quatrains*. "She will learn them much faster than I," thought Marie.

An hour passed. Françoise, engrossed in reading, had only half a mind to the birds. Every now and again they would wander away and then she would jump off the stile and chase them back with a stick. Turkeys were like people, she thought. They must conform to the way of the flock or else be lost.

She looked up, startled. What had made her think that? It had been one of the arguments advanced against her the other day by Uncle Benjamin, pretending he was a priest of Rome. She had been on the other side and in the end had found an answer to it. But now the answer evaded her and she was left with the fact itself. Obstinately she reassured herself as to the fallibility of her assumption. If one thought thus, all freedom would be lost. One would become like Madame de Neuillant in her damp-fogged château among her musty curtains. Freedom of thought and worship was what all Huguenots had fought for, what her grandfather Agrippa d'Aubigné had fought for. And though in France the Huguenots were now penned birds, no longer free to fly as they willed, their minds were unfettered and so would remain.

"They burned down our churches, leveled our walls. They will not give our sons preferment in the army or the navy. At every turn they humiliate us, persecute and seek to injure us. But in spite of all, the faith will remain."

An old man, one of the itinerant pastors who had spent much time in the Netherlands, had stayed one night with Uncle Benjamin and had spoken thus. She wished she could recall his name.

She listened to her own thoughts, one finger held to mark the place on the page. Often her mind would hurry ahead of her understanding, like the little brook that ran near by the stile. At times she would see a thing from all angles in a manner that could not be explained even to Tante Arthémise. Once she had attempted to do so and been reprimanded. No one who had not definite views, her aunt

45

said, could attain to an understanding of anything; they would have no politics, no philosophy, no religion.

And yet was not Tante herself a living example of moral change, denying all the cut-and-dried notions that Madame de Neuillant accepted without question? These were not matters she could discuss with anyone.

No, she would always be a person whose innermost thoughts were concealed because they had no outlet. She saw herself now thus, and also as a small grave girl seated on a stile guarding turkeys, regarding her own sabots thoughtfully.

There was someone coming now. She waited, while the book still lay on her lap. The person was hurrying and as he drew near she saw it was her cousin Philippe. She wondered what had brought him. He should have been with the Chevalier at this hour, pretending to work at the classics but in reality dreaming of ships. Since Constant's death he had become withdrawn and silent and rarely spoke, but she saw his eyes follow her often.

She smiled, the small closed mouth curving graciously; her eyes shone. Philippe caught sight of her and broke into a run. Marie called a greeting unheeded.

Françoise slipped off the stile and went to Philippe. She had the notion that something was wrong. Philippe's eyes stared as they had done on the day of Constant's death. *"Ma cousine—"* he began.

"What is it?" she said to him. Her mind ran on disasters. Was Tante ill? That would be the worst thing that could happen. . . . The sight of Philippe's hands, gesturing helplessly, brought a twist to her heart.

"It's not Maman. It's not that, it's— Oh, Bignette! They have come to take you away!"

He turned suddenly from her and burst out weeping.

Bewildered, she stared at him. He had jerked an arm in front of his face; the crimson pattern of the stuff of his sleeve came to her clearly, she would remember it. The whole world seemed to have shattered in pieces, and to have resolved itself unfamiliarly again. Philippe's voice came, oddly gruff and ashamed. "They do not know I am here to tell you," he said. "They will be waiting to break it to you at home. But I saw the royal *officiers* ride up and I waited above in the gallery while they took out the writ and handed it to Papa. I saw his face when he read it, Bignette, and then he called Maman and the two of them read together. He's an old man and it—it—they were fond of you, and I know *she'd* sent before, but they would not hear of it, and they said I was not to tell you, only now, I—I—"

"But to whom am I to go?" she said bewildered. The bright day had converted itself to nightmare.

"Madame de Neuillant. And we are Protestants and have no right of claim."

Of course she should have known. What had the Marquis said? "You are a bone of contention. It may be that they will try and claim you, although God forbid that should happen." And Murcy, with its kindness and clear air, would soon be a dream, remembered, as once in Martinique, with longing between sleeping and waking. The royal *officiers* had ridden up, the royal word could not be gainsaid. Cruel Anne of Austria, of the snow-white arms, signing away the fate of an obscure little girl who happened, by the grace of bad fortune, to have been baptized into her mother's faith and not that of her father's; what could she know of all this, or care?

In any event there was nothing to be done. She closed the little book carefully; the worn brown leather of its binding was familiar to her fingers. She told Philippe calmly that she would come with him, and accompanied also by Marie, who had gathered the tidings across the field and come to them with a face from which all color had fled, she went again down the path that led from the hill.

Madame de Neuillant had not come herself to fetch her charge. After goodbyes had been said, Françoise was put in the coach. She was in the misery of bewilderment that swift change brings; recollections, jumbled like colors in an embroidery bag, peeped out at her, without relation to time or relevance. The little white curtains of the bed upstairs

47

came to her; she would never see them again. The eight great towers; Constant's pond; the dairy. Tante's face, swollen with tears. It had been unlike Tante, the calm and gracious and bountiful. Of course, of course, Tante had promised, they should meet again . . . and then in the next breath had enjoined Françoise to be steadfast, no matter what the years might bring, to the things they had taught her at Murcy, the love of faith and truth.

The years! They stretched before her, terrifying because blank. "These things are not for girls to learn . . . you should be instructed in the arts of sewing and cookery and housekeeping. More than that is above your station. Suzanne does the spinning, Louise cleans the shoes, Françoise chops the wood, stokes the fires, feeds the horses in the stable, washes, mends, scours. . . ."

She knew very well what Madame de Neuillant would make of her.

VI

MADAME DE NEUILLANT was exasperated. She could feel the chagrin and annoyance grow, shooting up in all directions like weeds through the raked earth of her soul which should have been arid for God. For the whole of her life she had striven, in her own way, for this order; on the face of it, all one had to do was assemble one's way of living in straight lines, neat pathways made flat with a spiritual hoe and stone-gray, no color anywhere. Lately it seemed that she had achieved that end, the Lady of Neuillant surrounded, at home and abroad, by her array of placid daughters; keeping the fasts, relaxing at feasts, giving a tenth of all she had to the Church, obeying its precepts, attending Mass, succoring the poor, saying the prescribed prayers at the hours recommended. This done, not once but every day, regularly as a clock that ticks when wound, Madame began to have hopes of heaven; sometimes, while praying, she knew a state which resembled ecstasy, although her confessor warned her to beware of that. It had been during such an experience that it had become apparent to her that God wished her to become the guardian of Françoise d'Aubigné. Madame had had a sudden clear vision of that beleaguered soul, and of herself as the instrument of its salvation. Clearly she foresaw what should take place consequent on the adoption; a reclaimed Françoise, led by the hand to God's altar, and Madame herself having earned the gratitude of Heaven enabled to bask in the agreeable glow of duty well done, with earnest of garlands later.

That had been the vision. But now, as Madame too clearly saw, the reality evaded her. The reality was a stubborn, contentious, dark-eyed girl, who not only argued with tiresome clarity on matters of faith until she won, but grew so fast that all her clothes, within a short time of leaving the Château de Murcy, were too small for her. And as Suzanne, Madame's eldest daughter, was short and thick-set, the benevolent intent Madame had had of putting Françoise d'Aubigné into Suzanne's cast-off garments could not materialize. That, then, was an added expense; and of all things Madame abhorred expense. She began to watch every morsel that found its way into Françoise d'Aubigné's mouth at meals. Having decided that her ward was eating too much, she reduced the portions allotted; but still Françoise continued to grow, and the sight of her tall thin figure, carrying pails and measuring oats for the horses, began to irritate Madame with the very sight of it and the general air it had of not being cared for when God knew everything had been done to make the d'Aubigné girl feel that she was one of the family. It was not, either, that one could find a flaw in the way the middens were stacked, the fowls fed, or the oats given out in the stable. Madame had herself checked the measure on two occasions, and there had been the exact amount given, no more and no less. It was not right for any child to be so precise and so certain. Something must be done to make my lady realize the extreme dependence of her station, the amount she owed in gratitude to others. Something . . . but what? At first, when Françoise had come from Murcy, Madame had had her up to her chamber, as on that first day, treated her to little talks, intimate as befitted those of a foster-mother to a reclaimed heretic daughter. But what had the brat said? What had her answer been? Invariably Murcy. "At Murcy we did this and that." If religion was mentioned, the girl's duty to God and the Church laid down, or certain angles dwelled on, it was Murcy again and Uncle Benjamin. *They* had said that God was approachable to any of His creatures in the same degree. *They* had spoken prayers made straight from the heart. *They* had sung psalms and made their own interpretations of the Bible regardless of their own fallibility, and ridiculed the Host as a piece of bread and the Mother of God as any woman. All this Françoise d'Aubigné made apparent to Madame's ears, not in any hysterical fashion but rather in the attitude of a stern young judge. Her feet in their ridiculous sabots might still scarcely touch the floor, but she had confounded Madame on every occasion and lately, when he had been brought in out of desperation, Madame's confessor also. *Mon père* said he had never encountered anything like it.

"She is very wilful!" he said in perplexity.

"She is completely given over to the devil!" snapped Madame.

The little talks had stopped because she told herself she could not endure to have Françoise d'Aubigné near her. It was like having a governess, a preceptress, in the house. The Chevalier de Méré, no doubt in search of silver, had offered to come and continue the d'Aubigné girl's instruction, but Madame would not hear of it. Françoise had been taught to be pert enough.

However, *mon père* had other views. The little Huguenot might, he said, have an adverse influence on the children of Madame. Would it not be better for all concerned if she were removed to some institution, say that of the Ursulines at Niort?

Madame thought of her daughters. Placid Suzanne sat at a window, sewing Court braid on her gown. The insistence of bands of gold or silver braid for every lady in attendance on the Queen made one consider, although of course there was no option but to buy it. Suzanne, moreover, had done very well. Always dutiful, she had pleased her mother by the final conclusion of her betrothal to the Duc de Navailles. That would be one more off Madame's hands, and it was unlikely that Suzanne would know contamination from Françoise d'Aubigné. Nevertheless Madame thought it as well to ask.

"*Ma fillette*, has Françoise d'Aubigné ever approached you regarding matters of faith?"

Suzanne wrinkled her high pale forehead in perplexity. She tried to remember when Françoise d'Aubigné had last spoken to her of anything at all. "No, *ma mère*, I do not think so."

"Well, then, if she does you are to come straight with it to me, or put it into your confession. Françoise has the misfortune of her upbringing very strongly rooted in her head. You are her godmother and must do all you can to save her soul."

Little Louise, when questioned, could remember only one extraordinary thing about Françoise and that was how she had cried when asked to mind the turkeys. "She does not mind doing anything else, Maman. She polishes the floors and fetches water. But when I took her to the field and she saw all the gray *dindons* she cried. As a rule she says nothing."

Nevertheless *mon père* persisted. The influence of Huguenots, he said, was often so pernicious that it was not apparent even to the parties themselves. A word, a habit noted, might plant the seeds of false doctrine in a young mind. Madame listened, and hedged. She was thinking of the expense of boarding Françoise with the Ursulines.

Françoise raised her head from contemplation of the stone floor and rested her weary body back on her knees.

The flags had been scrubbed and soon, when they were dry, she would scour them again with chalk to give them surface. In spite of her weariness of body she knew an almost fierce satisfaction in a task well done. It had fortified her in the hundred-and-one sordid labors she had been compelled to do. She could lose herself in the physical exhaustion of it.

Drearily, seeing the sun beyond the high windows, she thought of Murcy. On a day like this they would all be out in the fields, Philippe and Marie with baskets to fill with the fruit which would be ripe. They would pick all day in the sun and then go home with their mouths and fingers stained with juice and the baskets overflowing. They would be laughing, having forgotten her, happy and gay.

Had they indeed forgotten her? Little Marie had come over one day when she minded the gray birds of Madame de Neuillant. It seemed that those birds would be with her always, having taken on the aspect of symbols in dreams. They had been with her when she was carefree and now again, when she was miserable, she had beheld their outstretched necks and heard them gobbling. Marie had run to her and hugged her and said how thin she had grown. . . . "And, oh, Bignette, your poor hands, how chapped and rough they are!"

Things were just the same at Murcy, said Marie. Papa had sought a fresh injunction with regard to the State's ruling regarding Françoise, but Protestants had few rights. Marie shivered. "They billeted soldiers on the Hogue family near Rochelle. They acted like beasts and the girls—" She did not finish and Françoise was left to imagine the fate of the girls. She had heard of such cruelties and the thought of their closing in on Murcy through her agency chilled her. "Tell my uncle that on no account is he to expose himself to any injury for my sake," she begged Marie.

Rather than influence them in any attempt to act further regarding her, she said less than she might have done regarding her own treatment by Madame de Neuillant. Tante Arthémise had sent marchpane and assorted sweetmeats, a cake of her own baking and a little round yellow cheese.

Françoise shared the food with Louise after Marie had gone, as Louise also was sometimes hungry.

During the silent evening meals at Neuillant, where after crossing themselves in a brief grace Madame and her four daughters would sit down to a frugal table, Françoise would survey the faces behind the high candles and think of Murcy. There, it was true, they had had longer grace, sometimes until the meat grew cold, but afterward there was enough to eat for everyone and still later the intelligence of cheerful talk. Her mind cried out for an hour of her aunt's good sense, her uncle's sharp dialogue that had taxed her wits to the utmost in reply. Here nothing at all was said by anyone; the sparse light shone on a silent table where Madame and the frightened daughters ate in silence. This world was nothing, claimed Madame; it was of greater importance to fit oneself someday to meet God.

Somehow she felt it would be better if Marie did not come again.

Madame had sent for her later. She had been angry about Marie. She said that she would not have her house contaminated by the presence of any Huguenot and if Françoise persisted in bringing them here she would have her shut up in a convent. "I am myself Huguenot, Madame," said Françoise. Madame had raised her hand and struck her across the mouth.

She rubbed the place on her lip where Madame's ring had cut it. It did not bleed now, but was stiff and swollen as though by a sting from a bee. She reflected that she would not have been sorry to get away from the Château de Neuillant, but the thought of a convent chilled her. There was no entry there for the light of day and Tante had said that nuns were ignorant and stupid women who were bundled into a cloister when it was despaired of finding them husbands. But Madame had proved ignorant and stupid enough and it was doubtful if the nuns could be more so than she.

Again and again in that upper room she had come up against a stone wall, with Madame's face peering sharp and white from round it. The smell of moths and of *sachets de violette* were bound up in her own mind with this distrust of change. However logical the assemblage of a thought, as answer to stock questioning; however heavily the dice were loaded for probable against improbable on her side, the answer ran always thus; the Church says so. Always, fortifying Madame in her assiduous prayers before a carved Mother of God decked in gems and silk. Madame had that assurance; Françoise had nothing but her wit. The candles shone before her tired eyes, the many little silver tokens gleaming on their cushions of red velvet so that it seemed that all vision consisted of tiny stabs of light. Mesdemoiselles de Neuillant would kneel in trained gowns, primly marshalled, to receive Communion, and come back smug and smiling with folded hands. Smug and assured, the entire Neuillant family, by virtue of that strength which was given them daily . . . whereas she, Françoise d'Aubigné, compelled to attend, sat breakfastless also but without the satisfaction that that condition brought.

Alone seated among the kneeling servants, stolid to all outward appearance in that air heavy with the scent of flowers, incense and guttered wax, she tried to recall the image of Uncle Benjamin and his clear faith to her mind. But the image began to grow blurred and alien, the turn of his wit less rapier-sharp; the priest, facing away from her toward the lit altar, had silver hair that shone like his. The sudden sweet clangor of the Mass-bell stirred her senses; suddenly, in the tingling the sensation brought, she caught sight of the face of Madame. It was raised and pale; its exaltation sickened her. This languor she now felt might end so; this, then, must be the beginning of that state against which she had so often been warned, the senses' call aiding a gradual subsidence into conformity; final acceptance of that drug that satisfied so many, dulling the questionings of the brain. Uncle Benjamin himself, how would he have fared had he been exposed to this scent, these sights, from childhood?

She turned, in desperation, to the Lord's Prayer. In Madame's Mass-book they made use even of that, but perhaps God would deliver her. But in that place where the relics of martyrs lay veiled in golden shrines she began to hear other voices come faintly, half forgotten; and had to stir herself to anger, almost, to remember the martyrs of La Rochelle.

VII

THE TIME approached for Mademoiselle Suzanne to go to Court and to her marriage; one day a letter with blue seals arrived by courier for Madame. Immediately the château was thrown into a flurry of expectation; the family, it was made known, would go to Paris in the autumn. Little Louise would remain behind; it was not disclosed what would become of Françoise.

Madame sent for her, after the last stitch had been made ready on Mademoiselle's trousseau. There had been a great deal to see to regarding that, and the preparation of the coach, which required padding and gilding. Madame's relative, M. de Saint-Herman, would accommodate them in Paris. It would not do to make a shabby entry, thus giving rise to adverse criticism of the future Madame de Navailles. Hourly Suzanne was deluged with instructions, none of which she required to heed greatly; whatever happened, she would never put a foot wrong. Every day lately a dancing-master had come, to perfect her in that art for Court, and her squat figure performed the complicated patterns well enough, if without inspiration. Suzanne's life would move according to such patterns, nothing ever occurring to lift it to extraordinary heights.

Her little Huguenot godchild—already a head taller than she was—watched, and while she did so Madame's word came, and Françoise turned from the ornaments she had been polishing at the end of the *chambre* and went. The tinkle of Suzanne's spinet to which she performed the dance followed her downstairs. For almost the only time in her life curiosity beset her to taste, only once, the sensation of taking part in a Court ball or ballet, of moving her body to the sound of music, expressing emotions with a feathered fan. . . .

One would soon weary of such things, she thought.

Before Madame she was grave and the Comtesse ran her eyes over her, seeing as usual in irritation how she had grown so fast that the sleeves of her gown were again too short and the wrists stuck through. It struck her as a further manifestation of the little d'Aubigné's ingratitude that she should, on entry to the Neuillant household, lose the dark child's grace she had had and instead grow tall and pale like an upshot plant. In addition the Regent had asked in her letter about the progress of the conversion that Madame had undertaken to attempt. It was galling to have to answer nothing, nothing but the expense of butter eaten, of good portions of mutton and beef and salted pork devoured. It would be bad for Suzanne if her mother were forced to admit at Court to failure, all through the obstinacy of a little, gawky-limbed Huguenot fit for nothing but to argue of Murcy and stuff her thin frame with food.

"How awkward you are!" she said, partly in an attempt to overcome the feeling of inferiority this calm child always aroused in her. She raked over Françoise' person in an effort to find some flaw. "Hold out your hands," she said at last. "When did you last clean your nails, Mademoiselle?"

"I have been cleaning the silver, Madame."

"Do not answer me. It is now eight months since you came to us. You have done very little in that time to earn anyone's affection here, or to show gratitude for being housed at Neuillant."

"I did not ask to come, Madame."

Madame de Neuillant restrained an impulse to slap the girl's face. She had tried force with her before and obtained

56

little reward. Her own children would weep and cringe, but with this adult brat it had become a matter of feeling oneself a fool and the switch in one's hand a child's own weapon. The proceeding had been unsatisfactory; she had obtained neither sobs nor prayers from Françoise d'Aubigné.

How to be rid of her? Was she, for the rest of life on earth, to be saddled with this incubus, this refractory young she-heretic who was most surely fortified by Satan? Sometimes Madame had felt the blind urge rise to take the girl and beat her senseless, pinch her about the body and arms till she broke down the reserve that was so infuriating. *Mon père* had warned Madame against this desire and said that she must not give rein to her passions. Then he had recommended once more that Françoise be sent to the Ursulines.

Now with the girl standing here before her she thought of it again. For long her desire to be rid of Françoise had wrestled with her fear of the cost. Besides, if payment were delayed there was no one to insist on it. At a pinch this Tante, the inevitable guardian angel of Murcy, might be prevailed upon to bear her share of the expenses provided her affection for the girl stretched so far. Grimly Madame dwelled on the satisfaction it would be to charge the Marquise de Villette with the expenses of a Catholic convent for her niece; compensation, doubtless, for the amount she had had to endure in the form of digs about Murcy, comparisons made between the conditions here and those at Murcy, the superiority of the Villette housekeeping, the intelligence of M. le Marquis compared to that of anyone at Neuillant. . . . In spite of the fact that she looked always towards the next life, it need not mean that she was impervious to darts in this.

Madame looked again at Françoise d'Aubigné. If only it were possible to find the force that would convert her! It would be a triumph as complete as having married one's eldest daughter to M. de Navailles. Madame knew herself to have lost all sense of proportion regarding the triumph of it.

In how many weeks could the Ursulines achieve her object? Would it be possible—one dared not hope it probable —to have brought about the conversion in time to report it at Court?

"The grandchild of Agrippa d'Aubigné has embraced the true faith in the *convent des Ursulines*. . . ."

And everyone would know that hers, the Comtesse de Neuillant's, had been the guiding hand. Who could say what promotion might not come of it! The Regent was devout, as befitted a daughter of Spain. . . .

Madame never afterwards ceased to surprise herself with the recollection of how rapidly the decision was made in her mind. She turned to Françoise d'Aubigné.

"*Eh, bien*, then, Mademoiselle, you shall not long remain here, as you do not desire it."

The flush of color on the girl's face made her look suddenly beautiful. "Madame—"

Madame de Neuillant savored a small enjoyment. In spite of the fact that she knew it to be improbable, the girl's mind dwelled still on returning to Murcy. With this card in her hand Madame's triumph grew. To render this d'Aubigné, even for moments, foolish! She could not but succumb to the temptation to drag the situation out, making her believe that, in fact, she was indeed to go back to Murcy. She must be careful to utter no falsehoods, leading the victim unsuspectingly along the path. The longer she could preserve the illusion the keener would be the disappointment. Ah, if only it were possible to do so until the very convent gates were reached!

She allowed the joy to linger in Françoise d'Aubigné's eyes. The sensation of power over another was very sweet to her.

"I am to go back to Murcy," Françoise thought.

She said the words over to herself, trying to achieve in repetition some semblance of a reality which she could not feel. As on the voyage home from Martinique, the image of Murcy came as in a dream. It did not yet seem possible that she should return there, and with so little struggle. What had become of the State order? Could even Madame have it annulled?

Jolting beside the Comtesse in the coach, her belongings beside her in a small bundle, she looked at the road. She was barely conscious of Madame beside her, or of the *sachets de violette*. Soon the air would be clean and fresh and she could eat till she no longer felt hungry. Perhaps she was becoming greedy to think so much of food. Madame seemed to survive, and to expect others so to do, on very little. The fish they had had yesterday had been stale, there should be no need for that on an estate where there were stocked ponds. But now again she was criticizing Madame. . . .

"Madame, this is not the Murcy road."

Madame plumed hat inclined a little in acknowledgment. "No, we are going first to Niort."

Françoise said nothing to that, but suspicion grew in her mind. And yet, surely Madame would not play such a trick. It would be the act of a child, stupid and mischievous, and yet . . . and yet not impossible to Madame. Françoise could remember still the curious gloating in Madame's eyes as she had prepared to beat her . . . so much so that no matter how painful the beating had been it was imperative to stifle all crying till Madame had gone, burying her face then in the pillow and giving way to humiliation and pain. Perhaps there were some who enjoyed giving pain. It was useless to speculate.

The buildings rolled past. Down one street was the prison, where Françoise herself had been born. Papa and even Maman seemed very far away now. They had had word from Maman lately, she had been again in difficulty regarding the lawsuit and had obtained an apartment in a noblewoman's house in Paris . . . but only until the autumn, when the room would be required. After that no one knew what would happen.

Did anyone know, now, what would happen? The door at which they stopped was set back from the rest of the street and cut in its face was a little grille. She got down from the coach with Madame and was told to bring her bundle with her. From then on she was certain that Madame

59

had indeed been deceiving her and that it was not to Murcy she would go, but the realization came slowly like the thawing of a numbed limb and it was not until she had followed Madame and the portress down the corridors smelling of beeswax, and into a scrubbed inner room, that she knew.

Everything was clean in the convent. She noted that first, with a little lift of relief. It would not be so unpleasant to polish corridors that were already clean. There were few hangings here and everything was scoured and poor and bare; a crucifix hung on the wall, its figure carved in light wood, with silver for the crown and nails. The table was old and into its surface were hollowed spaces, at intervals, such as peasants with large families used instead of dishes for their soup. She wondered if this were where the nuns ate and if so what kind of room were used for the *pensionnaires*. The portress disappeared and presently the Superior came and Françoise was presented, and then after a little talk the nun went away and she and Madame were left looking at one another. The rustle of the Superior's skirts died away in the silence. She and the portress had worn black coifs, draped over *collets* about pale faces. Françoise felt that she would not readily distinguish one from another again.

Madame smiled. In the austere room her perfumed clothes looked tawdry. She began to twist the ring on her glove, looking down at it as if she preferred to have some object on which to fix her notice. Presently she began to talk to Françoise as though they were strangers.

"You are disappointed at being brought here? What makes you prefer Murcy?"

Françoise said nothing and the Comtesse continued to talk, as though she had answered. "Happiness is a fleeting thing; not all of us are lucky enough to have known it. You say you were happy at Murcy; of that I cannot judge. It is of little value to be selfishly contented now, and burn hereafter. That is what comes to those who persist in error."

"I am not in error, Madame. I am a Huguenot."

"And that is error, in that it goes against the tenets of the one true Church. Who are you to say that you cannot err? You are full of vanity."

Françoise began to tremble. The Comtesse watched in some satisfaction. This nervous, labile creature was not the same who had come to her last year and sat stubbornly throughout the progress of Holy Mass. If it was necessary to become as wax in the hands of God she, the Comtesse, had aided the process. A few months more and Françoise might have been whipped into shape like a young horse; for an instant Madame regretted the possibility. But remembrance of the expense guided her, and the activities for which she preferred to be left free in Paris decided her. It was a relief to put the onus on the Ursulines. Who could accomplish anything, if not they?

"You will be well looked after here," she told Françoise coldly. "Do as you are bid, and cause no trouble if you are wise. You are of so refractory and stubborn a nature that it is a hard task to undertake the curing of your soul. When I hear that you have had a change of heart, I may consider returning you to Neuillant. Until then it will be better for you to remain under supervision here. Perhaps," she added with a flash of malice, "it will be apparent after a time that there are fewer luxuries here than even at Neuillant."

She studied the girl closely, anticipating her reaction. In this last meeting of theirs for no one knew how long, she found dislike take hold of her. She would have enjoyed tears, pleading to be taken back to Neuillant, but there were none. Madame felt disappointment rise; there was no change of expression on the set young face; even the eyes did not darken as they would sometimes do when there was no other sign of feeling.

Madame felt an inexplicable weariness. "Well," she said sharply, "have you nothing to say?"

"No, Madame."

The girl must be stupid. She was thankful to have her out of the house.

VIII

LIFE IN the Niort convent resolved itself almost from the beginning into monotones. Remembering it, Françoise could not recall any color clearly. That there were subtle grades she knew, and on the other hand sharp blacks and whites so dominant that she could not ignore them. Personalities also were sharply defined, the more so for the lack of colors to obscure them; she began to wonder after a very few days how she could ever have thought she would fail to distinguish between nuns.

Everything was clean at Niort, free of association and fuss. The girls ate out of wooden bowls; no one bowl was any particular person's, any more than a coverlet was one's own, or a coif. Every morning the straw pallets lining the dormitory in long files were tidied, the blankets cleared and stowed in piles at the end of the room. Every wash-day coifs and collets were handed in, laundered by the sister in charge, threaded again with black ribbon and issued regardless of identity. It was possible to lose oneself completely in the anonymity of day to day.

That she was a Huguenot was of course apparent, but she did not find that the *pensionnaires* looked at her askance or singled her out for ridicule. They were mainly peasants and held her, as a relative of Madame de Neuillant, a little above themselves; this even when it was discovered that Madame had paid not a sou toward her upkeep, making of her a partaker of the nuns' charity. An attempt had been made to induce Tante to pay her convent fees, but although the Marquise sent many gifts of food and warm clothing to her "little victim," Françoise was glad to learn that she had refused to gratify Madame in this respect. She knew very

62

well the upset it must be to her good aunt to learn that she was placed in a convent at all.

She was not unhappy, having learned long since to take the days as they came. She was obliged by virtue of her dependent status to help with the heavier domestic work, but life at Neuillant had toughened her and accustomed her to menial tasks, and moreover she was pleased to oblige the nuns, who were kind to her. Although she found after a time that this kindness was partly activated in hope of effecting her conversion, she was grateful for it and even found herself able to return affection a little, notably to Sœur Céleste.

Sœur Céleste worked in the laundry. Although she occupied so humble a position in the life of the convent, taking no part in the teaching or finer work, for which the nuns were famous, Françoise did not think she was a peasant. It was not permissible to ask from where she came, and this the girl never discovered, but the kindly face of Sœur Céleste and a certain calm she had reminded Françoise of Tante, although of course Tante would have disliked the suggestion extremely. Seeing Sœur bending valiantly over a mountain of starching in the *blanchisserie*, she felt bound to help her. "It is the *collets*!" Sœur was heard to moan, shaking her head as though that, too, was no more than a matter sent to try one and insure fitness for entry into the next world with more facility than might otherwise have been possible. "The *collets* take so long!"

Françoise stole down one night into the laundry and starched at *collets* through the long hours till beyond the trefoil window the day broke and she could hear birds singing. When Sœur Céleste came down before Mass she would be astonished by the sight of so many starched *collets*; their laundress, pleased but exhausted, had flung herself at last on her small flat bed, with hardly half-an-hour to lie there before it was time to rise again.

With Sœur Céleste she was trustful, but the teaching nuns who sounded her with regard to faith met with the same lack of response as Madame de Neuillant had done. Now that her senses were no longer flooded by the sight of richness and the perfume of banked flowers—the Ursulines were poor and their chapel bare, there was no singing of Mass even at high festival—she found her reason assert itself. That reason was cold and metal-hard and crisp, a legacy of tempered steel, from old Agrippa d'Aubigné, and tested again by adversity. Proudly she would fling the fact of her Huguenot ancestry in the faces of the bewildered nuns, contentiously argue, as she had done at Murcy and Neuillant, point beyond point of dogma and doctrine until the poor ladies, having beheld each weapon in their armory brought forth, examined, and calmly returned as unusable, besought the Superior to petition Madame de Neuillant to remove her young charge, whose intractable spirit could hardly but injure the budding intelligences committed to their care.

The Superior weighed the advantages of Françoise' diligence at laundering and housework and needlework, proficiency in penmanship and the expression of thoughts in a letter, her quick mind and retentive memory which were a joy to the teaching nuns, against these demerits. Reluctantly at last she wrote to Madame in Paris, confessing that in spite of some months' care and instruction in the matters of the Faith, Françoise d'Aubigné remained as Huguenot as ever. But it took more than one letter to elicit from Madame any reply.

When she heard at last that Madame had sent for her, Françoise knew a moment's fear. How angry the Comtesse would be she could only guess, and her real anger would undoubtedly be fearsome, rather cold than hot, rejoicing in malice and in injury by any means. Moreover, in spite of her rather conscious flouting of them, she would miss the nuns' kindness and their cool voices and calm eyes. Here the world was shut out for a little while, removed with its color and jostle and strife. It would not be desirable to remain here all her life, but for a time it had been pleasant.

Nevertheless she was conscious of the fact that she had beaten them all and she was proud of it. Tante and Uncle Benjamin must be remembering her in their prayers for

God to have sent her the answers to so many questions, to have preserved her foɪ the Protestant faith in sight of so many altars.

When she went to say goodbye Sœur Céleste said a thing she would remember. She had been stacking linen in the great cupboard where it was kept, and the warm smell of lye came to Françoise strongly, bringing with it a remembrance of the linen of Murcy and the way it was always folded away among herbs. The linen had a fresh smell then that made it a pleasure to lie down to sleep, but one would say nothing of that to these women who denied themselves all luxury as an aspect of God's will.

The nun turned her head in its cumbersome coif and regarded her for an instant before speaking. Then she said, "You are going? I wish you well."

"And I too wish you well, *ma sœur*, wherever I go I will remember you for being so kind to me, and I—"

"I will pray for you."

The gray eyes surveyed her, not as the *pensionnaire* who had starched the collars but as no one and anyone; a soul before God. Françoise was conscious of resentment and a feeling of loss. Had nothing that they had shared been worth remembering? Would Sœur Céleste recall her no more than a dozen others? Her vanity was piqued, remembering the *collets*; she managed to smile, to hide her hurt.

"They will say I am in need of prayers, *ma sœur*, but I am firm in my own faith."

"You do not yet know your faith," said Sœur Céleste.

She went on stacking linen. "Later on you will perhaps realize that it is your own will you worship, and not God," she said. "You have rejoiced, have you not, in setting it up against that of others? Because they tried to make you do what you would not, you convinced yourself that what they desired for you was wrong."

"I did what my aunt and my uncle desired for me, and they were the best people I knew. They helped the poor wherever they could and were kind to me and made me happy. They loved God, yet I am told to believe that they are heretics and displeasing to Him. Yet those whom your

Church describe as being of the true faith I have found mean and comfortless and cruel. How is one to explain this, *ma sœur*? I have no doubt whatever that my aunt of Murcy will see God before Madame de Neuillant."

She felt the flush of anger die, and seized the nun's hand and kissed it. "Ah, *ma sœur*, I do not know to what I am going now! It may be that I shall need your prayers when I learn what is reserved for me."

"Poor child," said Sœur Céleste.

She had learned with relief that Madame was not to come for her. Madame was in Paris, busied with great affairs. A servant came to escort Françoise to Neuillant, and on the way there she learned that a place had been booked for her on the stagecoach to Paris on the morrow. What Madame would do with her then had not been specified, but in the meantime she was to be delivered to the Hôtel Saint-Herman.

Françoise was nervous. Paris seemed far off and too imposing, and the anger of Madame had only been delayed. Neuillant was unfamiliar and full of echoes, the furniture in the unused rooms herded together away from walls, spotted with the damp. Accustomed as she had been to the rustlings of pallets in the dormitory at Niort, Françoise found the quiet of solitude disturbing. It had never been hers and it was not for a long time yet that she would crave it for what it could give.

In the morning, dazed from lack of sleep, she was put very early into a corner of the passing coach for Paris. With her in a basket were two hard-boiled eggs and a small loaf to sustain her on the journey. She hoarded these for as long as she could, as the journey was a long one and she was afraid of hunger, but the crush and stench of the other passengers within the coach caused her appetite to desert her and she had, in the end, no wish to eat. So many things had happened in the past few days that she was already bewildered; another shake of the dice-box of her life had come, and how was she to know what sort of personage would this time emerge from the mêlée?

After many hours, lulled by the jolting of the coach, she slept. Madame had ridden this same road in her gilded carriage many weeks before. The whole world knew of it, and the city to which it led. Presently the scattered huts and occasional great châteaux among their wooded parks would thicken and cluster into streets and houses; old Paris, the Paris of Saint Louis and Jeanne d'Arc and Henri Quatre, beckoned and would absorb her. Above its ancient roofs a new dawn shone, thinly as yet but with promise of breaking out soon into broad day. A boy in his apartments in the Louvre had ceased to care for toys; presently he would resent the dominion of an Italian Cardinal and a Spanish widow over France, taking the reins into his own hands one memorable day while clad in a hunting coat of scarlet and a hat with a gray feather.

But before that, war would come. Already it was apparent in the grumbling hungry crowds, the banding together of silly society women who tossed the name of Condé from lip to lip and pinned small bunches of straw on the breasts of their gowns. Paris was hungry, and resentful of hunger. Paris would go to war. Somewhere among the gray roofs a cripple was writing scurrilous rhymes about the Cardinal. Presently they would catch the favor of the crowd and his printed *billets* would scatter wildly among them like leaves in a gale. Gossip was all of the Cardinal and of the behavior of Mademoiselle de Montpensier, and the price of meat and the impossibility of obtaining any vegetables. No one would notice the shabby coach clattering into its terminus on the Quartier Saint-Denis, or the stiff descent from it, after all the other passengers had alighted, of an equally shabby little girl. No one could read the future, or if they could, would have believed in it. Françoise thought nothing of it at all, being occupied with the wish for sleep and the necessity that was hers of facing Madame, at the Hôtel Saint-Herman, on an empty stomach.

67

IX

MADAME DE NEUILLANT had long made use of the town
house of her brother, Jacques Tiraqueau, Baron de Saint-
Herman, during her sojourns in Paris. Jacques was lenient
and his wife indolent, and the obligations that arose from
the task of being the King's *maître d'hôtel* made it necessary
for them to be often absent, so that the house was Madame's
to do with as she pleased.

She was therefore able to order the arrival of Françoise
d'Aubigné and receive her when she did arrive, without any
tiresome explanations given. It would have been possible
to entertain an extra person for many months in Jacques
Tiraqueau's household without his ever noticing the difference, but this Madame did not propose to do.

She watched the shrinking child cross the carpet. It gave
her pleasure to wait in silence until she should have done
so, knowing very well the tumult her conscience must be in,
this intrepid Huguenot. As the child came, she studied her
appearance. She wore a plain gown of buff-yellow serge.
Madame had sent a roll of the material herself, having had
it in gift of someone and knowing it too ugly for Suzanne,
but being so thick and strong that hardly anything could
happen to it, it was the very thing for Françoise. Here in
the splendid *hôtel* with its woven hangings the child looked
awkward, provincial, out of place. Madame permitted herself
to speak at last; there was triumph in her voice.

"And so you have had an agreeable journey, Mademoiselle?"

The child's great dark eyes looked at her. She was too
much afraid to speak. The smooth voice went on.

"You consoled yourself, no doubt, with the thought that

68

every turn of the wheel brought you nearer to Paris, which in your dependent state you had scarcely hoped to see. It would suit you, you decided, better than the life of the convent, where there are no diversions and the food is poor."

Françoise stared at her. Why was Madame so gentle? Horror assailed her as it so often did when Madame wore that terrible smile and spoke scarcely above a whisper. Her voice, she found, when she tried to answer, was dry in her throat; she could not speak, and she saw Madame's smile broaden.

"You are silent, Mademoiselle? That is not the report I have of you. It was said that you were contentious, argumentative and stubborn. You took a delight in impertinence to your betters, to such an extent that it was found necessary to arrange your removal. You are such a well of iniquity that the very Church itself is not sacred to you. You are obstinate and ungrateful to such a degree that even my patience is exhausted. Yes, Françoise d'Aubigné, I wash my hands of you. When I can find the leisure I will conduct you to your mother. Perhaps when there you will have a better sense of values and of what you owe me. Your mother may see what she can do with you. I can do no more."

If she had hoped for the reward of emotion, she almost won it. The child's face, which had been pale and shadowed after her sleepless journey, grew now so white that Madame thought she would faint. She began to talk in a low voice, clasping her hands together as though to strengthen herself by their contact; her words came rapidly; often Madame did not know what she was saying.

"You say what, Mademoiselle? *What?* That I cannot return you to your mother? Indeed I can, and with all speed too. . . . Poverty? You should have thought of that sooner!"

The child knelt to her. Madame withdrew her skirts from the clutch of her hands, remarking coldly that she would soil the satin. "Rise, Mademoiselle," she commanded. The spectacle of Françoise d'Aubigné kneeling before her surpassed her expectations of what a threat could do. She would not be in too great a hurry to deliver her to Jeanne.

She began to deliver instructions to the weeping child who knelt still on the carpet. She could remain, Madame said, in the Hôtel Tiraqueau until such time as she might be conducted to her mother. Meanwhile she would make herself invisible, inaudible and useful. She would eat what was put before her. She would refrain from gossip with the servants. "I will not have your reason for leaving here discussed with anyone, do you hear me? If I hear that you have done so I will not contribute a sou to your upkeep, and you will starve. If my relatives return before you leave you will not approach them. I shall tell them you are a servant, which you resemble. Do you understand me? I will not have my relations penalized for your ingratitude."

The contradictory ordering went on, hardly understandable to the child, who wept as if her soul were lost. To be sent back to Maman! Maman, who hardly knew how to keep herself even on the starvation-fare she contrived! Maman, crazed with lawsuits and long poverty, and the excesses of Charles! Maman, who would rather anything should happen than that she should be compelled to support her, Françoise, with things as they were just now . . . who had imagined her safe in the care of Madame de Neuillant!

Truly God persecuted those who were faithful to Him, sending no comfort at all. "If I had said I would be Catholic at the beginning to oblige Madame, she would have kept me at Neuillant," Françoise told herself wretchedly. In the worsening of her state, which must be extreme when it made her think of Neuillant as almost paradise, the glow of martyrdom forsook her; she understood how Huguenot Jacqueline of Holland had felt when they took her out, half-frozen and naked, and whipped her in the public market-place and then strangled her for aiding Protestants against the Catholic might of Spain.

The Tiraqueau family returned with the inconsequence that attached to all their doings, and Mademoiselle de Saint-Herman, aged seventeen, prepared in spite of the war to fling herself with zest into the Paris season. Mademoiselle

found zest for all she did, whether it was walking out, with
her hazel curls becomingly disposed under a large plumed
hat, to the Hôtel de Troyes to meet the *monde* in company,
of course, with Suzanne de Baudéan, who was a trifle dull
but had her uses as a chaperon; or repairing to the Jardins
du Luxembourg of a morning to receive the protestations
of such heart-sick gallants as were not with the army; or
dancing all night at the Louvre. But, of course, that was
unlikely nowadays, with the Queen so worried over the war
that she was prepared almost any day to fly the city with
the little King. Well . . . life was much less agreeable, at
any rate, and Papa had had to leave her short of money to
spend, although to be sure money was little use nowadays
when things were not to be got. M. Scarron, the cripple,
over at the Hôtel de Troyes, had written a very witty piece
in his usual style and ended by observing in rhyme that he
would give almost anything for a good fresh melon.
Mademoiselle felt likewise. At first it had been exciting to
think of living in a city under siege, but now the siege had
grown wearisome and Mademoiselle grew tired of living on
salted meat, and longed like poor Scarron for some fresh
fruit or an *omelette aux fines herbes*. Even Scarron's *salon*
had begun to pall, with most of the talk either above her
head or else so vulgar that she pretended not to understand
it. Paris itself was dull, a thing that Mademoiselle would
never have believed could happen. And so it was that one
day in search of diversion she took notice of the little creature in hideous yellow serge that she had observed, on more
than one occasion, creeping to the foot of the table at meals
or flattening herself between the wall and the stairs.

"What is your name?" she asked the little girl, and then
when she had heard that, asked her age. When this was
given she showed surprise. "Why, you are only two and a
half years younger than I am! What have they done to you
to make you remain so small?"

And the child, stung by this remark out of the odd reserve
she had shown in replying, answered that on the contrary
she was as tall as Mademoiselle, only darker and not so
plump, which made her seem smaller.

"Oh! Oh!" cried Mademoiselle de Saint-Herman in scandalized laughter. "Measure yourself against me!"

It was no longer possible for two young ladies established back-to-back to remain strangers to one another, and on discovering that they were, in fact, exactly the same height, Mademoiselle de Saint-Herman bore no grudge but on the contrary made much of her visitor. "Why were you so shy with me when I spoke to you first?" she scolded. "One would have thought you did not want to know me."

Françoise flushed and cast down her eyes. "Why, you odd little thing, what are you blushing for?" demanded Mademoiselle. "You are my aunt's protégée, aren't you?"

"Yes—I—no, that is, I was so, Mademoiselle, but now—"

Suddenly, in face of this rather pert kindness, she burst into tears. Mademoiselle, who had a kind heart and more common sense than her conversation made apparent, cast her arm round her, led her to her own *chambre,* sat her on the bed, and commanded that she unburden herself. "For it is not right for anyone to look as unhappy as you, even although there is a war," she added. "Oh, this war! How it upsets everybody!"

Françoise gave a watery smile and scrubbed away her tears.

"There, that is better," said Mademoiselle, "and now you will have a sweetmeat. I lie all night and nibble sweetmeats, which is very bad for my teeth. Papa sent me these from Lyon. He knows how I adore them. Now tell me what is the matter with you, and why you are crying."

Under the commanding blue eye which was fixed upon her, Françoise stumbled out her story. All the time she was frightened that Madame would return and find her in Mademoiselle's room. Had she not forbidden her to have converse with the family?

Mademoiselle's room was very pretty. Even at Murcy there had not been such splendid furnishings. A portrait of Mademoiselle herself had been fashioned in wools to make a small screen. It stood in front of the fire and did not resemble Mademoiselle very greatly; the cheeks were round and pink like those of a doll and the hair frizzed and embel-

lished with ribbons. Mademoiselle saw her regarding it and
at once informed her that that was how they dressed now
at Court, and that she also thought it very ugly but one
must be in the fashion, or else die. "But you, you poor little
thing, have never had the chance to be in the fashion at all!"
she exclaimed.

She whisked about the room, picking up mirrors and
trinket-boxes in her agitation and setting them down again.
She announced then her intention of rescuing Françoise.
"My aunt cannot leave you to starve!" she announced.
"She is a murderess!"

"Oh, no," said Françoise in distress. How unthinkable if
Mademoiselle told her aunt so! "No, but . . . she is *reli-
gieuse*, and it grieves her that I will not change to the
Catholic faith, and I will not."

"Why will you not?" said Mademoiselle reasonably. "It
seems to me that half your troubles have come from no more
than that."

Françoise regarded her gravely. How to tell this butterfly
of the tenets of Murcy? It was so long since she had heard
them herself that they were remote now and a little vague.

"Be a Catholic, and stay here with us," said Mademoiselle.
"Nobody nowadays is martyred for a particular kind of
religion."

The flippancy of this remark was in a degree never encountered by Françoise before. She was shocked, and said
so, rather primly. "I could not reconcile it with my conscience to accommodate myself with such ease."

The nuns of Niort would have been chilled into with-
drawal; Mademoiselle de Saint-Herman laughed, and hugged
her. "Why not?" she persisted. "You have endured enough.
Think what the difference would be if you would only conform! My aunt would be so overjoyed there is nothing she
would not do for you. You could come into society and wear
pretty clothes; Madame would be so anxious to show you
off as her convert that she would see you met all the right
people. You could come with me when I go to the Hôtel de
Troyes, to meet the *monde* at Scarron's—oh, that Scarron!
He is a little man, a paralytic, and so wicked it is a delight

73

to listen to him. He smothered himself in honey once for a carnival and stuck feathers all over himself, but while he was capering through the streets everyone he met pulled a feather off, and in the end he was left stark naked and they chased him into the river, because he was an abbé, you know, and it was all very dreadful. But poor Scarron caught a chill in the water and gave himself a *rhumatisme,* and ever since then he has been doubled up, but he writes very clever verse."

She chattered on, while the grave girl on the bed sat and listened. Not all of Mademoiselle's heady talk was noted by her; the novelty half shocked and half amused her. This was the manner in which the *monde* lived, the gay world of Paris. In her drab life there had been little enough time for gaiety, except at Murcy, and that had been of a different kind. But already the cheerful kindliness of Murcy was overlaid by dreary memories; it was so long since she had seen Tante, long since she had even poured out her heart in a letter, as these were suppressed. She was without means of succor, and the glimpse Mademoiselle afforded of a world of brilliant intellects was like a flash of brightness in her gray sky. It would be diverting to meet clever little Scarron, pleasant to read his verse; welcome to talk to those who could reply on other subjects than the life to come. She must be unworthy, she told herself, to desire it; she would never be a Jacqueline of Holland. She would never be anyone, if she went on as she was doing, except a drudge, whom everyone shunned.

Here was a creature who did not shun her. On an impulse she turned to Mademoiselle, "Ah, if I am sent away, do not forget me!" she begged. "Intercede with Madame de Neuillant for me! It would mean so much . . . if I could only remain a while!"

Madame de Neuillant's response on being begged to allow Françoise to remain a while was to drive with her straight to her mother's.

On the way Françoise had a lecture read to her regarding

74

her suborning of Mademoiselle de Saint-Herman. She had abused, Madame said, M. le Baron's hospitality. She would have filled the head of his only daughter with pernicious ideas of her own. She was full of the devil, deceitful, untrustworthy, and a liar. Her mother would be told all this when she was handed over. Françoise heard it dully, no longer caring very greatly for that or for anything. Going east, the trees of the Luxembourg left far behind, she watched the streets narrow in squalor. This was to be her life, and the other had been a dream. Children ran about filthy, starving and almost naked, diving between the coach's wheels. Would she some day come to look like these, or like the sleazy women about the doorways? Beggars whined at every street corner; often a skinny arm was stretched forth almost into the carriage windows; the high demanding note followed them along the way. Give, give, give, cried the beggars of Paris, who had nothing at all. It was not the war that had made them so, but because they were so the war had come. That she knew . . . very soon she also would be hungry. The hunger of these people had given them words. Often on a wall or doorway there would be posters shown, their shabby corners fluttering in the wind. These would be the *Mazarinades,* that little Scarron had written. She wondered when she had heard of Scarron; it seemed a lifetime ago.

The house they reached at last was in the narrowest of narrow alleys. Maman must be in great poverty to live here. The windows, slatted and high in the manner of those built before the religious wars, were broken, their casements hingeless and often stuffed with rags. Madame de Neuillant was not sparing of her disgust at the matters left on stairs and alleyway, and Françoise knew a sudden silent rage; what would *she* do if she must live as Maman, for years now, had lived; work in the places she had done? "She would have need then of her *sachets de violette,*" the girl thought bitterly. She followed Madame up the fetid stairs, from habit holding her own skirts high to avoid the refuse.

Madame d'Aubigné lived on the fourth landing, a woman told them. Françoise felt the eyes, red-rimmed with the dirt on her face, follow them. She called something after them as they mounted the stairs.

"What did she say?" asked Madame.

"She asked for silver."

They came to a door. Madame raised her gloved hand and knocked; within there was silence. Presently there came the sound of shuffling footsteps. After a while the door opened and an old woman stood there. Her voice came high and peevish with a whine like that of the beggars', asking who they were and what they wanted.

"If you are from Madame Gondrin tell her I have no work ready. I have been ill with a fever and I cannot work. Tell her I will send—"

The words trailed off piteously and Françoise stood looking into the face of her mother.

An instant only they stood thus, and the Madame's voice cut into the silence. Madame, cruel Madame, intent only on another world than this, could she see the things that were wrought by this world and still feel nothing? For Maman was old. Her hair that had been mostly brown was all gray now, and straggled thinly. She wore a cap that was not clean. Her hands, which Françoise noticed then, were twisted like a cripple's hands, swollen at the joints and with dirty hollowed nails. They were the hands of a washerwoman, a scourer; a carrier of pails in wintertime, a grubber among refuse for food. They would not hold a needle now without botching, or write a fine hand with a pen, or curl hair. Wherever she went, those hands would reveal what had happened to Jeanne de Cardilhac. Françoise clenched her own small roughened ones on a fierce resolve.

Madame bent her plumed head and preceded Jeanne into the dreadful room. Here was poverty, as bad if no worse than that they had met with in the streets. The rats had come and eaten at the legs of the table and the single chair. Madame would not sit on it. Standing, she handed Françoise over, as she had promised, to her mother. The girl heard the words of the formal little speech as though they came from behind a veil. That other world, the one of Mademoiselle de Saint-Herman, did not dream of this. If it ever had its dreams would have aroused its conscience before now, and help would have come. But there was none, from anyone, anywhere, and Madame was saying now that she did not feel inclined further to contribute to the upkeep of so refractory an ingrate as herself.

Maman said nothing. Maman who had, even in the Martinique days, a storehouse of bitter words to her command, was silenced now. One knew she would never, in this most barren of all worlds, reply again to taunting. A broken-down animal, Maman, little more; a pitiful, vulnerable animal still, for at some of Madame's unkinder words tears welled up and started to run, thick and unheeded, down her face. She made no effort to stop them or to wipe them away; such action would have involved will, and Maman had no will any more. She had battled and fought and lost, and this was what courage had left her; a ragged scarecrow figure, aged too soon and unclean; poor twisted hands that hung loosely, having nothing now that they could do. Madame talked on, and, in the end, took her departure; and Françoise was left watching the tears as they ran without hindrance down Maman's face.

X

"YOU DENY that God's Church is infallible?"

"I deny that any human being is infallible. The Pope is human."

Mon père laid down his catechism with a sigh. Opposite him on a high chair sat the d'Aubigné child, with her finger in a Bible. It was a Huguenot version and neither threats, cajoling, nor force had hitherto been sufficient to wrest it from her. To everything he said she found an answer. She appeared to know the Bible through and through.

He began again. "His Holiness the Pope is a man, true, but in his position as the Successor of Saint Peter his pronouncements, made *ex cathedra,* are infallible. This is a part of the beliefs of Holy Church and indeed her very foundation stone."

"Peter was an extremely fallible fisherman," said Françoise.

"Ah—compare the man *before* Our Lord's Crucifixion with what he became after. 'Thou art Peter, and on this rock will I build my Church, and the gates of hell shall not prevail against it.' And so we find this rock willing to lay down his own life with great suffering at last for the sake of that belief."

She inclined her head once, gravely, as if to concede the point to him. "But, *mon père,*" she said presently, "there is nothing there that says the Pope is infallible. It is possible to be a rock without being perfect. Even rocks have flaws. It does not prevent their making excellent foundations. They are unable, you see, to give way."

He stared at her. "Like yourself, Mademoiselle!" he shot out. A gleam in her eyes surprised him and he regretted losing control. It would be possible to sit here night after night with this little Huguenot and always, when a corner might seem to have been turned, she would double back again. Who was she? Where had she come from, before her mother, the widow d'Aubigné who sometimes scrubbed for *mes sœurs,* had begged to have her accepted as a charity-boarder in the Convent of the Faubourg Sainte-Anne?

Mon père raised a hand and surreptitiously rubbed the back of his neck, where a boil troubled him. He was at his wits' end and had used a great many candles in this argument. The hour a day originally set aside for Mademoiselle d'Aubigné had drawn out to two hours, three; and still he was no nearer victory, and still there was nothing to report to Madame la Supérieure. *Mon père* went in some little fear of Madame, who had a sarcastic tongue she was inclined to use, forgetting their respective positions, to himself. But to be bested by this child! It was humiliating. . . .

* * *

"You are an unbeliever, Mademoiselle. You are like Saint Thomas, who would not believe until he had seen. Blessed are those who have not seen, and yet have believed, were the words of our Lord to him."

"And yet your Church makes Thomas a saint," said Françoise. "Why is that, *mon père?*"

"Saint Thomas was one of the blessed apostles. All were saints," said the Vincentian shortly. He was growing very tired under the d'Aubigné girl's questionings. She differed in so many respects from the docile children of the *quartier* that he was not, any longer, able to enumerate the differences. He felt himself making no headway with her, and was depressed. In what way had he failed?

He looked at the child who sat opposite. She had lost flesh since she came to the convent and the eyes in her face were enormous and dark. In spite of himself *mon père* was reminded of a portrait of the dark little Baptist by a painter of Spain. That mystery of shadows lay about so many of the children of Paris now, with the privations of war.

Françoise thought of Saint Thomas. If they had said that he was a saint because he believed after all, having seen, would not that have been so much more satisfactory? But everything in this rather angry thin man's reckoning was wrapped up in little parcels, with labels attached. It was tidier, no doubt. If only he would answer her, instead of thundering! At nights his face made her afraid, she would see it still when she lay down to sleep in her cell, with anger dilating its nostrils and the candlelight throwing into relief the sharp high bones of the cheeks. If only those at Murcy had been near!

Suddenly *mon père* turned on her and his voice was very bitter. "We waste time splitting hairs," he said. "Either you accept, or you do not. When a simple thing has been accepted without question, the rest follows in time. I will pray for your soul, Mademoiselle, that grace may touch it, but I cannot undertake to instruct you further until you cease to argue with me."

"But how can I believe without reason?" she cried. He regarded her gravely.

"There are times when reason is less pleasing to God than simple faith. In His own good time He may send grace to you. Meantime I can do no more."

XI

"THIS PLACE, where to live is worse to me than death," wrote Françoise to her Aunt Villette. "So-called, the house of God!"

During those days she was more nearly out of her reason than ever again; poverty, hardship, ridicule, loneliness would come, pass and leave her. But now every cruelty was intensified, every shadow substance in her mind; her intelligence, holding fast to the standards she knew, found those standards broken and not capable, any more, of sustaining her. She would pray at night and wonder if she were praying to the devil or to God. She would see herself as her preceptors described her, in their desperation of achieving anything with her by ordinary means; pig-headed, ungrateful, heartless, ignorant, stubborn. She must be made of wickedness; her own mother had never loved her, nor she Maman. She was unnatural, loving an aunt, who was a heretic, more than her mother, who was faithful through all her afflictions to the one true Church. What had the Huguenots done for her mother? They had stripped her of all her possessions. It had been left to the Church to shelter her, feed her when she was starved and house her child when she could not support her.

Murcy was lost to her; she remembered how Madame de Neuillant, at Niort, had made the nuns send the bill to Tante and Tante had refused to pay, for although she grudged no generosity to her besieged Bignette she would rather have had her dead than in a convent. And if Bignette should yield to siege? There was no doubt of what would befall. Tante, the daughter of Agrippa d'Aubigné, would wash her hands even of one she loved. "Better that one eye should be lost!" How often Françoise had heard her say it! It would be goodbye to Murcy, if she accepted the alien faith, goodbye except in memory and dreams.

"But what else have I?"

She thought of it, lying at night on the cold straw. If she were to yield? Often, since that first time at Neuillant, the sweetness of the Mass-bell called her. These were the urges of the senses, against which she had been warned. She would not be deceived by them. But if—if—the Church could convince her in her mind!

Often, in the state between sleep and waking, memory would return to taunt her. Besides Murcy there came Martinique, the hot sun with flies, the harshness of Maman who had once jerked a comb through her hair so hard that she bled, and struck her for crying. Maman again in the dreadful room where they had both lived on almost nothing, and in which Françoise had at last fallen ill with a fever that left cramps in her bones. If she had been a saint she would have worked for Maman, gone out to support her by scrubbing, perhaps, or sewing. But she had been ill and useless and so was brought here.

Was God angry with her for ingratitude? Her hatred of the Church they said was wickedness. One should be grateful for the sustaining of life itself, the daily meal however poor, the warmth in the thin *bouillon,* the bulk of the harsh bread. That, in the end, was the immediate necessity; to preserve life, waiting for it to be apparent what God wished one to become. "God, show me," she prayed.

Maman had once said a strange thing. Kneeling by the box which held the few things she would take to Bordeaux, where she had obtained a situation, she had held up a rosary in her twisted hands. The beads caught the light; it had been hers, she said, when she was a girl. "I have kept it although so much else has gone. If I thought you would ever use it I would give it to you."

There had been appeal in the voice, but Françoise said

she could not promise yet to use it. She watched Maman put the beads away in the box and shut the lid. She felt that she ought to have been grateful to Maman, perhaps loving, but it was too late to start and in any case Maman had never liked her, bearing her a grudge, she felt, for her birth. Suddenly Jeanne had looked up and Françoise had seen her eyes, regarding her with clear gray depths; their look surprised her. Maman must have been, she realized, once pretty and young. Strange that one had never thought of that. . . .

"Well, I will take them with me," said Jeanne. She smiled with closed lips. "Either way you will be a weapon for the Church, *ma fille;* I've prayed to Saint Teresa of Avila. She was another who wanted to know the reason for everything." She turned away, continuing in her task of packing. "Remember me occasionally in your prayers, as I will you; I don't think we shall meet again."

And Françoise felt her heart contract in sudden fear that Maman should be going so far away to work, when she was ill. But with employment so hard to get, what was one to do?

It was only later that she remembered the thing Maman had said, and by then she was gone and one could not ask about it.

Mon père's arguments having failed, other force was resorted to. At one time this would have increased her stubbornness, but she was ill. The weakness of her body made her mind shrink; her terrors became very great. In the uncertainty under which she labored it seemed that every road led to hell. Could Tante blame her, could God do so, if she took the easy-seeming way whose answers were provided?

Mes sœurs, going about their various concerns, were used to the sight of the thin little figure in its gray gown. Most of them were honest simple women, who carried out the tasks they were allotted and asked nothing of themselves or anyone else. They had been told that this was a stubborn young Huguenot who resisted instruction and they regarded her as such, mentioning her name for salvation in their prayers but seldom, if ever, saying a direct word or meeting her

82

clear dark gaze, which disturbed them. But at the end of that winter there came to the Faubourg Sainte-Anne a young nun from the sister foundation in Dauphiné. She was silent at first, as is the way with new arrivals, and then one day she spoke to the child.

"If they would answer my questions, *ma sœur,* I would listen to their reasons. But when I ask I am reported for insolence. How can I believe what I do not understand? It would be a greater wickedness to pretend than to continue, as they say, in error."

Sœur Basile listened, carding flax with dexterity as she did so. "Put the carding ready by the distaff, and listen to me," she said. "It is of no use to expect fair answers unless one keeps an open mind. Hand me the flax; we must finish all of this before collation."

Françoise thought how this was the first nun she had met since Sœur Céleste who had mentioned an open mind as a thing that was not evil. What a pity it was that so many nuns were stupid women! Could one say so?

The nun smiled. Here face had a cheerful calm, different from the unhealthy ecstasy one had seen on the face of Madame de Neuillant; different again from the waxen look of Madame la Supérieure. Sœur Basile was fresh, sane, cheerful, not coarse or earthy but somehow approachable; it was possible to express oneself to her without fear of ridicule or punishment. During the days that followed they talked often, in the evenings carding the flax or sewing, with the small fine stitches of the convent habit, at wimple-hems or shifts. Françoise learned easily of the saints she had been brought up to despise; shy Thomas of Aquino, who out of modesty was thought a dolt at school, later disclosing the brilliant mind whose written thoughts would outlast centuries; Maman's Saint Teresa, torn between visions of God and the devil and wresting a great Order out of the effete material of Spain; gentle Francis, not only a lover of all things God had made but suffering, in himself, the agonies of Christ. There were so many of whom she had never heard, in that haven of Murcy which had, after all, excluded this knowledge. What other things had Murcy excluded? In spite of herself curiosity rose to see and experience the other, forbidden things.

Madame la Supérieure sent for Sœur Basile and questioned her regarding the little d'Aubigné girl. She must beware, she told her, of nourishing her stubbornness.

"Kindness has been tried, and makes no headway with her. The only method left now is compulsion. Sooner or later, if left to herself, she must yield. In the meantime it is inadvisable to encourage her persistence."

Sœur Basile ventured, with respect, that she had not found it impossible to make headway with Françoise d'Aubigné. "She seems to me an intelligent child, whose mind is hungry for knowledge of the right, and reasonable in accepting it," she told Madame.

The Reverend Mother viewed her with disapproval. Was this newcomer, discreetly boasting aristocratic blood in the shape of her hands and her nose, to set herself up against the Vincentian Father, the entire community at Niort, and herself? Such affectation would be bad, she felt, for discipline. Sœur Basile knelt, raising her intent face to Madame.

"Let me, I beg of you, *ma mère,* be with her a little longer! I assure you, in a little, I may bring word that she will yield!"

The Superior hesitated, then gave way. "Well, use your discretion!" she told the other. "If you can indeed accomplish so much, it will be for the honor of the house—and a joy to Holy Church," she added as an afterthought. A rider was added, by way of preventing Sœur Basile from forgetting her station, to the effect that not enough flax, in the Superior's opinion, was being spun.

A few evenings later Sœur Basile came to Madame with a proposition. Françoise d'Aubigné begged the favor from Madame to permit an argument between a Huguenot pastor and a Catholic priest, she herself to be present during it. "Whichever side wins in logical argument, Françoise promises herself to that religion," said Sœur Basile. Her smile was placid. "Madame, have we not won a soul for God?"

"Irreverent nonsense," said the Superior coldly.

*   *   *

She granted the request under pressure from a horde of relations. Villettes, Neuillants, the new Navailles household, Jeanne d'Aubigné, still in Bordeaux careful of the welfare of her child's soul—all these wrote, stormed, requested, begged, threatened. In the end, beleaguered as if by an angry swarm of bees, Madame yielded. A Huguenot was found, with difficulty in those days; with equal difficulty, was persuaded to enter the precincts of a convent; a priest, not the Vincentian, co-opted for the defense. Mademoiselle d'Aubigné, armed with her Bible, sat behind a grille.

The argument began. Piece by piece the antagonists dealt with the Articles of Faith. Strong in the room was the memory of how old Agrippa d'Aubigné as a boy had pestered a cardinal until the sweat rolled down his brow in great drops. The child who was his granddaughter sat now, silent, very erect, following with her small roughened finger the passage under fire in the Bible. It was true, she thought, that the Huguenots said Catholics had little knowledge of the Bible, but *mon père* appeared to have read it. As for that, the pastor had read it too, so thoroughly that he grew excited once or twice and rose from his chair, declaiming on the corruption of all priests and how they had misled an unlettered flock. That was not fair, thought Françoise, and *mon père* gave no rein to abuse. In fact, he seemed both calm and amused, letting the pastor rave on without attempting to stop him, simply saying once, perhaps twice, something in answer to the wilder accusations. . . .

Françoise felt a little lump grow in her throat. It was true, the pastor was talking of many things wildly.

"Your answers are all cut and dried! How can you have a finite answer regarding that which is infinite?"

"You cannot," said the priest smoothly. "I can, not of myself, but by reason of the power handed down from God."

"A laying on of hands cannot make a man what he is not!"

"Do not then deny that it drives devils out. Look at your own Bible."

"Any man can drive out devils who has strength in belief."

"We are becoming removed from the issue."

And so on, hammer and tongs, and the little *frisson* that went through the room signified listening shocked veiled ladies, none of whom had ever heard the like before. On and on, until the pastor's round face grew crimson and *mon père* crossed one leg over the other beneath his gown.

Time passed. When had she last been in a state of conviction about anything? It was as had been said, there was no finite decision regarding matters infinite. She herself was very ignorant and had tried to stand alone against all the might of centuries. God had humbled her, having been proud; had confounded her, having thought herself wise.

"I have no faith in any particular," she thought. "God guide me."

If there was a point, any one single point, whereby one side could trip up the other; any given word, repeated phrase, of which to make a peg and hang one's cloak on it . . .

God, she thought, would send her a message. God would show her a word.

It was at this point that the pastor garbled a passage in the Gospel of John.

For many years afterward the nuns of the Faubourg were to talk of that day. They would have talked of it in any case, whether or not the child had ever been heard of again. According to their own reckoning she was marked with God's finger like the Prophet Samuel. One child had heard a voice in the night and the other had cried aloud behind a grille.

"Monsieur, Monsieur, you have garbled that passage!"

And then a sound of sobbing, come—as they themselves had to admit—from the remembrance of all that she had endured, which was now ended. The battle had been fought, they said, and was won; Françoise d'Aubigné obeyed her

86

promise; *mon père* had won the contest of words; her soul was henceforth in the Church's keeping.

From the narrow gate of the convent word went forth. At Murcy there would be despair and bitterness, with the long estrangement Françoise had feared; at Neuillant, rejoicing. In any case, whatever the results, the decision was taken. The grandchild of the Great Agrippa had renounced Agrippa's faith; henceforth she was no longer Huguenot. But even so there was one condition made by her, having accepted the faith that dispenses in its absolute validity with all conditions. She would kneel to God on the altar, but only if He would promise one thing.

"Say that my aunt Villette will not be eternally damned."

Françoise watched with detachment the joy of the nuns as they prepared her for her first communion. They had accepted her as possessed now of the glow of grace, but she felt none. She did not delude herself that she was an imposter. In the gray bargain between herself and God there was no ecstasy. *Mon père* in preparing her found her now docile, but still down-to-earth in the questions she raised. He knew better than to be shocked at the logic of Mademoiselle d'Aubigné.

To the question of Tante Arthémise he gave consideration. The dark eyes regarded him and he felt that to hedge would be futile; nor dared he, as with a peasant child, give the direct denial. Subtlety was for subtle minds; no one could say that this child was banal. He would trust her with the delicate conception of invincible ignorance, staking all on the intelligence that lay behind the eyes.

"We cannot say to what extent circumstance has played its part," he told her gently. "Wilful denial is one thing. Your aunt does her best according to her lights."

"Then the Church does *not* say she will be eternally damned?"

She reminded him of a careful housewife, hesitating before spending a sou. What a weapon might this child not be in skilled hands! It was for him, in this instant, to make or mar the steel. An instant's hesitation, and she would have been lost to him. *Mon père* did not hesitate. He gave her her answer.

"If your aunt loves what she knows of God, then she has hopes of heaven."

Françoise gave her little, grave bow. "Very well, *mon père*, when you will have me, I am willing to be received."

She asked no more questions.

Her reception took place in early spring and the streets were still powdered with snow. Now that she was to enter the Church the rigorous discipline of the Faubourg relaxed and she was able, once again, to receive visitors and to go, chaperoned, abroad. Mademoiselle de Saint-Herman came to see her, wrapped in furs, her cheeks rose-pink with the cold. She was ecstatic at news of the conversion. "We shall soon have you out now! Why did you remain here all the cold winter, you stubborn little thing?"

Mademoiselle turned up her nose at the smells of garbage in the Faubourg Sainte-Anne, but she promised to be present at Françoise' reception. At the ceremony there were others present apart from the nuns who were there in full number to recite, when the time came, the *Veni Creator* with her. She saw, as she made her way, curiously cool, down the side aisle, a well-known back before the altar, and a great hat with plumes surmounting jet-black hair; the lady had just lit a candle.

It was true, she thought, what Mademoiselle had promised. Madame de Neuillant had returned to her, or was it she to Madame? Afterward there would be the sharp embrace and the odor of *sachets* to contend with. Madame, pleased now, would have the approval of the Regent sustaining her. Madame would shortly air her convert in the world.

All these things were clear and separate in her mind as she went, without faltering, between the faldstool and the confessional.

XII

THE MARRIAGE of Françoise came about in this fashion.

During the chatterings of Mademoiselle de Saint-Herman, she had mentioned the name of one Cabart de Villermont. Cabart shared rooms with the poet Scarron. It also transpired that he had been in Martinique. Françoise had a bewildered picture of him, in those days when life moved rapidly without any propulsion of her own. He had come one day and stood by Saint-Herman's mantel talking to Madame. Françoise came into the room when bidden and saw a tall man in a fair *perruque*. His eyes widened a little as she approached, and as she curtsied she heard his laughter. It was deep and rich and affected her curiously; since Papa's death she had not heard such laughter from a man.

He took her hands, disregarding her shyness and Madame's frowns. "But, name of the saints, can this be possible?" said Cabart. He turned to Madame and explained how in Martinique days she had been a little, little creature —"Oh, but small enough to blow away with a breath! Every night I cast a card with your father Constant, and by the time he had won my silver you were abed. So little a creature, and now this!" His cool, smiling eyes never left her. "Madame must be proud," he said smoothly, "of the beauty of her charge."

Madame had answered coldly, but Françoise, thinking of it afterward, felt herself flush with pleasure. She was surprised at the importance of one word, only one, from a man with a rather ugly pock-marked face who had known her in Martinique. Beauty! Cabart de Villermont had said she was beautiful. Such a thing had not come into her

89

reckoning before, among the people with whom she had been. She cast, when that night she passed a Venice mirror on Saint-Herman's stairs, a glance at her own reflection. The shadows thrown by the candle she carried thrust up and flickered over a small pale face and she did not dare look longer in case Madame would see. Her own eyes had looked back at her like still pools.

Whom could she tell of this adventure? Mademoiselle would have understood it, but she was in the country. Françoise undressed and lay and wondered in her small bed, pleased and half-frightened. If Reverend Mother knew of what she lay and thought, instead of, as they advised at the convent, heaven and one's approaching end! Gravely she reflected on it, and told herself that in the *monde* there would be many more like Cabart who, if it were true, would say such things again to her. There was therefore no reason to behave as though anything had befallen out of the ordinary.

Nevertheless, she was pleased when a few days later word came for Madame and herself to attend a gathering sponsored by Cabart in the apartment of the poet Scarron at the Hôtel de Troyes.

She climbed the stairs in the wake of Madame de Neuillant, hearing her raised voice as she talked to her younger brother, M. de Candé, who had returned to town in time to accompany them. Madame was very grand, as befitted a visit to one of the most-talked-of personages in Paris. Françoise had spent an hour assisting her into her dress and lacing it tightly, and one of the laces had broken, being old, and Madame had raised her hand and slapped her, once, twice, across the face as she had been used to do before the conversion. Françoise could still feel her cheeks tingle a little; between that and the fright she was in at seeing the *monde* closely for the first time, she was near tears. She felt them rise and bit her lips fiercely. To make a fool of oneself so, on the very first visit to a house of the great in Paris!

That Scarron must be great was, she saw, indisputable.

Madame was saying now that his pension had been stopped because the Cardinal had see one of the *Mazarinades* and would not continue to support a man who could write such things, but however that might be the visiting *monde,* apparently, was fed. . . . The *appartement* was crowded to the very walls; Françoise had never seen so many personages at once. Madame had to thrust her way, aided by de Candé, between the wide skirts of the women, avoiding the men's dress-swords. The universe seemed stocked with silk-clad legs and rosetted knee-buckles and shoes. There was a chatter of many voices. Somewhere, in an inner room, some pastime was in progress; a woman's laughter rang out, high and shrill, followed by others, and on the instant the room seemed to swell and vibrate with the coarse, rich laughter.

What did they laugh at? Someone had said something; someone in the inner room. Françoise would have liked to know at what they laughed, and at the same time was thankful that she did not . . . and still, not knowing, felt alien, unwanted, provincial and too young; brought here, to the amusement of the satins and brocades and velvets, in her ugly yellow serge gown.

Ah, to be dressed like these opulent beautiful women, to have their assurance! To be able to talk, as Mademoiselle de Saint-Herman could do, with knowledge of the latest scandal—and how often these revolved about M. Scarron! A nun, whom he had loved in youth, a lady of good family, had returned to care for him in his infirmity although he could no longer be her lover or any woman's. Another noble and beautiful lady had donated her petticoats to make a chasuble for the priest in Scarron's little oratory; yet another had embroidered with her own hands the cover for his bed. Françoise could remember Mademoiselle, scandalized and giggling at it all; she herself had listened to all these enormities, digesting them in her mind like unripe fruit. In Mademoiselle's *chambre* it had seemed strange enough, but here, among the very company that saw and perpetrated such things, how shy she felt, lacking all knowledge beyond that of books. . . .

She moved timidly behind Madame and Saint-Herman,

eyes downcast in the manner of the convent so that full skirts, brocaded coats, and great-tongued shoes were all she saw. Once a bunch of ribbons, negligently knotted below a knee, reminded her of flower-colors, making her look up to see who might possess these.

The owner was a courtier, bearing the silver braid and the great dress-sword of those about the Regent Anne. His expression was at once haughty and oddly challenging; he looked at her, then his glance traveled on. She remembered, clearly conscious of the detail, the way in which his own dark hair hung in shining curls over his shoulders and chest.

She felt the hot color mount again in her cheeks; she would recall, she thought, that face, which was like that of a young demi-god in Agrippa's pictured *Aeneid,* long lost or sold. Madame le Comtesse had noted it also; Françoise heard her ask who he was. De Candé's voice held a trace of amusement as he replied.

"The young man with the ribbons? But where have you been? That is Villarceaux, *ami de Ninon.*"

Then Madame tossed her head and gave a little laugh and was silent.

They made their way at last to the inner door, from within which bursts of that same laughter had come again and yet again. De Candé bowed to this and that acquaintance; Cabart de Villermont lounged in the doorway. Françoise looked at him, glad to see a known face; he seemed less challenging, less terrifying, than on that other evening which had been, surprisingly, only four days ago. He came now and bowed to Madame and to herself and then made them precede him into the inner room from which the laughter had come.

A burst of it met them at the door; Françoise felt as though she had again been struck in the face. In her present nervous uncertainty it seemed incredible that it should not be herself at whom they laughed; she, the figure of fun, in her too-short yellow serge gown, brought from her convent to make an hour's diversion, like the monsters at fairs.

She trembled; the whole of her body was shaking, and her eyes were blurred with tears. Through them it seemed that the world was yellow; she was in a yellow room. Gradually the mist cleared and she saw that it was true; she was in a bed-chamber hung with yellow, walls, windows and bed having saffron curtains. On the floor before the bed was a box, and out of the box protruded, slightly awry, a man's head. His eyes, which were large, blue, and oddly childlike, squinted in divergent directions. He had long silk-fine hair which was turning gray.

"Scarron," said someone to the man in the box.

Françoise stared, not believing her eyes. *This* was Scarron! At the back of her mind she was conscious that Cabart de Villermont talked on. "Our little friend here, Mademoiselle d'Aubigné . . . has been in the Americas . . . this rascal, Scarron, wishes to go there, thinks it may restore him to the shape of other men. Perhaps Mademoiselle will help you, Paul. But fresh from her convent . . . have a care what you say, rascal . . . his powers are atrophied, Mademoiselle, but his tongue is the tongue of a debauchee. . . ."

And on, and on. She was aware of the growing horror of the thing. How dared they speak of this crippled man as though he were devoid of hearing? His eyes now fixed on her, converging slightly; bright and inquiring, with that odd look still of a child. One eye, she now saw, was a very little darker than the other. But what a face, and how it mocked, containing in it all the expression that the poor boxed body could never obtain! Only the eyes were sincere, wistful, and a little lopsided; their surrounding flesh not set like the rest into wicked lines. She waited for Scarron to speak, wondering what he would say, when he did so.

"Mademoiselle thinks now that no monster she ever saw in the Americas is remotely like to me. Is that not so, Mademoiselle?"

The voice mocked and challenged. Night and day, she thought, he must keep this up; a buffoon, that being his livelihood; not vulnerable to pity, or all present would tire. . . . As it was the crew, like Circe's horde that she remembered from the days of the turkey-field and Marie,

93

closed round, gaping, listening, jaws ready to part presently with that stock tribute of facile laughter. One must make them laugh, always, Mademoiselle, Scarron's eyes said to her; that is the only hope now; give way, for an instant even, to the desire for a soul of one's own, and the *ennui* on their faces will spell the end of this vogue which is Scarron. . . .

They were waiting for her to answer. Madame de Neuillant waited, mocking in the awareness of her charge's ignorance. Cabart waited, anxious to see how this little daughter of Constant, now grown, would do. Everyone, eyes fixed on her ridiculous ugly clothes, waited, amused even now before she should have spoken. And Scarron waited, with his self-deprecatory eyes on her face.

What should she say? What might she say? She dared not hurt the crippled man; no answer that she could make would fail to do so, she knew. "Yes, M'sieur, I saw many monsters so. . . ." Or "No, M'sieur, there was nothing like you at all!"

And so she could not answer and she burst into tears. Through them she heard the laughing commiseration of the crowd; the voice of Scarron, quickly breaking in, she thought, to save her—"Ah, among the fish that fly, and the apes that hang upon trees, and the root that groans when you eat it, and the giant oysters that have swallowed their own pearls, there is nothing, no, nothing, even remotely as I am, most completely in the form of a Z!"—and Cabart de Villermont's hand on her shoulder, kindly enough; and more talk, and more of the heartless laughter; and last of all the voice of M. de Candé, after many hours seemed to have passed, suggesting that Mademoiselle was tired and that they might all go home.

When Madame announced her intention of returning her to Niort, Françoise was surprised at the strength of her own resentment.

During the days of the Faubourg Sainte-Anne, she had forgotten how to feel. Now, with the glimpse of the world that she had had, that feeling returned to her; slowly, unrecognized until now, growing out of her appreciation of the talk of Tiraqueau and of Cabart de Villermont, who had traveled in every known continent of the globe. The *frondeurs* in the Hôtel de Troyes had scared her but she had been interested in them and would have liked to know more of their world . . . and now, after sacrificing her Huguenot faith, the respect of Tante and all those at Murcy, to be cast back, as though it had never happened, into the company of vapid nuns!

"I cannot go back!" she wept into the arms of the inconsolable Mademoiselle de Saint-Herman, "Madame wishes me to become a nun myself; it is her only way to be rid of me."

"Not so," said Mademoiselle shrewdly. "My aunt would be unlikely to part with a dowry for you, and without that you could not be received into any Order. In any case, they don't take unwilling nuns."

But to the weeping Françoise it seemed that Mademoiselle only spoke so blithely because she could have no knowledge of what she spoke. How to explain the effect of day to day, the growing feeling that there was nothing beyond the convent walls, no end but the common end for all to attain, no discipline but that exercised continuously down the silent corridors, the unpictured cells? If she remained long enough at Niort she might become a nun in spite of herself.

Mademoiselle was practical. "We must see that that does not happen. You must write to me, often, and I will write to you, telling you all the doings of Paris. *Chérie*, it is not so bad as it might have been in the Faubourg Sainte-Anne! At least you are not being sent back there—although," she added mournfully, "had that been so I could have come to visit you. But next winter, my aunt will bring you again to Paris!"

Françoise was not even sure of that. Next winter! How far away it seemed! And Mademoiselle, although of a good heart, was worldly and would undoubtedly forget her as soon as she was over the doorstep, despite her affectionate words.

But in this she maligned Mademoiselle.

* * *

95

Back at Niort, everything seemed small, gray and drab. In spite of the fact that she was now a Catholic, she found that she had no joy in the common life of the convent. The sermon at Mass she found provincial, listening to it with the critical attention a Huguenot would give. The priest in the confessional failed, she thought, to understand her problems; he dealt with her as with any peasant girl, discontented with her lot in life.

"Show gratitude to your guardian," he told her, "if it is the case that she wishes you to be provided for within the shelter of the Church. Try to overcome your will to meet her wishes. What other alternative is there for you?"

What other, indeed? She must be wicked and ungrateful, frivolous, desiring not what was best for her soul but the things which flattered her body. "Madame must indeed be proud of the beauty of her protégée . . ."

Cabart had admired her. If only—if only the young man called Villarceaux had done so! Why was it that his handsome face, the upper lip darkened with the little mustaches that had come to be ultra-fashionable at Court, the blue eyes mocking, would come so clearly to her mind?

What was it she wanted? For what did she wait, and hope? It might be that she would never see Villarceaux again. Why should that be so important, with a person on whom she had set eyes but once? What had there been in the face of Villarceaux that had made it mean, for her, suddenly, the whole of Paris?

> "*Que donneriez-vous, belle,*
> *Pour avoir votre ami?*
> *Je donnerais Versailles,*
> *Paris et Saint-Denis,*
> *Les tours de Notre-Dame*
> *Et le clocher de mon pays . . .*"

A frivolous little song, a wicked song, that Mademoiselle de Saint-Herman had hummed often in the room with the worked-wool fire-screen, saying it was come straight from the troops of M. de Condé and the war, with every week a new verse added. A song that had nothing whatsoever to do with the gray-flagged corridors and the smell of beeswax, the placid veils of the nuns and their calm unquestioning faces. And with it all a voice would come, lazy and amused, having seen so many *affaires* like this and answered so many queries from foolish women.

"The young man with ribbons? But where have you been? That is Villarceaux, *ami de Ninon*."

She should have asked Mademoiselle de Saint-Herman to tell her who Ninon was, but for some reason she had been afraid.

Mademoiselle did not forget her as she had supposed, and indeed wrote as often as Françoise would have wished, conveying in amiable ill-spelled script the latest news of Paris. For the younger girl to reply at any length might have been difficult; the days, containing nothing new, dragged out their length; summer darkened into autumn, the days grew short and the nights long so that candles were lit sooner. That was all; and vespers and compline, prime and terce and nones, followed each other. They might have been dull letters, and by rights should have been. Perhaps they were, Françoise thought; perhaps Mademoiselle was bored. For a long time no answer came, and she was certain that Mademoiselle had, at last, forgotten her. It must have been her own fancy that she had wit with a pen on paper, that the bare walls of the little cell had blossomed as she wrote, in an air grown bright with images and ideas. But no, she was dull, she was convent-bred, she was forgotten.

Then one day a letter came.

She carried it back to her little room, suppressing the excitement she felt on seeing the blue seal, with the Saint-Herman device. It was a measure of her confinement here that she should find Mademoiselle, whom she had once thought frivolous, a diversion. She felt the letter; it was thick. Precisely, with the small neat movements which were a part of her, she slit the seal, and opened out the paper and read.

Her brows arched in surprise. Mademoiselle had shown

her letters to Scarron. They had talked often together of Françoise, whom he called *la petite Indienne*. He had thought at first sight she was dull, but now, on reading her letters which Mademoiselle had assured him would give him entertainment, he no longer thought so. On the contrary, he was enraptured. Françoise was left with a picture of the twisted man, eyes bright with pleasure over her letters, hands—now, with the progress of disease, the only mobile part of him—gesturing in his joy. Scarron wished, Mademoiselle noted, that Françoise would write to him also. He still had a great desire to see the Indies. He had begged Mademoiselle to enclose a poem he had written on the subject, submitting it for the approval of Mademoiselle d'Aubigné who was a judge both of letters and of the conditions of that climate. Françoise found it difficult to reconcile her memories of Papa's drunkenness, Maman's harshness, with Paul's lively picture of seas where the best fish swam for nothing and one kindled fires with ebony and traded in pure gold.

> *"Et le sucre que j'aime tant*
> *Aussi bien que les confitures . . ."*

A little boy, she thought, might have written that; one who had the gift of verse.

She wrote to Scarron, finding after the first that her natural stiffness deserted her; his replies were so amusing, with so much of the *gamin* in them as well as the man of letters, that it was almost like writing to Charles. Gradually she began to look forward to his letters, as she had done to Mademoiselle's; and did not in the end notice that Mademoiselle's had ceased. It was possible, she found, to live entirely in the mind, accompanied by such a one as M. Scarron; and assuredly what else had the owner of that poor boxed-up body done these many years? If Scarron could remain gay and amusing in spite of his infirmities, then surely she could do the same, having her four limbs and all her strength, even though it were within four walls?

But just at it began to seem that all the world had forsaken her with the exception of that one correspondent, Madame de Neuillant wrote to say that she would come to fetch her in a few days' time and this winter again would take her to Paris.

Françoise was overcome with joy. It did not manifest itself in any outward manner, and the nuns noted only her shining eyes. They were fond of her, but they made no secret of their relief in seeing her go; no one, to date, had paid them any fees for her upkeep, and although she was willing and docile she could not help but eat. Besides, they, like Françoise herself, were persuaded that she would never make a *religieuse*. She was too unwilling to accept without question, all her life she would want to know the reason for everything; she needed the challenge of other minds, the scope of books beyond those the convent's list provided. They did not know what to make of her; she did not know what to make of herself. She packed her few things into a bundle with dexterity and pleasure, picturing the waiting world as a sea swimming full of fish.

She smiled, remembering the line in Paul's poem that had made her think of that. She would be able, she thought, this time, to meet the cripple without crying. . . .

Madame came, surveying with her hooded eyes the girl's face and figure as she came to her across the scrubbed hall. She was aware of a difference in Françoise although her features did not betray surprise or emotion regarding it. It emphasized, she told herself, the difficulty that would now be hers in settling the d'Aubigné girl suitably, as she had been stubborn about refusing to enter a convent and in any case there remained still the obstacle presented by the dowry. She wore still, Madame saw, the dark woolen gown and starched coif of inmates; beneath the coif her face showed oval and delicately colored. During the past year she had become a woman. The dark eyes showed a new awareness. Madame watched the progress of her protégée with coolness, seeing that the days of the meek follower in ugly buff serge were over.

Thoughts passed in procession through her mind like cows for market. They bore little labels and names, each one having a relation to the last, all having a bearing on Françoise d'Aubigné. Round and round, in orderly progress. No more expense . . . a settlement. One must be very careful not to scare off Scarron. It was not, of course, possible that he would ever make a husband in the ordinary sense. But what of that? The expense would be at an end. One must move carefully now. . . .

"My dear Françoise."

"Madame."

The Comtesse pecked the girl's cheek with some degree of warmth. It was colored by the sun and smooth as a petal; for an instant some emotion, which she could not name, assailed Madame. It passed, and she forgot it. Françoise stood stiffly to receive the embrace. She was unused to and shy of physical contacts and, in endeavor to escape from this one, took refuge as usual in the awareness of a variety of odors; the beeswax and harsh soap used about the hall, so familiar that one had ceased to note it until today, when it conflicted with Madame's *sachets de violette* which were as always a little stale; and the lead-powder on Madame's face, perfumed also and giving to her flesh that scared-ghost whiteness between the wrinkles, where it lay thickly; and also, because it was winter, the salty smell of the furs Madame wore, which had lain too long in storage.

Later she wondered at her own innocence with regard to Scarron. Almost the very day she arrived again in Paris she was taken to see him by Mademoiselle de Saint-Herman; and then that damsel, departing in a flurry of dimples and skirts looped *à la mode*, would not stay with her.

"I know nothing of books," she pouted, "nor of poetry either. You two leave me far behind."

Françoise and the twisted man were left regarding one another, in the yellow room which was empty now, by contrast to that other day, when the *monde* had thronged it. The scratching and chattering of a monkey on a stick was loud in the silence; had it been there last time? She knew that the same shyness overcame Paul Scarron as herself; both of them sought for the next word to say.

She remembered that he had complimented her on her letters; seeing, no doubt, now, no longer the fanciful correspondent whose wit matched his own, but the awkward little girl who had embarrassed him on the last occasion of their meeting by bursting into tears for no cause. That must be the reason for his helpless, curiously intent gaze; he must be wondering what to say to her, fearing lest she should behave so again. To relieve his fears, the silence must be broken; she did so, not without effort. "I have always," she said primly, "found it of greater ease to write than to speak freely."

"So?" said Paul Scarron.

An instant of his whimsical, tragi-comic smile transformed his face; then suddenly he began to talk, as though she had been anyone. "I, I can do both," he assured her, in answer to her last remark; and with a great waving of hands began to discourse of most things under the sun, but chiefly of Paul Scarron. "I have come of a line of talkers, lecherous lawyers, boastful bishops, and barons without any brains," he said. He told her of his childhood in the house of his father, an unlovable notary who was known as The Apostle from the habit he had of carrying Saint Paul's *Epistles* under his arm wherever he went. "But practice what he read, that the greatest of these is charity?" said this Paul, "never!" He had disliked The Apostle, a figure of fun in the old suit he wore of the time of Henri II; and loathed his new stepmother, Françoise de Plaix, whom he had plagued so greatly that in the end his father had sent him away while still a boy to a relative at Charleville, and Paul had hardly been home since.

"Then, *vois-tu*, they decided that I must be an abbé, and for a little while I was a great success at that; I have had success at most things. But I went to Italy and had too much pleasure and caught the pox, and as you see I am not as other men now, but am the ugliest being that was ever seen."

She listened without changing her expression or withdrawing her grave gaze from him; in return for the honesty he had shown in not, for some reason, telling her that tale about feathers and honey and the ague caught in a bog, she did not shrink from him. In any case, he could not have touched her; could not raise, beyond the wrists, his kyphosed arm toward her; could not turn his head, when she should go, to bid her farewell. Now with the twist of expression she was to come to know, at once comic and unbearably pathetic, he began to recite the lines on himself which he had once sent to his friend Sarasin.

> *"Tout tortu,*
> *Tout bossu,*
> *Suranné,*
> *Décharné . . ."*

"Ah," he said, "but your eyes hold pity!"

Almost every day after that Françoise went to the Hôtel de Troyes. It seemed that never had Madame had fewer duties for her to perform. Moreover, with the Court still out of Paris few of the *monde* had returned from the provinces, and only tradesmen and beggars walked in the half-empty streets. After the seclusion of the convent, the sensation of being in a town's streets pleased her; she began to look on it as an adventure to walk from the little side-door of the Hôtel Saint-Herman, down through the lane of narrow houses which leaned toward one another from the upper stories and almost blotted out the sky. The things in the small markets, the dark shops, intrigued her; she began to know the prices. Food was dear still because of the war and the meat was often fly-blown and bad; green vegetables were always scarce, and fruit was hardly ever seen.

Her gravity amused Paul and he took delight in trying to upset it; after the first he grew careful what he said to her, modifying his habitual coarseness. She did not laugh, he found, so often as she smiled; she did not talk so often as she remained silent. She was restful, kind, upright, freshly charming and something of a prude. He did not know of a single thing they had in common, and found it novel.

She also, with less reason for inquiring why, enjoyed his company. In her mind, still narrow on account of its environs, the comparison, half-formed, once came to her; flotsam, both of them, she thought, remembering the ownerless things cast up by the waves on the shores of Martinique or watched, half-seen and floating, on the restless seas between there and here. Nobody claimed her, and no one would claim Paul Scarron; his sisters, two of them, one a nobleman's mistress and the other a confirmed drunkard, troubled him little now that they were provided for.

His house was kept in a shocking state and she had enough leisure now from the demands of Madame de Neuillant to wish to improve it. Having asked shyly if she might do so, she astonished Paul with the industry and energy she displayed, the manner in which, once she had made her mind up to a task, she would perform it with thoroughness. Seeing the dust lie thickly on his table and the chest where his papers lay, she fetched a cloth and whisked and polished, disposing the litter; Paul watched in solemn amazement. "Why did none of my servants think of doing such a thing?" he inquired.

It was not in his nature not to repay her. One day when she went as usual to do one task and another for him, she arrived in the room to find a well-known figure standing, hat in hand, before the fireplace; M. le Chevalier de Méré.

Remembering afterward the things that befell in those days, it seemed to her that, right from the first realization that M. de Méré was no longer quite the same person, everything else that followed had come; culminating in the discovery of herself, as a force in the *monde*, a personality. . . . Of course, it did not happen quite like that. But impressions remained with her, such as the admiration in the Chevalier's eyes, different from the grave regard he had had for her in the days of Murcy; and the discovery, which filled her half with pleasure and half with fright, that the lessons he wished to give her now were not only those of Arabic and the classics but also the things which Tante had said she would never need to learn, such as how to curtsy and hold a fan and dance.

At first she watched in amazement, seeing the posturing little man removed, it seemed to her, from every kind of dignity he had ever had. But these movements were, he explained, the latest thing at the young Court of His Majesty, Louis XIV; the King himself, generally dressed as Apollo or some other deity, had begun to take a leading part in the ballets, which some said were only large-scale flatteries of himself.

"More likely large-scale devices to keep him amused, and his eye off the Cardinal and his doings," put in Paul drily. "A pretty state of affairs when all power in the land is vested in the illicit spouse of an onion-woman."

But M. le Chevalier looked so shocked it was doubtful if he would ever come back. Françoise guessed that his connections with those at Court were all but a religion to him.

He continued to come, however, to the Hôtel de Troyes; and the reason was herself. For the first lesson he had done no more than make her walk, again and repeatedly, toward him across the room. There was a way, he said, in which even that should not be done. To her surprise he complimented her at the end of it.

"Mademoiselle has a natural dignity, a certain *hauteur*," he explained. "She should strive to maintain it."

He taught her the mode of entry of a room at Court; he taught her the rules of Court etiquette, of precedence and of the dance. Scarron looked on like some gnome, only his eyes moving. Once or twice he was not alone and then others would stay to spectate. This at first made Françoise nervous, but de Méré assured her she had nothing to fear. "They cannot compare with you; they are envious," he assured her. "Do not let them see that you are afraid."

Once a very tall slim woman with fair hair came. She also remained in the memory with curious persistence; one might devote many hours to asking why and find no answer. There was an unusual quality about her, although what it was Françoise could not decide. Perhaps it was her very indecisiveness. The gown she had worn swirled about her figure in a manner seldom seen now when stiffness was all the mode. Its lightness, and her quick graceful movements, and her odd, mobile, attractive, dimpled mouth, made her memorable. The mouth laughed always, whether at herself or another was doubtful. It laughed at Paul, boxed in his gray chair. It laughed at de Méré, in his threadbare punctilious clothes; reducing all his pretenses to cobwebs and idleness, making great matters small and small ones the pivot of the universe. Ninon, the fair woman's name was; Ninon de l'Enclos.

Françoise had trembled so greatly at the introduction that Ninon laughed at her also.

That night she could not sleep at all and lay awake filled with strange longing. Scarron, the Chevalier, the yellow room, herself; all had dissolved and she was someone else, although where and wherefore she did not know. There were matters here beyond her understanding and only the mocking eyes of Ninon knew, and could understand.

She asked Paul about Ninon and he told her; he did not seem surprised at her question.

"That immortal Ninon! The Queen of Paris! It is unlikely that she will ever be old. . . ." And he went on to tell her of how this Ninon, whose father had been an indulgent notary and her mother a lady afflicted so deeply with religious melancholy that she had made of Ninon an atheist for life, had been left an orphan at the age of sixteen and, quite simply, made her own world thereafter and lived in it as she chose.

"Everything that Ninon does, or says, is elegant. She is never dull, never clinging, never wearisome, never possessed —for longer than it pleases her—or possessing. She has discarded many lovers but kept them all as friends. That in itself is a very great achievement." Ninon's house, he said, in the Rue des Tournelles, was open to all those who were elegant or witty as long as they remained so. A *mot* by Ninon in the morning would have gone the round of Paris by night. "Then, you see, it is time to think of a new one," said Paul gravely. "That in itself will entail a great deal of labor, is it not so, Mademoiselle?"

Françoise could not think of Ninon in connection with

labor, and said so. Her heart was hammering out a question which she dared not ask.

Paul did not answer it, therefore, but he said a thing which astonished her. Ninon was now more than forty years of age.

It had not struck Françoise that Ninon de l'Enclos would show any interest in herself. When she looked, as on that night of Cabart's visit, at her reflection in the glass at the Hôtel Saint-Herman, she saw only her own grave face, slim hands and ugly gown. How could such a creature attract the elegant, the witty, the desirable Ninon, whose *ami* Villarceaux was, who must know every nuance of the fine-lipped, sardonic mouth, whose long white hands must so often have touched the shining hair?

Why would she think of such things? She must be wicked. . . .

But next time she went to the Hôtel de Troyes Ninon was there, and had brought Villarceaux with her.

How had she seemed to him? For days she could think of nothing else than the memory of him: his smile, faintly mocking as on that first day, and the manner in which one fine hand was flung along the mantel idly, as though he owned the house. What he wore she could not tell, and what they said she could not recall; only the voice of Ninon, light, teasing, charming, elegant, had gone on, and her laugh that tinkled like silver bells had tossed back and forth for them all, for Villarceaux, Paul, and now herself, the little discovery who was to parade before them and show off how well M. de Méré had groomed her.

"The protégée of Madame de Neuillant. . . ."

Murmured approbation, inquiries, directions. Françoise felt her heartbeats strong and loud, her face and throat suffused with color. She must posture and turn and walk, curtsy and simper. Then he would go home and forget her for other things.

The Chevalier's voice. "Show Mademoiselle Ninon and M. le Marquis how one makes the *grande entrée* to the

King's chamber. Three curtsies, in the *façon du haut monde*. Regard," this to the others, "how she has progressed for me!"

But it was not for the Chevalier de Méré that Françoise came slowly across the outer room, dropping at stated times the three great curtsies demanded by custom on entry to the presence of His Majesty, Louis XIV. Nor was it for Paul, who watched from his chair, his bright child's eyes holding many things she did not see. Nor for Ninon; least of all for her, that charming and amoral person whom no one could resist, dislike, or ever forget. Villarceaux was Françoise' king, as she came toward him—Villarceaux, watching between lazy eyelids the little acquisition of Scarron, whose eyes, skin and hair held promise of beauty once her *gaucherie* should have been shed and her figure maturely rounded. She saw him as she had never before seen any man, nor would again; a god, a super-being infinitely to be desired with the innocence for which desire has no name. Because of this he was above her, unattainable as a star; of what avail were *hauteur* and a natural dignity to the serving-maid of Madame de Neuillant?

She heard their applause, dimly as with a matter far off; saw the twisted smile of Paul, the satisfied joy of de Méré. The latter was like a showman, drawing forth praises of the young dignity of his pupil's bearing, the grace of her movements. "Her proportions are admirable, her coloring perfection!" He gestured in appeal to Mademoiselle Ninon, that *connoisseuse;* did she not think, as he did, that in a year, months, weeks, this little d'Aubigné could be the rage of Paris?

Ninon said little, smiling her slow amused smile. The tall graceful child who had just been demonstrated to them had, she thought, eyes like a bird, bright-dark. They ranged inquiringly from herself to Villarceaux, and back again.

Ninon's voice came then lazily, having a quality and richness as though honey lay in her throat. "And M. le Marquis, who is silent, what does he think?"

Villarceaux was her lover. For some time yet the passion between them would burn fiercely, destroying everything that hindered its flame. She watched him idly, knowing him very well; remembering from how many fleeting interests he had always returned to her. No woman had ever denied Villarceaux. How handsome he looked in his coat of dark velvet, with the veiled lazy regard in his eyes! It was desirable for a man to be brutal, a little; most women preferred it so.

She had no fear that he would forget her for this charming young girl. His answer, when it came, was contained in that one word.

"Charming," said Villarceaux, and smiled and moved his hand, so that the light glinted on a ring he wore. Françoise hung her head.

The change came one day when Françoise mounted the familiar stairs and found Madame de Neuillant sitting with Scarron.

She could tell from the expression on her guardian's face that she was not pleased. Paul, on the same count, looked embarrassed. The expression was so foreign to him that she stared, forgetting her fright; and was called sharply to attention by the voice of Madame.

"So I find you!"

She launched then into a tirade of the many times she had looked for Françoise and found her out of the house. Françoise listened in amazement. She had a fair idea that Madame had always known where she went; it would never have occurred to her to try and conceal it. Now, listening to Madame's talk of duplicity, deceit and hoydenish behavior, she felt the color rising in her cheeks as if she were guilty of a fault.

Scarron tried to interpose; Madame brushed him aside. It was not to be supposed that he, she said, had been aware of the harm he was doing. To a man such things were second nature, and her godchild's reputation not a matter that could be supposed to encumber the conscience of the most fashionable *écrivain* of Paris. Françoise might have known better had she been less strictly reared. No doubt the innocence of the convent remained with her to such a degree as to veil even now the seriousness of what she had been doing; but in any case it must stop. "How can I allow such visits to continue, and soon have all Paris talking of my ward's loose behavior?—classing her, no doubt, M. Scarron, with those who have come here already, and were less innocent? No, no, I say that the thing must cease, and that there shall be reparation!"

Françoise dared not look at Scarron. What had happened? Why should those few words of Madame have made what was innocent seem harmful, poisoning the very air of the yellow room so that she felt she never wanted to breathe it again? It should be so easy for herself or Scarron to tell Madame all that had befallen; the talks they had had of Tristan l'Hermite, of Grandfather Agrippa and the playwright Corneille; the lessons in deportment given by M. de Méré; the thousand and one things they had enjoyed together, the dusting and polishing, even, as it had been at the Hôtel Saint-Herman only with more joy thereto. . . . But neither of them said a word, and she knew that the twisted man must be as embarrassed as she.

It seemed a long time since she had heard Scarron's voice. When it came she looked at him; but he would not meet her eyes. Françoise felt herself lost in a sea of bewilderment and misery. Had Paul, too, turned against her? Would he see her as deceitful, in the hideous way mentioned by Madame?

She saw Madame waiting, a bird of prey. How often she had thought of her as such, without consciously forming the simile! After this moment she thought she would never forget it again. The hooded-eyed face, with the little wrinkles caked and filled in with white cosmetic and the neck strung and lean, was like a waiting vulture's . . . why did Madame hover so, and what did she will Scarron to say? For an instant the yellow room waited, weighed, brooded, together with Madame. Then Paul spoke.

"I will repair the damage done to your protégée—Madame."

His voice was smooth. The Comtesse's face, from being

hostile, maintained a careful lack of expression as she awaited his reply. Now she would reap her reward of the patience shown while this *frondeur* dallied with the little d'Aubigné! She was watchful not to allow optimism to creep into her tone.

"Damage, Monsieur? Such damage is irreparable," she told him. "A young girl's reputation—a man such as yourself! I do not mince my words; out of fondness for one who is not my own—"

"Such fondness, Madame, is known to be without parallel," said Paul. His eyelids drooped wearily and he grimaced as though he were in pain. "It cannot be . . . permitted . . ." the voice died for an instant until the spasm passed, then resumed as though nothing had happened —"that Madame should further subject herself to excursions such as today's. The relief of such a charge will be enormous, and I will therefore do all in my charitable power both to assist Madame, and to undo what harm has been done."

His eyes moved to the scared girl by the wall and his voice became gentle.

"Tell me, *chérie*, you would be happier, would you not, out of the care of Madame de Neuillant?"

"Ah, no gratitude," began the Comtesse, "after all I—"

"Be silent, Madame, or go to the devil," blazed Paul. "Answer yes or no, my child, and if your reply is 'yes' I will see to it myself that you are provided for."

Françoise felt the world spinning about her. Where would Scarron send her? There was no time to think. . . . "Yes," she breathed, "yes."

"I have nourished a serpent," said Madame.

Paul gave a little flicker of his eyelids; his face was white. "*Ça suffit,* Mademoiselle, there is no need to say any more," he told her. With the effect that he could contrive of having turned toward Madame, although unable to move, he added, while his mouth smiled, "Rest assured, Madame! It will give me the greatest pleasure on earth, since you decline to provide your charge with a dowry, myself to offer her one, in order that she may enter a convent."

XIII

Mademoiselle de Saint-Herman was distressed beyond measure. For Scarron to have failed them! Scarron—to offer a convent!

"What is the matter with him?" she asked herself. The plot had gone wrong. It had been so suitable, so unusual, the future she had permitted herself to map out for her little friend Françoise d'Aubigné; in her situation, with no money whatever, no vocation whatever, there could not have been found a better. Scarron, who required a good little housekeeper; Françoise, who would so appreciate a tutor! As for the rest, Mademoiselle was not so ignorant; but that, she thought, would right itself in time, very few women of *ton* at the present day did not have lovers, and one might be considered fortunate in fact in possessing a husband who in that respect was no encumbrance. It was true that in many others poor Scarron would be a burden, but *la petite* Françoise would make an excellent nurse.

It had all been so suitable, so desirable, almost too adaptable to plan . . . and then for the chief actor to have behaved so, right in the middle of the main scene. . . . Heaven forfend, a convent! The very thing poor little Françoise d'Aubigné had been trying to avoid!

She dared not speak to Françoise. She had seen the poor child, white-faced and terrified after the ordeal at the Hôtel de Troyes and the following few days of purgatory—she had refused, Madame made known, M. Scarron's generous offer, and with her old persistence and demon-supported nature, Madame's life was a trial to her, just as it had been in the days when the little d'Aubigné would remain Huguenot. What did it matter to Madame if Scarron married the girl or made a nun of her, provided she was off the Comtesse's hands? At first, it was true, his offer had been a shock. Then she had come to see the worth of it . . . but by that time Françoise d'Aubigné, stupid regarding her own best interests as usual, had blurted out a refusal in face of M. Scarron and then turned and run out of the house. It had not been possible for Madame to do anything then but follow her, although when she got her home she had had her whipped soundly, as she deserved. The fear was now that M. Scarron might withdraw his offer in face of such pig-headedness, and where would any of them be then?

"I will have her on my hands," said Madame, "for the rest of my life." She regarded her brother's child angrily. There was little doubt, she thought, that her niece was to blame for stuffing the d'Aubigné girl's head with nonsense. Marriage, indeed! She should be lucky to have a roof above her head and clothes on her back. "If she lets the offer go by, I believe I will kill her!" announced Madame.

Françoise certainly believed this. In those days of renewed terror she found that her mind almost ceased to function. Madame to her reckoning took on the aspect of a devil; determined by whatever means to break down her opposition before Scarron should tire of his offer, she missed no means of assaulting her, body and spirit. The most menial tasks became hers, such as before had been fit only for scullions and gutter-sweepers; she carried them out, sick with fear and with the memory such things aroused in her of the dreadful winter in the Faubourg Sainte-Anne when she had been deserted by all the world. Had the sacrifice she had then made led only, after all, to this? Was she to spend her life walled up with foolish women, never hearing of or seeing the world outside, with her mind like a bird beating against bars, till her brain atrophied and her spirit broke? If she had remained faithful to Murcy and the Huguenot teachings they could not have done this to her; perhaps God punished her so. Had she indeed been wrong, unfaithful, a renegade; had she lost Murcy for this? "Tante, Tante, you would not have used me so," she would breathe pitifully, lying on her face in the hard bed at nights with her body smarting from the blows of Madame. Of what avail to write to Tante, who could do nothing? If she had not saved her from the Faubourg Sainte-Anne she could not save her from this.

Once Mademoiselle de Sainte-Herman came to her, shading a candle with her hand and walking carefully, so as not to wake Madame. Françoise sat up in bed and greeted her joyfully; she saw that Mademoiselle was still dressed, grandly as though for a ball. "Ah, that!" said the young lady impatiently, when the other remarked on the becomingness of her blue silk. "I made Papa bring me away early, for it did not divert me. I had a great desire to talk to you. Hush, say nothing, *petite!* I know very well my aunt has forbidden it."

"She says that I am possessed of a devil," said Françoise. Trembling, she told Mademoiselle of her considered intention at last to accept the offer of Scarron. "I do not know if I am doing rightly. But who is to direct me? All those whom I have consulted tell me I am foolish to refuse. How can I hold out longer?"

Mademoiselle de Saint-Herman leaned forward and took her by the shoulders.

"Listen, you little fool, do you *want* all your dark hair to be cut off and buried under a linen strip for the rest of your days? It's very beautiful hair, I have been admiring it. Others will do so too, if . . . if you will give yourself a day or two's grace. Do nothing till I send you word again, in case Aunt prevents my speaking to you. Promise me that, at any rate; do nothing quickly."

"What will you do?" said Françoise fearfully. The candle-shadows leaped in the room.

Mademoiselle was already at the door, a finger on her lips. "Hush," she said, "I thought I heard my aunt stir. Leave everything to me for a little. Will you?"

"Yes," said Françoise from her bed, "yes," as she had done to Scarron. Only time was short— "Please do it quickly!"

It was two days later when a note came to her from

Mademoiselle. If she still wished to accept M. Scarron's gift, it said, she must go and thank him for it in person. If she asked Madame's permission, the Comtesse would allow her to go.

Françoise folded the note again with a little resigned firming of the mouth. Of what avail had been the interference of Mademoiselle? She had accomplished nothing.

She herself was almost resigned now to the will of God. Perhaps that was the way of these disguised vocations; resignation came gently, unacknowledged and unwelcome at first, merging at last into a blessed acceptance. In any case she could not accept Scarron's gift coldly without further thanks. She would make known to Madame her wish to accept his offer of a dowry and to thank him for it in person.

"You've left it late," grumbled Madame, concealing her relief. A formal letter was dispatched to the Hôtel de Troyes. Would M. Paul Scarron be pleased to receive Mademoiselle d'Aubigné at a date and time specified? Françoise thought dully of the days when she had been used to run upstairs to the yellow room without thinking, untying her cloak as she went. Those days were gone forever.

The reply came; it was noncommittal. M. Scarron would receive Mademoiselle.

When Françoise saw the twisted man again she was aware of the change in him.

He had been ill, she thought, reproaching herself; was he not always ill? But this day he seemed as if some long added trouble had weakened him, bleached the flesh on his contracted bones and darkened and enlarged his eyes. He was like an animal that has pined and grown smaller. He watched her as she stood by the door.

"Monsieur Scarron, I have come to thank you for your generosity."

How pitifully thin and stilted her words sounded! She must make it sound as if she really desired the convent; as if she esteemed his offer. She swallowed, feeling her throat dry. How was one to begin to lie?

"*Attends*," said Paul softly. "What have they done to you?"

"To me, Monsieur?" She was bewildered. His eyes held her.

"You are like a little wax candle that has been burned almost away. There are smudges under your eyes; you are thinner. What have they done to you, what has that woman done, that they have made you accept this offer which you would die rather than accept? Answer me."

"They—I—" Ah, she must not make him feel that his offer was so unwanted! She began to blush and stammer, forgetting her rehearsed speech. M. Scarron must not think her ungrateful—she was not used, that was all, to generosity . . . it had required thinking over, she had concluded, after all, that what he purposed would be for her good, and she—

"Do not sell me that stuff like wares for market!" he shot at her. "Listen now! Do not thank me, Mademoiselle, for what no longer exists." He glared at her. "Not a sou will I give in order that you may enter a convent. *Je ne le veux plus!*"

Françoise gave a great cry. It was useless, then!

"Madame will kill me. Monsieur Scarron, dear Monsieur, she will kill me if I return without the dowry!"

She knelt to him. Dimly she saw herself, acting in a way to which she was unused; kneeling to Scarron, to a little crippled man in a gray box. She heard her own sobbing, and recalled how he must think her a tearful fool; she had wept on first seeing him, and now this.

"Monsieur, Monsieur, what is to become of me?"

"Listen to me," said Scarron.

She raised her tear-filled eyes. Of what use to storm so? Whatever became of her now would be her own fault. She had dallied too long, while M. Scarron grew wearied. It was as it had been with her conversion, putting off for one reason and another till everyone grew tired of her. She wondered what Madame de Neuillant would do when she got home.

"You are not fitted to be a nun."

Not fit for a nun, not fit, even, to be as Sœur Céleste, rubbing and starching at linens for the glory of God. Unfit, still more, to be a contemplative, in that most exacting of all vocations, kneeling perpetually in the spirit in prayer. Unfit to glorify God's altars even with the flowers of summer. Unfit to be a drudge even to the woman one hated, who was mean. . . .

"You cannot understand . . ."

That well-remembered, halting speech! What would she have become had she had to endure affliction like Scarron's, racked every few minutes with excruciating pain? God had given her health, which she had abused. . . .

". . . the extent of the sacrifice you would make. Will you become my wife?"

Mademoiselle de Saint-Herman waited with impatience. An hour ago she had seen Françoise set off. Yesterday she had spent two hours persuading Scarron; today, a less welcome task, she had to placate her aunt. "You use me!" that lady complained, but Paul, with more reason, had not done so. How difficult it had been to convince him of this necessity nobody but herself would ever know; and that not on account of aversion to Mademoiselle d'Aubigné, but on the contrary by reason of aversion to himself. *"Tout tortu, tout bossu, suranné, décharné!"* How could he, aware as he might have been of Madame's machinations, see himself as the husband of a charming young girl? "She will be beautiful, accomplished, desired! How can I tie her to myself?" His poor hands had tried to gesture, his tongue to protest. Did he not think he could love Mademoiselle d'Aubigné? Mademoiselle had asked.

But that had been a cruel question. "I am not as other men! How can I love? And yet—"

Of course he loved her, thought Mademoiselle. Aloud she said, vaguely aware of the torment Paul had been in these past few weeks, "Put away your modesty, Monsieur! You will be shelter for her, both from the world and from the veil. She is in almost as much terror of the one as of the other."

"The poor child," said Scarron. Then he remembered that he was the clown of Paris and must make, for this occasion, a *mot* that would make Paris laugh. It would divert no one to hear of his megrims and his sighs.

He allowed the old, wicked grin to overspread his face; the eyes diverging above one hunched shoulder leered up at Mademoiselle.

"I can do her no harm," he said, "but I can teach her a deal. Oh, what things I shall teach my wife! She will be the wickedest woman in all Paris."

Mademoiselle de Saint-Herman did not repeat this remark to Madame de Neuillant on her return.

The girl Françoise came in slowly at last and Mademoiselle caught her as she was loosening her cloak preparatory to mounting the stairs.

"You look as one who sleep-walks," said Mademoiselle teasingly. "When are you to go to the convent?"

She had been prepared to burst out laughing, to tease and cosset and caress. Such things were in keeping with a bridal-to-be, even a bridal with Scarron—poor Scarron! But although the girl flushed and murmured with down-dropped eyes, "I am to be married to M. Scarron," for some reason Mademoiselle found her voice desert her and her congratulations die in her throat.

Françoise went on talking primly. "He says that his servants misuse him, which I can very well believe," she said. "Also his friends will visit him more often if his house is made attractive. It is understandable; he cannot go to visit them, and he is fond of company."

Her cloak was off; she took her candle from the rack and prepared to mount the stairs to her room. Desperately, Mademoiselle sought to lighten the moment; the reassurance was rather for herself than for that other, who remained so unmoved. "And did he not—M. Scarron—give a single reason as to yourself? Any old *concierge* would have sufficed, it seems—from what you say!"

"He says that I have beautiful hands," said Françoise. "Also that I am shapely, and not devoid of wit."

"Merciful saints!" said Mademoiselle. This time she allowed the other to ascend the stairs in silence.

To have become the *fiancée* of Scarron carried with it certain disabilities, and Madame de Neuillant, having accustomed herself to her original relief, announced that it would be more proper for Françoise to leave Paris for a while.

Heaven knew, she said, that it was not the betrothed. He at least was static, and having written, and obtained, permission from Jeanne d'Aubigné in Bordeaux, there was no point in pretending that he would give any trouble. But the *monde* had come inquiring for the lady he was to marry, and besides the jeopardy to Françoise herself in her singular state, it was an expense, on which Madame had not reckoned, to measure out glasses of Madeira wine for the Raincys and du Ludes and the d'Albrets and Villarceaux, and every other young blood who thought that the bride of Scarron was an object of curiosity and possibly of desire.

She stared coldly at Françoise d'Aubigné during the journey south. The girl had made no demur either at leaving Paris and her grotesque *fiancé* or at being lodged, once again, with the Ursulines at Niort. A battle still raged about the payment of expenses there, but so far no one had made Madame pay them and it would be a saving of money to place the girl there until her wedding, instead of housing her at Neuillant. Doubtless the Marquise de Villette was good for little more; she had ceased all communication with the girl since the conversion was made public, in spite of her once-avowed fondness for her. How stubborn Huguenots were!

Well . . . this girl, sitting silent in the corner of the carriage, watching the jolting past of the mud-rutted roads, owed her the fact of her marriage, her establishment in some sort in the world. "But for me, Mademoiselle, you'd still be living on the charity of others; don't deny it. I haven't done more for my own daughters. When you are settled in Paris, remember me."

"M. Scarron intends our going to the Indies, Madame."

She had not turned her head from contemplation of the roads, nor unclasped the hands which lay idly, ungloved, on her lap. Madame de Neuillant suppressed irritation at her apathy. Where had she learned to sit so, as though she were a duchess with servants to come running? One could not, for some reason, mistake her for a *bourgeoise,* still less a maidservant. Madame raked back over the d'Aubigné and Cardilhac ancestry; rogues, the d'Aubignés, all of them, but Jeanne's father, old Pierre de Cardilhac, the Governor, had had a presence. Madame shrugged. For what it was worth it might do very well in the Indies, that high-handed manner; provided they ever got there, she and that bag of jumbled bones no one could call a man. . . . Doubtless little Scarron pictured himself as being able to restore his functions in the sunshine.

"Well," she said aloud, "you as a good wife will make no demur about accompanying him. It follows that one must preserve the spirit of this marriage, even though the practical side lacks substance. It would hardly have been possible in your state to find you, with honor, a normal suitor."

Françoise stared still at the gray roads and fields and the sky, and saw none of them. Her awareness was in layers, each one of them dealing with separate things; the upper sensing the wheels of Madame's coach, bowling and swaying ever further from Paris, further and further from M. le Marquis de Villarceaux, who had come to the Hôtel Saint-Herman and, with the rest, surveyed her as though she was, shortly, to be for sale. It had not needed the care of Madame de Neuillant to keep her by her side.

At Niort, Françoise received letters from Paul as though he were her lover. The impossibility of there ever being physical love between them made his pretense the more passionate. "I love you more than I had ever dreamed," he wrote. *"La malepeste que je vous aime, et que c'est une sottise d'aimer tant!* For God's sake return soon. I stare at myself and imagine that I am worse than I am, twisted from head to foot, without also suffering from this damnable complaint called *l'impatience de vous voir. . . ."*

She stared at herself, likewise, trying to conjure up the person that Paul saw, or wished to see. She was so unaccustomed to the terms of expressed love that she did not know whether his words were common or strange. Pretense was not easy to her; her replies, written from Niort and a sick-bed (once or twice, since Martinique, a tertian ague had assailed her), were prim, unable even through the stimulus of fever to attain the ease of fancy that had blossomed from her pen a year ago. Paul then became gay, seeming in his reply to personify the young, able-bodied lover he would have given his soul to be; jesting on paper with an ease contrasted to the bitter quips that physical nearness seemed to draw from his twisted body. "Let the fever turn to quartan," he wrote, "and we can share it all winter!" He wrote also that their stay in the cold of Paris would not be for long; he had found a means of procuring the three thousand livres necessary to join the new *Compagnie des Indes* which had been formed, that year, by a band of those as anxious for the sun as himself.

The method of his procuring the passage-money was typical. Almost everyone, Paul himself included, had forgotten that he was, in fact, an abbé. On being reminded of this disposable asset, he sold the interest to the first comer, a gentleman desirous of the benefits of Church living. Now, he wrote joyfully, deliverance was at hand! A nuptial feast —a new gown for Madame Scarron—a sojourn in the provinces pending the Cardinal's return to Paris (the possibility that that dignitary would revenge himself on the author of the *Mazarinades* was never very far from Paul's thoughts) and then, on board one of the two new vessels which the *Compagnie* was about to float, a voyage to the land of sun and of all desire . . . three thousand livres! It was the beginning of everything.

*   *   *

They were married on the 14th of April. Françoise had come back to a Paris fearful of siege; picketed at every street-corner were men-at-arms who called out, impudently, in Spanish or guttural German, as the party passed. She would see the dark bulls' faces of the Spaniards, the brutish fair Saxons, in her mind that night when she slept. Paris was strange, on edge and frightening. After the peace of the convent the noise assailed her. She would be glad, she thought, when she and Paul had gone.

She thought of Paul, realizing how little she had seen of him since their betrothal; never the two of them alone since the day he had asked her to marry him. The feeling of having been stage-managed overcame her; she was a puppet, moving to pulled strings. Glancing up at the face of Pierre Tiraqueau, who was to give her away, she found it remote; Madame's brother had been kind to her, but would be glad when his duty was discharged. She continued on her way in silence, looking straight ahead.

The *chambre jaune* was as it had been that first day, filled with people whose faces seemed a blur. There was no sign of Paul, who had been wheeled into his oratory. Leaning on Tiraqueau's arm, Françoise made her way slowly in and knelt. She still felt unreal and as if at any moment she would wake up, once more, in her narrow bed at the convent.

The altar-cloth was of silver mesh embroidered with great golden flowers. Someone, a woman, had given her veil for it, thinking to please Paul. Françoise wondered how he felt, if he regarded this ceremony as a sacred thing or not. She heard him make the responses in a low voice, seated in his chair.

The ceremony completed, she was met and kissed by various people, among them Madame and Tiraqueau. The procession re-formed and they went, she walking by Scarron's chair, back to the room where a feast was laid. Someone had arranged flowers in a crescent-shaped basket. Françoise stared at them from her place in the center of the bench, eating little. Every now and again would come a burst of laughter as a result of something Paul had said. It was so like that other day, with the sense of the whole world pressing in, avid for laughter.

She was conscious of herself, the bride, seated there in the midst of it all, but not of them. Wherever it was she belonged it was not here, among mirth. She did not think that she would ever learn to laugh much, and wondered if her husband would find her dull.

Her husband. The meaning of it was made clear to her when, after they had all gone, the valet came and asked her to assist Monsieur to bed. There was no one else, he said, tonight, the other servants having gone on holiday. She saw the man's frank, lewd gaze as he spoke to her, and was suddenly afraid. There had been, after all, protection in the house of Madame de Neuillant that she would not find here.

Well, she herself must be her own protection. She went with the man and assisted him to lift Scarron, still a trifle drunk after the feast, from his gray chair. She had schooled her features to show no change unguardedly, but the sight of that pitiful body which few saw shocked her. The joints were so contracted that it was impossible to straighten the limbs; his very head on his neck was wry. The valet left them after he had undressed Paul; Françoise was alone with her husband, a lit candle between them. The great shadows behind his head made the bed seem an abode of ghosts.

"You are comfortable—Paul?" Even his name had become an effort to her. She saw his eyes, and that he was in torment. Pity overcame her.

"Madame." His wry lips twisted in an attempt to smile. It had been all he could do to maintain his flippant humor in this hour. The light showed him the girl's face, pale against the candle-flame and the darkness of her eyes. Her hair hung loosely, shining and chestnut-dark; beneath the shawl she had hurriedly flung on to come to him the young curve of her breast was outlined against the white pleated shift. "Madame—" What a travesty of a name, that, for her; not a wife, not—dear God, for one hour of himself as he had used to be, only that . . . but to be left only a brain in a shell of torment, with the pain that racked him zigzagging down the nerve-paths of every limb!

"A man like a Z. No man. *Quelle nuit de noces!*" She had to bend low to hear him; the eyes never left her face.

"Tell me, child, were you . . . shocked . . . when you saw me as I am? Did you wish that you had chosen a cloister, rather than—this? This blasphemy? It is no marriage for you."

She saw that he was in pain. "Tell me where to find what will ease you." The valet had told her where his powders were kept. Paul indicated the chest with a glance of the eyes. "Bring them to me . . . in a little water. Ah, to have you do this!"

She opened the chest and found in it a little box containing gray powder. It had a heavy, greasy feel and sweetish smell. She measured out the amount into a cup of water and brought it to Paul; surprised at her own hands' steadiness. To drink he had to have his head raised and she slid her arm under his neck and hair. His head was heavy; so large a head for the small wizened trunk, containing all the wit of Paris.

She watched him drink. Presently his eyes grew light and calm and she settled his pillows. "You are better now?" she said. "You will sleep?"

"I never sleep. After a while the drug wears off. When they gave it me first it was better."

His head rolled pettishly and she saw that he was shy with the sense of his own hideousness. Hesitantly, she tried to ease the pain. They said that gentle movements, up and down, regularly, not too hard at first, on the limb brought relief.

"Your hands are gentle." But sometimes he would cry out sharply with pain. Slowly, she lost her unfamiliarity at the touch of flesh, her vestige of shrinking from him. Sometimes he would drop into a light doze and she would go softly to the door, but always his voice sought her and she came back; he was better, she began to imagine, when she was there. Outside the night grew silver and the stars, which

123

had been bright in the sky, shone less clearly. It was almost dawn when she found her own bed. She did not sleep, all weariness having gone; but strangely, her mind was lulled and she did not feel unrefreshed. It was no more possible to tell what tomorrow would bring than it had ever been, for her, from one day to the next; but somehow now at the back of her mind there had grown the certainty of being wanted; for now, at any rate, there was someone who needed her and for whom she would be willing to live. She fell asleep at last during the unfamiliar Rosary, which she tried to say every night but which would never, as long as she lived, come easily to her mind.

PART II

The House of Impecuniosity

I

PARIS OF 1653 had a new interest. His Eminence and the royal family, finding the capital safe again, had returned from their sojourn in the provinces; but the Second Fronde still raged, in desultory manner, about the banks of the Loire. It was uncertain now who waged the war or which side anybody was on. Now that the young King was growing up, no doubt it would shortly cease. Paris speculated much about the King but seldom saw him; in the meantime everyone must turn elsewhere for diversion, and as so many old ties were now severed it was a question in which direction to do so. Writers? They were outmoded, and found it difficult to live. Corneille, someone said, wrote plays for the price of a loaf. Tristan l'Hermite was starving. Scarron? Ah, Scarron! He had been heard of again.

It was not any longer a matter of the yellow room, the *Mazarinades*. Scarron had a wife now and at first everyone had laughed. From the Court down it had been so. "A woman?" had said that Venus, the Regent Anne. "A woman must be the most useless piece of furniture in his establishment." But among the new houses that arose along the Rue Neuve-Saint-Louis this establishment revealed itself and those who had been there once returned. The green Seine spoke of it to the leaves that fell, that autumn, on its surface below gray bridges, in the place where it parted to embrace Notre-Dame. An intriguing *raconteur* in a box! A young no-wife, whose dark beauty was so unusual that it was certain sunnier climes had accounted for it, and it was true that she was known as *la belle Indienne!* And above all this no money, none at all, and a house full of new furniture. All this was undoubtedly a thing to go and see.

127

So they came, the *galants* to whom the beauty of Madame Scarron was a challenge; and found when they saw the phenomenon for themselves that rumor had not overstepped itself. Never, one was assured, had there been seen so charming a young bride. Her hair, of that deep chestnut that was almost black, set messieurs rhyming and sighing; the turn of her neck, they swore, would ravish, the curve of her bosom cause the senses to reel. It was said that her husband had married her because of the beauty of her hands. What torment, and what privilege, to be this Scarron! Many had observed the milk-and-carnation loveliness of Madame riding in her coach last year, when Scarron had brought her back from the provinces, where he had gone, it was whispered, in fear of Mazarin. Was there not also some tale of his having joined the *Compagnie des Indes?* As well, if so, that he had not gone with the expedition. As well as robbing Paris of its sight of the so charming wife who would, assuredly, have beguiled any journey, the *Compagnie,* as everyone knew, had been unfortunate from the start. One leader had been crushed to death between two boats, another murdered; their goods has been dispersed in transit before leaving Lyon; those that had, in the end, made the voyage had suffered from every imaginable disorder including pirates and the flux, and only a few had in the end come home. Well enough for little Scarron that he had not risked his pitiful limbs in the same manner as his three thousand livres! And *la belle Indienne,* who it was said had professed herself ready to accompany him wherever he chose, was better in the Rue Saint-Louis where messieurs could visit her.

Rivalry was intense. In the wine-shops and picture-galleries wagers were laid on who, among the gradually steadying list, should head it for the favors of Madame Scarron. The situation was intriguing; a *mariage blanc!* Where was the man who could resist such a challenge? Connoisseurs watched the Sieur de Raincy, that young man whose fortune had been made in the Huguenot business of banking; the gifts he brought to Madame Scarron would surely afford him headway . . . old du Lude, who ought to have known better, was never away from Madame's side, leaving his wife to the diversion of the *monde* in the upper room with Scarron . . . the Chevalier de Méré, who it was believed had previous knowledge of Madame (her origins were so mysterious, where could she have come from? Someone had said she was a relative of Madame de Navailles), had laid his heart at her feet, in so charming a manner that one could forgive him for being, *enfin,* a trifle outmoded.

And Villarceaux!

It was noticed, right from the beginning, that that charmer of hearts was *épris*. This had happened before and might have been expected; when Madame yielded, as she must undoubtedly do before long, the Marquis would be seen in the Rue des Tournelles once more. But, knowing Ninon, his former mistress, no one was surprised when, at one of those conversational evenings there for which she was so famous, Madame Scarron was present as a favored guest . . . it was all so diverting!

Was Madame witty? they said. *Oui, oui, oui!* Had she not saved the situation more than once in that impoverished household where the guests, as everyone knew, had to bring their supper with them? And on an evening when for some reason this had not been attended to, the valet, who was everything else besides, had leaned over her as the meal progressed and whispered, "Madame, for the love of God an anecdote! There is no *rôti* this evening!"

It was odd, after all that, to be assured then by so many people that Madame Scarron was shy as a nun. . . .

Françoise Scarron moved the curtain cautiously aside in order to survey the carriage in the courtyard.

It was always as well to insure that there was no one of importance to see her husband; the other day Turenne had come, a fierce little man very plainly dressed, in his own carriage. Françoise liked to have Paul prepared and ready for such occasions, his hair brushed and his nails clean; the valet was careless and would forget these things if she were not there to remind him. Moreover, there were often flagons littered from the previous evening (where *bons vivants* would have come and forgotten to take them away again), and as Françoise usually retired when the conversation grew too boisterous she could not always see that everything was cleared at the end.

But there was no one, apart from those who came almost every day, and perhaps she might have a little time to herself in which to read the book Paul had mentioned to her the other day, and which had just arrived from Sarasin.

She found the book, lying still in its wrapped covers on the table, and opened it with a knife. The flyleaf showed a printed title; the *Nouvelle Allégorique*. She smiled; there was a picture of Paul on the inside cover, fiercely represented as the captain of troops of the Queen of Rhetoric, leading a charge against the King Galimatias. The wry head grinned at her from behind a lifted hand, brandishing a pen as a spear.

Françoise closed the book. The allusion had made her think of Paul. She thought, now that he had settled down to work again, that this time the play might succeed. *Don Japhet d'Arménie*. He had dictated a great deal of it to her yesterday, when they had respite from callers for awhile. It was a better occupation, she was sure, than writing unpaid libels against Mazarin.

A little frown creased her forehead. If only they could lay their hands on some money! At first she had been so overwhelmed with having a house of their own, a room of her own, with furniture she herself had chosen, and gowns for which Paul paid . . . it had been a shock, after a while, to realize that he had nothing with which to meet the bills. His generosity was unbounded, but he had not the wherewithal to indulge it. It had not been so bad as long as they lived in the house of Paul's sister in the Rue des Douze-Portes, or stayed in the provinces where things were cheaper, but a house of one's own in Paris was prohibitive, and this eating the meals brought by the callers could not last indefinitely, she was sure.

"Do not worry, *chérie!*" Paul would say. "We are both of too much importance in the *monde* for it to allow us to starve. Tonight we have d'Aumont, de Mollier and Mignard. Pierre

will bring a capon, Cabart the *vin du pays,* Monsieur a collation of *filet de veau* and some artichokes and a melon. Do you
remember how impossible it was to obtain melon? *Tout ça
est passé."*

Nothing, she had found, would diminish his gargantuan
appetite. It was as though Providence had returned the
energies of which his other parts were deprived and deposited
them in his stomach. "I will eat all day, like an ox in a stall,"
he told her, and it was true. She was torn between affection
and despair of him. He had no idea of the value of money
and, when he obtained any, spent it without loss of time.

Françoise moved about the room, touching with light preoccupation everything in which she had taken such pride.
Even yet it brought a little glow of pleasure to her; the
tapestries, woven in scenes from the Bible, with Rachel and
Susannah and Judith regarding her from the walls; one
recognized Judith by the head she carried and Susannah
because she was naked. Or were they Salome and Eve? The
Venice glass Paul had also brought her, saying that she
should have leisure to look at her own beauty instead of
having to hurry past on Saint-Herman's stairs. There was a
cabinet of pearwood and a vast pillared bed, softer than any
in which she had hitherto slept. After the hard boards of
the convent or Madame's attic pallet it had seemed as if she
were the queen of all France.

Beyond the satin sheen of the carved wooden pillars her
own reflection gazed at her. She observed it curiously. How
had she come to resemble the fashionable women who
thronged, with their husbands and lovers, about the house?
It was true that Ninon had shown her how to dress her hair
to best advantage while dispensing with the need for a *coif-
feur* Françoise could not afford. Her deft fingers had worked
at Françoise' hair till it hung majestically, thick and lustrous
and dark, over one shoulder in curls *à la Vénus,* in no way
quarreling with Ninon's own smooth fair style. But how
could she outshine Ninon? And yet . . .

She caught her underlip between her teeth on a little
gesture of pain.

She could not recall the first time Villarceaux had come

to the house. This was not odd, as with their two floors, thronged with visitors, he might have been in Paul's rooms while Françoise was in her own. Lately it seemed that he was always here. It was true that when he was not, she was thinking of him.

Desperately she had turned to religion, finding, in the newly learned forms and seasonal austerities it involved, a little solace for her hurt. She had made a bargain with God; she would keep her side of the bargain to the last iota, weighing bread for fast days, picking at a herring while Paul and his friends enjoyed their feast. Paul laughed at her herring, as he laughed at her lovers; would have so laughed, she knew, had she indeed regarded this *mariage blanc* as the world did, ignoring it. But the pathos of that wedding-night was there for her in all their life together; while she lived she would never forget the torment in Paul's eyes. However she might appear, however Paul and others saw her, she must preserve her integrity or the foundations of her life would crumble.

She strove to know herself, seeing the strange new being in the glass. Assaulted on all sides by the attentions paid to Scarron's wife, she had developed the *hauteur* de Méré had recommended; he was among the first to suffer from it. "She is cold," they had begun to say. It accounted for their own lack of success in a manner credible to themselves; how they would have mocked if they had known the truth!

Cold, then: the wife of Scarron. She regarded her face, a fuller oval than hitherto; a lily, someone had told her, on the tall stalk which was her throat. If there should be less of that talk from now on because of her alleged coldness, she would be better pleased. She would be able to devote more time to Paul and the task he had undertaken of reading Spanish plays with her. And lately she had undertaken to withdrawing from the *foyer* with a few chosen friends, women, to this room; and established on her bed in the manner of the famous *littérateuse,* Madeleine de Scudéry, she and they would talk privately and with enjoyment among themselves.

One of them was Madame de Villarceaux.

* * *

132

She turned again to where a little portrait hung on the wall. Villarceaux had painted his wife as the Magdalen, in profile with a blue veil. What irony that Madame de Villarceaux should have brought it to her as a gift! At night she would lie and look at it, from where she lay in bed; the face, sweet and remote, told nothing, the downcast eyes hiding many things.

What would it be to exchange, for a day, with Madame; to be, between two gray dawns, the wife of Villarceaux?

She must not think of it; must not succumb to this longing. . . . It was a thing without name, to which if she yielded disaster would follow, the breaking down of every barrier of restraint she had set herself. Why should one man's eyes, one man's tall form, his hands, his voice, mean so much more than another's? Why need she count the hours till he came again?

She sank to her knees before the wooden crucifix that had been carved in Spain. The eyeless face regarded her, held sideways against one shoulder beneath thorns. The head was held like Paul's, she thought; like Paul's.

She said her deliberate prayers and rose refreshed.

Paul was waiting for her that evening when at last she had leisure to seek him. In the manner that came with ease to them now they had little to say to one another. For one who had always to earn his living by words, it was gratifying on occasion to have silence.

He watched her as she moved about the room, lighting candles. She wore a gown of flesh-color, the taffeta of the skirts rustling faintly; over it was a little flowered jacket. Paul liked the way she dressed. It was simple and not expensive, and gave her a thousand times the appearance of the other fools of women who had to have every yard of their clothing stiff with paillettes and embroidery. Yes, she had grown into a beautiful young woman, the poor child who had come to his notice first by reason of her tears and her damnably ugly yellow gown.

"Do you remember, *chérie*—" he began, then stopped; of

what use to remind her? She had grown so, expanding like a butterfly in the sunshine; at first he had been afraid of her shyness at the Dutch banquets over which it was necessary that she preside, until one day when, suddenly, she had looked up from her silence and come forth with a very witty, very concise little tale. Since then his friends came to hear her talk as well as his, although the difference between them remained in that there were things one could not say to Françoise. Astonishingly, he thought, for her, Cabart and the others held their tongues.

Without a doubt she was beautiful . . . and virtuous . . . and she had wit . . . and she was the good nurse, the perfect secretary, copying out by the hour in her fine script his rough-hewn ideas till they made sense and saved his fingers.

Ah, God in Heaven! What was he? An insect smitten with a creeping paralysis, stupefied half his waking life with drugs, having written his own epitaph with its expressed hope that at last he would find a night's sleep! A useless fool . . . even his last play-subject had been stolen by Corneille, and the latter having the use of his legs had seen that his version was the one to be played, while Paul's was forgotten. It was so with many things; they had asked him to write a weekly gazette of the gossip of Paris, but he could not get about to cull it at the street-corners, and without that basis there was nothing on which to write. It was not as it had been in the days when all one need do to live was insult Mazarin. And so it went on, and he had had to sell his *Vision of Saint Paul* that Nicholas Poussin had painted for him, by request, in Italy. And shortly Françoise would ask what had befallen the silver spoons and he would have to admit that Guillemot, the urchin, had disposed of them also by request. *Bon Dieu,* how could one help such things? There was oneself and a spaniel and a monkey and magpie, two servants and a cook, one beautiful wife, a gutter-brat and occasionally a sister who was much too fond of wine. All these had to live. Friends would not last forever. He must think, think, think of a new idea, some astonishing thing which would shock the world out of feeling so pleased with itself.

His wife sat down at the table near him and took up a quill ready to write. The quill was worn and neatly, deliberately, she set herself to mend it. Her bent head was richly piled with exquisite dark hair. How beautiful she was! Mignard had requested, once again, to be allowed to paint her. Perhaps when he found time to do so he would bring something to eat. This *hôtel de l'impécuniosité!*

II

CHARLES D'AUBIGNÉ stretched his shapely legs and leaned back in an attitude of comfort, from which he was able to survey, not without amusement, his sister's *salon*.

How had Bignette achieved it, in the name of God? From nothing . . . from less, a little slut, a little out-at-elbows, beaten and starved kitchen-wench, married to a cripple. And now marquises, duchesses, the wives of the respectable of town were here; if a man brought his wife anywhere it was a recommendation indeed.

But not always so. . . . Charles heard among the murmured voices the deep, caressing tones of Villarceaux. Did that elegant ever fasten his attention on anyone now except the wife of Scarron? And to no purpose, if one were to judge from the scrap of reply that came to one's ears; other replies, he had heard, had been made in allegory, learned rhymes, indirectly, always negative.

"You say I am a jailer, Monsieur. I take no pains to make captives; it gives me no grief to lose them." Which, thought Charles, is most palpably a lie; she would regret, as surely as a female spider that has lost its fly, the nearness of that burnished head to hers, daily, hourly.

"You are as cold as the moon, Françoise, and so much

135

more beautiful. I should like to paint you as Diana. When will you permit me to have such pleasure?"

Françoise murmured that she already had her time fully occupied by M. Mignard. As if asking help from the importunities of the tall young man with *châtain* curls, her eyes sought out the little, black-clad figure of the painter. He, surrounded by an assemblage of ladies, was declaiming, as he nearly always did if there were listeners to impress, of the beauties of Italy. "That *poseur!*" whispered Villarceaux. "He only paints you, *chérie,* for the social advertisement it will afford. But I, I would paint you because I desire to have your picture before my eyes in your absence, and shall so till I die."

"It takes a strong emotion to last until death, Monsieur," said Françoise coldly. She gave a little inclination of the head and moved away from the discomfited Marquis to where Scarron sat, surrounded by his crowd. D'Aubigné put a hand up to his face to hide the grin that had come there. As well be in love with Lot's wife after she had changed into a pillar!

Later, he left his seat and lounged toward Villarceaux.

Afterward he taxed his sister with her refusal. She colored, was silent, and steadily, although he knew the subject displeased her, Charles pursued his advantage; Paul was present.

"Why do you prevent her?" he said to the cripple. Scarron's eyes turned to him, their expression sardonic.

"I? I prevent Madame? She is as free as the air. Anything she wishes to do shall be done. I have sown my field and it is full of tares. Why should she have to reap them?"

"Paul, you have had too much wine," said his wife repressively. "I do not wish to sit for M. de Villarceaux."

"Because you doubt your own virtue, *chérie,* or lack resistance?" murmured Charles.

Crimson, she listened to the softly mocking tone. She sat very straight at her wheel, spinning. Charles was sorry her hands were occupied; it gave her support, and he had wished her defenseless. He continued with his gentle assault, a word here, a hint there. It was like pulling down a bastion, stone by stone. Once the foundation-stone was reached the whole thing would crumble. He was aware of crippled Scarron watching them, and of his eyes. The whirr of the wheel came endlessly.

"A friend at Court . . . a rich man . . . a patron for Paul." Charles said nothing of his own ambitions, which were unlimited.

Françoise' thread broke and twisted up against the spindle. Both now heard her little indrawn breath.

"Of what use are patrons to Paul? They give him no silver."

"She is angered now," thought Charles in triumph. He knew that sooner or later he would win the wager he had made with himself, and that Françoise would sit for her portrait.

Ninon also threw her support into the scales. Françoise and Villarceaux should have her yellow room, she swore. The clear light hangings were good for the eye, and moreover Villarceaux was pledged to discretion. She herself would be in and out, to watch the painting progress. It would be so much better there than in the Rue Neuve-Saint-Louis, with its small windows and filtered light! Moreover, there would be no disturbance from callers, unless by invitation.

"Promise then that you will not be cruel to him, *ce pauvre Marquis!* It will give him great pleasure, and anything that gives such pleasure cannot in the end be wrong."

All this was said in the drawing on of a single elegant glove. One might as well have read in the words, "Take my lover, whom I can recommend. All that is finished now, at least for the time being. I never allow *les affaires* to drag. Take my Villarceaux, and after that you will lose him, but *quant à ça?* There is love and there is also friendship. In any case one cannot chain the spirit." And looking at the woman before her there rose in Françoise' mind, unbidden, the face of a little widow who had come once to talk with Paul; her husband had killed himself, it was said, from despair, although it was true that it had happened in a duel with Ninon's name not openly mentioned . . . Madame de Sévigné.

The first day of the sitting, Ninon, as she had promised, was present; seated where the sun would slant on her, on a little couch with gilded legs, near by the easel. Villarceaux was preoccupied and unfamiliar, mixing colors in a long smock of bleached linen; his hair hidden under a cap. He spoke little, only pausing to alter or rearrange some fold of Françoise' draperies as the sittings changed. She had sat already for Mignard and was capable of stillness for long periods without growing tired.

She stared downward, regarding her own foot as Villarceaux had instructed. There were to be angels, the Marquis had said, sustaining her in the finished work; also Paul's spaniel, which had accompanied her on her walk here held by a lead. Its large brown eyes had strained obediently up toward her for a while and then it had scrambled free. Villarceaux would, he said, insert its likeness later when the main portraiture was done. The picture was to be an allegory.

"And the moral?" murmured Ninon, while Françoise pondered on the acquaintance of angels with the goddess Diana. Villarceaux smiled slightly. "That remains to be seen."

As the days progressed Ninon sometimes looked in on them and sometimes did not. Although Françoise was on her guard against Villarceaux, she had no reason to complain of his conduct. He was, she guessed, enough of the artist to think of her meantime as a model rather than as a woman. In any case they had little to say to one another. Would it have been so if he had not been painting? She had the notion that he thought of her always as a body without mind.

Often, drowsy with the heat and the aromatic smell of paint-oils, she would see them all three in a detached way; herself, Villarceaux and Ninon, dancing always in a *pas de trois* of love and friendship and desire. The masks on their faces were those of Circe's horde and no single one of their movements were unplanned. . . .

It was hard to remain detached, seeing the sunlight slant

down on Villarceaux' cheek; watching the line of the jaw cream-pale and austere with no hairline to soften it, and picturing her own mouth warm against his, so that their breaths mingled.

"The portrait is finished," said Ninon. She was smiling.

She took Françoise to see it. Villarceaux was absent. Françoise stood before the easel and beheld her face, neck and arms as Villarceaux saw them. The shining eyes of the little spaniel stared up as in life. The angels were plump and naked.

She made some murmured speech of approbation, sensing a mixture of satisfaction and disappointment from the fact that he saw her face as did Mignard. She looked like a doll, she thought; face a full oval, long-lidded eyes that held secrets. Perhaps no one ever saw themselves without a sense of bafflement. One's thoughts were not, then, visible to the outside world.

Why did Ninon laugh so, without a sound from her lips?

Some weeks later Charles d'Aubigné went early to the rooms of Villarceaux and stayed very late. One by one the other gamesters, who had won or lost their silver, rose and departed. D'Aubigné yawned, desirous of his own bed. He knew very well that the Marquis wished to talk to him of Françoise; he himself was not sure how much he ought to say. One could ignore the episodes of Maman, of the floor-scrubbings at the Château de Neuillant. No need to make a man think he desired a drudge for mistress. And Charles himself was in search of fresh employment since the army had dispensed with his services.

Villarceaux did not return and Charles discovered in himself a desire for the privy. In this new house which the Marquis had recently taken, it was a matter of dislodging curtains. One fumbled for long enough along half-lit passages, opening doors and led nowhere or into other gaming-rooms. Once he came on old du Lude, drunk and slumbering, the flagon beside him half-empty, the candle dying. To be old, to feel in oneself the stink and corruption of all decay, beginning before the appetites had ceased to function! *He'd* not make old bones himself—God knew, any more than poor Maman, dead long since in Bordeaux.

He found the privy and on leaving it parted a curtain on the other side. A chink of light in the room beyond was accompanied by the sound of voices. Villarceaux was still occupied, then, with the guest to whom he had risen to bid goodnight. The curiously deep tone of his speech reached Charles clearly.

A moody man, Charles thought—an artist. Not an easy man to handle, if . . . but already there were diversions. One saw, in this room which must be the Marquis' bedchamber, a naked woman. The fact that she was a woman of paint on canvas made little difference; woman, flesh, she was, achieved somehow. Desire rose in d'Aubigné's throat and wetting his lips cautiously he moved a little forward. Awkward to be caught, when all was said, in Villarceaux' own chamber. But he must see this . . . a damnably illusory piece of work, enough to give a certain satisfaction from where one lay, doubtless, in bed, although the genuine article would be even better. What flesh that woman had! Pale, clear as ripe fruit, the sunned flesh of a pear under glass; breasts mounded, full and firm, in rose shading out of ivory. A perfect body, a goddess, Venus; down from the slender-pillared thighs, the very toes were separate for desire. . . .

His glance traveled upward. What a purchase to have made! Conventions, he saw, must be served; the goddess was preparing for her bath; a couple of nymphs or angels upheld the fair limbs, also a spaniel. Dwelling on that one realized that it was not, in fact, Venus who was represented, but Diana, and that, thought Charles, was a misnomer. Diana was a virgin goddess, cold and chaste as the moon, and this —no, *assurément,* this was Venus masquerading as Diana, and no afterthought of little white moons set in the dark hair would serve to deceive anyone, unless—

Pondering thus, Charles took his eyes from the moon-crown and rested them, last of all, on the lady's face; and gave a little oath. Presently surprise, or whatever the emotion had been, passed, and a grin of enjoyment spread over his face. Françoise!

He withdrew, laughing quietly.

For a long time he held his peace. Affairs came and went; it suited him to billet himself on the Scarron household and he made no haste to move. Bignette, he found, was a house-keeper *par excellence;* Charles' food was hot, his bed-linen clean. For such a one as M. d'Aubigné (he no longer styled himself "Capitaine," trusting that memories would shorten with lack of allusion) this was enough; if he had had ample silver at his command he would have been happy. As it was, a man was embarrassed by the refusals of wine-keepers to advance credit, and of women of substance to permit oneself the *entrée* to their salons.

He grumbled about it to his sister. It had been impossible, again, he said, to arrange a marriage for himself with a little heiress, the daughter of a Picard gentleman lately deceased who had been resetter of jewelery to Her Majesty, the Regent Anne. (How impossible it was to stop talking of "the Regent," although now the little King was old enough, at eighteen years of age, to take the reins into his own hands, as far as that was possible in the presence of M. le Cardinal!) Françoise must give him countenance, he said, must allocate him a little more silver; of what use was it to be trailed every-where only at her apron-strings, and when dowagers in-quired as to his prospects to have them told, "None!"

"I cannot hang about here all my life," he informed her. She raised her head from her sewing and regarded him calmly.

"Then do not," she said.

Charles gaped at her, the fumes of the wine lately taken mounting to his head and making him touchy. "What, you?" he told her. "You sit there, my own sister, and will do nothing for me, nothing? Three years ago you were a little scrubbing-maid at the tail of Madame de Neuillant. I will not have it," he said expanding.

Françoise threaded her needle. It had been almost seven

years ago, she thought, not three. The error corrected in her reckoning, she returned to Charles. It had been at the back of her mind for some time that she must speak to him. Paul had enough ado to support himself and her; he could not billet Charles indefinitely. Charles was drunk now and this could not be the best time to speak, but when would it be so? Always there was some hindrance, other people present, the loud-mouthed laughter beckoning from Paul's rooms, to which Charles would go.

"*Cher*, you know I wish only for your good," she began, but with a grandiose gesture of the hand he detained her.

"Good? Good? Ah, you talk a great deal of that!" Something in the way he leered caused her discomfort and she rose, laying down the sewing, and stood away.

"You must listen to me, Charles. You cannot stay on with us. You know yourself how Paul is situated, and that it is not easy." Looking at him, she thought with sudden contempt of how he had battened on Maman all those years, taking every sou she could give him and doing nothing in exchange; the expense, he had said, of life in the army was such that he had nothing left over.

Now he would do the same by Paul, unless prevented. Thought of Paul made her voice sharp; who else was there to protect him if not herself? He had given Charles enough.

"You must go," she said. Charles laughed at her, and she tried to thrust him away.

"You cannot get rid of me so easily, *ma sœur*. I know a thing or two."

Something, a cheapness as though of bought scent, was in the air. Whatever street-woman he had been lately with, the odor had clung to him . . . a memory, repeated now, of wine-heavy breath displeased her. She moved away. Charles laughed.

"Little prude, Madame oh-so-correct Conformity Scarron. What would they say, these duchesses and maréchales who come to your salon, if they knew what I know, saw what I have seen? Were Madame de Villarceaux, who comes here to sit with you, to go to her husband's lodging by the Palais-Royal she would find a thing, as I did. Yourself, Madame, naked as on the day you were born, as you've often been for him in the *chambre jaune* of Ninon . . . the 'Queen of Paris!' Everyone knows of her. . . ."

She stared at him, her face white. What did he mean? Men were revolting in the looseness that was theirs after drink, even Paul said things that made her writhe inwardly, seeing the faces of those who heard them. But this . . .

"How dare you speak so? How dare you lie to me? There is nothing of that. . . ."

"There's nothing of any garment in that portrait Villarceaux did of you. I confess it made my mouth water till I saw who it was. My girl, you should habituate yourself to that sort of thing. You've the body of a fine whore, and there's money we can make, you and I."

He lurched to the window. "I'm sick as a dog. Bring me a ewer, there's a good girl, and I'll see if I can get any of this wood-rot out of me. Damned if they don't poison my drink because they know I can't pay . . . but you, Madame, can supply me."

"Charles." Her voice was urgent. "Where did you see this—picture, this—abomination? Who else . . ." Her voice faltered. Charles retched sullenly with a finger in his throat.

"Very well, if you will not, you will not. . . . No one but myself was there; and, we'll take it, those, if any, whom Villarceaux takes to bed with him will know, that's all. His valet. . . . Bignette, child, you've a cold heart, leaving the man to console himself with a canvas only . . . should be there with him . . . fine fellow."

"Abominable. . . ."

He became aware of her attitude, standing with bowed head and face hidden in her hands. "Bignette," he began. Clumsily, his hand reached out to her. She felt him move, and grew rigid. "Don't touch me," he heard her say. "Don't speak to me."

Villarceaux. Had he painted, over the draperies she had seen that day, her body as it formed itself in his mind? Had he studied her through the stuffs of her dress while he painted? Or had he—this thought was the more horrible—borrowed, in fancy or reality, the body he knew, that Aphrodite, epitome of all desire, the woman whose flesh he had often beheld in every aspect of their passion, the ageless, pagan, beckoning, incomparable Ninon?

Or any other woman he could have bought from off the streets.

She turned in sudden cold fury to Charles and bade him take his things and go.

She never spoke to a living soul of the portrait.

Only in this way could she conquer them all, the chance sightseers, the gossiping enjoying tongues; Ninon, who must have guessed and therefore laughed at her simple gaping, knowing what was to come. Was there anything that Ninon did not know? She would not, thank God, speak of it.

Would Paul hear? If Françoise made no attempt to justify herself, would he, with the world, believe that she had given her body to Villarceaux, while he—ah, but if any were determined to believe, they would do so no matter what she might say.

So she was silent.

For a time she lived in dread of encountering Villarceaux again. She shut herself in her rooms with her books and had it given out that she was indisposed and would receive no callers. She began to know a fear of faces, feeling that every dropped glance, every discreet smile, would contain admission that they knew. Gradually the first rawness abated; she began to go about her household tasks again, to be seen in the streets.

She had much need of Paul as a companion in those days. Strangely, she began to find in him support by contrast to his accepted leaning on her. It was true that she still catered for his body. But for the first time in those many years she was able to cull relief from the quality of his mind. In spite of the inroads disease had made, it was simple, direct, and lacking in pretense or any hypocrisy. He had an instant grasp of all situations that were brought to his notice. His understanding took facts and digested them like food, which his fancy embellished. Nothing stood in the way of this;

he was a creature with less heed to his own fortune than anyone she had ever met. "You would throw away position, future, everything, for the sake of a pun!" she told him one day. It was true. How many times had he yielded to the temptation of that too-easy ridicule of Mazarin? It had lost him his pension, on which they might have lived comfortably. . . . At times he was her despair. And then, with a flicker of his odd eyes, he would charm her again with his talk of Villon and Descartes and his own rival Corneille and also a queer player-fellow who was beginning to be spoken of, Jean-Baptiste Poquelin, who had wandered back to Paris by way of Picardy and, having imbibed the headiness of the air there, begun to sell plays which poked sad fun at everybody, using the name of Molière.

Company, as the summer drew on, was scarcer. There was always Anne Gallois, that sister of Paul who preferred, as he said, the bottle, spent all her money on it and then came wailing to the Rue Neuve-Saint-Louis for more. Françoise *l'avide* was with her old Comte at the country-house he had given her, together with her brood of bastards by him. "For the dozen presented to him by his own wife," Paul said, "he does nothing at all." Bored, he changed the dedication of a poem he had written to his sister's little bitch-dog, Guillemette. Altered, the dedication ran, "To my *chienne de sœur*."

There were others, who never left town. Paul had names for everybody who came. Whited sepulcher, *beau parleur*, flower-shop gallant, *clabaudeur*, brute, stinking man, sycophant, *inviteur à diner*, fool—these were common—ignoramus, *goguenard*, parasite, buffoon, the king of bores.

He hated fools. Often she would have to drive away by force those who came, as Paul weakened, exhausting his strength so that his good-humor gave way and he snapped and demanded. She would see these signs of exhaustion about his eyes and mouth, the flesh growing sunken and bluish against the skull; and the hands, that when he was lively were capable of expressive movement, would droop like the ends of a plant when it has no water. She knew, now, how welcome a refuge was in which one could find solitude; but Paul had no refuge, none, against those who came and stayed and stayed, gaping after folly or maundering like fools. "I cannot endure it!" he would scream at last, against the laughter bursting out again at sight of his twisted fury, his comical flapping hands. They would not put bread into his mouth by the gift of a sou, yet they came and demanded wit and rhyming of him with the rapidity of a goose laying eggs, he said, and he was tired.

Yet without company he was not gay and without gaiety he could not write. Often she would sit and bear him company, the quill in her hand ready to take down the words, any words, relevant to the new work he was writing, that *mélange* of the doings of ordinary people leading extraordinary lives that he had called the *Roman comique* till he should think of a better title. Françoise would watch his eyes grow weary and his tone dull, and his notions dry up so that nobody would buy them. It required the Segrais, the Guillemots of this world, to fan his smoldered genuis into flame. She could not do so, any more than at the time of the Gazette she could go out into the streets and pick up the small, spiteful, toothsome pieces of gossip that he required. She had known then, and she knew now, that in that respect she would always fail him. It remained to make the other ways succeed.

She was not well that year; the fever which returned at intervals plagued her, and with the warmer weather came the fear of plague itself. Paris was dust-laden, and foul in the heat; Paul, immobile and helpless in his gray chair, was tormented by flies. But Françoise, even more than he, now found the heat unbearable. The continued strain of nursing Paul as the disease progressed and drugs grew useless, the lack of sleep and of fresh air, drained her. She grew thin and wan and there were great shadows under her eyes. Ninon, returning from a visit to Orléans, called in one day and exclaimed at her appearance.

"Why do you not go out of town in this heat, the same as

all the rest of the world? Ah, *nom du ciel*, why talk of money or the lack of it? You look fit to drop."

"Paul," said Françoise. Ninon snapped her fingers.

"Paul will be happy enough with his dinners *à tous* and his concerts that last till all hours of the morning. You've already tried dragging him to Avesnes by coach; it was too much for you. No, you're coming away with me; I have been home two days and already this town stinks in my nostrils. Dearest, I am going into Vexin, to the château of M. Valliquierville, whom you have met, and you will be able to rest there and get the color back into your face. No, don't argue with me! And say nothing to me of Paul. How many years have I known Paul? I will speak to him."

And she stood at Paul's door like a cool scented orchid and found him, with Guillemot, busied with alembics and a fire. "Name of my God!" said Ninon. "Your wife pines in this heat."

Paul turned his eyes absently, and reaching him she saw a change in his appearance. His hair was quite gray now and the look he gave her was childlike, almost bland. "Ninon, my Ninon," he murmured. "I shall discover the philosopher's stone."

He began to stumble out a theory he had invented which should be infallible as the moon and the stars. Only let him obtain a little more mercury, which the apothecaries had not delivered. "One heats it by little degrees, and presently it changes," he explained. It took him a long time to carry out the complicated business of holding and striking a tinder. The mercury, he said, turned scarlet. It was the beginning of a discovery.

"Paul, dear lad, your Françoise is not very well. Shall you be happy alone with your mercury and Guillemot? Word will be sent to us at once if there is anything you should require."

She told him in a few words of the château, the garden where fruit hung ripe, the herb-plot and the many green walks where one could sojourn in peace. His big head rolled slowly from contemplation of the elixir of life; she saw his reckoning, as if from behind clouds, focus itself and be renewed.

"She shall go," he said. "What does she not deserve? I owe her everything."

There were tears in his eyes and Ninon, lightly, kissed him. Going to the door she saw him, with the same delayed progress, turn to his metals again, talking meanwhile to Guillemot in a low lewd voice about the times when he had been a wicked little abbé in the meadows about Le Mans.

III

THE TREES about Valliquierville's château were green with summer. Afterward remembering that Vexin interlude Françoise would see it always as in a bower of green trees. Pastoral, also, were their pursuits, after the close air and habits of Paris. How many years would it be before the *monde* recognized such things as delightful, turning consciously shepherd and shepherdess with little lightly held gilded crooks? They had anticipated that recognition, she and Ninon, who in her hat of wide straw would cast off her shoes and stockings, bathing her charming feet in the stream that ran by. Often they would eat out of doors, carrying their meal with them in a basket after the manner of Tante Arthémise . . . but the volume of Pibrac's *Quatrains* and the little home-made cheeses had been replaced by what M. de Valliquierville was pleased to call ambrosia for the delectation of goddesses. Satin-coated apples, delicate nectarines culled from his garden-walls of mellow brick; thick goats' cream in scoured wooden bowls; *vin du pays* carried in little straw holders that the peasants plaited and sold; white bread. It was so delicious to obtain eatable bread once more. . . .

She grew brown and well in the clear air of Vexin, carnation-cheeked and with eyes that shone. So swiftly had the time flown that it seemed none at all since they had left town; soon they must return. "You were made for a country-woman," Ninon said idly, the long eyes that saw all surveying this added beauty and committing it to her thoughts. This seemed like a different creature from the pale wife of Scarron, wilting in Paris from the heat that brought the plague. What a good thing it was to relieve oneself of constant company for a while! All company, Ninon maintained, even the most delightful, saving one's own, would at last pall.

But that there was pleasure in other company she would have been the last to deny. It was not until they had been a week in Vexin that the plan she had made was revealed. Françoise, coming in from the fields, saw a horseman ride up; she made no inquiry, thinking him a friend of Valliquierville's. That this was so might be true enough, but it did not lessen her anger when she knew. What right had Ninon to bring Villarceaux here, under the same roof as herself?

Ninon met her reproaches with calmness. "Why disturb yourself?" she told the younger woman. "Nothing that befalls us can do so without the direction of our own will."

Ah, had *she* had volition toward the thing that had befallen last autumn, and which had brought to her so much shame that she had not to this day come face to face, alone, with Villarceaux?

"How dare he come here?" she thought, and then, remembering the manner in which she had heard of the portrait, understood him; he did not know that she knew.

He was waiting that evening when they assembled downstairs for wine; he was cool and assured. Françoise found the color in her face mount hotly; it would always betray her. Strong in the room was the awareness of the *pas de trois* again, dancing. Ninon smiled and watched and said nothing and drank her wine. The firelight played on all of them from the great hearth.

Villarceaux' voice whispered in Françoise' ear; the deep

tones troubled her. She wondered how she could ever have forgotten his voice. Ah, but she had not so. . . .

Time moved in a cycle, she thought. It was all as it had been, so many times in the Rue Neuve-Saint-Louis. And again, and always, all her life, she must pray. . . .

The days followed one another in pursuit of pleasure and sunshine. Valliquierville joined them oftener now in the *al fresco* times by the stream. The four of them talked together on every theme, ranging through the brevity and art of life to embrace many things. As her unease faded in the golden warmth of the sun, Françoise began to feel the old, irrepressible enjoyment rise at the sound and skilled play of words, uttered now less often for their sense than for the rise and fall of the very phrases on the ear. "Avoid that!" Paul had told her, speaking of writing, "Too many fools take a pen and pour forth syllables like a diarrhea, taking no thought as to what, if anything, they may mean. Know what you would put down and why, then do so. That way of writing will make sense." But in this air that was heady with *vin du pays*, sensation rose and engulfed one like a scented tide. And it was not always only the senses, the emotions, that were dwelled upon; in the swiftness of pun and riposte that followed one another in that most brilliant of company she, too, shone.

She felt herself a new person. If only she had been so! If only memory, duty, faith itself were dead, and she—ah, but what would she become then? Pagan, as Ninon was? A being who would cease easily with stilled breath, becoming no more than a cloud of dust, blown hither and back on the wind? But for the present it would be joy.

Villarceaux prepared to transport her to that pagan world. After the long winters of his siege of her he saw, he thought, for the first time signs of yielding. The hours spent gazing at his mind-picture of her flesh made him, in that flesh's presence, bold; but still cunning as hunters are to snare a quarry. It was not the first day, or the third or fifth, that he pressed the siege; and not in Valliquierville's garden where every moment there were shadows in the grass and they would be disturbed. But one day losing Ninon and her *ami* in a wood where mallow leaves grew high and dark, he walked with Françoise a little way, and then further. He had more charm than almost any man in Paris and could make even the wife of Scarron forget her danger, for an hour. And then at last seating her on a fallen tree that lay forgotten and silver-gray among the high ferns and mosses, he turned to love and talk of love and hoped to find her weakness in the fact that she had been unprepared.

He was Saturn, he told her, she was Vesta. An English poet had written of it. This was a glade far back in time beyond Olympus, beyond Ida and all the follies of Troy. "The earth is young again," he told her. "You and I will renew our youth. Of what use is it to lose the hour which soon passes? *Belle, cœur de mon cœur,* I have loved you for so long!"

He saw her, seated there, the great liquid eyes startled like a caught wild thing; her lips had parted slightly. How red her lips were! He was aware of her beauty against the background of delicate leaves; the sunlight slanting through them cast lace-like shadows on her face and breast. The artist in him was roused to inspiration; the lover fanned to flame. He felt within himself the approach of passion in an onrush of hurtling, effortless words; the nearness of her white flesh maddened him, with that particular blue-pale shadowing of curved arm and throat, that translucence as of a shell he had obtained, only once, and desired always. . . .

A little wind stirred her hair and he saw that she was trembling. He could no further restrain himself from touching her; he caught her to him.

"*Mon âme,* do not torment me longer, do not be cruel! Have you not known how passionately I worship you, how I treasure your every breath? You have mocked me, and I have paid; they laugh, how they laugh through all Paris . . . knowing how I burn for your coolness, and that you deny me always. . . ."

His mouth sought hers, as she had so often imagined it; his lips were soft and warm. "I kiss your mouth, your eyes, your throat. . . ." How was it that this soft mouth bruised her so? His kisses marked her flesh, she would feel the brand till she died. "Villarceaux, Villarceaux, leave me. . . ."

When his hands grew bolder she regained control; she would not yield to him. Unresponsive, she lay stiffly in his arms. He might have held a dead woman. She sensed his bewilderment; it was a new weapon. Her mouth no longer responded to his.

"He will find a greater satisfaction in his canvas," she thought. The remembrance brought strength.

Villarceaux released her; she might have struck him. For a long time she was to remember the ugly twist of his mouth.

"You are a figure of ice," he said, "that fascinates from a distance. Have no further fear for your propriety, Madame, or your virtue. It is understandable why you make such a feature of it. I am unlikely to trouble you again."

He rose then and turned on his heel and left her. She heard the sound of his footsteps die away in the silence, and presently the quiet rustle of a bird among the leaves.

She went quickly to her room at the château and gathered her things together without fuss. Ninon asked no questions when she said she was returning to Paris. Villarceaux did not appear again before Françoise left; she made her adieux to Valliquierville and departed.

She had not permitted herself time to think of what had passed. As the carriage wheels turned along the jolting road she tried to focus her mind on other things. It was not easy, it was sometimes not even possible. To look forward, not back, was the only way, otherwise . . . *cœur de mon cœur, mon âme* . . . yourself, Madame, naked as on the day you were born. . . .

And Paul.

Paul was lying in his gray chair doing nothing. She imagined that he looked thinner. His eyes lit up at the sight of her, standing by the door.

"I had not expected to see you return so soon," he said simply. She made her way toward him across the floor.

"Paul," she said. Suddenly, in an abrupt way that was not natural to her, she knelt by the chair and took his hands in hers, laying her cheek against them. She was unable to speak.

Scarron looked at her bowed head with a little twisted smile. "And so?" he said gently.

"No—Paul. You knew, then?"

She raised her face. He had known of Villarceaux! She stared at him, seeing in the well-known features many things. A *mari complaisant* . . . and yet . . .

"You are young," said Paul, "and whole. Who am I to deny you what the world can give? It was not in our bargain. And I have had my own turn."

All expression was denied him. He could not shrug or smile widely, or turn to her or take her in his arms. She felt the bitterness of his lot as if it were her own pinioned body, boxed, till death released it, in a closed gray chair. Tears rose in her eyes, rolling down her cheeks as they had done on the day he first saw her. She remembered the wild beating of her heart as she had lain in Villarceaux' arms, the desire that had come to her to yield. No one must ever know of that; not even Paul.

But Paul knew.

"Nom d'un nom d'un nom d'un chien!" he swore softly. "How the world uses us both!"

His poor hands, the only moving part of him, caressed her hair. She felt the touch of his fingers, hesitant with paralysis; in her mind was the seed of a growing joy. How would she have felt now, had she betrayed Paul with Villarceaux or any man? It was better to endure whatever the world might send, for the sake of the gratitude in his eyes.

"He said I was cold." How much better to be called cold than wanton . . . as the wife of Scarron, who found protection so.

That others would laugh, she knew. *Madame Scarron n'a point fait le saut.* So wrote Tallemant; the legend of a cold intellectual spread about the *monde.* Françoise cared nothing,

153

said nothing at any rate. And Paul? A little later, while he could still write, he did so to a friend. The long purgatory was almost over.

"My only regret," he wrote, "is that in dying I shall leave few benefits to my wife, whose worth is infinite and to whom I owe every conceivable thing."

IV

THE PROGRESS of disease began to bring Paul grandiose dreams.

Hitherto he had been *mens sana*; now he was not. The crowds who still came and battened like parasites on a falling tree made louder laughter to his greater folly. Hitherto he had been witty little Scarron; now he was their prey. He grimaced with agony; he was a monkey, *un chien*. His eyes rolled divergently, he was growing deaf, his food dribbled from the palsied mouth. He was conscious and yet dead, an interesting phenomenon. He had not the power in his whole body that most men had in a nail, yet he made, he said, his wife write letters to Court offering his services as porter, overseer of haulage and wharves. *Quelle divertissement!*

The Queen of Sweden sent for him to inspect him in his gray chair. She was eccentric, in course of a long visit to sovereigns no little embarrassed by the honor; she had lost a kingdom, changed a lover, become involved in the murder of a servant, and she wore high boots and a frizzed wig like a man. She stared at the cripple and he stared back, and the Queen threw back her head and roared with laughter.

"I will give you leave to be in love with me," she told him. "You shall be my Roland."

Roland was carried back to his house in which, in a room

bare now of its early furnishings, Mignard's portrait of Françoise still hung on the wall. In the facile method he had acquired of painting (Court beauties, all of them, a matter of eardrops and a pose only, of a pout or a smile, ringlets, and white hands caressing a spaniel, and *voilà!* four hundred louis), Mignard had not, altogether, overlaid the character of this sitter for whom his services were given free. The young woman in the canvas had turned half away, facing round again over one shoulder to display the symmetry of back and breast. The richly disposed draperies were anyone's, not hers; a Court lady, not that wife of Scarron who had used to wear a flowered bodice and a taffeta skirt and kerchief of *point-de-Gènes* lace. In a moment she would, Paul thought, execute the three great curtsies of the *grande entrée;* how long since de Méré had taught her, and he had watched! But the long bright-dark glance, the intelligence of the brow, and the probity of the small red mouth were the same.

He watched, focussing his unequal eyes which were beginning to grow dim. Pôussin's *Vision of Saint Paul* . . . he'd sold that . . . no need also to sell Françoise. She'd be there, always, to look at; relief to do so, after that ugly bitch in *bottines*. But soon, soon he would have to sell—what next? The other night it had been good eating, he had had twenty-one *littérateurs* at his table and Mademoiselle, what was her name, Madeleine, Isabelle, Marguerite Saint-Thomas?—from the Théâtre du Marais, had danced with so much feeling that they had all wept.

In the spring of that year Françoise took him away from Paris. Françoise' *l'avide* had a country-house at Fontenay-aux-Roses. "She will not be there?" Paul had said ungratefully, adding again the old quip that one sister thought only of men and the other only of drink. "No, she will not. But we may use her house when she does not require it, which is kind."

"Bah!" said Paul. "I poured money down their throats in an effort to get them married, she and Anne Gallois."

It was with relief that at last they left behind the streets of Paris, already blowing with the dust of summer. How was it possible so to love and hate a place, to be glad of absence and equally glad of return? Paul's face in the light from the carriage-window seemed drawn like that of a corpse.

"Do you remember our first carriage-journey, when we went to Avesnes?" But he could not and, when she repeated the name, smiled a little and said, "Avesnes? Avesnes?" as though it were a new word he had learned.

At Fontenay he revived a little. There was no company to distract him and before he began to pine again, as she knew he would do, for the variety of torment at the *hôtel de l'impécuniosité*, he wrote two comedies. The ill that pervaded his body like a blight served to floresce and magnify his brain. Each cell saw men as giants, birds as grotesques; the norm of an idea engorging till it turned, swollen, into fantasy. She prayed that his creation would continue, that the hunger and thirst for the company that killed him, while it succored him, would cease. But soon he grew restless again, his eyes turning always to the long windows beyond which parterres of flowers bloomed. "How weary I am of vegetables!" he said one day.

Coming in out of the sunlight with the flowers in her arms she found him, once, painfully laboring from the gray chair, turned to face the wall. He had not heard her enter and on drawing near she saw that he was making a map. The jagged fantastic outlines met her eyes.

"This is the *empire goguenard*," he said, "of which I am king." His voice was low and she understood that, although he could no longer hear her, he knew that she was in the room. "This is the Creek of the Pedants where many fools were once wrecked many years ago because their ship had no bottom and they stuck in the sand. And these are the Mountains of False Supposition to climb which takes a great deal of skill, because no sooner does one take a step upward than, without volition, one is propelled two steps back; it is better to ascend them backward. And this is the River of Misguided Thought which waters all the realm."

She looked at the infinite fancy in the laboriously constructed kingdom. Often Paul had scribbled faces on margins; he liked to draw. But here were strange birds, gargoyles and sea-serpents and tritons, swamps and water-falls. Deep down in her remembrance images stirred; the picture he had evolved for her of that mythical Martinique where no trouble and only bliss existed had had such trees. Out of his bitter notions beauty came; she regretted that he had not drawn on paper, it would have been worth taking the *empire* back to the Rue Neuve-Saint-Louis.

But Paul only babbled when she tried to make him understand; the effort had exhausted him and he succumbed to one of his worst spells, when nothing, not even her persuasion, would rouse him from what he gradually sank to become. And yet some memory of the idea behind the drawing must have remained with him, for after they reached home again she heard him mutter of it.

"Can I pin my chimeras on the wall for the approbation of Mignard? They have laughed enough; it is finished now, and so am I."

V

SHE STOOD on the balcony in the Rue Saint-Antoine and felt the press of humanity on all sides. Behind, around and below was packed the waiting city, come to see the entry into Paris of the King and his new bride. The eye could see only heads, the ear catch murmurings. Everyone talked of the same thing. Françoise shut her eyes against the crushing heat and tried to pick out, from the varying odors, the perfume of herbs with which the streets had been strewn early this morning.

They had been in their place for many hours now, she and the d'Aumonts and Mademoiselle Ninon, who had come to the occasion garbed in silver cloth. It was an opportunity to see all that passed; the Hôtel d'Aumont was situated almost opposite to the Hôtel de Beauvais, where the Queen-Mother sat. The cruel Venus of the fair white arms of early nightmares had passed away with time; Françoise gazed curiously at the plump *veuve de France*, talking now with expressive gestures of her still beautiful hands to a small brown harassed creature in black, the Queen of England.

"There is the English Princess Henriette, who is to marry the brother of the King." Madame d'Aumont nudged her excitedly. "As well marry her to another woman! The Cardinal dressed Philippe as a girl when young, in order that he might not oust his brother; and a girl he has remained, they say, ever since. But it is different when one is royal."

Yes, different, different, she thought, watching the group below the crimson canopy; if that young girl with the slight figure and beautiful eyes were a doll to be disposed of, she herself had once been so . . . did they feel at all, these royalties, playing their artificial part in each day's ceremony, like forced flowers under glass? Had the little brown widow of England grieved for her beheaded husband? Had there been any romance at all in the whispered marriage of the *vendeuse* with Italian Mazarin?

Mazarin, Mazarin. Wherever he showed himself one heard the name, whispered like the rumors that circulated of him, half true and half false. Paul had ridiculed him so that it would never be possible for him to be free of sniggered laughter again. Did he know that she stood here before him, the wife of Paul? And in fact there was so little left of the butt of the Fronde that even Paul, if he had seen him now, would have known him for an ill man . . . beneath the scarlet biretta M. le Cardinal's face was yellow as a louis. This was his triumph, this marriage for which he had worked between France and Spain. It was also his leave-taking. After this he might die.

"They will not come," yawned Ninon, "for another hour." Françoise made no reply, finding diversion in the sights in the street. Crowding the pavements, Paris also waited, fenced in by double rows of halberdiers. Paris was docile, weary, but still, with expectation, gay. A little shiver took her in this city of two souls; what would be the outcome now if the crowd burst its bonds, flooded the streets which were cleared for the royal approach, scaled the decked balconies which held the hated Mazarin and his crew, and cast them down like carrion against the waiting stones? It could be done; it almost had been, a decade ago. What power was in a crowd!

"They need a leader," Paul had said. "Their energies must be directed so that their will is heard. It is not that they have no further grievances, or that they are better off than they ever were in the days of the Fronde. One day, not yours or mine, they will rise again. Then it will be like an eclipse of the sun and the whole world will be re-fashioned out of a sea of blood." She still heard the laughter that had followed; what fantasies came from Scarron!

She shrugged a little, denying with the light movement the feeling that took her. Why should she feel an omen in this innocent crowd? They were talking now and shouting for the young King, popular ever since the day, last year, when he had walked to meet his hesitating *Parlement* whip in hand, attired for the hunt in gray and scarlet, and due in an hour at Fontainebleau, where he had told the ladies to wait for him. "I will not have orders of mine contradicted or even discussed. Henceforth any word of mine is law. You will conclude the minutes of our last meeting, *M. le Président;* there will be no further hesitation." Then he had clapped the great hat with gray feathers on his head again, turned and, striding out of the building, had ridden back to Fontainebleau in time for the promised hunting-party.

Now all about the streets those words were repeated, whispered and laughed over in admiration and a growing hope. Little Louis the offspring, by accident of one stormy night, of the *vendeuse des oignons* and the melancholy monarch who had been estranged from his wife for eighteen years! It was the hand of God that had directed the late drenched King to his wife's bed for shelter. And now this child, so mercifully conceived by arrangement of Providence, had emerged from the shadow of that yellow ecclesiastic seated up there, who would have diverted his mind with

ballets and other frittering nonsense. "Henceforth my word
is law. There will be no further hesitation." Ah, there was a
little king! Now *les affaires* would be dispatched promptly;
there would be justice for everyone and no more civil war.
"I am the State." There was the grandson of Henri Quatre!
Praise be to Heaven for the reign that was ended, of women
and foreigners and fools; and for that begun of the triumph
of France, the Sun-King in whom all promise lay and who
would return, today, to his own capital of Paris, with the
beautiful daughter of the King of Spain he had ridden south
to marry. A good thing, when all was said and done, that
the Princess of Savoy, who had been on the *tapis*, had after
all not been chosen; or the Princess of England, whom
everyone knew lived on French charity for long enough
with holes in her vest. No, only the most beautiful daughter
of the greatest of kings would have done, and the greatest
king of all being Louis, why, recourse had to be had to
Spain, for the second greatest. Ah, little wonder the time
seemed slow to pass, waiting for a sight of the King and
his bride!

At last the trumpets sounded. Far down the street there
was a cloud of dust, glittering as though gold-powder had
been thrown among it. The great carved arches of stone
spanned the way; down the street the escort was coming.
The guns of Paris thundered in salute. The crowds jostled
and roared. Windows, balconies, were packed with faces;
the very walls seemed to move.

To have such power, thought Françoise. Surely no other
human being had it under God.

She watched, seeing the long dark lines of a thousand
monks, the sad low sound of their chanting half-heard, their
carried candles burning. The furred scarlet and black of the
Faculties followed; then archers; trumpeters; guilds of mer-
chants; mayors of corporations. The Chancellor of the Kingdom passed by on his caparisoned horse. His Majesty's
Musketeers displayed their white and blue.

"*Les muguets* are coming," whispered Ninon. "This is
worth all the rest."

Les muguets were the elegants about Court. Françoise glimpsed that averted, elfin face, bearing the suspicion of tongue in cheek that accompanied all Ninon's profounder statements. The veil of lawn she wore was quasi-nunlike, accentuating all her fascination. The cruel, dimpled mouth was whimsical today. *Les muguets* passed by in every variety of gem and plumage, saluted the Queen Mother and also Ninon. "Stand forward, *chérie*," murmured that lady, "or you will miss them as they go by."

She thrust forward the wife of Scarron with a little push. So it was that Françoise saw Villarceaux ride by, with the queer twist of the heart that always came at sight of him. He was distinctive, she thought, even among that throng, with his erect bearing and darkly burnished hair. His horse was restive and he had difficulty in curbing it. . . .

Madame d'Aumont clapped her hands. "Look, I demand of you, look! The Swiss Guards are magnificent!"

Guards. Marshals of France. Heralds, resplendent in their surcoats whose bearings shone with gold. About her the applause swelled and grew to a shout. "The god approaches," murmured Ninon.

The cheers were deafening. Alone on a Spanish bay, in a space cleverly stage-managed beneath a gold tissue canopy, rode a slight boy of twenty-two. His dark curls clustered richly beneath a great hat whose plume was clasped by diamonds. His coat and harness were heavy with silver embroidery. He smiled, but not from the eyes.

"He treats *la mère* with great deference," observed Ninon. "They say she will still outshine the Queen."

The boy swept off his plumed hat gracefully, bowing toward the place where Anne of Austria sat with his aunt, the Queen of England. He managed his bay with ease, sensing the degree of control needed to keep it within its place beneath the canopy. "He will do so with all things," Françoise thought, "or else he will not undertake them."

She was left with a curiously strong impression of the coldly smiling, efficient, pampered, gorgeous boy. After he had passed, the excitement of the crowd died. The new

Queen in her coach was a disappointment, being less beautiful than rumor had said. Her short thick body was plastered with jewels and her smile, with the heavy Hapsburg lip, was vapid and void of intelligence. Paris looked at her frizzed fair hair and sighed, remembering the beauty of young Anne of Austria when she had come, in exactly this way, over the Pyrenees to be their Queen. "A dwarf, this one," Françoise heard them murmuring in disappointment. "A little painted dwarf out of Spain."

The carriages passed and the dust-clouds settled, leaving a million crushed sweet herbs in the streets.

Back again in the Rue Neuve-Saint-Louis she found Paul lying in his chair, ailing and cross because she had been absent. "The day has been long," he grumbled. "I thought you would never come."

He showed no interest in the day's event, turning his eyes aside fretfully when she tried to speak of it; she guessed that he was in pain. She fetched him his draught and when he had taken it, instead of drowsing without further speech, he started to talk again; he must, after all, have taken in something of what she had to say.

"The King. The King. I am glad you have seen him. You, Madame, have a natural *hauteur*, it will do very well. I shall obtain a Court appointment. It should have been done long ago. I have enemies who are against me. But see, over there you will find it. There shall be no more of this, no more," and he started to mumble and presently, as she had hoped he would do, he slept.

She stole over to find the letter, fearful of waking him. It was almost illegible, painfully composed in his crippled fingers throughout that day which had seemed so long. It was an application, set out in formal terms, to the King's Majesty to demand the post of historiographer to the royal house.

"In the manner of *mazarinades?*" she thought. The pomp of the world had faded in her mind and she recalled the present bitterly.

VI

THINKING AFTERWARD of the death of Paul, she found that she was unable to remember it as an isolated event. So many things seemed to have happened before and after; at no time would she ever again be the person she had been. The milestones of conversion, marriage, widowhood, marked the way whitely, at the same time seeming like little graves.

Which of her memories was the strongest? Always there seemed to be voices, calling about the street under the windows. At first she had thought them horrible with their callous hawking of news; Scarron is dying, Scarron the clown is at last grips with King Death. They whispered about the doors and noted who came in and went out; for two pins they would have come chattering and prying about the poor corpse that was not yet dead. She formed a little guard of the friends who had loved him: d'Aumont, the Maréchal d'Albret, Elbène who had held Paul as a child when he was christened. These she could trust, until such time as there was no need further to stem the flood-tide of bailiffs and creditors, tradesmen and quacks and professional rogues, and the idlers and busybodies who were never distant. These friends could slip in and out, quietly, past the mob that waited outside; convey food and little luxuries in gift to Paul, who could no longer heed them. These she would send, at last, on the errand of final need. When she broached the subject to d'Aumont he and the others protested.

"Paul was never devout," they said. "It is different for yourself. He took no heed of the Church, ate meat on Fridays, laughed always at the idea of contrition and the rites for the dying. Let him die now in peace, in the way he would wish."

"His is the greater need," she said, and they stared at her; she knew, for she had heard them talk, that they thought of her as a bigot. "It is necessary," she said. "If no one of you will fetch a priest for my husband I must go myself."

And so at last, seeing argument was useless, d'Aumont went and fetched the parish priest of Saint-Louis and smuggled him into the house. There were no catcalls and laughter from beyond while Paul made his confession and received the viaticum. Nothing was known until it was all over.

He seemed peaceful; grateful, as she could tell in some way, for her insistence. He could no longer speak much or with lucidity except at intervals. Once he awoke and, casting his eyes round the few of them who waited about his bed, he saw that many wept. *"Courage,"* he said. "I have made you all laugh a great deal more than I will ever make you cry."

He did not forget her, searching for her often with the eyes that had always seemed to her like a child's who uttered enormities. "See, my wife," he told the company, "she must wed again, but not a paralytic." And then he jested to himself and her about the taste he must have given her for marriage, so that it behooved her soon to wed again for fear of worse ills by reason of that.

A handkerchief would have held his bones. She thought of the quiet interment by night in the little church of Saint-Gervais. The audience that would have watched his struggle with Death had not troubled with the corpse from which all strife had departed. He had made "the best end in the world"; and now his sisters, herself, the others and Elbène, were alone at his burial. The younger children of his father, old Apostle Scarron, had come, like the crows she remembered after Constant's death, for pickings; but there had been none and they had taken themselves off, having announced their intention of claiming a share in any inheritance, and returned home to Beauvais.

The pamphleteers were busy; she was accosted by them

on the way back from the funeral. In the guttering light of a lantern papers blew, demonstrating Paul's decease in terms mock-heroic or libidinous, and his reappearance after death to herself, his widow, begging her to moderate her grief a little. D'Albret beat the pamphleteers back and she reached home.

Home? The word still made her smile. Paul had long ago disembursed such poor stuff as was still salable. To rid the house of importunate newcomers was the most urgent need; by dawn they were on the stairs. Odd spoons and forks, a needle-box, a sugar-sifter, a salt-dish; four torches that had once lighted the doorway of the Hôtel de Troyes, went to them. The *hôtel de l'impécuniosité* was chaff, that the wind would soon blow away.

Françoise examined her own state, when she had time, in the little bare room that d'Aumont had found for her at the top of the building owned by the sisters of La Charité near the Palais-Royal. It was the first leisure she had had; notaries, creditors, auctioneers, servants to be dismissed, accounts to balance . . . she had seen to everything, with a few francs in hand. The clan of Beauvais would meet with disappointment.

Paul had died on the seventh of October. Now, looking from her casement over trees from which the withered leaves had long since blown, she searched for his face in her mind and could scarcely recall it. That part of her life was closed, as the part in the Hôtel de Saint-Herman had been when she married Paul. Already the well-known features had blurred in her recollection; softened, as they had been in death, all satyr-lines smoothed away, all mockery silent. She remembered how peaceful he had looked at the last, and hoped again it had been by reason of the ease of soul she had tried to bring him. They said that after speech and even consciousness was gone some faculty, some inner ear, could hearken to the spirit.

That he would have mocked she knew. The epitaph he had himself written contained only a prayer for sleep. To that tormented body the only heaven would be cessation of awareness of itself. The tortured nights he had known! But surely God had arranged it so that to all eternity little Scarron should exist as an eager mind. Mind, brain, senses; could one at all employ the finite things in a matter infinite? The priest and the pastor in the Faubourg Sainte-Anne all those years ago had argued over it for so long. . . .

And surely Paul's valediction was more genuinely contained in those lines he had already written, long since, on the eve of that voyage to the Americas he had desired so much for its healing suns that would enable him to be her lover.

> *Adieu Cour, adieu Tuileries*
> *Jardin des simples, Luxembourg,*
> *Beaux lieux où la ville et la Cour*
> *Vont faire leurs galanteries. . . .*

Paul had loved Paris. Tears blinded her, as they had not done on that day when she had bidden farewell to him, the crippled limbs oddly relaxed and straightened, peacefully lying between four candles. The crucifix on his breast mocked her. "Why have you laid this on me," she heard him say, "and why the weeds? You cannot pretend to grief, *ma mie,* and in them you resemble a spider." Almost she looked for the bitter note of his laughter from the still mouth; so often, masklike, he had lain, unmoving, as he lay now, the dead man in the silence.

"Sleep well on this night," she said. Rising from her knees, she had gone at last from the room. That night and many nights she would spend in fervent prayer. Peace for him she desired most urgently, at the end of that long journey his soul must still make.

She stood now watching till at last a dried leaf fell against the window. It hung there damply, caught by the flaked paint on the decaying wood of the frame. Presently the wind came and tugged it away.

Leaves were like souls, she thought. Paul's night would be as secure as any prayers could make it, away from debt and change and the necessity of earning a living. But what of her day?

PART III

The Wit of Mortemart

I

THE *laitier* who was making his rounds in the horse-alley
that backed the houses of the great stopped, setting down his
pails, when he came to the Hôtel Richelieu and paused, seeing
in the distance an approaching figure. It was early still and
there were few abroad, so that he hoped it would be the
bonne, who would bring him a vessel for the milk and with
whom he might exchange a few words and possibly a kiss,
for she was very pretty. He listened for the clap of her clogs,
easing at the same time his shoulders that the length of wood
had chafed. He always traveled the streets with this lathe
across his back and at either end the pails swinging, swinging; and at first there had been sores on his skin when he
got home at night, but of late years he had grown used to it.

But the figure bore no vessel and walked quickly, silently,
and he saw that although it was a woman dark-gowned in the
manner of servants she was no *bonne* but the widow Scarron.
He shrugged lightly, picked up his pails and went on. That
woman was a familiar figure going about the streets, he
wondered at himself that he should not have known her. She
would have come down from early Mass in the Rue Saint-
Jacques or in the chapel of Saint Francis of Paula. Most days
a week she did that and then disappeared, like a swift black
shadow, into the Hôtel d'Albret or the Hôtel Richelieu.

Passing the widow Scarron, he stole a side-glance at her
out of his eyes. She had been good-looking once, he decided.
As far as that went, she still might be so, if she were to dress
like other women. One might as well be a nun as attire oneself so, in a high *collet* and a gown of black serge, and a black
veil. It argued great devotion to the *mari;* what had he been?
A poet? A painter? In any event he was dead now and had

been for many years. Madame should put by her mourning.

They passed; her dark veils brushed his sleeve. She kept her glance fixed on the ground coldly, as though not seeing him. What did she think of? She was a queer woman. Like a servant, only not so, Madame de Richelieu's *bonne* had said. She would run errands for Madame and answer doors, and if she were not there Madame would call for her angrily. Yet in the evenings, when the great ones came, this widow Scarron was admitted to their conversation and often, when the company broke up too late for her to be admitted to La Charité where she lodged, Madame would beg her to stay the night. And sometimes to this same La Charité the carriages of the great ones would themselves come. It was all very puzzling.

Well, who was he to care for such things? He watched the retreating figure out of sight and then forgot her.

Françoise hurried on and felt against her veiled face the cold of dawn abating. Presently the twilit mist would clear and the dews resolve in the pale sun of early morning. She was thankful, feeling the thing that had come with darkness depart, already, in the light of day. And in any case it had not been her affair . . . might even, truth to tell, not exist save in her own mind.

But that there had been something evil in the night she was sure; felt as she hurried swiftly, out of the shadows that had hidden in the Rue de la Tannerie. It had been only by chance that she had been there, having sat late, as she had promised, with the daughter of old Mère Maillard who had been ill. *La Mère* was bedridden in the Charité and had worried, worried, about her girl, till in the end Françoise had promised, as a means of setting the old woman's mind at rest, to go to her and see if there was anything that could be done. But so filthy had the house been in which the girl lay, the very rags with which she covered herself soiled and devoured by rats, that it had taken many hours to cleanse her and make her comfortable, and even with that and the soup Françoise had brought, it was likely enough she would die.

Coming out into the dawn she had seen, shrouded in mist,

the wretched street, the houses seeming bodiless, floating among wreathed vapor near the ground. It was a miasma, composed of all the vileness of Paris. She must see what she could do to get the girl out of that house, that street, if she should live till morning.

The ground was uneven and rutted with holes. Stepping carefully, she wished that she had brought the maid, Nanon Balbien, with her. Nanon, remembered as an apple-cheeked serving-girl at Murcy in the old days, had come to her when Tante died. She was a big raw-boned woman now and feared nothing, having taken even her own conversion as a matter of course. She would have made little enough here of the heaps and runnels, choked with mud, round which one must pick one's way. To Nanon, everything was black, or white; necessary, or unnecessary. To serve Madame Françoise one must be Catholic. *Eh bien,* she would be so, forgetting her early days . . . and Françoise herself, holding high the skirts of *étamine du Lude* that were serviceable and cost so little, giving a better appearance than the faded colored silks that gentlewomen of no means so often afforded, would fix her attention on avoiding the mud and forget them also. But that house, that house with its poverty and filth . . . how unwillingly it made one remember!

Mud and shadows; certain of them moved. There were many here who had no shelter to go to, even so wretched as the one she had just left, and who spent all night in the streets. Over there was a house where, so she had heard in the roundabout way of these things, clairvoyants lived. A light shone at a high window, showing them up early or—could it be?—not yet abed. Figures waited about the door.

She would not have raised her glance, taking less interest in them than in the safe preservation of her skirts from filth, if it had not been that the figures moved. For the first time, although the unconscious knowledge was always with her, she thought of footpads. There would be little enough in her purse, God knew, but to keep to the middle of the street was wise.

The clear sky at the street's end showed grayly. If she were to hurry she could reach there. Coolly, for she was accustomed by now to these dangers, she surveyed the moving figures, deciding at last that they were not making toward her and that, in any event, there was a woman among them. A lantern bobbed as she passed them on the way; she heard a voice, urging to be careful.

"Do not shine it so brightly here!"

They broke off abruptly, as if silenced. In the queer half-light they made their way past Françoise, withdrawn near the gutter. Something in their silence and the swift muffled sounds of their footsteps made her unwilling to be accosted by them or to speak. They passed, and she was left with the strong awareness of two things: a perfume, subtle and evasive, of verbena flowers; and the sight of the woman's face beneath her hood. She was very beautiful, and her eyes had the staring lost look of someone who walks in sleep. It was impossible to say what evil had taken place, but that it had been here, in this street tonight, was certain. And the victim? Françoise crossed herself in the shadow of her veils. "If I knew her name, I would pray for her," she thought. She became aware that the street was very cold, and pulled her cloak about her.

That had been in the dawn. Now, having heard Mass and taken the sacrament, she felt strengthened, as if the filtered evil in the air had been purged away. At such times a great peace would come to her and she would feel that perhaps, after all, she need not fail to give pleasure to God by living humbly and serving where she could. There was so much to do in little ways; perhaps that was her task on earth, and if so she would fulfill it gladly. Already the d'Albrets and the Richelieus relied on her for small things which another would not have done. It was little enough trouble in return for—what? "Society, *ma mie*," she heard Paul's voice, mocking her. "Madame la Duchesse, Madame la Marquise—could you bear it if they did not continue to call you friend?"

No, she could not. It made life infinitely brighter to be able to look forward, in the manner of the Rue Neuve-Saint-Louis, to witty talk; to the cultivation of friends, their entertainment. "Ah!" had said Madame d'Albret, who never knew what to say to guests, "you, Madame, have always the right words for any occasion." And Madame de Richelieu liked, when she awoke in the morning, to be met with freshly made hot chocolate, as only she, Françoise Scarron, knew how to make it. All these ways . . .

"Madame, you think too much of the world," had said her confessor, the Abbé Gobelin, blinking in disapproval behind his spectacles.

She hurried on and up the steps that led to the back entrance of the hôtel and swiftly to the kitchens. Madame liked her chocolate brought to her at an early hour and she would complain a little, fretfully, if it were not ready. Françoise fetched the silver pot, heating the ingredients meanwhile on the fire that was already kindled. When it was ready she carried it carefully upstairs to Madame.

The Duchesse de Richelieu was in bed, her face devoid of last night's rouge, unamiable and pettish in the morning light. "Why, there you are," she said. She lay and watched Françoise throw back the closed shutters. The full day flooded in over an array of littered garments, velvet, silk and lace, flung heedlessly over sofas and across chairs. A perfume lingered, of mingled wine and violets grown stale with the night's dying.

Françoise poured the chocolate, handing it wordlessly to Madame. She set herself then to collecting the garments, selecting a bed-gown of *point-de-Venise* and draping it about Madame's shoulders. Her face was expressionless, the eyes dark and secret; her movements made no sound.

"What are you thinking about?" said Madame suddenly. She had been watching the widow Scarron for some time curiously. Being a woman of no imagination, it did not occur to her often to recall the house on the Rue Neuve-Saint-Louis. There, it was true, Madame Scarron had held her *salon*, which, now one remembered it, had been amusing and successful. But the wife of a twisted curiosity, who diverted the *monde*, was one thing; this was another. How had the widow managed to insinuate herself so that one could not do without her? Even so, one had to be careful. *Nom de Dieu,* had not Madame d'Aumont been mortified a year or two back, boasting as she had of the aid she intended to render this destitute case? In the end widow Scarron had piled all the firewood Madame sent in gift onto a barrow in the back yard and returned it. "I have no need of almsgiving," she had announced. Since then everyone had been circumspect about her. Madame la Duchesse began to chatter heedlessly.

"How long is it since I saw anyone worth talking to? It will be necessary soon to show ourselves in the *monde,* when the Court comes back from Fontainebleau. What do you think of the talk that the King intends to invade the Low Countries? The war will be a diversion . . . not like having it on one's own doorstep, and I daresay everyone will go. His Majesty makes a spectacle of these things. I make no doubt he wearies now for action; ballets, fêtes, all that sort of thing, pall after a while. La Vallière, too, is fading. That type of soft fair pretty little creature runs quickly to seed, and everyone knows she gave birth to the King's child in the room where *mesdames* were going in to dinner. "I have colic!" says she, and writhes, and everyone killing their laughter over this colic, which was no such thing. They say the other child is hidden in Colbert's house. Of course she'll never hold the King."

Madame yawned. "Not noble blood. Her stepfather, they say, was a cook. Blood always tells, as they put it, in the long run; now there's somebody coming to Madame d'Albret this week—such a beautiful, witty creature, and married to a religious fool. He—Montespan—was even a little beneath her; but of course it was difficult to overcome that, she being a Mortemart—the Rochechouarts, you know, Madame d'Albret's kinsmen; one of the oldest families in France." Madame preened herself. "Even so, they say that old Gabriel Mortemart is so riddled with debts that he could not pay his daughter's dowry. In any event, she comes here—Athénaïs —to sit with me on Tuesday a while and drink Madeira. She has so little time to spare from her post at Court, it is useless asking her to a *soirée* or a ball. You'll come, won't you, Scarron, and talk to her for me also? She is so witty—the wit of the Mortemarts, you know, is proverbial—she will make a butt of poor me without my knowing it. Only you can cope with her. You always have the right word."

Françoise left her at last, carrying the chocolate-tray downstairs. The sound of the carping voice disturbed her thoughts and threatened, a very little, to invade the peace that had come to her, having hastened in the early dawn to meet God, to taste the body of Christ.

"You think too much of the world." Was it the confessor's words to her that morning that had made, to a greater degree than usual, the words of Madame la Duchesse seem shallow? However it might be, she saw him in her mind, that saintly man who had been a soldier before he became a priest, and so knew a good deal about the world he scorned. The eyes burned in his thin face with a light that was steady and clear; already it outshone the candles in silver sconces, polished for the *monde*, in the Hôtels d'Albret and de Richelieu. And Athénaïs, who had wit in her blood, meant nothing at all to her.

How was she to have known what would befall, or that she would always remember the day she met Athénaïs de Roche-chouart? Even at the beginning she felt that strange bond forged of pity; the pity one has for a lost child, wandering in the dark. What would they have said, the elegant ones, if they knew? The widow Scarron, on her pension of two thousand livres a year *grace à la Reine,* has pity for the glorious, the well-born, the fortunate, the spirited, the beautiful Marquise de Montespan, who by raising an eyebrow could buy and sell her and her few miserable possessions!

Yet it was true.

She had paused on the threshold of Madame de Richelieu's smaller *salon* and there beheld a very beautiful woman drinking wine. The woman sat with crossed knees and one foot swinging, swinging as if the energy pent up within her would not allow a moment's stillness, she must get on, get on. . . . Her hair was abundant, the color of ripe wheat, drawn back

175

from the low white forehead in little, rippling waves that were caught at last in a great knot of Ceres behind her head. She was dressed in green, the bodice of the gown laced impertinently with silver so as to resemble the King's guard. Seeing her, Françoise was aware of paradox. The gown was high-throated, the style of the hair severe, but the effect was one of fruitfulness, invitation, voluptuous promise. All eyes were drawn to the high full bosom, the swinging calf beneath the green silk. Here was an animal, healthy, physically perfect, insolent in perfection; a foil for desire.

Here was the woman of the Rue de la Tannerie.

"Madame Scarron."

The low voice dwelt on the syllables carefully. Athénaïs de Rochechouart rendered one gloved hand, an instant, in salute; she did not trouble to rise from Madame's Dutch chair. The hand that had been raised returned again to its task of slapping a little silver whip, rhythmically, restlessly, against her thigh. Great sapphire-blue eyes raised themselves, surveyed Françoise and fell again, hiding a sparkle of malice behind creamy lids. The full mouth smiled.

Françoise heard the Duchesse chatter on; herself, her history, was being dwelt on. She felt the awareness of shock recede and disposed herself in a chair. Wine was brought; she sensed the wrought relief of silver wheat-ears about the flagon, cold to her fingers' touch. She sipped the wine.

Presently she found herself and the fair woman talking. In the aridity of thought that often surrounded her now, she was quick to appreciate an intelligence akin to her own. This the Marquise had; she knew of, had heard of, Paul; had read his plays.

"*Typhon* I love best; and of the verses, his ode to the little dog. He had a fancy like the Italian poets, but, I think, less insipid. One can read Italian poetry and drown in the beauty of phrases; there is often no sense."

She threw back her head and the room was filled with the sound of her rich laughter. "So many fools emulate other fools, that to read at all grows tedious. Savages are happiest, who can say and do exactly as they prefer. Do you not think this probable, Madame Scarron?" Her eyes mocked the widow's *étamine* and veils; she dimpled with laughter.

"In a savage tribe the customs, they say, are more rigorous, and the restrictions less reasonable and a good deal more severe," said Françoise. *You,* Madame, she thought, would let no customs bar you; the world is a ripe fruit, and your little white teeth ache to bite it. And yet—how much I like you, and how much pity you!

The conversation flowed on and she listened to Athénaïs talk of her husband, who was, she said, a bore, and of her little son, the Marquis d'Antin, whom she adored.

"I can endure Montespan for the sake of my child, and for that reason only. He's unreasonable, pedantic, jealous; follows me everywhere, and denies me money enough to keep myself in decency. How can I help running into debt? I'm not a gambler, but to make an appearance at Court one must contrive now and again to hold cards. How can I help it if the luck's against me?"

A gleam, no more, between the lids, showed, then they dropped; the Marquise surveyed her shoe. Its buckle, set about with brilliants, pleased her; she twisted the foot to and fro.

"Luck," she said again. "Luck's everything." She laughed. "What is your opinion on that, Madame Scarron? But I shock you, I believe."

"No," said Françoise, rather sadly. "No, Madame."

In the way such things happen she saw Athénaïs often after that, chance having once drawn them together insuring, as it were, that their orbits would transect again, and yet again. Their planets by compulsive pull would be together, and then apart; shocked into strange orbits, forever becoming to one another as moon to body, satellite to earth. They would never travel completely out of range again.

Athénaïs was present at Mademoiselle de Pons' marriage. Françoise hid herself, having hurried at an early hour to fit the bride out in her finery and left herself, when the time came, no leisure for her own toilette. Mademoiselle was a friendly laughing creature who reminded her a little of the Saint-Herman girl of long ago. "Promise that you will come!" she had said, and widow Scarron had kept the promise, hastening straight from early Mass to stitch, drape, lace, arrange and cosset. "How well you dispose my dress, dearest Madame!" said the bride, gratified. "Why do you not set up as an arbiter of fashion? Nobody else I know has so certain a sense of elegance as you, so faultless a knowledge of what will please."

She was radiant, standing there in her white veil and wide-skirted gown of pale satin looped with blonde. How many brides had had that mystic beauty, while she herself, never having known it, must be content to dress, and aid, and admire! But her help was invaluable. "I? Why; she said, in answer to the other's inquiry, "I am too old, and too poor."

Yet she was handsome enough, she knew, to be noticed still, in the severe garb of her choice; the *étamine,* at a louis an ell, was cheap enough to make full and becoming skirts. Her dark eyes sparkled with wit and health above the snowy *collet.* That her appearance was unusual she knew; she took pride in it. Madame thinks too much of the world. . . .

But today she had lost herself in the world so completely as to forget even her appearance, having her hair bundled up beneath a cloth to keep it out of the way, and her mouth full of pins, when the bride gave a little shriek. *"Nom de Dieu!* Here is the company coming, and you, Madame, are not dressed!"

She had stolen then from the room with last of the pins and wrappings. In her coarse apron and head-clout, she was sure, if anyone noticed her at all, she would be mistaken for the cleaning-woman. Later she returned, cleansed, attired, and *point-de-vice;* the eyes of the new Madame d'Heudicourt danced with laughter in answer to her own.

"They nearly caught you!" she whispered. She was delighted to show off her friend to the company. How distinguished Madame Scarron looked, like a raven among thrushes! Ah, now she was married it would be possible to do more, a great deal more, for one who had been so kind.

"Athénaïs," murmured the watchers, as a very beautiful woman made her entrance into the room. . . .

Later, in the disrobing-room the bride chattered of Madame la Marquise and how she had kissed her. "Was she not *ravissante,* more so than anyone there, in that cloak of pale satin, and the little high collar of fur? They say—" The bride dimpled, shrugged, looked mysterious, and finally gave all her attention to her curls, which were limp with the heat of the ceremony and needed crimping. "Oh, well," she said, as Françoise wielded the irons, "there is no need to say anything yet until one is certain. But such things are very entertaining, do you not think so, Madame? La Vallière is such a fool! They say the King snubbed her publicly for driving her carriage ahead of the Queen's to meet him in the Franche-Comté. How silly to curl one's hair merely to go to bed!"

The last remark having nothing to do with those preceding it, Françoise left the owner of the curls with M. d'Heudicourt, who appeared gratified by the result. Making her own way home to the narrow attic in the Charité, she felt tired, but pleasantly so. It was always a pleasure to serve others, particularly when they were as easy to please and as grateful as the laughing creature she had left. There had been so much laughter about that wedding today; she thought of those two happy young people, and then remembered her own.

II

MADAME D'HEUDICOURT'S high voice twitched with excitement. She was happy. It was good to be married, to be young and rich. It was a satisfaction also to have assisted Madame Scarron. That she had done so she was in no doubt whatever; did not everyone wish to be invited to this banquet in the presence of the King? "As it is, *chérie,* only three hundred well-born ladies have obtained the *entrée.* Half Paris sighs because it has not been chosen. And you, Madame, you are to come and sit with us, and watch the King dine! Can greater bliss be imagined? They say—"

"It would be greater bliss, surely, to dine ourselves," murmured Françoise. She stitched determinedly, having resolved to show nothing of this fatuous—one could not help thinking it—general adoration of the King. What was he but a man, after all? "And a fallible one, by all accounts." But she could not damp the young woman's enthusiasm, and truth to tell she was not displeased to be included.

Madame laughed. "How dry you are! But of course we shall dine!"

That they would dine was obvious, on the night, to anyone seeing the lit hall, blazing with a thousand candles, which reflected themselves in silver and in petals drowned with wine. Everything seemed as if contained in the heart of a great jewel. Colors were thrown back, faceted in myriad points of light. The carvings on the pillars shone with gilt; the satins and white shoulders of the ladies gleamed. How beautiful it was, all this beauty of France, gathered to cheer the victor in what had after all been a fairly easy victory, the taking of the willing towns of Franche-Comté! And the food, as Madame did not hesitate to remark, looked, beyond all computation, exquisite. "If only," she sighed, "they would come in, and we could eat!"

"They are here now," said Françoise, "on the hour."

The trumpets blew. In spite of herself she felt a queer excitement. The years had rolled back and she was standing expectantly with Ninon on the d'Aumont balcony in Paris, while below the crowd milled and roared. How much had passed since then! Paul dead, the opulent white-fleshed *Reine-Mère* on the other balcony dead also, of a corroding cancer that ate away the bowel. So many shades, and herself, still, waiting while trumpets sounded the arrival of this same King.

A man in a dark perruque came swiftly in and the great sea of skirts sank, spread and rose again. Louis XIV took his seat and gestured that the ladies be seated also. "An honor," twittered young Madame d'Heudicourt. "As a rule no one may sit in his presence."

Seated, Françoise watched him, eating little as was her wont; the dishes passed her plate in procession unnoticed. He had changed, she thought, from the boy who had managed his horse so expertly that day of the ride through Paris. Men did so, showing often less of age than of experience; women, she thought, were the opposite. The face of the King now was that of a man, handsome, attractive, courteous; a trifle bored, she guessed, with his female company. It was the company that compelled her interest.

The Queen she knew. Marie-Thérèse had for this occasion dressed herself in cloth-of-silver with flame-colored ribbons. The plumes in her frizzed hair sat stiffly and she was loaded with jewels. A little laced doll, Françoise thought, with feeling enough, no doubt, beneath the silver. Her fear and adoration of the King were reflected in her timid eyes. Had she been so hedged about with etiquette, from birth, that humanity was a race apart? She must be lonely, the Queen of France.

Near the King also was a lame woman. Françoise had watched her enter, aware of that slight, invisible closing of ranks with which is greeted an alien in the herd. Once long ago in the turkey-field of Tante Villette there had been a chicken which had hurt its wing. The others had pecked it to death, and when she had cried Philippe had laughed at her. "They will do so with anything that is different from themselves," he said.

So it would be with this woman. For an instant it seemed as if a veil had parted, and she stood revealed naked, a lamb among wolves. The wolves kept in check only because they must. Otherwise they would turn and rend her.

She was not beautiful, or even, any longer, very young. She must have been pretty once, in the manner of a wild rose, which fades early. Although she had lost her youth she retained the pathetic helplessness of a young, thin thing. The limp was very slight. It gave her a dragging hesitancy, sufficient with the unease of her manner to brand her, in the watching eyes, with that difference. She wore a gown of dull-yellow brocade, tasteless and too ornate for her fair coloring, as if she had dressed to the command of someone else. Her brows were mobile, obliquely drawn on a high light arch which drooped at the outer corners.

"La Vallière." Madame d'Heudicourt's whisper reached her too late to tell her what she already knew. The young, sharp profile of Madame was raised and curious; suddenly, for the first time, she looked like a bird of prey. How urgent must be the need for succor of the faded girl up there, taking no joy in her public place at the banquet, drooping a little like a weary flower so that the silk-fine hair fell forward, helplessly, under the small gold veil!

"Why does she come?" Françoise thought. "It is an abomination."

Laughter rang out. There was another woman present, close by the mistress and the wife, one of three hundred whose eyes were for the King. The level gaze of Louis met that of Madame de Montespan, and was held by it. He smiled, and responded to her laughter; La Vallière drooped; the Queen listened. It was like watching a play, a play of no morality, all the characters present on the stage, their fates planned out by relentless gods anxious for any diversion. The end of one scene was now in sight, and another was due to begin. Those who saw all made pretense to see nothing. La Vallière, the discarded mistress, would feign least of any. Therein lay her torment.

"But now she is part of the pomp and must sit here. He holds them all captives in his Roman triumph. It is not only Franche-Comté that he has conquered, this King. Nothing that is his possession must be returned, allowed to hide itself, to withdraw. This will continue till that woman's spirit is broken with misery and shame."

Françoise felt her cheeks flame in the tell-tale manner she remembered. So lit with anger was she that the knowledge brought no distress. Let them see what she thought of it all, if any chanced to look her way! She would make of him no god, this King.

"He is spoilt," she thought. There had been too much flattery. Adoration, adoration, from every woman in sight, from the mother who worshiped his slightest whim to the meek wife, the meeker mistress, the women who watched the food enter his mouth as if it were nectar to some celestial hive!

But Madame Athénaïs would never adore him. Athénaïs adored no one but herself. "And therein," thought the widow of Scarron, "lies the variety."

She was soon to know of it.

The nuns of La Charité by the Palais-Royal had an objection to make. She received too much company, they told her. It was not convenient to have, at all times and seasons, the carriages of the *monde* outside in the street. Neither was it seemly that Madame Scarron should be so often out to such a late hour that the gates were closed and she be seen returning next day, with no explanation given. Such habits might pertain in the world, but this was not the world. Would Madame please to conform a little? The other *pensionnaires* would otherwise follow her example. What would be thought if Madame Maillard, the widow of the army captain, the two unmarried ladies of middle age on the *troisiéme étage,* were to do likewise?

"We cannot have it, Madame," said the regretful Superior. "This place is a place for the poor and needy. If Madame is no longer so, then she should go."

Madame was so, to an extent that she was very nearly unable to pay for the cost of removing her few belongings. Where to go?

"I think too much of the world." Always the words of the Abbé Gobelin were in her mind. Now they returned to her, strongly, reproachfully. She had ignored them; she had vexed the nuns. It might be true that they were silly and prudish here, but the fault was hers.

"A middle-aged widow!" She spoke of it, laughing to hide her hurt, to Madame d'Heudicourt. That young personage was all sympathy, offering a room in her own home. "It will be to a degree more comfortable than a drafty convent, and you can see all the company you choose."

But Françoise smiled, thanked her, shook her head and said that she had already made arrangements to lodge in the Convent of the Ursulines in the Faubourg Sainte-Anne.

It was strange to be back here.

Her cell was the same. She had asked for it, and they had given it to her; anxious, she now saw, to give way to her every wish, in a manner that would cause her to become spoiled if she were not careful. They remembered her— "You, the little Mademoiselle d'Aubigné who had so tough a conscience that it took many months and the argument of *mon père* and a Huguenot pastor, at last, to convince you. Ah, that was a famous day for the convent! It has never been forgotten."

She had been remembered all those years, when old faces went or changed, and new ones lingered. Sœur Basile was still here, grown old now. She greeted Françoise with the same calm as before.

"You have come to be among us." Then with her straight directness, "You have never thought of being one of us?"

But Françoise shook her head. "I am too fond of the world, my confessor says. It is true; I would not part with it."

"Perhaps you have a task in the world, my daughter," said the nun.

Françoise smiled, sighed a little, and threaded her needle before replying. "I am thirty-three years old and it is not apparent yet. Perhaps I am one of those who may serve God in little ways. I like to think so; in this, perhaps, is my conceit."

"You guard against that danger in knowing of it," said the nun. "God is patient."

"I would I too had patience. Sometimes I ask myself for what purpose I was born. I am happier now than I have ever been, and yet—of what use is it all?"

III

ONE EVENING Françoise returned from sitting with Madame d'Albret to be informed that a visitor waited in her room.

She hurried upstairs. It would, she thought, be Madame d'Heudicourt, of whom she had seen little enough lately, her Court duties keeping her always occupied. This Court was a pivot about which all things revolved. To be outside it was to be of the *demi-monde*.

But the figure which waited, cloaked and hooded by the window, was taller than Madame d'Heudicourt. The woman looked out, with a curious fixity, over the roofs of Paris.

Hearing Françoise' quiet entry she turned, and put back her hood. To the world it might seem impossible that Athénaïs de Montespan should be here, in this poor room which her beauty illumined like a candle. But if Françoise felt surprise, she showed none.

Athénaïs smiled now, coming forward. She was completely mistress of herself. "You are surprised that I have come?" she said. "But we are old acquaintances now, you and I, Madame Scarron."

"In what way can I serve Madame?"

Athénaïs' eyes narrowed. "You're quick. How did you know I needed service?"

"I did not know. If you have come for no reason but acquaintance I am honored. If not—"

"Ah, you know very well not," said the Marquise. She stripped off the gloves she wore, flinging them on a chair. "What a small room this is! You're quick, as I say—discreet. That was why I came myself; I'd no fear you would betray me. Otherwise I'd have sent d'Heudicourt, who suggested you. She and my cousin d'Albret sing your praises daily."

The imperious figure stood poised, aloof; the slim hands idle, only when one moved a jewel caught the light, then another. Where had the daughter of old Mortemart, who was riddled with debt, obtained jewels worth a ransom? Everything about her spoke now of precious stones and metal. Her hair was liquid gold in the cell's faint light.

Françoise remembered, from far off, what she had been saying, and was curious. Betray Athénaïs? What did she want? Why had she come?

"Madame—" Françoise began, but the other, with a tiny gesture, interrupted her.

"Let me speak; I'll be gone soon, leaving you to your prayers and your devotions. I said I shocked you, that first day; do you remember?"

Her smile, teasing, charming, melted the heart. She began to move about the cell, talking the while, examining everything.

"How tidy you keep your things! I can't do so . . . Montespan, my husband, used to be in despair of me. He's one of your tidy men, methodical as an old maid . . . it's unnatural, I think, in a man. He writes to me to come now to his place in the Pyrenees. 'Consider, my dear Athénaïs' —all his letters begin so, as if they were essays, and I a pupil who must read them for their style. 'Consider the incomparable mountains and blossoming groves, over which you would reign like a presiding deity, were you here'—but when I begged him at the beginning to take me away from Court, he would not hear of it, saying I only imagined the King's attentions to me, saying—" She bit her lip, stopped, flushed, drew back, began again. "What have I said now? But you know of it . . . though everyone does not know. We've been discreet . . . but, Madame, Madame, unless you will aid me, both of us, now I am lost! How can I conceal it? I won't return to Montespan, it would kill me, and yet . . . and yet *he'd* kill me, too, if he knew. I dread what may befall if—if the thing becomes known, because by law the wife is still the property of the husband, and all that she owns is his."

"Let me be clear as to this, Madame," said Françoise evenly.

The other stared at her. *"Clear?* But haven't I just been saying—"

"You have said a great deal, while still saying nothing. I am discreet, as you say. If I can help you I will do so, provided always I do not go against my conscience. Let me know in a few words what it is that troubles you, and in what way I can aid you." She spoke coolly, desirous as she was of establishing order in the other's mind and her own. Athénaïs went on staring for a minute. Then she broke into harsh laughter.

"Hear me, then, and I'll risk my name against your conscience, Madame. I am with child by the King."

Now that it had been said, defiance took her; she began to talk rapidly, often in a low voice, so that Françoise scarcely heard; justifying herself, it seemed, to her own mind as much as the listener's; glossing over the truth, evading, lying.

"It began on the Holland campaign." The tale took on the aspect of a recitation. A door in Françoise' mind opened and against the darkness a woman stood, the light from within catching her golden hair. A short step from there to the King's bed, a first unfaithfulness, the prelude to many. Louis the god, bored with an easy campaign, an easy mistress, a Spanish dwarf for wife. Louis the conqueror, who must have food for conquest . . . and this determined woman. The voice talked on, plaintive in self-deceit; the King had followed her, the King had seduced her. Françoise prayed for charity; I know, she thought, hearing, that it is not true; that it was you, yourself, who tempted the King.

Athénaïs turned suddenly and on her face was a wild fear that made it unrecognizable. "What am I to do?" she almost screamed.

Suddenly, in a flurry of silken perfumed movement, she came to where Françoise was and knelt. "Only you can help me," she said. "Only you—discreet, wise, experienced, without ties, not a nun, not a courtier. Say that you will not refuse me—promise, promise!"

"I?" said Françoise. Bewilderment was with her. She stared down at the bowed fair head. That Athénaïs was acting a part came as no surprise to her; that she was being used brought little grief. One expected nothing, in this world, and by so refraining, gained much.

"Find me a house in Paris. A little, discreet house, to hide the child. I daren't come—yet. But you can watch over him. You can tell me, without suspicion, how he does, if he's well and—oh, many things! You'll be paid handsomely . . . oh, I know you've little means. Do not be proud . . . or unwilling, Madame—I'll be so much obliged to you. Later, there is nothing I will not do to repay—to atone—"

"*I* undertake your child?"

The room spun round her. She was conscious of a medley of things. The fair face upturned at the level of her knees seemed suddenly grotesque. "Rise, Madame," she said stiffly. "I cannot do what you suggest."

"Not for me—not for me—ah, then I am lost indeed!"

The lovely eyes were bright with tears. Françoise stared at her. "Does the King know?" she said at last. It came to her mind haphazardly, among the other things.

A flood of sobbing was her answer. "What can he do, when he knows? Even he can't undo my marriage. The child's my husband's, by law; nothing alters that. Ah, if you'd only help! It would mean so little to you, so much to me. I can contrive the birth. La Vallière did so with her three and, though she is such a fool that everyone knew and laughed because of it, she showed herself in public immediately after and they could say nothing at all, her cheeks were all covered with rouge and the child was hidden, by that time, in Colbert's house in Paris. If she can do it, so can I. It's necessary to be discreet. . . ."

She laughed suddenly; the sound was harsh after her sobbing. "*You* didn't guess, did you? No one has, I've laced myself so tightly. They needn't know." She had risen to her feet and now moved closer to Françoise and began to speak softly, urgently. The tears on her face had dried by magic; she was beautiful, persuasive, calm. "You come to me wherever I am, when I send word. The King will give me money, which I'll send."

She held out her hands to the woman before her. In the small cell they were as light and dark; Athénaïs' cloak, in the pastel she affected, drawing the light together with her hair, so that the other seemed part of the shadows and the silence.

"I will take this appointment only from the King."

Athénaïs drew back sharply; the consternation on her face left it blank. An instant later a flicker grew; an ugly look passed in her eyes, and then was gone.

"So, Madame?" she said sweetly. "You do not take my word?"

"I do not doubt your word. Such fabrication would be folly."

"Then—then—"

Françoise moved slightly. "I will take this child, not irregularly, but at the direct request of His Majesty. If that cannot be obtained, then it is not consonant with my position, Madame, to accede to your request."

"How correct you are!" said Athénaïs.

She regarded the widow Scarron with carefully blank eyes. Within herself she felt an uprush of laughter. What a rendering she would make of this scene to the King!

But now, for this widow who would rise in the world, she allowed her manner to become gravely calculating. "That would be a question of a Court appointment," she said. "Unofficial, that goes without saying." She bit her finger reflectively. "I will see what can be done."

She knew very well that there would be no difficulty with the King.

After the King's mistress had gone, Françoise stood for long at the small window, looking out, as Athénaïs had done, into the street. Long before, after the death of Paul, she had stood so at another high window, watching the barren trees. Her life then had finished, as she thought, with all that youth and love and emotion might bring. Henceforth she would be a shadow, a servant; living only to serve God through His creatures, feeling no more, as feeling hurt so much. But now the forces of day and dark were circling once more to encompass her, the web of living to spin her about, so that whichever way she turned she would feel its toils. For the first time in many years she thought again of Villarceaux. Why should his face come so strongly to mind tonight? If he came now, what would he think of her? How would she receive him?

"There need be no more fear," she thought, looking in the glass. Her youth had gone, and beauty, as Mignard had seen it; as Paul had done. She was thirty-three and looked older; her face was fuller, her figure heavier, and there were lines of endurance about the mouth and eyes. But these last still had, as Paul had pictured it, the bright-dark glance of a bird.

"I have no gray in my hair yet," she thought. What had made her say that? She looked down at the shining coins Athénaïs had left in her hand. They reminded her of the golden smoothness of the Marquise's hair. Ninon, too, had had hair of spun gold. How much beloved the bodies of such women had been, and her own never! She was neither flesh, fowl nor good red herring; neither maid, wife, nun nor mother.

"A bystander," she told herself. What had she ever had to do with children? Curiously she recognized in herself a passionate jealousy of Athénaïs de Rochechouart for being, even most sinfully, with child.

It is never easy to picture oneself as repellent.

She knew, even at that first meeting of theirs, that the King disliked her. She had not been prepared for it, and was surprised at the depth of her own hurt. Why should the King have feeling, of any sort, regarding her? She was a subject, prepared to serve him. It was, she knew herself, even something of a favor she might be rendering him.

Therein, perhaps, lay the stigma; Louis preferred to dispense his favors. It was a part of the nature of the man.

"I need not be beholden," she thought. She had found a little house on the Marais, as she had promised. It had not been a task of undue difficulty, in that quarter which she had known blindfold in the days when she was married to Paul. She had also found a woman.

"She is reliable, and will act as wet-nurse. Her own child will be born a month earlier."

Everything was according to schedule, planned and neatly disposed of. She had prided herself, a very little, on the clockwork of her arrangements. The King, she had heard, was a man who liked order. He was never late for an appointment by the fraction of a second.

Certainly he had hers arranged on time. She had been driven in a plain coach along the long flat approach to Versailles. This was the new palace, they said, on which the King was spending millions, adapting it from a hunting-box of which his father had been fond. They said it had cost a fortune alone to have the marshes drained and that four hundred workmen had died of swamp-fever; a short-sighted place for a palace. She remembered passing the site once on a jaunt with Ninon in Saint-Aignan's carriage; then the building had been scarcely begun. Now it seemed that the world was yellow, again, like that first day of all in Paul's chamber. How the color pursued her! Slabs of yellow stone lay waiting, in company with mortars and cranes. The dust about the paths and beds was thick. A stone faun leered at her from among the trees. In the distance was a great sheet of water.

She was met, discreetly, in an alleyway and taken up little dark flights of stairs to nowhere. She could hear the echoes of their footsteps sounding through the empty rooms. The courtier who accompanied her, a little man with a long nose and impertinent manner, whose name was Lauzun, chattered knowledgeably, gesturing with his hands. She guessed that he regarded her as provincial and undesirable, even odd, in her dark clothes.

"His Majesty detests black." This he said sourly, casting a glance over her while hurrying on. "These rooms are in process of being made very magnificent. Downstairs are the reception-rooms, whose ceilings will be ornamented in time with renderings of His Majesty as the Sun King driving his chariot through clouds. Then the tapestries, as you will have heard, are from Gobelins. They will show His Majesty in process of his various victories, garbed in the manner of the siege of Troy. You are looking at the emblems? That of course is His Majesty's chosen insignia, that of the Sun. If Madame will step this way—"

Down, by a narrow stairway, to a curtained apartment whose windows drew the light. Inside was a group of men, talking. One sat at a desk, and she recognized the King. The blue, slant-set eyes met her gaze coolly.

"Madame Scarron."

The tone held no query. Françoise made her obeisance, feeling a little warmth at her heart. Here was a man who was no fool and who would transact the business in hand with dispatch and reliability. For the first time she felt relief from her doubts at having undertaken the task.

The King began to speak. Oddly, she had the impression that she was not being talked to, but at. Impossible, her mind told her, for so greatly occupied a monarch to conduct business in any other way! And yet she was conscious of disappointment. Had not his affability, accessibility even, been talked about, to the admiration of Mesdames d'Albret and de Richelieu and d'Heudicourt? "He makes everyone feel," they had told her, "as if he talked to them alone."

But there was none of that for her, and she began to have the feeling that he despised her faintly. Also she felt the gaze, which never wavered, of that other who stood behind the King, a big gross man, with a heavy face somewhat resembling an ox in its determined blankness of expression. He also, she told herself afterward, disliked her. Dislike? Why need such a thing enter into it at all?

"Louvois," said the King to this man. "Louvois."

So that was who he was, thought Françoise. Briefly she replied to the King's questioning. Yes, she had understood the position. Yes, she had found a house—she saw Louis nod briefly at that, as if it had not displeased him. Other inquiries followed; she was not unaware that, by this apparently guileless means, her every origin was being checked, gone over, established and noted down.

"You were the wife of Scarron. For how long?"

"Eight years, sire."

Louis nodded. "So. You would, no doubt, have contact with the *monde* through that connection."

His tone was cold. She felt herself flushing, and held his gaze. "It is true that my late husband's connections were wide—sire. His talents brought him many friends."

"Among them those whom, in his humble capacity, he could hardly have hoped to attract otherwise. We have not forgotten the pamphleteering of the late wars—Madame."

Françoise would have answered, but he cut her short with a gesture, "*Soit.* We will leave that. What was your name before marriage?"

He knows very well, she thought. Aloud, she answered. "D'Aubigné."

A pause. "That is a Huguenot family, is it not? But you are not Huguenot."

"I was converted, sire."

"From conviction, or for convenience?"

Heavens, how the man disliked her! "Conviction, sire."

Louvois bent toward the King and whispered something. The King nodded, replied in a low voice and surveyed her, again, an instant, before resuming.

"See then that there is orthodoxy in this charge of yours, Madame."

She curtsied. The cold speech continued. He never took his eyes from her.

"I understand from—a certain person—that you expressed a desire to obtain this charge directly from myself. That, Madame, was correct."

Correct, but he had been worsted, she thought; almost embarrassed by that correctness. How much more convenient it would have been for him had she accepted the charge, without official recognition given, from the mistress and not from the King! It was the first time, doubtless, that he had been overcome by legality in this particular connection . . . the *Roi Soleil*.

"For me," she thought, "the King of Ice would be a more suitable appellation." She began to feel the strain of standing there, motionless, beneath the lens. Thus, one imagined, a speck of living dust might feel, at one end of that new invention of the Dutchman, Mynheer Leeuwenhoeck; a speck magnified, so they said, to the size of a walnut, so that one could watch the workings within. How like the speck she felt!

As if he had read her mind, Louis smiled slightly. "It will not be necessary to detain you longer, Madame. Nor will it be necessary for you to come here again. I am given to understand that you have discretion, which will repay you; if indeed you should ever feel, as time passes, that your zeal goes without notice, remember this; although I am not seen, I see all things. Devotion does not go without reward."

He nodded briefly and she knew that the interview was over. Curtsying, backing, finding herself at last outside the room, she felt the repressed emotions of the last quarter-hour return in a flood and almost submerge her. "I see all things!" Who was he, that he should so emulate God, and meanwhile tell her—ah, she knew very well what his words implied! "You may have thought to attract notice, Madame, by your insistence, but you will be very far wrong. Yes, you can do your duty, with that thoroughness of yours, in little secret houses on the Marais or elsewhere. You will be watched there, but invisibly; you will keep your distance from the Court. All this for embarrassing me, Madame, to the extent that I must own to a state I am not yet prepared to admit. There are limitations even to the power of the Sun!"

Lauzun was at her elbow, preparing to lead her from the Palace. She had no desire, she thought, ever to see its tasteless aridity again. Let the King and Athénaïs build a great hall of mirrors so that whenever they passed up or down it they could see, like Narcissus, their own reflected beauty, and bask in its splendor and the adoration of the *monde!*

She'd not see it; had no wish to. She had her own life, her own circle, her books and—well, if an extra little house on the Marais were added, why need it make such difference as to upset her so? She could hear them now, in that room that she had left, the King with the chilly blue gaze and the stolid Minister of War, discussing her, and before dismissing an unwelcome subject the final valediction of King Louis.

"I detest black!"

But, at any rate, she would do her duty.

When the summons came it was a wild night with the storm beating hard against the windows. She woke at once to the hammering of hands on the door. Dressing, she thought of the little house on the Marais that she had found, waiting ready; its rooms partly furnished, all except that single, small, above-stairs chamber warmed with lit fires to keep the damp from the walls. There, everything was ready; the curtains drawn, the crib of dark pearwood that she had found in a little shop by the Seine lying waiting, filled with soft baby-clothes. Until now it had all seemed a dream that it should ever be filled; the placing of the chair, the dressing of the crib, had had a sense of unreality.

Downstairs a coach waited. She climbed inside and lay back while it drove off, hearing the clip-clop of the horses' hooves above the noise of the storm. The dark box of a coach jolted abominably and was full of drafts. She drew her hood about her.

They drove at speed. Looking out, clouds tore away from a watery moon. The streets of Paris swung past. She had the feeling that she had done it before, this driving through the night; that it was a part of her life, to be experienced again and again. She had that foreknowledge even then.

How often the pattern would repeat itself! After what seemed many hours, the coach lurched at last to a standstill, and she was helped to alight. The pale bulk of a great house confronted her; high trees compassed it, bowing and sighing in the dark. At one window there was a light and, seen above, a figure holding it; a woman.

"Madame must hurry." It was the voice of the escort. "It will not, they say, be long."

Stairs, darkness again; a great room, full of shadows. There lay in the great bed someone whom she knew to be Athénaïs. The shadows hid her face. A woman came forward and Françoise saw her to be the one who had stood at the window; she was small, with narrow eyes.

"Madame has not come too soon," said the girl, whose name was Desoeillets. "She will deliver before morning."

Françoise made no reply. A grunting, half-rhythmical sound came from the bed. She stood back and watched the busied figures of midwives and nurses. A man's figure was in the room and she observed him narrowly. It did not seem right that he should be here. He was muffled in a cloak still, but the long ugly sharpness of his nose showed between his upturned collar and the heavy perruque. Lauzun, whose duty it would be to take word to the King.

The sounds continued. Athénaïs, the fruitful one, would not delay her labors. Presently she began to scream and with a sharp gesture the midwife beckoned Françoise forward and instructed her to hold the sheet over Madame's mouth. Françoise exclaimed and Lauzun smiled faintly. "It is her own wish that that should be done," he murmured. "It is not desirable that there should be any publicity."

Not to be desired, then, the open light of day. When this was over Athénaïs de Rochechouart would rise from her bed and go and sin again and bear children in adultery yearly. Even now the germ of power, her beauty, was visible; seen in the pregnant ivory flesh, the pillared throat, the gripping hands. She would have no more trouble than an animal. Like an animal, she opened her mouth and screamed.

"In God's name stifle that!" said Lauzun. He strode forward. Françoise bent over and stuffed the woman's mouth with the edge of the sheet. Athénaïs strained to deliver and Françoise could see, perforce from where she stood, the miracle of the birth take place. At the end she stood back and felt, out of the welter of shapes that had begun to blur before her eyes, the cessation of pains as though they had ceased in her own body. Out of them triumph grew; the child had cried.

She eased her hands, finding them stiff with the pressure and the fact that Madame had seized, at the end, her wrists, pulling on them as though they would break. But only now was her part to begin and they thrust the baby, swaddled and wrapped in shawls for concealment, under her cloak. She was hurried downstairs and away from that room, out into the night again to where the coach waited, into it and off, with an order given, away from the house and the sighing tall trees and back, on jolting wheels, to Paris.

She lay back, as exhausted as if she had indeed given birth. The child had not cried again and she knew, with the strangeness of its tiny warmth against her, a fear lest it might have been smothered in the press of shawls. She parted them fearfully. A small red hand, like a minute sea-anemone, curled there; the face was closed and plum-like. The child yawned suddenly; the glistening helplessness of the palate and gums intrigued her.

They drove on, while the sky lightened. She was beset by fears that they would be seen. How warm the child was! She held it to her; it curved against her breast naturally, contentedly; it slept.

IV

THE Chevalier de Méré was perplexed.

He was on old man now and, having at last admitted the fact with reluctance, his chief delight lay in gossip of men and things. It was a subterfuge, he admitted with a shrug that was still elegant; a sop to dissolution, a candle against fate. But he himself, although his physical powers had failed, could give delight, he was assured, by *bons mots;*

a turn of phrase that slipped over the tongue like cream, a witticism of style both pungent and correct.

But very few would listen.

"The time is past for the elegancies," the Chevalier would say sadly, as some young buck in side-curls and the King's gold braid stared meaninglessly in answer to the best of his remarks. No one was interested; the talk was all of wars, and the days when one would fight a duel over a split hair or a pearl from a lady's ear were done. Everyone had other things to do, there was real fighting with gunpowder instead of swords, for countries instead of countesses, with no high feelings, real or pretended, on either side. Presently they would all march off to war again and leave him alone, an old man in a tavern drinking wine.

"And even the wine is not as it used to be." Nothing was the same. Once in Poitou he had taught a little girl the classics, she had been pretty and intelligent and he could have made something of her, but now she moved, it was said, close to Court circles and would have nothing to do with him.

What *did* she do in the house on the Vaugirard?

Who had told him of it? Madame de Sévigné. Madame, when not occupied with writing interminable letters to her daughter Madame de Grignan in Provence, would favor him, sometimes, with gossip. Madame sat almost every evening with Françoise Scarron in this house that Françoise had acquired. Her conversation, one was assured, was the most delightful in Paris. "But who taught her to turn a phrase?" thought the Chevalier dolefully. "I."

He had loved her once, he recalled, when she was married to Scarron. She had been so beautiful it was not even necessary to talk. Now she had lost her beauty, become a nun. Or almost; what difference did it make whether or not one took vows? She had never been in lately when one called. Now she was domiciled, with a mystery become the greater for the increased size of the house, on the Vaugirard, and no one ever saw her. At least, Madame de Sévigné did so; and Madame de La Fayette, who was always ailing. And Rochefoucauld. And Madame de Coulanges. And the Abbé

Testu. They made, one was told, a cozy little circle in the evenings, drinking tea.

He had written to Madame Françoise, hearing that; he had written twice. The style had been impeccable, his praise of her almost fulsome. He had received two little prompt cold notes in reply. They promised nothing.

"She forgets those who were good to her once," pouted the Chevalier. His old eyes gazed disheartened into his wine and he pictured the world in it. What was Françoise doing that was so secret? Madame de Sévigné had told him that she seemed to be looking after a child, the daughter of her friend Madame d'Heudicourt, and educating it. All that great house for one child! But once the Chevalier, passing near by, had seen a gilded coach, without arms, at the door; and a masked lady slipping into it who was too tall for Madame d'Heudicourt and who was not Madame Scarron, for she wore the gold braidings of Court on her silk gown.

Ah, there was a mystery! How tantalizing not to be permitted knowledge of it, so that one could drop a hint—no more, mind you, but only a discreet hint—here and there about the town. How elevated one's prestige would be!

Françoise was hanging curtains.

Standing on the step-ladders with her mouth full of hooks she waited for Nanon and surveyed herself. The time was past when she had found any limit for the things she must do. Amusement was with her, lightly and warm as it often came in these days. She could hang curtains and rig up beds and market for food and cook it. It was impossible to let workmen or servants into the children's rooms in case they talked of what they had seen.

"No one knows." She felt triumph, standing there on the steps. In the early days concealment had been agony. She had even had herself bled, once, to avoid flushing when Athénaïs or the King were mentioned at the Hôtel d'Albret. That had been before the intrigue was suspected.

"One little house was enough." But when it had become a matter of one, two, three little houses, each in a different *quartier,* she had rebelled. She could not, she said, undertake concealment of indiscretions so scattered and so numerous. Her friends already suspected a mystery; she had been seen, hooded and cloaked, driving from place to place. So there had been obtained for her this Vaugirard house, and she had left her own on the Rue des Tournelles and come here, the children with her.

She thought of them. They would be playing below in the garden, whisking in and out of the shadows of the great trees. Mademoiselle de Nantes would be leader and Vexin, who had been sick again yesterday, would have to be restrained from following her. Maine would not run at all because of his thigh. She had done everything in her power to heal up the fistula that had broken out there, but it had issued for a year now and she greatly feared the leg would shorten and he be lame. The little d'Heudicourt girl would play with him.

Anxiety took her. She must run, only for a moment, down to the garden to see that all was well. It was not possible to see from this window, and one of them might have strayed beyond the gate. . . .

"Nanon." The woman entered with the seamed stuff she had been altering and held it, bundled in her arms, up toward Françoise. "Take these—" her voice came muffled, through the hooks that she still retained. "I must go down."

"It is unnecessary, Madame, I have just been, and they are all busied like the angels," said Nanon equably. She was used to her mistress's unremitting sense of duty. Why should Madame trouble herself so, getting up during the night, creeping in to observe these infants who invariably slumbered peacefully? Then their food! Every scrap must be supervised, personally chosen and cooked by Madame herself, and served on the nail. The children's digestions would suffer, Madame said, if it were not so. To disturb oneself so for children! What matter if they were royal? There was a good deal of insolence to put up with on that account, notably from M. de Louvois, who came here monthly with his face of an ox and went over the expenditure of the *ménage.* "And he has never, for all his sour ways," Nanon thought indignantly, "found us a sou out!"

She gazed upward at Madame with fierce adoration. God only knew what she endured, Madame Françoise, and all for the sake of no reward in particular, that one could see. Certain it was that the children were good children, as far as that went; although young Mademoiselle was pert at times and Vexin was ailing continually. And now there was to be another, God knew, and they would have the house filled again with infant squalls that must be concealed, so that it was necessary to shut all the windows. Nanon had had her fill of the days when there was a little house for each. . . .

"There, then," said Françoise. She had turned and was fixing hooks. "It will be easier, now, to light the rooms up at night. I did not dare to use more than two candles before."

"*I'd* not ruin my eyesight," Nanon snorted. She helped her mistress down from the wooden steps. "That Louvois ought to have seen to the furnishings long ago. They've enough to spare for their own pleasures."

The dark eyes turned on her showed no signs of strain. "I'd not ask more from 'that Louvois,' " said Françoise. "We manage very well."

"Oh, well enough for middle-class brats, I grant you that. Wouldn't have done for your aunt, whose soul God rest, or yourself even, at Murcy. There was God's free country there, and the fields to run about in. The King has plenty of space at Versailles and Saint-Germain. If he's ashamed of his bastards he shouldn't father them. That's what *I* say."

"Nanon, Nanon, you are never to mention names here!"

In spite of herself, Françoise remembered Murcy. How different everything would be there now! The old people were dead, and Philippe was married, as she had heard only last month. How she longed to see it all again!

"Nanon, when—if ever—we can get away for a little while, I'd like to go back there, to Murcy; only to see if anything has changed."

"Places change less than folks," said Nanon. She stared at

her mistress, hands on her apron. *"You've* changed more than Murcy, I daresay."

"Ah—"

"Who has changed?" said a voice. "I grew tired of waiting for you, Madame, to finish the curtains, and so I came up to see."

A little boy stood at the door. He wore a suit of light blue satin with a collar of lace. He was slightly built, with curling pale-brown hair, and he leaned lightly on a small cane. His face expressed at once mischief and anticipation. Françoise went to him and took his hand in hers.

"So you have left the young ladies, *mignon.* That was not very polite of you."

"I do not care for girls, on the whole," said the Duc du Maine. He glanced up at her. "And as for ladies—" he smiled; the dimples at the corners of his small mouth quivered. *"You* are the only lady I have time for, Madame!" he announced. "When are you going to come and read to me?"

Nanon watched them, seeing the transformation in her mistress that always followed this, the beloved's, approach. They remained, for an instant, smiling at one another, the King's son, radiant with the kind of light that often shines about delicate children, and the maturely grave, dark woman who had once been beautiful.

"But now Madame is still so." Nanon, in her ponderings, spoke aloud. The fine eyes of Madame would contain their fire, she thought, when she was old; they were filled now with dancing lights and shadows. Her skin was still very fine. There was a quality—what was it? "It is not beauty she has, like the Montespan's," thought Nanon, who never minced her words when talking to herself. "I said that she had changed, which is true; how many of us have not? But now she is like a field of corn when it is ripe, or like a wine of full flavor. Without corn one cannot make bread. Who says that I am not also a philosopher?"

In any case they had not heard her. "They are very elegant curtains," said Maine.

V

In 1673 the King sent for Françoise and informed her that he would have the children legitimized by *Parlement*. She expressed neither surprise nor pleasure, although she felt both. She folded her gloved hands and waited. Whatever change this would bring to her own fortunes, one must ask nothing, only wait. It was always so with this King.

"They will be princes of the blood," said Louis. His hand, well-kept and tanned, a little, along the backs of the fingers, played with a pen. He did not look at the woman who stood before him. He disliked Athénaïs' *bel esprit*, he had told her. But it could not be denied that she was useful.

He looked up suddenly. How could this woman make an appearance at Court? She was like a crow in her black serge. He, Louis, liked bright colors; gaiety and witty, worldly men and women. It was so easy for oneself to become *ennuyé* without reason, with the melancholy like a miasma that crept up when one was without diversion or company. *He* wasn't one who could find satisfaction within himself, like certain others. Perhaps if he had had more education . . .

He gave his cold smile suddenly. "My children shall not lack for instruction," he told her. "In yourself they have had an admirable preceptress. Will you continue with the task at Court, Madame? You have been allotted rooms next to those of Madame la Marquise de Montespan. There, you will find it easy to obtain access to the children. Officially, *voyez-vous*, they are mine only, princes of the blood by an unknown mother. . . ."

He talked on, easy, cold, assured. No one had dared gainsay him since the day long ago, when, clad in hunting-dress, he had worsted the *Parlement*. He took it for granted now that it would accede to his request. To the drab woman before him he scarcely gave a thought. For her to express any wish regarding her piece of good fortune would be undesirable; to deny it altogether, incredible.

Therefore when he heard her do so Louis was incredulous.

He stared at the widow Scarron. She held his gaze and stared back. It came to him, as an item to be pigeon-holed somewhere in his mind, that she had fine eyes. They regarded him now steadily without change in their expression, dark and blank, opaque almost; unreadable.

"I have no wish to come."

"Madame?" The King's delicate eyebrows raised themselves. He waited, silent; he had stopped playing with the pen.

Françoise waited, also; she endured the silence. Finally he was forced to speak again. "Your reasons?" Dear God, *he'd* be glad enough to dispense with Madame's services! But there was no doubt she was learned, and Athénaïs—

At the back of his mind the thing festered. Versailles! She'd rejected Versailles!

"Well, Madame?" His voice was short. This hermit—this nun! *She*, saved from the gutter—he'd heard—and his palace still building, which was to be the miracle of all palaces, symmetrical as Athens, brilliant as the sun! Saint-Germain wouldn't hold them long now—there was going to be another —no, Versailles was the setting for Athénaïs, for himself. He'd have the children . . . little Maine, witty and coaxing; young Louise, with her robin-brown eyes. The other boy had died; a pity—not for lack of care, the governess had *that* attribute, she was careful, meticulous. . . .

No, it was necessary that he have Madame Scarron at Versailles.

Madame appeared to ponder. "I must ask the opinion of my confessor. It may be that he advises me against it. If that is so, I will not come."

Louis concealed his amusement. "Your confessor fears perhaps that you will catch the contagion?"

She made no attempt to fence with him. "I have no force

204

but prayer against the devil. If I am tempted daily, I may yield."

The King heard her curiously, studying the sincerity with which she spoke. "You take, then, every detail of your life to your confessor? You find he answers you?"

"I find he hears me." The answer came swiftly, with the ghost of a smile.

There was a pause. "I have no quarrel with your conscience, Madame," said the King at last, coldly. "If you are undecided, take your doubt on this matter to the Abbé Gobelin. Reflect that, if you come to Versailles, you will do me a service. I told you once; my faithful servants I do not forget."

Françoise made her obeisances and went out, reflecting that it was typical of the man to have possessed himself of the knowledge that her confessor was the Abbé Gobelin.

The Abbé was hesitant.

That precious thing, Madame's soul, he had in his keeping. He had cleansed it from the pride of too much wit and had abated in it the vanity of appearance. Now a fresh dilemma beset him; how would he confess Madame in the sinful palace of Versailles?

"For me to go there would be to condone the sin," he told her pitifully. Nevertheless he thought—or, as he knew in his soul, M. de Condom thought, and had approached him on it—that the royal bastards' benefit from the presence of Madame might outweigh the disadvantages to which her soul would be exposed. She was a pruned vine; they were tender plants. She should go, he told her.

She was quick with the riposte. "If you think I may conscientiously remain there, it will be difficult for you to avoid coming there yourself from time to time. You surely must come to me where I am?"

And so a little trembling priest in spectacles was seen on odd occasions emerging, with lowered eyes and secret lips, from a plain coach in Versailles courtyard; thence to reappear again, an hour or so later, hurrying off the way he had come, avoiding any prolonged view of the yellow buildings which had begun to grow up like flowers toward the sun. He was not noticed; someone said that he was La Scarron's confessor, and everyone giggled and then forgot it. They had laughed already at the sight of Madame Scarron, discreetly introduced as the *gouvernante* of the pretty little brood His Majesty had had over the years previous, by that termagant, Madame de Montespan. *That* secret had been kept close enough! Where had they been hidden, those children of bright eyes and clean limbs, attractive as lovechildren always are? They contrasted so admirably with the Dauphin, who had never been known to utter a word that was not in some way connected with food. It went to prove the dullness of virtue in a way hitherto undreamed of. The Queen, who was very little seen in any case and hardly ever visited, lived, as was more convenient, on the second floor; Madame la Marquise had her apartments on the first. In the adjoining rooms lived the children, and somewhere there was fitted in this crow, this oddity, who had once been married to some poet, or was it a clown? There was no need, at any rate, to stand aside when she went past, in her absurd black clothes; a relief, in a way, for a Court with so many irons, some of them irretrievably, in the fire. It was so difficult to know where one stood. The King, at the recent visit of an ambassador, had greeted him by dancing a ballet with on one side, as was to be expected, Madame de Montespan; and on the other, by way of consolation, Louise de la Vallière. But it was said that *she* desired to enter a convent.

VI

CHARLES D'AUBIGNÉ had not found it necessary to trouble his sister during the period of her obscure widowhood and lodging in the Charité. Now, however, he felt it incumbent on himself to offer his services to one who, so newly at Court, would be unaware of its many pitfalls.

But when he saw his sister he was shocked, and said so. "Michael and all the angels, Bignette, you can't be seen at Court in that garb!" he told her. He stared in horror; what had come over the woman? She was only forty, was it; forty-one? No need to rig oneself so, as though for the grave, or the cloister; he wasn't sure which. Bignette had always had the makings of a damned chaste nun, and now to look at her one would think she had become one. Even the gold bands on her skirt were narrow, as if in apology that they should be there at all. And her hair was all hidden. Bignette! Bignette! What would happen now if she crossed paths with Villarceaux?

Françoise listened to him; she looked strained and tired. "Charles, *mon ami*, you should not have come," she murmured. "Go, my dear; I can do nothing for you."

Charles spoke of Murcy. He had the charm that had been their father's when he wished to please and she saw, listening to him, the towers of Murcy clear in her mind. Dear Murcy, with the old cobbles and the moss like spilled sun on the roofs; with the dear faces, the quiet voices, the happiness of lost years.

"If I could have one hour of it," she thought. Beyond the window of her chamber here she saw the arid courtyard. Men and women, top-heavy from this view, strolled in perruques and hoops in the sweltering sunlight. Everywhere was the yellow dust. The flowers rose stiffly. Far in the distance pleasure-boats sailed idly on the lake. The King and Madame were going tonight to a water-party; there would be fireworks. Then they would all return and some would dice in Madame's rooms till all hours, so that the children would have their sleep disturbed, and she was tired.

To go away. . . .

Ever since the Abbé and M. de Condom had outlined her task in coming to Versailles she had felt, after the first glow, a terrible weariness. To save the King's soul! How could she, a woman, without a woman's weapons, without youth, beauty, riches, do so? By prayer, they had said to her. God knew she had prayed, with every other devout soul in France. But then interrupting her communion with God would come laughter and voices; the rattle of dice, the ring of gold coins changing hands; oaths, *risqué* tales whispered behind curtains, lewd actions, indecent sights. Often the King would come to Madame in the afternoon while Françoise knelt praying, and she would hear their murmured voices through the wall.

"Be strong," the Abbé had said. But she was weak, and even he and his spiritual superior, the Bishop of Condom, could not sustain her weakness. The very children were now less hers than formerly. Maine had his own tutors and she saw him, if at all, briefly; enough to know that he was not happy, homesick for the house on the Vaugirard, dazzled, then weary at the splendor and at being kept up half the night. Mademoiselle de Nantes and the baby, Mademoiselle de Blois, were ailing on rich irregular food. Ah, if she could but have *carte blanche* with them as it had been before! But how could that be, with their mother next door, alternately cosseting and raging?

Small grudges filled her mind. Last Tuesday Madame had taken the baby for a drive and had forgotten to have her fed till past midnight. The child had cried and Madame had slapped her for crying. Mademoiselle de Nantes was being taught to be impertinent. Nothing Françoise herself said was heeded. If only the King disliked her less!

"I do not like your *'bel esprit'!*" Somehow, in the way in which such things travel round, word of that had come to her. She was again surprised at the little stab of hurt that accompanied it. A *bel esprit*, an oddity, whom Madame la Marquise would make ridiculous! She had heard too much of Athénaïs' apt, cruel mimicking of courtiers to flatter herself that in absence she herself would be exempt.

And then sometimes Madame la Marquise would fling her arms about her and call her a good creature, and such was her charm that it was impossible not to feel for her as though she had been one of the children, and forgive her all. . . .

"Give it a year," M. de Condom said. He had the same advice for La Vallière when she wished to enter her convent. In her case, he feared weakness; in the case of Madame Scarron hoped for strength. He, Bossuet, had tried all means to save the king. Last Easter he had thundered at Louis from the pulpit; this year he would do so again. To Madame la Marquise he had preached also. She would reply with facile tears, profess herself repentant, go to Clagny for a spell and then relapse again. There was no peril like the peril of the flesh. The Bishop prayed for them.

But now this discreet woman, this pruned vine, had come. She was a willing instrument; she was a child of God. To have such a one in the Palace was of more value than a flock of priests placed there. The known dislike of the King? "Prayer, prayer!" said M. de Condom. "That will overcome it!"

He felt his own tremendous spiritual energy outflow in prayer. He felt it as he felt his power in pulpits; fertile, resounding, forthright, unafraid. The widow Scarron was an instrument for power, unyielding, stubborn for the right, meticulous, honest. Bossuet could not understand her tiredness, that wilted the vine in its season of bearing fruit. He waved away as temporal the desire in her mind for retreat.

"A place of one's own!" It became a crying need with her. To escape, once and forever, from this arid world; to breathe clean air again, feel her own mind fresh, her will unfettered in the pursuit of doing good. Ah, she would do so much if only she had the power! There were girls like herself, poor but of good family, for that reason not enabled to beg, permitted alone to starve by the laws of gentility. These she would like to help, teach them useful things, needlework, cookery, to spin . . . leave them, perhaps, with a little dowry, so that they might marry or enter a convent if they wished. There had been one she had helped so in Paris, another at Clichy, others elsewhere . . . of course, it was difficult when she had only a little money of her own, and nowhere to place them. Lately she had been talking to Sœur Basile to ask if it would be possible to rent a little house, somewhere in the suburbs, perhaps Noisy . . . and place six or seven, say, under direction there. She had saved a little money since Paris.

But her own place, for herself, must be particularly chosen. She laughed. Who was she, to choose? They made a game of it, she and Maine. Driving out with her, he would point to some great château. "That one, Madame?" "No," she would say, "that is not good enough for the place I will have instead of you." "Very right," said Maine gravely. "It has a great many ugly corners, and no moat; it is a new château, like the one La Grande Mademoiselle is building at Choisy. But she had so much money she doesn't know what to do."

And they would drive by. In any case the châteaux would all cost far too much. The one Françoise saw at last was quite out of the question. But she loved it; it reminded her of Murcy. It had great woods and little towers; it had a broad deep moat in which the whole of itself was reflected, and avenues and ponds, and a bridge. Seeing, she permitted herself an instant's idle dream. How perfect to come here, between Versailles and Chartres, off the high road, near the world but not of it! She could have her little chapel; she could have her days to herself. If she wished to see company she would do so, in the evenings when lamps were lit; Maine would come and see her, and little Madame de Sévigné, and dear d'Heudicourt and her little girl, and—and—yes, Charles! But he must not take advantage of her . . . and he would not stay long, for she would live very simply. There would be no need to trouble about appearance. "I would look like a portress," she thought. And then there would be new books, and spinning; writing, a little; keeping the calendar; giving alms. No more trouble, no more disgust and weariness, no more high tasks that she could never fulfill.

And yet it was only a dream. She did not delude herself for an instant. She was a solitary woman, an employee, to uncertain wage, of the King, who disliked her and, although he had spoken twice now of remembering her services, could hardly be expected to reward them to the extent that it would mean to purchase this château, which was called Maintenon. It was therefore much better to put it at once out of her mind.

VII

THE JEWELS given by the King to Madame de Montespan were fabulous. As Françoise became more familiar with Versailles, she began to assimilate its profusion of ornament as one grows used to a rich diet; but the gems were in a class by themselves. They lay in tiered cabinets, after the manner of the King's own. Often, when he would visit Madame's rooms, Françoise would see Louis pick up a jewel, turn it to the light, and stand thus, appreciating its color and flawless purity; the deep-blue sapphires, rubies with glinting flame in their hearts, diamonds clear as water, pearls smooth as milk. They would be set and re-set, destined to do the utmost justice to Madame's white skin. Athénaïs was greedy about jewels.

The crown of Agrippina had come from Rome. It had three hundred—was it?—Françoise never could remember—stones; sapphires, diamonds, emeralds, turquoises. Athénaïs had laughed joyously, holding it high above her head in the gesture of coronation, fitting it among the piled gold of her hair where it sat in barbaric beauty. "The mother of Nero," she said, "had compensations."

A little dark-eyed Italian, the Princess Mary-Beatrice of Modena, passed through France about that time on her way to her marriage with James of York, the brother of the English King. Mary-Beatrice was fifteen, beautiful and very devout. There were fireworks in her honor, feasting, water-parties.

"They say one day she may be Queen of England." Charles II had no legitimate heir, his brother might one day inherit. A sigh went up about the Court of Versailles for pretty Madame Henrietta, Charles' sister, who had been married to the brother of King Louis and who was dead these four years, they said of poison. *She* would have welcomed the Italian child and chased some of the doubt out of her big dark eyes. But now there was only German Charlotte-Elizabeth, who had been married to the widower shortly afterward, and who hated everything and everyone here, spending her time writing interminable scurrilous letters to her aunt, the Duchess of Hanover. Liselotte was ugly, squat and bitter. She wore high boots like a man's and read her Bible. *"She'd* scare the little bride out of her wits by the mere sight of her! We must think of some other diversion."

The King asked for Agrippina's crown to be brought. He wished to display it to the Princess. The crown was brought and Louis received it, running his fingers over the beaten gold. Suddenly he frowned; a slight flush stained his cheekbones. "Madame, these stones are false," he said. The blue eyes looked levelly at Madame de Montespan.

"I was never so mortified!"

Sobbing, recriminations, tears, protests, scenes. Madame had sent the jewels to be re-set, she said. The jeweler was sent for. Athénaïs raged up and down her rooms in fury. "To accuse *me* of being a thief, a common cheat, a swindler! That is what it amounts to—no one knows what I've endured—in public, too!"

Tears filled her eyes, Françoise murmured soothingly. "The King will find out for certain. His Majesty does not err in such ways. The thief will be found."

"Doesn't err?" said Athénaïs angrily. "Then you believe it too?"

Her eyes narrowed. Scarron always sided with the King. Much good might it do her! Louis couldn't endure the woman, laughed when she mimicked her to him in private. Oh—confound Agrippina's crown! Why hadn't she had the stones verified when they were returned?

"Of course I do not believe it. The jeweler will be questioned."

But the jeweler had left for Bombay.

"I'm afraid of the King," said Athénaïs. "*You* see him. Talk to him; make him see reason."

She twisted her hands nervously. "He will be so angry! I don't know what to do—not an heirloom, really, not replaceable either. Something quite unique. Oh, *mon Dieu,* why didn't I leave it to Louis to have the wretched stones cleaned? That is what comes of—"

"But His Majesty gave you the crown."

The governess sat demurely, stitching away at tapestry by the window. Athénaïs darted her a glance. "No, he did not," she said crossly. "I borrowed it. I would have returned it."

"*Soit,*" said Scarron. She threaded a needle. The pale thread drew itself in and out.

"Madame—Madame! See the King for me." The voice was pitiful.

"But it is certain," said Françoise equably, "that the King dislikes me. I have so little chance of success."

"No—no! It's only that I—only that I— Oh, dear God, why must he do everything *to schedule?* That damnable clock goes round, goes round, and if the skies were to fall he would not come here a moment later, or a moment sooner."

"Some would give much for him to come at all."

"I cannot endure it. I shall go to Clagny."

"I will see the King," said Françoise.

When Louis came she could see that he was angry. There was a whiteness about his mouth. Why was it, she thought, that to be made to appear ridiculous should be so much more important than anything? The Princess of Modena's suite will carry word to England that the King of France's mistress has returned him a trinket stuffed with false gems.

"Where is Madame?"

Françoise answered levelly. "She has gone, because she was afraid of Your Majesty."

"Afraid of me?" He made a little, contemptuous gesture with one hand. "Athénaïs was never afraid of anyone in her life. Request her to attend me, if you please."

"Madame la Marquise has requested me to deputize for her on this occasion."

"You?" he said, and his lips twitched. Suddenly he shrugged, and walked to the window.

"*Eh bien,* then, we will converse, Madame, since you refuse, I take it, to carry out my wish. There was a time when you declined to accept the orders of Madame la Marquise as a substitute for my own. That your attitude has changed I can only attribute to the stress of circumstance. Have you found Versailles as rewarding as you expected?"

"I have asked no reward," she said quietly. He swung round, as though she had struck him.

"No, by God, you haven't . . . and a single jewel, I think, would be riches to you. But you do not, I imagine, covet jewels, Madame. What is your ambition?"

She thought of it. A less propitious moment could hardly have been chosen. But it was now or never, as she knew, with Louis. She faced him squarely.

"I have ambition, sire, when I have served Your Majesty, to retire to a little property which I have seen, which pleases me greatly. But at this present time, although I have saved a little, I must confess that the amount exceeds the value of my services. If it could be borne in mind—"

He cut her short, frowning. "Never mind that. What is the name of this property?"

She told him. "Maintenon?" His brows drew together. "For a solitary woman it's extensive enough. Or had you other purposes?"

He referred, she knew, to marriage. Every now and again the question cropped up. The other day they had offered her the aged Duc de Villars, who in his state of decrepitude had volunteered, she heard, to bestow his title on her in exchange for being nursed. She had declined firmly, to the surprise of everyone. "But you would be a *Duchesse!*" they told her.

"I have already had enough trouble in a situation which

is singular, and pried into by everyone about me, without going to look for more in a state that brings misfortune on three-quarters of the human race," she had replied. An urge came to her to say something of the kind to Louis. His brows, which had been drawn together, flew up in surprise. He laughed.

"Your opinions, Madame—" he was beginning. But she had her hobby well under way by now and in this hour, which had been so unexpectedly allotted, she would tell him of it.

She talked rapidly and concisely, her assurance growing as she warmed to her tale. As she talked on her eyes brightened, her cheeks flushed; her hands were expressive and, he noted, beautiful. What was it he had heard about this woman's being the high-light of gatherings years ago at the Hôtels d'Albret and de Richelieu?

"She delighted everyone with her wit." What, then, in God's name, had changed the fascinating *raconteuse* of those days into this pious crow? He could see, now, the other self emerge as she talked, forgetting him in this dream she had of providing for poor girls. Respect for her facts and figures dawned on Louis. She'd obtained flax and wool on her tiny pension, was teaching young women to spin in a house at Noisy.

"If I had Maintenon, I would import weavers from Holland. With the amount that is spun, we could soon make cloth. There is a demand for that, as Your Majesty knows. Enough is obtainable from the grounds and the ponds of Maintenon to support such a community as I have depicted. They could plant, grow corn, launder the linen, fish—"

Louis listened. The novelty of hearing of such things from a woman's lips intrigued him. It was refreshing, also, to have no fear of that recurrence, the coquette. Pleasant to have an hour, in this manner, idled away, instead of the heat and perfumes, the demands and scenes and reconciliations of *l'amour* . . . how much less expensive if he could only do without it!

"To spend all on good works," he thought, "like Madame." A little, nagging ache made itself felt between his eyes; he had been troubled with a migraine lately. At first he had thought of it as an accompaniment, natural enough, to the scenes made by Madame la Marquise. How he loathed recriminations, shrill voices raised! It was easier to give in to her, when she demanded so; easier to yield.

He put a hand in front of his eyes. At once the widow's voice stopped. He heard it again presently, solicitous—servile he'd called it to Athénaïs—concerned, and even.

"Is Your Majesty unwell? It would be better to sit down."

"No—no," he said, confused. "It is the sun." But he sat, as she had suggested, and leaned back and closed his eyes. Waves of pain swept behind them, and passed.

A change in the shadows made him look up. The widow Scarron was moving about the room, quietly, adjusting blinds. The sun no longer glared as before. "There," she said, as though he had been Maine. "There. That is better."

"Madame troubles herself," he said coldly. He would not yield with quite such ease. Presently he began to invent excuses, to himself and to her, for this weakness, the denial of physical perfection in the Sun. He—who had never known a day's illness, except when fever took him in the early wars! Marie had nursed him then, Marie Mancini the Cardinal's niece. He had loved her, wanted to marry her. She had been tall, with dark eyes.

"My mother used too many perfumes," he said aloud, remembering the scented, darkened boudoirs at Saint-Germain and the Louvre and Val-de-Grâce. "It made me so that even as a child I suffered from headache in her presence. Someone today was using perfume. I think it was Madame du Lude."

He sat up, blinking away the last of the headache. "So be it, Madame," he said formally. Suddenly he smiled. "You have very effectively, have you not, forestalled my anger? It is true that I was angry. It is a mercy, however, that the crown was not acquired by the English usurper, Cromwell. He would not even have left us the setting."

With a slight, formal bow he left the *salon*. As he did so he had an impression of the widow Scarron, standing regarding him after having risen from her curtsy. A memory stabbed at him; it was Marie's. She was in Italy now, married to the Colonna. But this woman also had dark eyes. They had met his own steadily.

VIII

THE KING had a spinster cousin, La Grande Mademoiselle. Of all the faces at Court Françoise had found hers familiar, making the mind hark back to those early days when, shortly after her marriage to Paul, she had wakened early and, hearing the sound of horses' hooves, pulled aside the curtain that veiled her window. Below in the street had been a hooknosed young woman, boldly attired in an *ensemble* at once reminiscent of the latest mode and of the wars of Greece and Troy. She was followed by a train of chattering excited rich young men and women, mounted like herself on horseback and adorned, every one, with bunches of straw. Paul, who had missed the spectacle, grimaced when she told him of it.

"That is the modern Jeanne d'Arc, *soi-disant,*" he said, "on her way to help Condé. What a mistake it is for a woman to have too much money! She will only make a fool of herself."

And so Mademoiselle had done, for although in her brief glory she assisted in the siege of Orléans, she had been led away by her enthusiasm and fired on the King, whom many had been certain she was to marry. Cardinal Mazarin, who noted the shot, smiled, and observed, "She has killed her husband."

There was, then, no husband for poor Mademoiselle, who at one time had been at even odds for the position of Queen of France. Growing old was tedious, in Courts as elsewhere; and in the course of this process Mademoiselle fell in love with a ridiculous little man. This was Lauzun, whom Françoise remembered as a sharp nose, an impertinent manner, a muffling cloak and a burden. Why his charms should appeal to women at all was a mystery no one had solved; but they did so, and to the susceptible Mademoiselle in such measure that it was whispered at last that she and Lauzun were married.

No one was sure what happened next. Lauzun, the news leaked out, had been arrested. Mademoiselle was inconsolable. Lauzun had been taken to the furthest borders of the kingdom and confined in Pignerol, an impregnable fortress in the extreme south.

There matters rested. Mademoiselle, however, would not rest. Year followed year, and still she pleaded, with tears, to the King to have Lauzun released. To those who knew Louis years were nothing; how long now since Fouquet, the disgraced Minister of Finance, had languished in that same Pignerol, and would do so till death released him? Moreover, although the King was fond of his cousin, he could not afford, as someone put it, to have little Lauzuns on the throne of France.

So time had passed. Françoise heard of that as an affair long done with. Often about the Court she would see a tall gaunt woman, with aquiline features and over-elaborate dress, the middle-aged ghost of the girl who had ridden by that day; very haughty—she was a daughter of Louis XIII's brother, Gaston d'Orléans—punctilious in the performance of her Court duties (she must, by some means, win again the favor of the King) and very lonely without M. de Lauzun.

Athénaïs introduced the subject one day when she and Françoise were alone in the *salon*.

The Court was at Fontainebleau, where Madame la Marquise could not go. It was in the archdiocese of Sens, whose archbishop had refused her absolution. She frowned, thinking how pleasant it would be to ride again through the cool woods. Someone had said that that old priest was *in extremis*. When he was dead she would go back. Louis should engage that someone less antipathetic filled the see. The struggles of Church and State bored Athénaïs. Why should she not be received when Louis was? And Fontainebleau was pleasant.

"How hot it is!" she said, and yawned. Françoise Scarron said nothing. That odd creature was restful, with her silences; and somehow, in her company, one was not dull. "It is your inner peace," the Marquise had said once. "How I wish I had it!"

A little draft stirred the curtains. Everything in this room was the same, Athénaïs thought, as when she had come here the year the *Reine-Mère* died. The hangings, showing the victories of Louis, were faded a little with the sun. She must have others. The gilded legs on the chairs and tables were curved like the claws of dragons. Scarron was the same also, stitching away at tapestry by the window. She always stitched, or read, or spun. Always there, like the stars. And yet—

"Scarron," said Madame. "You still speak of going away?"

The governess raised her head. "My work here is done."

The Marquise smiled. "I think not. Where would you go to?"

Françoise murmured something of some little place. The King's mistress smiled. Louis had spoken the other day of some château. Maintenon. "She deserves it," he had said, and then announced that he intended giving Madame Scarron a hundred thousand francs. Athénaïs thought of it. She had no great wish to pension off Scarron. She was a good listener, discreet, and she soothed the mind. A good woman. Athénaïs also would be good, if—if only there were fewer things in the way! Some day, she supposed, she would grow old. Till then—

A queer chill took her, seeing her mirrored reflection in the glass. She saw a very beautiful high-bosomed woman in a delphinium-blue gown. Her hair and skin were of dazzling fairness. The gilt edge of the mirror surrounded her like a portrait-frame. In years to come, when she was dead, when they all were, a portrait would hang so, at Versailles.

"Are you cold?" said the widow Scarron.

Athénaïs shrugged, and changed position so that she could no longer see her reflected self. "No," she said, "but a goose walked over my grave." She laughed, a little nervously. How could she expect Scarron to understand? The governess got up now, shifted the blind a little, adjusted the curtains, sat down again.

"There is a draft," she said prosaically, "and you have had an ague lately. They can be treacherous on a hot day. I'll send for wine."

"I shall go and take the waters. I shall go to Bourbon l'Archambault. It always benefits me."

Athénaïs relapsed into silence and began to plan the wardrobe she would take.

Presently Scarron spoke again. "The King says," she ventured, "that the little Duc would do well to go also."

"The King says!" Athénaïs felt amusement rise. Louis had not, she thought, been so outspoken in his dislike of the widow lately. No doubt her own cajoling had brought him round to see reason. He was a man very slow to overcome prejudices. She remembered how he had disliked *her*, Athénaïs, at the beginning, preferring that vapid little fool, Louise de la Vallière.

"It took time—and persuasion." Athénaïs thought of some of the methods of that persuasion. Her eyes narrowed. Some of those methods were very useful still, at times, when the *ami* showed a shade of coldness, a thought of taking one for granted, of looking elsewhere. . . .

She remembered Madame de Soubise. That bold lady's black eyes had, two weeks ago, been all for Louis, she was certain. And that little sleek cat, the Princess de Grammont, had had claws sheathed for a long time, but she was not at present at Court. In any case, a message sent by Desoeillets for a certain powder from the woman in the Quartier St.-Denis, given to Louis' cupbearer, and all would be well again.

He'd had headaches, though. She would have to be careful. Now she remembered why that attitude of Scarron's with the blinds had been half-familiar; she'd come upon her once, after that affair of Agrippina's crown which mercifully had blown over, and found Scarron pulling back blinds, saying the King's head had ached. Athénaïs had laughed, at the time, with that and with the relief of no more trouble about the crown. If it had been anyone but Scarron, she would have begun to be careful. But there was no danger there.

She recalled what Scarron had said about the Duc du Maine and frowned a little. A child with her at Bourbon would hamper her, with its demands and queries. And Louis-Auguste was spoiled, would not obey her. He would be better to go—where? Somewhere with widow Scarron. The south, the Pyrenees. Montespan had always raved about them. One drank goat's milk.

Yes, she'd suggest it. Not now, though; through Louis. As well to let him see that she took an interest in the children. Sometimes, she thought, he as good as accused her of negligence. There had been that time when she and Scarron had disagreed about the children's food. "I must speak alone with Your Majesty!" Scarron had said. It was one of the few occasions when she had seen her flushed and angry. And Louis had stared. "Certainly, Madame," and he had accompanied her to the further room. Athénaïs had heard her voice, floating backward in protest. "Sire, I cannot have them drinking *vin de Bourgogne* at twelve o'clock at night!" And Louis had come back and said that really, really, she must allow Madame a free hand with the children.

Louis and Scarron . . . and their woes. . . .

Athénaïs suddenly found in herself an inclination to giggle.

Her thoughts floated on. What was it she had been going to say to Scarron? This heat enervated one so . . . Maine . . .

"Scarron!"

"Madame?"

Athénaïs considered her gambit. She must go carefully. How would one begin? It might be possible that the widow, who thought always of the next world, had little time for the benefits of this. But surely for Louis-Auguste she would do anything. One would attempt it.

"Have you ever thought what is to become of Maine?"

"Often." The pale thread darted in and out. How placid the woman Scarron was! She might—for that reason— succeed.

Athénaïs appeared to change the subject. "The other day, you know, the King and I drove out to La Grande Mademoiselle's Choisy. Have you seen it lately?"

"I have not seen it at all."

"Then do so—why do you not?"

"To what purpose?" said the widow gravely.

Athénaïs yawned. "Oh, Mother of God, you are so serious, with your reasons, and your purposes, but I also have a purpose in this." She sat up suddenly and her eyes were hard and bright. "Because Mademoiselle has passed the change of life and it will therefore be safe enough to let Lauzun out of prison. Before the King does this of his own accord I will persuade him to do it. Mademoiselle will be grateful and I intend to make use of her gratitude. She has no heirs, and never will have. It will be becoming, I think, if she is induced to leave her money to Maine."

The coach bowled along the road between Versailles and Choisy and Françoise watched the Duc du Maine, who was on the opposite seat, fast asleep.

Louis-Auguste was not well, and Françoise was far more interested in his health than in Madame's mercenary project. Of course Maine was charming, as everyone said; of course Mademoiselle would be delighted with him. That went without saying; but Françoise herself remembered how the boy Vexin had died, and the first daughter, and how the fistula in Maine's thigh had never dried up, so that he walked with difficulty.

"Ah, God in Heaven, if he should die! He must not do so."

The King, God be praised, had agreed with her on the matter of their diet. She would have fought wild bulls for her children's sleep, but war waged with their mother was twice as wearing. There had been scenes over a long period; Madame had flung a vase at her head. Then she had been sorry and begged forgiveness, but that happening every day would soon reduce one's tolerance. And often, often, Françoise knew, Madame would mimic her to Louis, in that time the two of them spent together, setting off his rare laughter in a way in which malice was compounded.

Ah, it was hard to be an oddity with no opportunity of redress, and there had come that day when Françoise also had lost her temper and then the King had come.

"I must speak alone with Your Majesty!" And then, in the little anteroom, she had poured out her grievances to him, and the way her authority was overridden continually.

"It is impossible to have two directors. I can no longer contrive. If Madame can supervise the children's meals, their welfare, clothing, lessons, all the other things, and leave herself time for her social activities, good and well. I can then take my leave. But it is *not* good to have the children drinking wine at that late hour, and to have Mademoiselle de Nantes encouraged to flout me, and to interrupt the lessontimes with visits from frippery persons about Court. There is a time for everything, and without order no progress is made at all." And she told him of the baby's colic and the worry she had about the health of Maine, and spared him nothing, so that afterward she was surprised at herself. But Louis had listened, and even made helpful suggestions, and since that day she had felt that he was for and not against her.

La Grande Mademoiselle received Françoise and Louis-Auguste in the great new chamber where Lauzun's portrait leered incongruously down from above the hearth. Beside the hundred others of Bourbon and Lorraine and Orléans he was a gnat aping butterflies. His nose looked very red and he wore a perruque, which he seldom did in life. Athénaïs had said there was a space on the wall the day of the King's visit.

Mademoiselle embraced Maine in an awkward flurry of striped silks. Her hair was dyed with saffron, curled, and the paint on her face was as thick as that on the Queen's.

All her movements were gawky like those of a very young man. She talked to the visitors gustily, punctuating her converse with bursts of very loud laughter. Taking Maine's hand in her large one, she showed them round the rooms. Françoise followed silently, having been given the other hand to kiss. This woman must be very lonely among her hanging portraits of dead kings.

Maine knew his part, she saw. Mademoiselle unbent, overcoming the gaucherie she had with children, who as a rule stared her out of countenance. Louis-Auguste was all earnest attention. Mademoiselle told him about her own childhood and how she had always wanted to be a man. "Then I could have been a soldier," she explained. Maine nodded wisely.

"I should like to have been a soldier also if I had not been lame," he said wistfully. "As it is, the King has promised to give me the command of a regiment of infantry once held by Turenne."

Françoise listened in amazement. Athénaïs had instructed the little wretch well. She watched Mademoiselle's rapt face.

At the end of the visit Maine, with pathetic difficulty kneeling on one knee, requested Mademoiselle's permission to assume her liveries. This had already been broached and its acceptance was now a formality. Mademoiselle assented, as she was expected to do. But then the unexpected happened. Mademoiselle burst into tears.

The flood-gates were opened. Françoise, frozen into passivity, and Maine, still kneeling in astonishment, heard in a torrent of words of the love, the longing, the sorrows of Mademoiselle, and the bravery, the harsh fate, the sufferings and the innocence of the incomparable M. de Lauzun.

"Oh!" wailed Mademoiselle. "I would not traffic with that Marquise! So ill-mannered she showed herself to me, when they came here, that my cousin the King remarked on it. I do not understand why he puts up with her tempers. Oh, I grant you she's very beautiful." She recollected the presence of Louis-Auguste and sniffed, determinedly, into her handkerchief, then began again. "But *you*, Madame, have influence. You are gentle. You are not above yourself," the poor soul wailed, conscious always of her own blue blood before everything except M. de Lauzun. Her raised face was grotesque, with the runnels of paint and tears upon it, and bloodshot veins in the prominent blue eyes.

"Free him and I will give you the sun," she said dramatically. Then, as if realizing that this was perhaps a little too much to hope for, "Free him, and I will give you anything I have. One of my estates, perhaps. You have only to speak. I know, Madame, of your influence with the King. I know that you will not ab—ab—" she hiccupped dolefully—"abuse such influence. Ah, Lauzun! He is in misery, in rags. He has dug with his fingernails a tunnel the breadth of a man, and so long that it made its way under all except the very outside wall of the prison. It took him four years. When at last he got out a sentry saw him and conveyed him back immediately. It was a cruel disappointment. No one knows how brave he is, how unfortunate, how dear to me—how dear!"

The poor creature dabbed at her eyes with her *point-de-Venise* handkerchief. Françoise was touched. She could not comfort this descendant of a hundred kings. The rules of etiquette prevented it; she must not raise a finger. Mademoisell herself would be the first to take offense at the homely offer of a sustaining arm. What emptiness there was in pomp! To Louise de Montpensier, Lauzun was not an insolent little upstart with a vermilion nose, who treated all her passionate avowals with a tepid condescension. He was a fairy prince who embodied all the virtues and who would always be the love of her life. And it was true that the tale of that passage dug below Pignerol had raised much sympathy.

But herself? What could she do? How did it happen that Mademoiselle saw in her a person of influence?

"I can do nothing," she said, in compassion. "I am no more than a servant."

Mademoiselle reverted suddenly to the slyness of a grotesque wink.

"Well, there are different kinds of service," she said. She put her hands on her hips, like a washerwoman. "I'll leave my possessions to Maine. If anyone likes I'll give them to him now. Tell the King so. Tell that—tell that woman,

Madame de Montespan. Oh, *I* know what she wanted. But you, Madame, hold the reins. *Your* word's listened to; I've heard of it. Folks tattle, you know."

It was infinitely worse, this false heartiness, than anything that had gone before. Françoise left Choisy with Maine feeling, unaccountably, soiled. Who had been spreading about the word of her "influence" with the King?

Driving back to Versailles, moreover, she felt her conscience smite her. It was true that she had done nothing; promised nothing, left events to take their course. But she had been there, lending countenance to it; and it seemed like robbing the blind to beguile that hungry soul with promises in exchange for her gold.

Athénaïs was triumphant, showering Maine with caresses to an unusual extent when she heard that Mademoiselle would make over to him a portion of her estates.

"How clever you have been!" she said to Françoise. "Oh, you shall have your reward!" She lay back on the couch, and began to toy idly with the fringed cushions. "Lauzun will be released," she said. "It's as I promised it should be. Why shouldn't the old woman have her lover—now?" She gave a note of cruel laughter. "Who'd be royal? But they have advantages, *sans doute,* that we have not. What's a château to them?" She sparkled at Françoise. "Maintenon shall be yours, *chérie.* But I hope that you will not be leaving us. Are you so weary, then of Court? Of me? Of the children?"

She pouted and pleaded. She was, she thought, with child again. "Can you leave me at such a time?" But Françoise was adamant. Her race was run, she said. "I have found my true vocation."

"The instruction of girls?" Athénaïs' brow furrowed. "But you can do that also and still remain with us." The truth was she did not want to lose Scarron. Nor, oddly enough, did the King.

"She *wishes* to go?" he had said incredulously. He had been silent on the subject since. He was intrigued, Athénaïs thought, by the enigma of Madame Scarron. "What a series of contrasts her life has been!" he had exclaimed one day.

He was insistent, she knew, on the trip to the Pyrenees for Maine. Could Madame be persuaded to remain till after that? Surely she would not grudge that last task in their service?

Françoise yielded. Behind her eyes were thoughts no one knew. Maintenon was reality, with its silver water and the woods that in spring would be green. But other reality was the Abbé Gobelin, slipping bespectacled into his carriage in the courtyard.

"You must not go yet," he said. And then, "Pray for the King!"

Easter drew near and Madame de Montespan was afraid.

IX

MADAME DE MONTESPAN was afraid each year in Lent. She spent it at Clagny.

Bossuet, who feared nobody, brought the terror of God to her soul. "He will stand in his traveling-cloak and thunder at me," she said tearfully to Madame de Maintenon. That lady, who had accompanied her, raised her dark eyes, said nothing, and returned to her tapestry. The King was at the wars.

Athénaïs stood by the window and watched a peacock strut by. Down in the garden she had seven of them, trailing and proud, with jeweled tails that were moulting now, a little, so that one did not acquire the maximum pleasure from watching them. They were vain creatures; she disliked them faintly. Sometimes they would eat out of her hand.

How changed everything was! Not long ago she had been complaining of lack of change. Here at Clagny, it was true, things continued as ever. M. de Condom would come soon again and scold her, and make her read passages of the Scriptures. How easy it was to repent, listening to his powerful voice relating, earnestly, the prospects of continuing sin! She would listen and weep, and then he would send Louis the same passages watered with her tears, and they would both promise to do better. It was a sin to receive the Body of God if one was unrepentant.

Sometimes the horror of it would overwhelm her. To be cut off forever from God, because of sin! Once she had done a thing she had not mentioned. Dear Christ, she could not think of it, at such times, the time of the Easter festival when all she had mocked came true. . . .

No, she would not remember it. It had not been necessary, in any case, to go back to the house in the Tannerie; or that other place between Paris and Versailles, the place where a high moat fed fountains. *That* had been in adventure, desperation; in the spirit of any young fool going to a *sorcière* to obtain a love-potion. It had gone further, in the end, than one intended. Looking back, it was sordid and a little embarrassing. But not wicked, never wicked. Abandoned, a little. The woman's accomplice, who called himself an abbé, who performed the rite, had looked at her naked body with lecherous eyes.

No, the little powders fetched by Desoeillets had worked, in the end, as many miracles. It had not been necessary to go back in person to that woman.

Had she repented now? She should not be thinking, in that case, as though she and Louis would come together again after this season. Perhaps she had always known they would do so. Perhaps she was a hypocrite, a lost soul, possessed of the devil.

Possessed of the devil! She began to laugh hysterically.

Scarron—no, Maintenon—raised her head. Athénaïs must remember the title. Only a word from Louis, one day at Versailles; the daily greeting, asking for Madame's health.

"Madame de Maintenon," he had said. And nobody had addressed the widow as Scarron again.

X

MAINTENON was the first home Françoise had had since the days of her marriage to Paul. Even when she had no time to spare for it, it was always in her thoughts. So often she had longed for green trees, quiet paths, and water. Now these were hers she had little leisure for them. "You must not go!" the Abbé Gobelin had said.

She had pleaded with him. What further good could she do? She had no wish to make selfish use of Maintenon. Already she had made inquiry about the weavers. Never, she knew, in her life would matters be ordered the way they were for other women, whose hearths were their castles, guarded by a man's arm. The Abbé had asked her to use her influence to further the repentance of Madame la Marquise. She had done so; she had prayed for her and for the King. She would continue to do so till the end of her days. Would prayer be less real at Maintenon?

"Wait till this trip with the little Duc is over. Do not make plans till then."

She would make the trip, she would go to Barèges. She and Louis-Auguste would visit Charles at Cognac and see how well he did since he had been made Governor there. No one could say she had pushed for that appointment, or that she had tried to have Charles posted nearer Versailles. "Charles is much better in the provinces," she told herself firmly. She would do what she could also for Philippe de Villette and his children.

She examined curiously her late preoccupation with children. Until that night when she had driven home in the carriage with the King's child she had had little time for them, or they for her. That journey had released a well-spring in her. It had remained for the children of Madame la Marquise to break down the barriers between herself and childhood.

Now and again, by a chance word dropped, she would hear of a case of want. She could not relieve such cases of extreme poverty as were the lot of the La Charité sisterhood or those of Saint Vincent de Paul. It was true that she had started an office of charity at Versailles and, in the way in which such things become fashionable, everyone had put their names down for it and a great deal of good was being done, but her own mission lay elsewhere. . . . There were those who lived in a twilight world, neither beggars nor yet provided for; those whose names might once have been noble, who could not toil with their hands because they did not know how. The shabby-genteel. They were the most miserable of all, even the husks the swine ate being denied them. How well she knew their misery!

"You, Madame, have influence." The words of Mademoiselle de Montpensier ran in her mind. If it were true—and she knew now that, in little ways, it was so—then how she would use it, how she would employ it to serve the ends of God! The King had given her a hundred thousand francs, then doubled it. She'd use that too.

She smiled, remembering how that had arisen. Louis-Auguste had said something clever. He was sitting on the King's knee. His Majesty burst out laughing. He was more at ease with Maine, much more, than with the big dull son of poor Marie-Thérèse.

"He has sense," he said to the onlookers. "How much sense he has!"

"How can I not have?" said Louis-Auguste. "I was brought up by a person who is entirely sensible."

And Louis had doubled the hundred thousand francs.

Easter came. The King took the sacraments in presence of the Court. He sat listening while the preacher faced him with a charge of debauchery. Madame de Montespan sat behind him and the Queen, on a low chair. Everyone heard it.

"I am sensible of my wrongdoings," said Louis. "But I do not like them publicized."

He rode again to the front. Françoise and Louis-Auguste set off for the south parts, leaving the Court behind.

PART IV

The Conscience of the King

I

FRANÇOISE RAISED her head to smile at Maine, who had called to her for encouragement. For an instant her eyes lingered on the small toiling figure and then fell again. She was writing a letter, and in the full glare of sunshine it was not possible to see, for long, without shading the eyes with one's hand.

Above her, the network of goat-paths clambered. Maine advanced manfully, sometimes pausing to steady himself, clutching at dry tufts of grass. Everything here was brown and parched already, the days of pink almond-blossom and feathery green hill-slopes were past, and the skies, hot as bronze, drew the moisture from the ground, leaving dust that collected in the seams of one's clothing.

She would not be sorry to return, now, but it had been pleasant here in the south. Journeying along the incredible roads, drinking the sour red *vin du pays* and eating at little inns, they had watched the jagged peaks high and strange against the sky. Near by Montespan, the forsaken husband, brooded among his peach-clad slopes in the valleys he had once said were like heaven. He had not come to meet them, but all the rest of the world had. Françoise sent an account of it now to the King.

"Write to me," he had said, and she had fulfilled her promise, telling him every detail of the journey south, the way the towns had flocked to greet them, and how at Bordeaux they had gone by water to the thunder of guns from the Château-Trompette, and the music of forty violins. It had been a little royal progress; Louis-Auguste had been fêted in the manner of a prince. At Cognac they had dined with Charles, and at Blaye the old Duc de Saint-Simon had entertained them magnificently. She remembered being presented to his son, who was much of an age with Louis-Auguste and had a turned-up nose and inquiring, very bright brown eyes.

Louis in his tent at Latines would be pleased to read it all. . . .

She thought of Versailles, remembering it as pertaining to a time past and done with. She did not think, having completed this journey with Maine, that they would require her services again.

Maintenon was waiting. Françoise smiled a little, against the sun. There were fourteen little girls there now. As the years passed she found the names of those she had helped become blurred and often repetitive, merging into a general awareness of rosy scrubbed faces and slender hands. Anne, Louis, Marthe, Mathilde, Marie. She had hired two good nuns to look after them and instruct them in simple cookery and needlework. Soon she would go herself and continue in that instruction. Philippe's little girl, Tante's grandchild, should come to her too at Maintenon. She loved that child, with her mop of chestnut hair and her laughter. It had been like coming back from the grave to see Murcy again, visiting there on the way south; although Philippe's wife was young and careless and did not keep it so well as Tante had done.

Ah, she must be growing old! Why should the weeds on the path at Murcy so distress her? It was no longer home; that was at Maintenon. Soon she would return and then, set free, remain there till she died. No more curtsying . . . except that of her "little girls" as she came by on the daily round. The sound, too, of her new name pleased her. Françoise d'Aubigné she was at heart, the d'Aubigné arms were on her new carriage doors, and she was proud of that as embodying the bravery of dead fighters and the friends of kings. But this other had a stately sound, and she heard the children utter it with a respect due to the fact that she was now their foundress.

"Madame de Maintenon."

* * *

"Madame, Madame, I walked to the upas tree!"

"Madame, I went by myself to the place where the melons are!"

"Madame, I can walk, I can walk, I can walk!"

The peasants here, she knew, prayed to Santiago de Compostella, carrying his likeness on a medal of pewter or silver attached to the worn wood of their beads. If Santiago, or Our Lady, or the whole assemblage of saints, could accomplish Maine's cure, she would pray to every one of them. She did so, nightly, on her knees.

"There is nothing I would not give," she promised. By day she teased Maine.

"The commander of Turenne's former infantry will march in soon, with flags flying, to greet the King. Courage, my little one! Think how pleased the King will be . . . and how proud it will make me, when you walk to meet him through the great door of Versailles."

"Without my stick!" said Maine.

At last it seemed that that might be accomplished.

Françoise had written daily to Athénaïs of her son's progress, partly out of assurance that it could not fail to interest her, partly out of the pride and joy she herself had in Maine. She never tired of writing of him. The Governor of Cognac had been as impressed with him as La Grande Mademoiselle. What joy it had been to turn her own shameful associations with Château-Trompette into a remembrance of glory!

Athénaïs' replies were rare. The King had freed Lauzun. He might not come within thirty miles of Paris (poor Mademoiselle!). He disported himself with Mademoiselle Fouquet and other young ladies at the waters; he showed no inclination to return.

"The King promised Lauzun his *freedom*," the emphasis ran maliciously. Françoise felt weary of it. Why deny the poor woman her lover? She had paid dearly enough.

Maine, the beneficiary, was now so much improved in health that she and he, with the chaplains, tutors, equerries and persons of the household, returned a day or two earlier than was expected.

On the way to Versailles a coach met them. At sight of the grass-green liveries she recognized, and was prepared to greet, the inmate. Athénaïs' lovely face peered at them, laughing, behind the glass. With her in the coach was her sister, Madame de Thianges. The Marquise lowered the window.

"But how delightful! Madame! My dear! And Maine!"

A torrent of words greeted them. Madame la Marquise was full of information, queries as to their journey, their happiness, their health. She looked superbly beautiful; on her breast lay a great opal. Its many facets kindled little fires as she moved. She seemed to glow with happiness; for them? It was doubtful as to that. . . . Madame de Thianges' face was alight with mischief.

"You're going to the Palace? But of course! The King is not at home tonight. He will be available tomorrow morning, at ten. Why, Louis-Auguste, you do not find that suitable? But certainly . . . you wish to surprise the King. Very well, then, at ten . . . but of course we will not tell him! In the study."

The window shut again over their muffled laughter. Françoise bowed, smiled, instructed the coachman to drive on. She suddenly felt old and tired. It was not over, then; had never been. That Easter repentance had not lasted forever. Only for a year, until the next approach of Lenten fasting, confession and cleansing of the soul. Only a token cleansing, because it was convenient. A sop, no more, to God.

She was therefore not unprepared for the look in Louis' eyes the next morning. Over Maine's head, when the little boy had made his *entrée*, successfully and hardly limping at all, to the King's desk, the King turned and looked at her. He had shown great joy at seeing the child, exclaimed at his improved appearance. He spoke then, with the ease of habit, about her letters, and how the one at Latines had been supplemented later by those Madame la Marquise had received and read to him.

In that statement lay his defiance and apology. The blue eyes met her own with an expression hard to read. "I have enjoyed your letters, Madame. I have missed your society.

I am glad that it is returned to me, for I am not as you knew me previously. My dear Madame, I have fallen once more into the sin of David. She is so beautiful I cannot resist her, and I have just ridden home from the war."

Above the heads of all of them Athénaïs' portrait mocked and beckoned. Her presence was strong in the room as though she stood there, laying, as several nights ago, her head on the King's shoulder in full view of those who played cards. It had come to the notice of Madame de Sévigné, who had hurried the news to Provence. But Madame's friend, who had once dined with her nightly in the days of Vaugirard, said nothing at all. Her glance returned to the child again. How pretty he looked, with his little face less peaked, and a slight color still in his cheeks after the long hours in the Pyrenean sun! That, after all, was her personal concern; the other need not affect her so absurdly.

"What fascinating letters you sent!" said Athénaïs.

She moved, yawned, crossed one leg over the other in the way she had and stretched her body agreeably, like a cat. As she moved, the scent of the verbena-herb she used among her linen came faintly, emphasizing the allure of her flesh. She was pleased, lazy, fulfilled, and embellished with the King's late gift of a diamond *parure* and two bracelets. She could afford, she thought, to give the governess a little pleasure. Poor Scarron—Maintenon—consoling herself that at last she had led them both, herself and Louis, back to their own beds and their separate altars! They had been almost hysterical that time at Clagny, herself and Madame and Bossuet in his clerical muffler, preaching the Word at her and roaring at her to repent. Repentance was a luxury, no doubt, but as such could not last.

Maintenon! Did the governess think she had acquired some kind of hold over Louis? It never paid to be too indulgent. . . . She should have made more trouble, really, over that time when the two of them drew aside into the anteroom. Setting aside her own authority over the children . . . ah, God knew, that kind of thing was the thin end of the wedge, if it were allowed. And then Louis had doubled that money-gift. One hundred thousand would have been sufficient. Oh, it was true that Madame had nursed Vexin for them, as the King said, but even so. . . .

But Athénaïs was pleased now. She smiled, with her eyes half-closed against the light. "The King said such an extraordinary thing when I read him your letters," she said to the governess, "that I am going to tell you what it was. He's an extraordinary man," she said flatly. "He's very ignorant. The only education he ever really received was as a young man, from the Cardinal's niece, Marie Mancini. She instructed him in English and Italian, and being in love he learned fast. But apart from that—phoh! The late *Reine-Mère* and the Cardinal made it their studious anxiety to keep him uninstructed in everything except the niceties of the ballet and the dance."

But the assured young figure in a scarlet coat, downing the *Parlement,* had emerged from that. "*L'Etat, c'est moi!*"

Françoise felt her color rise and her heartbeats, unaccountably, quicken. "And the remark?" she ventured, calmly. "What was that?"

"The remark?" said Athénaïs. "To be sure, I'd forgotten. 'She knows very well how to love,' he said. 'It would be a pleasure to be loved by her.'"

And Françoise remembered how Paul had first noted her through her letters.

Now that the change had come she could not follow, with any exactitude that would stamp matters on her memory, the progress of her friendship with the King. That the seeds of it had been laid long since she knew. He was a man whose slow speech held considered decisions. His life was a pattern, in many ways unalterable. From the hour at which he rose, with the progression of *petit lever,* he was surrounded always by ritual. It was like the Ark of God, said Athénaïs. Petty details of precedence, coveted by the noblemen to whom they were granted as their grandfathers would

have coveted châteaux and their great-grandfathers swords
—these were the reasons for which, at great expense, everyone existed; bearing the alternate drafts and stuffiness of
Versailles. Louis liked all the doors and windows open, but
the maids-of-honor in their attic rooms died of heat. The
King himself ate sparingly on journeys, but liked to see
everyone else stuff themselves. "But, Madame, you have
eaten nothing," he would say, perplexed, after the seventh
plate of comfits and *petits-fours* had been waved aside.

Françoise began to adapt herself to him. The warming of
the Royal shirt, the foretasting of wine, the buckling on of
Louis' shoes for which honor Ducs fought with polite insistence, were details known to her, but not significant.
Louis had, she guessed, fortified himself with these things
as men had been used to do with armor. She had no concern with them then or at any other time. For her, as time
passed, Louis became the fastidious boy she had glimpsed
that day in Paris, disdainful of a world he planned to master.
Also, somewhere, beneath the façade, was the young lover
of La Vallière.

Louise was almost forgotten. If she was mentioned, it was
with the amused contempt of the world's successes for its
failures. At one time she had been a cover for the King's
affaire with Montespan; since that had been made public,
she was superfluous. No one knew why she remained at
Court. A nun? Well, let her go and be one . . . at the
convent of the Carmelites, which she favored. "Why there?"
said Louis, distastefully. "She has the *entrée*, if she wishes
it, to the noblest foundation in France. I myself offered to
make her an Abbess. The Carmelites keep strict fast and
wear goats' hair, and open sandals. She is a gently nurtured
woman. Such a life is not for her." He said it was hysteria,
and blustered a little. That was much later that year, when
he and Françoise had talked often together and he could
speak freely of such things.

"Hysteria does not last for four years," said Françoise.

She knew that Bossuet, in whom Louise confided, had
advised her to wait again, and yet again. "Another year," he

always said. Françoise too was familiar with that phrase. "Do not go yet"—to Maintenon, home—always that "Another year!"

One day the King came to her. His face, as always, betrayed nothing. He asked her to come with him to visit a friend, who was ill. Until she saw the elfin face in the shadow of great bed-curtains, she had not known that the visit was to La Vallière. Now, pity claimed her. The face was neither young nor old.

"Madame la Duchesse de Vaujours." That was the title he had bestowed on her when their love faded and, ever since, Louise had born it unwillingly and with reproach. As on that day when Françoise had first seen her at the banquet in honor of Franche-Comté's fall, she was heavily, tastelessly surrounded. Then it had been a gown that was unbecoming; now it was hangings, furniture, everything ornate, heavy, tasteless, chosen without interest, dull. Louise's body scarcely raised the coverlet; her hands were paper-thin. "She has been following the rule of the Order for two years," said Louis, aloud as if La Vallière could neither hear nor understand. "I cannot see that it does good."

La Vallière looked at Françoise without replying and the latter saw an infinite understanding in the gently shadowed, speedwell-dark eyes. "I have given," the eyes said, "all my youth, my love; it did not bring me happiness. Now my torment of soul, my guilt, are unappeased; and I love still." A fierce hatred moved Françoise suddenly. What was this callousness that had overcome humanity in the King's heart, as though he could trample on the soul and spirit like the bodies of dead soldiers in the Flanders mud, and be forgiven because he was divine? "He has been as God to this woman, and yet she still knows God can be found elsewhere, with torment enough, it is true, on the way. But does *he* know that?" Seeing, one doubted; remembering the Apollo ballets, the emblem of the Sun-King on walls and stairs, the easy conquest of fair flesh, the silencing of conscience. Her pity was the greater for Louis in that he might never be brought to understand.

Going away from the room, he spoke of La Vallière regretfully, as of someone who has not too recently died. "If she desires it so, she can go," he said. "I was opposed to it, for the sake of the children and what I owe her; but she takes no joy in them, or pleasure in the life at Court. If she felt as she once did—" He broke off, coldly, as though a solecism had been made, and continued after a little pause. "I shall regret to lose her," he continued, as though speaking of a servant. "I have, however, seen Bossuet and he, although he advised her to give herself another eighteen months in the world, admits now that she is sure. I did not think she would have the strength," he said, and passed on to another subject. Françoise had not been able to say farewell alone. What could have been said, she thought, in any event? "I have loved with my whole heart and I do still, and for the rest of my life I shall pray for him?"

"Let her go," said Françoise. She had not spoken aloud.

When Sœur Louise de la Miséricorde took her vows crowds lined the streets of Paris. But the world that she had left was nothing to her; the man she had lost was all. Bossuet and Bourdalous might mount their pulpits in face of packed congregations; penitents, raised to an ecstasy by their eloquence, kneel by the rails. Outside in the streets women knelt, sobbing and praying aloud for the King. It was, M. de Condom said, a spiritual revival. From the Babylon of sin to the Carmel of repentance! What an example was there! They made a hundred converts in a night . . . and Sœur Louise, chilled in her bare cell, felt no false ecstasy or easy approach to God, and prayed for the King with tears falling between her fingers.

Athénaïs visited Sœur Louise sometimes in her cell. She took her little, spiteful pieces of gossip. When she returned to Court again she would discuss the looks of the new Carmelite, idly as one might relate the colors of a pinned moth. The situation amused her lightly. "Why love to that extent?" she said to Françoise. "That way one becomes, of necessity, an embarrassment; especially when the beloved is the King." Then she would laugh a little at the idea of anyone so loving

Louis. Françoise turned away from the subject as from a hurt that would not heal.

She looked often at the King, seated with profile toward her in the way he would be when, of an evening, he would come to inquire of the progress of Maine. He always sat in a certain chair, as though it had gradually become familiar to him. At first he had spoken formally, graciously, on various subjects, but lately he seldom spoke. She had discovered that he disliked silences, as though unable to derive satisfaction from his own mind, and she had fallen into the way of talking gently, lightly, amusingly, something after the manner of the days of the Hôtels d'Albret and de Richelieu.

Watching, she saw his changed face. The fine drawing that his features possessed was being overlaid, a little, by grossness, as though evil smoothed the flesh. She welcomed the offer of being permitted to solace his loneliness of mind a little. More she could not do yet.

By nights she would kneel in her closet and pray, with more intensity than she had ever done on behalf of anyone, for his soul. By day she would watch the efforts of Mesdames de Louvigny and de Soubise and others to eclipse Montespan in the favors of the King.

He was surrounded by women, like a comfit-dish with flies in summer. The assiduity of his vice had increased them, as wine-shops multiply for the custom of drunkards. Bossuet, now Archbishop of Meaux, whose funeral oration for dead English Madame had brought him fame that would live after him, could do nothing. "It was the double adultery," he said time and again. "For that I blame all."

"Something may be accomplished," Françoise said. "God will not forsake the King."

"No, but the King has forsaken God, Madame," said the Archbishop.

He spoke much with her, both directly and through the Abbé. She knew that both regarded her as having a foot in the camp of the enemy, and for that reason she must stay at her post for a year, another year. In her heart she cried aloud. Was she hypocrite? An image of the King's face came to her; the imperious arch of the brows, the contours of jaw and throat, reminding her of a young Caesar, only a very little marred by the world. Had her very nature betrayed her? Louis was five years younger than she. Was she like other women, and her concern no more than pique?

"I?" she asked herself. Her lips twitched, alone in the privacy of her closet where no one, not even Nanon, could see. Against the opacity of the window-glass she could see her faint reflection; grave-eyed, middle-aged, staid, unyielding, plain. Louis, the arbiter of high and peerless beauty, and herself! "I am not an aristocrat," she was to write. "I am a mushroom."

"He hated all of them," mocked Athénaïs' voice. "La Vallière . . . she was a little plain lame thing, of no family. Marie Mancini was nothing in the days when he was enamored of her sister Olympe. *I* was nothing . . . time and habit . . . at first, he hated *me* . . ."

Her laughter rang out clearly in Françoise' mind. It mocked, with a shade of evil. Why was she always so conscious now of the presence of evil?

"He hated *me*," she said aloud, "and now does so no more."

Sinful or not, she yet had pleasure in the thought. So often now she was able to smooth the way for him, establish *rapport* between his imperious, exacting mistress and himself. "He is tired," she would murmur to Athénaïs, seeing her primed to embark on a new tirade, a new demand for money or houses or jewels or, simply, attention. "She is overwrought," she would soothe Louis, her quiet voice dropping like stillness over water after the sound of Athénaïs' shrill demanding, the thoughtless cascade of her laughter.

And always later in the solitude of her own heart would come that gnawing doubt.

She consulted the Abbé regarding it and he calmed her.

"The devil seeks to weaken us in ways least expected. *He* is aware that you have influence with the King; *he* would imperil your confidence in yourself, break the weapon in your hand for God. Watch over the exercise of your own faith lest he enter in. Be more assiduous than ever in prayer, to leave no loophole." She must take the sacraments more often; she must strengthen herself against spiritual assault.

She needed all her strength. Never before had Versailles seemed so airless, so beset with the things of the flesh, so lacking in every cool draft from God that she wished, often, to gather up her skirts and run. Even the chapel glittered with false light. Pretty young demoiselles took each a candle, made themselves noticed at Vespers and Mass, with the lights held near their hooded faces, showing the freshness of throat and rounded chin. In the side-galleries they knelt in long lines, when the King was present, each seeing in herself a potential Montespan or La Vallière. When Louis did not attend, neither did they. The captain of the King's guard was a devout man and daily the sight made his teeth grind together. One day he marched his *corps de garde* out of the chapel, saying in clear tones, "Guards, retire! The King will not attend Mass today!" There was a rustling of disappointed skirts, a general blowing out of candles. The chapel was half-empty when the King came. When informed of the reason, he laughed heartily.

There was one who was of little importance about Court. In her apartments on the second floor, Queen Marie Thérèse lived, prayed, ate, slept, played cards and was unhappy. She had borne the King six children, one of whom had lived. On State occasions she was paraded like a doll. Françoise had often seen the little, stoutened figure, gorgeously attired in its gowns of metallic cloth with their trains a requisite number of yards long and faced with ermine, and its curious, loping walk overshadowed by the frizzed coiffure of yellow hair. She felt that the Queen mistrusted her, as being in employment through the offices of Madame de Montespan. She waited, her sharp pity for the poor soul being tempered by the queer dignity the Queen displayed. She had never, by word or look, lowered herself by reference to the affair of her husband's mistress.

"She has learned," said Athénaïs, and laughed. "When she

came at first there were scenes if Louis so much as spoke to English Madame, and worse ones over the business of La Vallière." And she went on to explain how that little, stout type of Hapsburg woman cared for very little in the end except the pleasures of food. It had been the same with His Majesty's mother, Anne of Austria. "They lose their emotions as they grow older," said the Marquise complacently.

II

FRANÇOISE SAT at a window, spinning. It was evening, and the shadows in the room had grown longer. Down in the park of Maintenon the "little girls" played, tirelessly. She could see the colored whisking of their skirts appear and disappear among the trees. The black hoods of the two hired nuns surveyed them, motionless.

How still everything was! The late sun bathed the leaves in gold; it shone in, gently enough, at her west window, no longer dazzling the eyes as it had done earlier in the day. A little creeper tapped, tapped on the open glass. She could hear the tiny sound faintly, accustomed as she was to the constant whirring of the wheel.

Other sounds there had been. All afternoon there had come the creak of wagons, bearing the great piled loads of flax from Noisy to Maintenon. Tomorrow there would be singing heard when they worked it in the fields, the little pipe of the children joined with the deeper notes of the Flemish weavers. Soon there would be thread spun, looms set up, work done for the linen for smocks for next year, sheets and *collets*. All from a little seed of flax sown, even as the handful of little orphans at Noisy and Ruel had swelled, in the end, into this school of Maintenon.

How happy they were!

Charles' little girl was down there, playing with the rest. She was a clever child and showed, God be thanked, no tendency to inherit ill-manners from her mother, that little Paris gossip Charles had married without consulting anyone. Philippe's child also was somewhere, having been rescued somewhat forcibly from Murcy, but no one objected to that. They loved her, those children, particularly little Marthe de Villette. When she had been brought away in the carriage she had, instead of crying for her mother, begun to sing.

Tante, they called her. How things repeated themselves!

She pressed the treadle, feeling the dear familiar pull of the spinning-yarn in her fingers. "Madame, Madame, will you ever be done spinning?" Louis-Auguste had said, on the holiday at Barèges last year.

Louis-Auguste. How far away he seemed! The house on the Vaugirard was sold now, all that time was past with necessity. The younger children of the King and Madame ran about openly at Court, and did not need her.

A shadow crossed the day, drowning the bright voices and shapes, bringing remembrance. Versailles, an hour's ride away, was a world to which she must return. At Versailles she had failed, even as here she had succeeded. The King was not yet parted from Madame.

"Will it last forever?" she thought. At Court now everyone was talking of the Dauphin's betrothal. He was to marry the daughter of the Elector of Bavaria in the spring.

They all grew up. Soon Maine also would marry. She remembered the King's frown on the subject. "Persons of that sort are better to remain single," he had said, thinking of the succession. He never failed to keep the division between affairs of State and affairs of the heart clear in his mind. But Louis-Auguste had made up his mind that he would be like other people. She remembered his child's face, rapt with an odd intentness, as he expressed his thoughts on the subject. "My wife must have beauty," he informed everyone, "but I do not mind whether or not she is rich."

The Dauphine of Bavaria would not be rich and there

were, as always in such cases, conflicting opinions as to whether or not she would be beautiful. The Court had its one fervent prayer on the subject; otherwise it was not interested. "Deliver us from another Madame Liselotte!"

But surely two such ugly brides could not come out of Germany. In any case it did not matter, as everything had been already arranged. Françoise herself would have little to do with it. How much she desired to have nothing to do with anything!

Except here. . . .

The trees sighed. Already, with evening, it was growing a little cold. Françoise stopped the wheel, rose and closed the casement window. *Mes sœurs,* below, looked up and she signaled to them that it was time the children went in. . . .

She stood and watched. The black skirts marshaled the colored ones, mustered them obediently like a flock of lambs. The small coif of Mademoiselle Françoise d'Aubigné was awry; a sister straightened it.

"Now, little ones, supper, and then Benediction."

She would go down, join them quietly at the devotions, then bid them good night. Later she would go round their rooms with a lamp, to see that they were sleeping. Her own meals she preferred to have privately here, in the room, where there was hangings on the walls from the house in Vaugirard.

This would be her old age. . . .

She lingered a little, still, by the window; remembering other times. Once she had stood and watched the leaves borne high on the wind. Now it was summer. Paul, little twisted Paul, what would he have said had he seen her now, patroness of a score of demoiselles, with her castle?

"You should have married again, *mignonne.*" She could see his wry smile. To Paul, the idea of a solitary existence had been anathema. He had drawn his very life-blood from the current of other life. How strange she would now have appeared to him, she who had always needed her silences!

A horseman was coming up the drive. She could hear from sound of hoof-beats steadily. It would be a message from

Noisy, or perhaps from Court. She hoped that Maine were not ill.

She waited, feeling the peace of the night disturbed. The horseman drew up to the door and dismounted and Françoise saw, from where she stood a little way back from the window, that he wore the royal livery. She went back to the wheel and disposed herself again, till he should be brought to her. When he arrived she was carding wool. The soft rolled masses fell one after the other into a wide basket, to lie there. She held out her hand for the letter, seeing its swinging seals.

The messenger waited. Françoise slit open the letter. Still she was conscious of absurd things. The man wore a livery of frog-green, with blue revers and braiding. His face was impassive. What was she to say to him? She was aware of the weight of the carders, suspended in her free hand.

"You need not wait," she told him.

Nanon was at the door, silent but curious. She waited till the man had gone. Nanon would ask nothing, she was too well-trained, but one could feel her curiosity like a nudging elbow; Françoise folded up the letter. She turned to the woman at the door.

"Send me up a little flagon of warmed ale and an omelette. And order the coach for tonight. We are returning to Versailles."

Nanon stood her ground. "To Versailles, Madame?"

"To Versailles."

After the servant had gone she stood, irresolute. How quickly her orderly planning could be upset! Of course, she would have no hesitation in declining the appointment, but first it would be necessary to see the King . . . and the Abbé. *He,* no doubt, would advise it. He had never been in favor of her retiral to Maintenon, even though the few days such as she had lately spent there were all that, in the end, she had contrived.

But to think of them as over was ridiculous. Of course she would not accept this appointment as first *dame d'atour* to the new Dauphine.

*　　*　　*

"She is not a beautiful bride," said Louis.

This pronouncement, coming as it did from a monarch who in youth had declared that the pre-requisite for the wife of any reigning monarch was beauty, had cooled the enthusiasm of several about Court who had been speculating as to the bride of Monseigneur. That personage himself, on being approached, had only ventured, "Has she any deformity?" and on being assured that she had none, relapsed into vegetable contentment.

But now the King's words fell flatly, for his listeners' minds were elsewhere. Madame de Montespan, Guardian of the Nuptial Casket, Lady-in-Waiting to the Queen, remained silent. Her attention appeared given to a miniature she held, set about with brilliants.

The King gestured, and with rather an ill grace Athénaïs passed it wordlesssly to Françoise. The blue eyes glinted curiously; the atmosphere in the room was uneasy, as if a word would be a tinder struck. Françoise looked in her turn at the portrait.

It showed a plain young woman, sallow and broad-nosed, one hand rather nervously smoothing a spiral of dark hair.

"They say," remarked Athénaïs, her teeth on edge, "that Madame la Dauphine is a prey to melancholy, and dislikes society. I trust, Madame that you will not regret your acceptance of the task of—*dame d'atour.*"

"We must not believe all we hear," said the King evenly.

His eyes met those of his mistress; their glance was cold. The heaviness in the room was the aftermath of passionate scenes. So often he had borne much from this woman, enduring all she brought him because of her undoubted magnificence of body, the fact that she was the mother of his children. But now—was it by contrast with that other, seated quietly in her chair?—he remembered each separate insult more clearly than was his wont, as if her voice still rang in the silence.

"That old woman." Of late she had begun so to describe Madame de Maintenon, as if age implied senescence, a denial of all else that was worth having. "That old nun—dowdy, unsuitable . . . a *dame d'atour!* Your Majesty could have searched the whole Court without finding more of a laughing stock . . . do you suppose either France or Bavaria will have forgotten the ridiculous Scarron? A *parvenue,* a *flatteuse,* hanging on to my skirts and those of Madame de Richelieu!"

Had the woman not received Maintenon? Athénaïs had raged. What more had she done that deserved reward? People would begin to say that the King was led away by witchcraft.

Louis had looked at her sullen flushed face; even in middle age she was beautiful. How could so fair a body conceal so resentful a mind? He began to remember other things he had endured from her. . . .

"Witchcraft." The word remained with him. "Ay, so they may say, Madame," he retorted.

And slowly the crimson flush had dulled on her face and neck, paling till it was the color of lead, of ashes. She had begun to talk very fast and sullenly then of Madame de Maintenon, and her reward.

"Give her another estate and more money, if you must. That's the way to reward these people." Desperately, she had whirled about, facing him. The trick, which had fascinated him in the old days, had a way of showing off her glorious body, compelling the eyes to the twist of bosom and waist, the arms' whiteness. "You and I, Louis, understand each other. Dear God, would that be unlikely, after so many years?"

Her glorious eyes, her proud winning manner, pleaded with him. She could be charming, Athénaïs, in obtaining what she wanted. And she wanted this appointment of *dame d'atour.* God knew he had not realized she might desire it, but some obstinacy in him now prevented his acceding to her.

She had pouted then like a child, seeking to cajole him. Why invest that old woman with importance at Court? All she was interested in was the life hereafter . . . and her old château of Maintenon. She doted so on it that it was depriving her of enjoyment to take her elsewhere, and was no real reward.

"In that case," Louis had said quietly, "she will take the appointment to oblige me."

"You must wear," said Louis, "gowns of gold tissue, embroidery, jewels. It is requisite for the *dame d'atour* to sparkle with the body as well as with the mind."

His eyes teased her, but Françoise knew him well enough to be sure of his displeasure if she did not comply. Somewhere behind the eyes was still the man who had once said, "I detest black!"

What made her accept? she asked herself.

Her life was changing, and she sensed it not only in the changed demeanor of those about her; the hate in the eyes of German Liselotte, the sudden ungraciousness of Madame la Marquise de Montespan. What was the King to her? What had he become? Why had she, when she heard of the furious attack made by Madame de Soubise, who had coveted the appointment and bearded the King with her grievance in public—why had she been almost glad to accept when she had intended to decline?

Or had it been, as always, the Abbé Gobelin?

"You must not forsake the King."

Always, always that phrase, as though the King were in danger and she had a sword. What more could they hope from her? What more could she do?

In the end she surveyed herself in her mirror and saw a changed creature. "It is I myself," she thought, but the assurance needed emphasis. This matured, graceful woman with dark-piled hair, whose arms gleamed as she raised them to fasten the clasp of jewels about her throat, was not herself. This was not the widow Scarron, who had renounced all matters of this world not of the mind and soul. This was—

The voice of Madame la Marquise cut through her thoughts, spitefully.

"I pity the young Dauphine," it said. "She cannot fail to be eclipsed in every way by her mistress of the robes."

III

Marie-Anne-Christine-Victoire of Bavaria proved to be a *farouche* young woman who showed neither excitement at her nuptial prospects nor sorrow at leaving her native land. She appeared, in fact, to be sunk in a dull torpor which, Françoise decided, would suit Monseigneur the Dauphin very well.

The meeting between Monseigneur and his bride was uneventful, the comments about Court varied; everything had become very dull. Emphasis was laid on the Princess's deportment, as it was hard to find anything of interest to say about her face.

The Queen sulked. Françoise, coming from her daily task of combing the Dauphine's hair, heard the petulant voice complaining, monotonously, from behind a door. "My family is superior to hers. There has been far too much money spent on the wedding. No one ever gave half that sum for a nuptial casket when *I* was married."

"I cannot even make her smile," said Louis.

He turned, gratefully surveying the approach of the *dame d'atour*. How well Madame de Maintenon looked, he thought, in her richer garments! Better than that dreary girl he had just left, who had no wit, no conversation, disliked company —even his—and would not come to Court.

How things had changed, he thought! He could remember the brilliant days, the time of young English Madame, when they had ridden through the woods of Fontainebleau and listened to music on the water; and fireworks had given pleasure and ballets caused delight, and *he* had danced, as the Sun King, and Olympe and Louise and Henriette had loved him. . . . But now when he suggested fireworks every-one shrugged, bored, as with children's toys; and since a certain couplet in a play of Racine's, he had sworn that he himself would never dance in a ballet again. And Athénaïs, the excommunicate of Sens, could not set foot in Fontaine-bleau, which made the pace there very slow; and even Lulli's music, somehow, had not the beauty once known. Ah, he was growing old; and without age's compensations. That dull woman, his son's wife, would bear dull children; no more might be expected, in any case, from his fish of an heir. What would become of France, when he himself had gone, with no one but those two dullards at its head?

"Ah, Madame. . . ."

She came, curtseying gracefully; where had she learned to move and walk, this woman? Always he had been taught to regard her as a freak, a crow; but now, even in the sober colors she had chosen, the richness of furs and silks enhanced her. There were some women who, when they were raised suddenly from obscurity, wore their clothes awkwardly, like borrowed feathers. Not so Madame de Maintenon.

She smiled; she knew what troubled him. "Your Majesty exercises himself without cause," she said gently. "Believe me, the Dauphine is not unhappy. There is a certain kind of nature that withdraws from the light; she is not suited to Courts, and she will occupy herself with reading, and with playing the lute. There are many worse occupations."

"But she is young!" said Louis. "When I was young they all wanted to dance."

How difficult it was for him to change! Françoise watched him tenderly. A deep affection had come to her for him, such as she might have given to a stubborn little child. Often she would see him in Louis-Auguste, and Louis-Auguste in the King. It was the partiality of the governess, she told herself wryly. There was really more of his mother in the engaging ways of Maine.

The Dauphine's dislike troubled Françoise. It had never been openly mentioned; only, combing those sleek dark locks of a morning, she felt it in the silence that must be endured. Madame de Richelieu, who at Françoise' own persuasion of the King had been allotted the appointment of *dame d'honneur,* could occasionally break this silence with her chatter of things inconsequential; Françoise could not. More than ever she felt her helplessness in making small talk. It required a warmer air for talk to grow and flourish, there is no germination from frozen seed. She could no more have thought of the ordinary, everyday things to say to Madame la Dauphine de Bavière than she could have danced spontaneously in the King's ballet.

She must have appeared cold and by her manner have frightened or chilled the young woman. She strove in every way to placate and please her, to win her liking, but without success.

She did not find out the reason until one day when, in passing from her own apartments into the Dauphine's, she heard voices, and hesitated at the door. The name mentioned had been the King's; there might be private business.

Then: "Do you suppose," said a voice clearly, "that he comes here every day to see your Royal Highness?" Silvery, mocking laughter. "Look again, my dear!"

The voice was that of Athénaïs. Françoise felt the color rise to her face. Madame had been much about the young Dauphine, more so since the King's visits. She had thought—

Other voices. "The *dame d'atour!* A *parvenue. . . .*"

"Worse than that, a woman of no virtue, for all she apes respectability."

"A whited sepulcher," said Athénaïs.

"Dear Madame, you should know, who rescued her from the gutter."

"And I," said a little, carping voice; Madame de Richelieu, who had liked her chocolate hot in bed.

"An adder, without gratitude." The words of Louvois came coolly. How strange to find a man in that circle! He would have escorted Madame la Marquise here.

"A friend of Ninon," sniggered someone.

"Villarceaux kept her, among others, at his country château for some time."

"It goes without saying . . . Scarron . . . a *mariage blanc.* . . ."

"They say the husband encouraged it. Grist to his mill, the *monde,* always."

"She gave out oats for the d'Albret horses."

"Constant d'Aubigné. . . ."

". . . and the brother, who is also profligate. How she has advanced him! The Governor of Cognac . . . and his wife, they say, is impossible."

"*She* was reared Huguenot," said Louvois.

"All these cattle change when it suits them."

"So servile to the King. . . ." Sniggers.

"The angle of religion is a new one."

"The old slut!" said Liselotte.

"After all you had done, Athénaïs. . . ."

"Seducing even the children!"

Still and cold; frozen almost, into an impossibility of movement, all sense resolved into hearing of the words that bit and wriggled and corroded. Those women, seated in a circle about the bride, poisoning her mind with lies made from twisting of the truth. Louvois, with his little drops of venom, fashioned from his dislike of herself and his passion, a well-known one, for Madame la Marquise. Rumor, a Virgilian monster, striding about the corridors of Versailles and over the roofs of Paris. The widow Scarron has succeeded where we failed. We will claw out the widow Scarron's eyes.

"Maintenon. The price of—"

"Hush, my dear, it isn't a respectable word."

"And to put her near your Highness!"

"Of all sins, I think that hypocrisy is the worst," said Athénaïs.

Françoise suddenly opened the door and went in. Her heart had stopped hammering and the color in her face was calm. She made her obeisance to Madame la Dauphine and sat down by her at the *tabouret* as though nothing had happened. The conversation continued sweetly and naturally about other things. The only honesty was the look of aversion which she saw in the Bavarian's flat dark eyes.

She took up her tapestry and began to sew.

IV

IT WAS from then on that her life began to be intolerable.

If anyone had used such a term to her a little while previously, she would have smiled. Intolerable! Anything could be tolerated; hunger, beating, cruelty, coercion; poverty, loneliness, desolation of the soul. But falsehood was a new thing in her experience.

All those who had ill-used her previously had done so with good intent. She told herself that, having used the knowledge over many years as a means of lessening her resentment. Maman with her bitter memories, Madame de Neuillant with her vision that compelled; Anne of Austria who had given Françoise, unknowing, into the hands of bodily insult and spiritual fear. They had all meant well by her, but this force that was now at work meant ill. It was the devil, hiding from her round corners. So often could she feel the smell of his presence and yet never come at a sight of him. Never in one instance did the gossip halt where she could hear it, and yet she knew it was always there.

It would be possible to go mad, she thought, simply from the knowledge of injustice being stated, repeatedly and unanswered, as though it were truth. And the mouths that spoke it were red and smiling and bland, the faces that listened and reflected it were angels' faces. That was the harm of the devil, to clothe his ugliness in light.

For who would fail to believe a matter so widely spoken of? And what could she do?

She could not go away. If she did, the reports would be doubled. "She went," they would whisper, "because she was ashamed."

"My God," she would pray in solitude, "preserve to me rightness of mind."

It was so easy to allow oneself to be led away, beguiled by the repeated whisperings into that most dreary of all sloughs of despond, self-doubt. And if she were to end by believing of herself all that was now said of her she would be lost indeed.

"Mortify yourself," the Abbé said. How could she fail to do so? They had it so fiendishly clear. Her love for Maine a mockery, clothing the obviousness of her planned intent. Her mildness to Madame la Marquise deception, self-seeking; a wish to advertise herself by virtue of contrast. Her friendship, at last attained with Louis, lust; no more than that, and flanked by ambition of such long standing that they were saying she had planned to be the King's mistress ever since she had first set eyes on him that day of the wedding-entry into Paris.

"It gave her her first taste of the spectacle of high life," someone said idly.

Athénaïs was her enemy now.

In the way that the King's attained regard had been gradual, so was this change. It was not a matter of, one day, Madame is white, and the next, black. It was a question of implications, nuances; very slowly, quite unalterably changing from shade into the next. Madame Scarron is a jewel, reliable, disinterested, loyal. Madame Scarron is so quiet one might almost never know where one was with her; she is rather cold. Of course we are grateful to her, the King and I. . . . The King and Madame de Maintenon say such and such. Madame de Maintenon is so servile, always. Madame de Maintenon is a serpent that I have nourished in my bosom. And so on, to the end.

Corneille and Racine had been in the way of coming to give readings in the *salon* of Madame la Marquise. Françoise preferred Racine, Madame preferred Corneille. The King came to listen. The discussions tore Versailles. It was as easy as that for a small pebble to set a snowball rolling. Everyone became weary of the sound of the playwrights' names.

It was not very long before Athénaïs encountered Françoise and told her plainly that she would prefer her absence from the readings.

"In matters of intellect, Madame, I am as well qualified as yourself. It is unnecessary that the readings should become the subjects of common wrangling about Court. I find my salons too crowded." She smiled broadly. "Hitherto, Madame, these have been subjects on which the King and myself have preferred to differ amicably."

Françoise looked at the golden beauty of the official mistress. The late sun made an aureole behind her head, darkening the hard set of jaw and lips so that their hatred could not be seen. The likeness of Athénaïs to a lost child in the dark came again to her mind and she remembered the first time she had ever seen her, and wondered what would be the last.

"How we could all hate, and destroy ourselves in hating," she thought sadly. She had spent many hours in her closet praying that that evil at least might be driven out of her heart, and with much vigilance it had been.

But, as before, it became necessary to preserve appearances. Therefore when an impertinent questioner demanded of her, on the next occasion of the readings, why she was not present, she said no more than she must.

"I am not further permitted to appear at these mysteries," she replied coldly.

She passed on. The questioner, somewhat taken aback, turned and stared at her retreating figure in something the same manner as the *laitier* had once done on the steps of the Hôtel Richelieu.

"A cold reward," he murmured, "the widow Scarron."

And then, "It will not be long before the King turns his eyes elsewhere."

V

"Her name," said Athénaïs, "is Angélique, and she is quite incomparable."

She leaned back idly among the cushions, and gazed up at the King. Louis had a little box of enameled silver in his hand and was examining its surface with a forefinger. Françoise, who sat near the window, stabbed at her tapestry frame. She had been bidden here this afternoon and was uncertain why, but Madame's sugary greeting had aroused her suspicions.

"She is up to something," she decided. The prim woolen birds who sat facing one another on her canvas stared, in agreement, from their symmetrical trees. Stitching at them, she was aware of the room's patent weariness. Everyone in it was wearied of everyone else, and there was no escape from anything. The King was tired of his mistress. Athénaïs was weary of the King. He had made love to her in exactly the same manner almost every afternoon for twelve years. The Court was weary in its innermost soul of them both and because, also, the new Dauphine brought no promise of gaiety such as everyone had long since ceased to expect from the Queen. And Françoise, the *dame d'atour,* was weary also.

She looked at the pouting spoiled faces, seeing the old unmasking of Circe's horde. At her feet sat Madame de Thianges, the Marquise's sister, with her loud talk. The carefully coiffured head that was a shade darker than Madame's nodded, always, over the exchange of little pieces of scandal with Madame d'Heudicourt. Even that friend of old days seemed predatory now, with her sharp profile beginning to resemble that of a parrot. Both women were sewing because she, Françoise, sewed.

261

Françoise stifled a sigh. It was a wearisome thing to start a fashion which would be followed not because the slaves to it like it, as she did, but because it was the thing to do. For the same reason every woman wore a little jeweled cross about her throat and it was called, Françoise had learned to her amusement, a maintenon. If they would act up to the standards implied by what they wore it would be different. Had any of these women hearts at all?

She heard the whispered talk now, speculating about the new beauty from Provence whom Athénaïs swore to be fairer than Venus and more graceful than Diana. It was sufficiently rare for Athénaïs to draw attention to the beauty of another woman, and everyone listened out of sheer astonishment. Presently the talk veered and a little draft, thankfully felt in the airless heat of the rooms, swayed the hangings and the long perspectives where fountains played. Only the King's eyes, curiously keen in the bored face, lifted from their contemplation for an instant; he set the box down on Madame's dressing-table.

"If you are the foremost to praise Mademoiselle Angélique, she must indeed be something extraordinary," he murmured. "When are we to behold this marvel?"

Athénaïs smiled, and languished at him. "Here, if you will; tomorrow; if not then, the day after. I can assure you it is a sight to be compared with nothing in this world. Silks, gold and silver also come from Provence. Is my geography correct, Madame de Maintenon?"

Françoise inclined her head. She had sensed the triumph in the other's tone. The furniture in the room had suddenly the appearance of crouching beasts, ornate and gilded, with dragons' legs and claws.

Marie-Angélique d'Escorailles de Roussille made her début at Court some time later, under the protection of Madame de Montespan. When Athénaïs had warned everyone to expect something quite beyond the ordinary she had not lied. To compare Mademoiselle's complexion to milk and roses was to sully a quality not of this earth by reference to mere flora and cows. Angélique's hair, which some classed as her only defect because its auburn was a shade too warm for perfection, cascaded about her shoulders in spirals of molten bronze. Her eyes were blue and languishing; her lashes of such length that they swept her cheeks. When she spoke, it was with an adorable lisp; and this celestial quality in her speech was the more prized in that she very seldom had anything much to say. "An angel, too rare for this earth," declared the gentlemen. The ladies said nothing.

Marie-Angélique lost no time. It was soon observed that she had eyes for no one but the King. Uncharitable people might have deduced that she had only one purpose in life. When Louis spoke to her she swooned with pleasure; when he looked in her direction she blushed like a rose. How different it all was from the stormy scenes of the Marquise, the piety of Maintenon!

Everyone watched. The King put extra plumes in his hat. In that Court where for him every voice was soft and every word dripped honey, Mademoiselle Angélique's tones were so mellifluous as scarcely to be heard at all. But they were heard, fairly soon, behind a yew-tree in the Palace garden, and intermingled with their bashful protestations enough, at any rate, of His Majesty's entreaties to make it certain what was the nature of the discourse. The Court hid its smiles behind its hands, not only for the discarded Marquise but also for the widow Scarron; reminding itself, as it did so, how it had always maintained that there is no substitute for youth.

The King made Marie-Angélique a duchess—the Duchesse de Fontanges. Now, everything was again as it had been in the days that all but the youngest could remember. The Roi Soleil, richly attired in his great plumed beaver and with jewels and orders sparkling on his coat, would escort the glittering new mistress to plays, balls, water-parties and *fêtes champêtres;* the music of violins was borne upon the night breeze, the woods were full of lovers, the world danced. And through it all Fontanges danced also, young and beautiful

263

and happy; known and adored about the streets of Paris by
reason of her gilt coach drawn by eight cream-colored horses.
The crowds would shout with pleasure at sight of her lovely
face at the pane, laughing with delight because she knew she
was beautiful, beloved, and wearing osprey feathers in her
hair worth a hundred and fifty thousand *écus*.

Madame la Marquise? She only smiled bewilderingly. Instead of showing anger at being ousted, she had with her
own hands dressed Mademoiselle Angélique for the Villers-
Cotterets ball. In days of old, one recalled, she had helped to
dress La Vallière. How time passed, and things resolved
themselves!

The widow Scarron had at no time been heard to say
anything.

VI

THE QUEEN summoned Françoise one day to her presence.
Mounting the stairs, she wondered at the cause of it, but not
very curiously. The days passed, she thought, and each one
brought its tasks to be got through. When that was over the
night came, and one slept. That was all, unpleasantness, and
whispering, and slanders, would pass, when all was said and
done. If one's own conscience was clear and could remain so,
the truth would win. She wondered which of them had first
carried the tales about her to Marie-Thérèse.

The stairs curved on and up. The King of France's mistress had not yet given way to his wife. Up in these rooms
on the second floor the little Spanish dwarf passed her days.
She was seldom seen now, unless going to and fro to State
occasions. Up here, these shadowed forgotten rooms; below,
the *salons* of the discarded Marquise glittering and empty.

She had left Athénaïs de Rochechouart striding up and down, up and down.

She passed the door. The Queen's men-at-arms clattered in salute. They wore padded armor and stiff high ruffs in the manner of old Spain.

"Madame."

The Queen was in bed. She sat there stiffly, the two spots of red paint standing out on her cheekbones. Her eyes had a dull filmed unhappiness. Her mouth smiled.

She held out her hand for Françoise to kiss. It was puffy with ill-health and whitened with cosmetics. By the fire two old duennas nodded. A crucifix gleamed on the wall. Near it, the Hapsburg lip of dead Philip IV jutted in its frame. His painted locks were combed carefully and hung straight down to his shoulders. They were the color of apricot.

"You are looking at the portrait of my father, the late King of Spain."

The flat weary voice pronounced its French with difficulty. The eyes were fixed on hers. What was there to say? The Queen pointed next to a second painting, hung in deeper shadow still. Cascades of that same silken hair framed a weak idiot's face with monstrous jaw and tormented eyes. "My brother," said the Queen. "He is King now."

Suddenly she began to talk, with the tumbling eagerness of the lonely person. The words fell over one another, mixed, slurred, abated. The Queen had hoped, she said, that Madame would come. She had heard so much about Madame, her devotion to the King, her goodness, her piety.

"I also keep the religious calendar," said the Queen.

The pathetic eyes never left her face. Françoise felt the shadows of the great room flicker and leap. So many unhappinesses had been here, both of the present and of long past ages, borne, in the inbred blood. Cousin married to cousin, uncle wed to niece, repeated thrice over the generations to produce that freak, that idol, on the wall. Kings of Spain! The devil was loose in that mad country, her rulers were witchridden and senile at thirty. What a heritage for Louis' son! And this poor soul. . . .

"We who love God are allies, Madame." For an instant Françoise wondered if she had done right. Marie-Thérèse, never permitted to embrace her own father except on occasions of high festival, brought up under the hoop-and-spectacles régime of Castile, would think it a solecism to have an ally; still less a friend.

But the Queen smiled.

"I have heard of you," she said again. Her eyes were trusting, like a dog's. "I never believed all that they said," she pronounced carefully. "I mean, that you were the King's mistress."

The words fell strangely, as though a child pronounced them. "Those others," said Marie-Thérèse, "have their purposes. I do not believe what they say to me. I shall tell the King that I do not believe it."

"Madame—"

She felt her color rise. Marie-Thérèse laughed a little. Her teeth were stumpy and darkened, and the gums showed. "It may not be soon," she said formally. "Next time the King comes." Her eyes filmed over; the painted mouth drooped at the corners. "He does not come now, often," said the Queen. "But when he does I shall tell him."

Her fingers clenched in resolution. One could see her mind repeating the order to itself; I shall tell him! I shall tell him! Awe of her husband had long reduced the Queen to a speechless cipher in his presence. Everyone knew that. Whether the courage would ever come to her to broach this subject to the King was a question. Françoise put out a hand.

"I beg that Madame will not trouble herself."

"No," said Marie-Thérèse stubbornly. "What I have said, I will do."

She fished under her pillow and after a moment clapped her hands, calling for Molina. One of the old women rose, shook her skirts, shuffled forward from the fireplace. A volley of Spanish followed. In the end a little flat box was found, and put into the Queen's hand.

"For you," said Marie-Thérèse. "I know what they say. If you wear it—"

"Wear it, Madame?"

Françoise' eyes filled with tears. In the box lay a little painted oval, set about with diamonds. From it simpered the face of Marie-Thérèse. She took it, carefully, out of its box. It depended from a narrow chain.

"It can be a brooch," said the Queen, "or a locket. See!"

She fastened it on Françoise' gown. Having done so, she lay back and looked at her handiwork.

"You will wear it," she said again. "Will you not? And come to see me—often. Unless—" her face fell—"unless—it is too dull here. They say you are very clever. Nevertheless it may please you to recite the Office with me, and the beads."

Hesitatingly, flickering upward, the dull eyes roved over the *dame d'atour's* face. Suddenly they showed concern. "Madame, why—?"

The *dame d'atour* was crying. Tears stood in her magnificent eyes. Marie-Thérèse was perturbed; could she have upset Madame de Maintenon? "Madame, Madame, I am stupid!" she said. She reached out a hand. "Do not—" Her voice held amazement. "But you are not to kiss my hand in that way, Madame. That is only for the King!"

Below, the footsteps of Athénaïs turned and sounded and then ceased. She was standing by a window looking down into the great park. The fountains were not visible to her; her own mind's images were clearer. She had employed a weapon, and the weapon had got out of hand. Angélique had served her turn too well. Little insipid provincial! A pretty picture . . . no wit, no fire at all. To prefer *that* to oneself; *that*, and the widow Scarron!

There were ways of ridding oneself of those one hated. Madame de Brinvilliers the poisoner had perished, but she had gone too far to avoid discovery. There were a hundred, a thousand others in Paris and throughout France who employed the same methods and no one knew . . . the woman, La Voisine, would tell her perhaps, or the sorcerer Filastre, who was more subtle.

"It is no crime," she told herself. "Or if so, then in a good cause."

The sound of laughter, borne from far away, came to her. She clenched her hands furiously till the sharp nails hurt her palms.

VII

FRANÇOISE HAD SEEN the King in many moods, but she was not prepared for his terrible anger when the whisperings about the circle of Madame la Dauphine were made known.

No one knew who had told him. Françoise herself never mentioned the Queen. She had gone about the Court in these days wearing the miniature of Marie-Thérèse like a talisman. With this sign of highest protection, many of the tongues would be stilled.

But it was not to be left at that and the little Spanish woman had, as she promised, conquered her fears and spoken of it to the husband she adored and of whom she was in such terror. In that marriage of an eagle and a wren much of necessity had been lacking, but Louis respected her. Therefore when Françoise was summoned to the weeping gray-faced young woman who was the Dauphine, she knew that everything had had attention. . . .

"Madame, Madame." The words were hardly heard for gusty sobs. The King stood, white-faced and implacable, by the Dauphine's bed. "Madame, I—Madame, I have said —Madame, I have listened . . . to things . . ."

"Madame la Dauphine would wish to tender you her apologies for certain scurrilous rumors which have arisen, and been spread from her circle."

How harsh the voice was! Although Françoise was the injured party, she knew a moment's fear. To have been the perpetrator and to have had to face those steely eyes, that presence! This was not the patient man who listened to the tirades of Madame la Marquise. This was the eagle, royal, cruel, relentless. Whoever had erred would suffer. Françoise felt pity for the Dauphine, who was *enceinte*.

"How was her Royal Highness to know?" she said gently. "She had come among strangers."

"Placed there by *my* orders, at *my* choosing! A certain person—"

The sibilants in the royal speech hissed coldly, the short clipped vowels scourged. Madame de Richelieu, the King insisted, should go. "Her gratitude is indeed singular! It was you yourself, Madame de Maintenon, who obtained for her this post at Court."

Françoise pleaded with him to reinstate Madame de Richelieu. He was so angry, she saw, that his hands trembled as they held the plumed hat. The lines that had begun to run from nose to mouth seemed deeply carved; the skin was blue-pale. He looked older. He was like a thoroughbred horse, she thought, that was being run to death. Suddenly her own ills seemed unimportant.

"Dear sire, if you send this person away from Court the world will say that I engineered it, and that the libels were true. Is that desirable? How much better to leave things as they are, showing thereby that there is no truth in them."

She broke off. Louis was looking at her strangely. "Have you no vindictiveness?" he said. "No desire for revenge? How unlike most women!"

"*Ach, ach!*" wailed the Dauphine. She had never been so much frightened in her life. The child, she was sure, stirred. Perhaps there would be a miscarriage. There also she would have failed, in this place where nobody liked her, refused to leave her alone when all that she asked was solitude and to be allowed to improve her mind by reading. And now soon again she would have to endure the company of this strange tall cold woman with the disturbing dark eyes. What was it that they had between them, her *dame d'atour* and the King? They looked at one another now as if—as if—

269

"It is Madame la Marquise who was the mistress," thought the Dauphine firmly. She felt melancholy settling on her and shifted, a little, in her bed. To have the curtains drawn against the daylight, and lie here for a while in the blessed half-dark till her woman, Bessola, came! That way she need not see the ugly stupid French faces, hear the foolish inconsequential talk. How pleasant it would be to be dead, in a narrow coffin! So much more agreeable than to live, and one day have to be Queen of France. She had mentioned that one day to her husband and he only wheezed with laughter and said that one must be alive to eat. They only thought here of eating and drinking, and making love, and making heirs. Pigs, all of them; pigs, the human race. She hated it. To die, to die! Pigs, pigs. . . .

"She can remain, then, as you so wish it," said the King. He still spoke of Madame de Richelieu.

VIII

ONE DAY Françoise received an abrupt summons from the King. She went, not very willingly; he was in Madame la Marquise's rooms, and surely she, Françoise, had had her fill of alarums and excursions for a little while. . . . It was in the heat of summer, and she felt very tired.

The room resembled a stage-set at the Théâtre du Marais. Standing with his hands tucked resignedly into his gown-sleeves was Père La Chaise, the King's confessor. His high, pale forehead was thrown into perplexed wrinkles. Raging up and down the room was Madame la Marquise. The Duchesse de Fontanges sobbed hysterically by the window. The King, with flushed cheeks, endeavored to calm both of them. Athénaïs turned on her rival with the violence of a fishwife.

Fontanges sat up suddenly and began to bawl abuse.

"Mesdames!" said Françoise.

The King took Fontanges above the elbows and piloted her forcibly from the room. Above her head, his eyes met those of Madame de Maintenon. "Help me with *her!*" they said. Françoise made her way toward the volcanic Marquise and tried, unsuccessfully, to calm her. In the end she achieved this object by the method of slapping her face.

"She is expecting a child," said Louis.

"They both are."

He fidgeted with his gloves; he was ill at ease. The woman by the window neither spoke again nor moved, and he felt the reproach of her silence. What did she think him, this quiet person? A profligate, a libertine?

She saw himself in her glass. He had rouged his cheeks again a little because Angélique, one day, had told him he was too sallow, and he had suddenly seen himself beside her glowing youth. Beautiful little torment, deriding him even while she caused him to put his hand in his pocket again, again, and again . . . but he saw himself in the mirror now and he resembled his brother Philippe, who aped women. A raddled roué, close to middle age.

But Madame de Maintenon was older than himself by five years. He looked at her placid face, and her complexion that showed nothing of the ravages of time. She was plump, a little, but that was pleasant. In spite of his chagrin, he smiled.

"You could give many of our younger beauties a pointer, Madame." She was a comely woman, he thought, standing there by the window. His eyes, jaded with the brightness of satin and gems, rested with thankfulness on the gown she wore; richly bordered, it was true, with deep fur, but modest and pleasing to the eye. Her hood was black, knotted loosely on her breast and revealing, set amid her hair, a commode of lace. Louis knew pleasure, watching her.

But Madame showed no pleasure in her turn and he knew that she was displeased with him. The sensation of that was novel and not unwelcome. Whatever happened, *she* would not cajole him—lie to him, with the purpose only of obtaining more money, more jewels! No, her ambitions lay in other things; things of the mind and of the spirit, desirable matters that would last. . . .

What would *he* have become in ten years, if—

Suddenly, harshly, he spoke aloud. "They weary me—all these women!"

Still she did not answer. Louis strode to the hearth and, holding his hands to the fire that blazed there, warmed them; the sun had gone and it was chilly. He did not look back over his shoulder; the woman would be still there, silent, judging him. "Yes, you see me," he said aloud, "and to what it has brought me—all this! You warned me, did you not? You and Bossuet."

He shrugged into the flames. "Well . . . you have seen and heard it. Sometimes I see myself as an aging man, an old fool, fair game for women who will deceive me . . . in the manner, I infer, that they always do kings, persuading them that they are for all time young and lovable."

"Kings, then, should use their common sense in not allowing the persuasion."

"Ah," he said impatiently, "there are things you do not understand. How could you? Angélique . . . you heard her today. She made me ashamed, but at other times she enthralls me . . . torments me. I cannot be free of her. The lure of the flesh, Madame . . . they say it is of the devil. God gave me a good deal of the devil's portion." He smiled, but his eyes were cold. "Sometimes, as today, I have the warning of experience; I see the look in the eyes of *mon père,* and in your own. At such times, with the nearness of the things of God, I feel, in the knowledge of my lust, the pains of hell. Other times it is as with a curtain drawn, and I see nothing."

He wheeled about. "And then I return to her again and she will have a gesture, a look, a pretty, adorable pout, that beguiles me . . . and she is an enchanting creature! She has no guile, no subtlety, she is entirely at my disposal, and she is so beautiful in the clothes I buy her, or in none."

He stared at her helplessly. "What does your Majesty require of me?" she said. Her tone was cold.

"What do I want?" A little frown, as though with pain, came between his eyes. "These damned heads . . . go to Angélique, Madame, persuade her . . ."

"To do what? To leave Your Majesty? I will attempt no less."

"Madame—" Why did he fear her scorn so? "Go to her," he said again. "Tell her—ah, do not look at me so! She is young . . . be her friend, if you can—you are so calm, so wise. Her family—"

He paused. The career intended for Angélique by her family had become well known. The King drew himself up and spoke clearly.

"Persuade her of the delicacies of her condition. Tell her of the harm she does herself by such scenes. Good God," he exploded suddenly, "have you women no sympathy for one another at such times?"

"I am scarcely qualified to dictate to the Duchesse with regard to a condition of which I personally know nothing."

"*Bon Dieu*," he said, impatiently, "did you not nurse Athénaïs through all hers?"

As he spoke, he regretted it. No wonder she thought of him—thus; small wonder if she had little regard for him, having no care for Courts and preferment. But what a friend to have! Rigid, they said she was; not for the first time an awareness of that inflexible quality came to him. Placid, disinterested, well-informed, reliable; where could one find a word that alone would describe this woman? Suddenly, and without any sense of ridicule, he found it; she was solid, Madame de Maintenon. "Your solidity." Should he address her as such? But it was not a time for jesting . . . he had seen those dark eyes of hers light with appreciation at other times, but not now.

"I will go, then, as Your Majesty wishes it." She spoke so low that he could scarcely hear her. He began to utter thanks, but the words were stilled. Françoise curtsied deeply and went from the room.

*   *   *

273

Fontanges had had her women unlace her and loosen her hair, which spread like a bronze cloud over her white, exposed shoulders. The bedgown she affected served more to reveal her beautiful breasts than conceal them. It was of priceless lace, as fine as cobwebs; small silver knots were threaded in the mesh. She looked like a lovely, exotic insect, disposed on her couch; pagan, quite unheeding, and lacking any form of mind but instinct.

Françoise spoke quietly. Fontanges turned her own foot this way and that. It was shod in a silver slipper, very tiny, heelless and covered at the front and along the seams with roses made from minute brilliants. In Spain, Louis had told her, grandees had been used to have even the soles of their shoes studded with real gems. What was this old woman saying?

This afternoon? A scene? Yes, it had been most unfortunate. Madame la Marquise was always making scenes. "She knows very well that she is growing old, and therefore getting sour; it's a natural process, like making vinegar." *That* hadn't been her own remark, it had been the Marquis de Chamarante's; how Angélique had laughed when she heard it! Chamarante said the most amusing things.

Angélique pouted, remembering that she was supposed to be ill. The King had sent doctors to pound her chest and belly. Heaven knew that if it were true she was with child they would do it very little good with their physic. She might be; she didn't know. She giggled. It was quite likely.

She moved her body, feeling satisfaction in its softness. They had bathed her that morning in asses' milk. Several ladies of the Court had come to pay their compliments. The King of England's mistresses, they said, received all callers in their baths, but Louis was strait-laced about such things. He was like one's father, really. Almost, that was. Madame de Maintenon was still talking.

What was that? *Leave Court?* Had the woman taken leave of her senses?

Angélique sat up and listened incredulously.

Afterward Françoise realized what a fool she had been. She had forgotten to whom she spoke in the urgency of her mission. She had spoken to that preening, pouting child as if Fontanges were not an idiot enslaved by her own body; as though there were more beneath that molten-bronze hair than wantonness, greed and self-seeking. All his days Louis would suffer from such women, unless by the arm of God. All his days . . . such was the fate of kings.

And Fontanges, her cherry-lips parted, had listened at first in sheer surprise, and then, by degrees, had hardened, fidgeted, laughed, coughed nervously and played with the little knots of silver on her gown.

"You sound as though parting with a passion were as easy as taking off one's shift," she said innocently.

When Françoise left her she was posturing before a mirror, trying the different degrees of fascination her full lips could achieve. She had begun to cough again, with a little light dry sound; her women, fussing and darting like moths, were again round her.

Fontanges began to wither and the King's passion faded.

They said many things. They said it was witchcraft. Much of that was known in Paris; a little philtre, a vial, being dropped in the food. Or it might be by ill-wishing. An image fashioned out of wax, with pins stuck in it, would warp and fade so.

Who could hate Fontanges? The Court shrugged, whispered. Madame de Montespan had disappeared for four days last March. Once near Saint-Cloud a coach had stopped, and a woman on the road had handed packages in at the window. The coach was Madame's. Someone had seen her face. These things were known in secret, never brought out into full light of day.

The image of a coach brought other horror. It had been, for Fontanges, a tale of Cinderella going to the ball. Now midnight had struck on all her pretensions. Enchantment had paled from the pumpkin-body, the escort of rats. One could see her still, driving between Paris and Port-Royal.

She was with child, which drained her vitality. Some said she had a rot of the lungs. "I spit blood," she said pitifully.

The voice was the same, high, childish and wandering. Otherwise she was totally changed. The bright metallic hair still, after many months, sprang from her fleshless skull. It seemed that even the thin blood was visible, coursing through the temple-veins, against the bone. Her hands were like claws.

Always the plea was the same. Why did not the King come? The child's mind held in a body of old age, death grasping backward with its hold on life, questioned and demanded always. The King, the King! He had loved her; now that she was no longer beautiful he could not have forgotten, would not fail to come!

Louis had not forgotten. When she was dying he would come. There were butterflies that only lived for a day, having no other use but beauty. And by then there were other matters clawing, like cold hands, at the King's soul. The arm of God had pulled away the curtain.

"Poor Fontanges," said the Court, and forgot.

IX

THE *chambre ardente,* which the King had opened for inquiry into the widespread poisonings of Paris, sat, month in, month out, in the Palais de l'Arsenal.

M. de la Reynie, the Chief of Police, long-chinned, patient and shrewd-eyed, presided. Beneath his hand was a paper, signed by the King. Every now and again La Reynie would look at it, finding support there when some woman of very high rank was brought in, to be interviewed and questioned.

"For the public good I command you to discover as soon as possible the traffic in poisons, with the purpose of striking at the evil's root. *Justice exacte, sans aucune distinction de personnes, de conditions ni de sexe. . . ."* And a remembrance of the cold blue eyes of the man who had written that would come to La Reynie and fortify him in the assault needed to break down the highbred composure, even insolence, of some marchioness or *Baronne*.

For these were the guilty ones. It was less surprising than it might have been a year or two ago, before that prominent little *empoisonneuse*, Madame la Marquise de Brinvilliers, had got rid of her own father and two brothers and one was uncertain exactly how many more. But that had been enough to finish the Marquise on the scaffold, in spite of her noble blood. Mesdames had clustered about the windows of Paris to see her in the cart, and they had jostled one another to watch the little, broken figure make its penance with a lit candle on the steps of Notre-Dame. But to be in the same position oneself would be a very different thing. Fear claimed mesdames behind their fans and in their carriages.

It had all been so harmless! As often as not one had gone in search of a little laughter. It was *ennuyante*, as everyone knew, to yawn in the salons of Versailles all day. And so one night mesdames—and mesdemoiselles also, in little hooded groups, giggling and secret—had stolen out, and into a plain coach, which then drove on along the flat familiar road to Paris, and after that roads grew less familiar, narrower and foul so that going was slow. But in the end they had reached the house in the Quartier Saint-Denis where great flambeaux burned at the door, and lanterns of different colors hung in the garden. It was jolly and hospitable, not in the least furtive or unpleasant. And the big red-faced woman whom everyone called La Voisin was amusing, with her *risqué* jokes and her knowledge of everybody at Court, and the fantastic robe she wore, all embroidered with golden eagles, that someone said had cost fifteen thousand livres.

But of course she did not wear this *robe d'empereur* for every caller, and one had to have the *entrée* to be allowed to observe it . . . and by then, somehow, it had become habit to go, and the little powders had become so indispensable that it would have been tedious to have to be again without them. Where was the harm in pleasure, after all?

And if indeed any harm should come there were other powders to take. These cost more and made one for a time feel ill, as La Voisin had warned. But they cured the trouble . . . or if they did not, there were still other things that could be done.

Sometimes, those who knew had to admit, things beyond this stage became a little frightening. And yet in one's own heart one could giggle, still, knowing that it was only La Voisin and her dressing-up, and the incantations and other things were simply to make an impression. And the old rascal she called M. l'Abbé had so enormously swollen a nose, the color of beetroot, that one laughed still. . . . But it was possibly a little shocking to hear the Mass as he used it. And in the concentration needed to say a Paternoster backward, there was very little leisure to inquire about the other things that were going on. In any case La Voisin had one's name and address by that time and it might be unpleasant if any fuss were made, so late.

So evil filtered, trickled into every chamber-wall, like water into loose soil. A monstrous weed, choking the life from the tree-roots of France. So La Reynie saw it; many laughed at him. Poisonings? They knew nothing of sudden deaths, stomach-aches, inheritances, blackmail. All they had done was spur on, by means of potions, a jaded or unwilling lover. It was true that a dose of too great strength, or one too often repeated, would go far to drive a man from his reason and cause him to behave regrettably in public. But no woman who was not a fool would wish her *amant* to behave so. Everyone had been most careful.

Some were sent to the galleys. Some were acquitted. Of those who were not, several cut their throats. Unknown persons who had no one to trouble about them languished in prison. Important ones were exiled. The questionings ordinary and extraordinary reached out, clutching higher and ever higher on the ladder of great names. The King's old love, Olympe de Soissons, the Cardinal's niece, left Paris. In the torture-chambers beneath the city's stones, La Voisin writhed and screamed. When the time came she would go cheerfully to her own execution; Guillaume, the public hangman, was a lover of hers. But in the meantime things were less pleasant. La Voisin looked at her jellied thumbs and wished in a way that she had remained quietly with her late husband, who had been a jeweler. The good days were over; what more could she tell? "Ah, *mon Dieu, mon Dieu,* do not put that on me again!" A name, a name! She had given thousands. . . .

"Who else?" The stern face of La Reynie showed clearly, and the light from a lantern flaring upward from his chin, throwing the top of his perruque into twin peaks like the devil's. "Do not call on God, Madame. He is not used to your attentions."

"Satanas! Satanas!"

But no help came. In the end she gave all the other names. Madame la Marquise would be angered, but she had done her best to shield her. In any case there was no more harm they could do. . . .

La Reynie nodded, satisfied. He ordered them to loose the screws.

X

MADAME DE MONTESPAN was laughing.

She lay back on her silk-covered couch, and gave her laughter rein. The gown she wore was of ivory color and accentuated her look of fairness, of belonging to the sun.

Madame de Maintenon, whose realm was night, sat opposite. The analogy came to Athénaïs amid her laughter.

Nevertheless she was grateful to the woman. Last year— was it? they had had differences. It was no use pretending that they had not involved the King. But now, with Fontanges spitting blood from the lungs in Port-Royal, these were settled; at least for the time being. There was, moreover, no denying that Madame had been uncommonly kind at Maintenon, where Athénaïs had gone at her invitation to be delivered of the Comte de Toulouse.

The Marquise stretched her body, feeling the return of suppleness to the muscles after the weakness, a little more protracted than usual this time, that followed childbirth. This latest child was a little angel, everyone said so; with golden hair and a placid disposition. He had been portrayed already, lying naked except for a wreath of flowers. He was beautiful, perfect, lovable, and gave no trouble to anyone. All the same, she hoped there would be no more births.

A shadow crossed her face. And yet—if that were so! It was impossible that she should not get the King back, this time again, as always.

Her lover. Yes, Louis was *her* lover. Had been, ever since she had wrested him from La Vallière. Now that the inquiries had come to light about the woman La Voisin, and her lover Guibourg, it was well not to remember that absurd affair of two pigeons' hearts, sacrificed with the names on at the altar of Saint-Sévérin. Louis and Louise, offered up to the devil at midnight. Well, she also had been young then, and it had all worked out as she had planned, in the end. Did Louise de la Vallière ever remember now, between terce and nones, office and vespers? Amusing to think of all that at this date; of course the affair would at any rate have had an ending. Little insipid thing out of Touraine. . . .

"Why were you laughing?" said Madame de Maintenon.

Athénaïs turned. "Oh, I was thinking of Lauzun. You knew he had been freed? Why, yes, at last! He came here—" she laughed on, helplessly—"in, believe it or not, his old uniform of the *Becs-des-Corbins* that he was wearing in the year he was first imprisoned. Imagine what a spectacle he created! That, and his uncombed greasy hair, and his scarlet nose! The women of course are all round him. Mademoiselle has not seen him yet. She had prepared herself to go and meet him in a triumphal carriage decked with flowers and drawn by six white horses, but Louis restrained her."

Françoise watched the lovely face. Not a tremor, not a doubt crossed it at mention of the King.

Her rooms were empty. Either she had the security of her own innocence or else had become so lost as to be unaware of guilt. The gilt-legged furniture waited, unchanging; the woven hangings did not stir. To Françoise the room was full of memories. Here she herself had come in the old days when, humbly and leading young children by the hand, she would experience the splendors of Versailles for an hour. Here bonds had been made and broken, passion echoed and laughter rung, like the lost woman's high, heedless laughter now. Fortunes had been won and spilled here; wit had sparkled, the spirit of an age been caught like a gnat in amber. Yet of all that which should have clung, like steeped sunlight, to the very walls, less remained than the growing shadow. The foreknowledge was with her, incontrovertible as doom, that after many years men would stand here and say nothing but this. "These were the rooms of Montespan, the King's mistress, the poisoner. She sold her soul to the devil, her body to the Black Mass. In the end she was forsaken; she smoldered to ashes alone. Her portraits were destroyed, her documents banned. There is no memory of her."

And the woman laughed and talked on of other things, and Françoise listened.

XI

How HAD Françoise first seen Louis since then? How had she known of what he felt?

In that Court where everyone whispered and guessed, there was no certainty, watching the King's face. Françoise, with a hundred others, had seen him go by; eagle-nosed, impassive, cold-eyed, formal, on the way to the great dinners of State, down the grand staircase of Versailles. The thousand eyes of the peacock's tail watched and waited. They grew weary after a time, discerning nothing.

"Is it true?" the voices whispered. "Is it true?"

Some would come to her, vapid, goggling, curious and eager for news of which they dared not ask. Perhaps the *Maintenaint* would know. Oh, undoubtedly! And so she felt herself under the same glare of inquiry as Louis must be. Every movement, every expression was watched. She gave no sign.

"The *chambre ardente* has been dissolved," said some. Why?"

"The mother of the King's children is involved," said others.

They sneered. *Justice . . . sans aucune distinction!* It didn't apply, apparently, to all contingencies. Madame de Montespan still had her rooms. The King's mistress had not been thrown into prison, questioned, humiliated in public, dragged in the mud. The King's dignity must be preserved. Exactly so!

Only Françoise knew what torment he must have endured, remembering the things that no one, except one other, knew.

He had sent for her one day. She had known then, seeing

his face dark and featureless against the light. The stiff immobility of his figure was like a doll's.

He bowed. Françoise made her obeisances, and went to him slowly. The room was heavy and silent, the desk at which he worked for so many hours each day scattered with used quills.

"You have come," she heard him say.

Presently he asked her what she had heard. It was easy to answer, and useless pretending that nothing was being said at all. "I have heard very little," she told him. She caught sight of his face and her words came softly. "Nothing is known, for certain," she told him, as if speaking to a child. "If Your Majesty wills it so, nothing ever need be."

"Will?" he said. "I have no will, no mind. They were dissolved by a harlot who bought my body by the use of certain drugs."

Suddenly, as though they had been in a court of law, he began to talk rapidly, precisely and coldly of it. He was like a machine reciting facts. Personality, feeling and reticence were absent. She listened, full of pity for him. Deep shock, she knew, deep mental pain, could do such things to a man.

"She procured me," he said again. "Athénaïs."

"Are the facts certain?" She was like a defending counsel, prodding skilfully. Her purpose was less to elicit information than to relieve his mind. Gradually the glaze of shock in his eyes receded and he resembled once more the man she knew. He had been, she guessed, the prisoner of his own thoughts these many days and nights.

"Long past," he nodded briefly. "Thirteen years ago she first went to conjure the devil. At the time, I had for my mistress Louise de la Vallière. You will remember that she —" His voice thickened, then cleared again. Sister Louise with her girdle of cord and her sandals receded once more into the shadows. The King went on.

"By means of conjuring the Black Mass, she—Athénaïs— became persuaded she could conjure me. She had several times attempted to win my attention, but I avoided her. I thought her bold, I remember." He laughed a little. "Dear God, if I had known!"

That young woman, the young golden she-wolf of the days of the Flanders campaigns, of Saint-Germain and Fontainebleau, had been persistent. "She beguiled me, I remember, by her cleverness at *bouts-rimés*, her quick play at cards. Poor little Louise had no talents. She would watch, in the evenings, while we two played."

Françoise listened. Absently, he had motioned her to a chair. A room of long ago was before her; the lit sconces shone on two fair heads, both of them intent on the King. Louise de la Vallière had watched her lover slipping, slipping, into the hold of that other who held the cards. It had been a thing of the devil. She heard the King's voice now.

"We played . . . then; and later made love. She was becoming, you see, desperate. She had already given her body to be an altar. It happened twice, if not oftener. Once she went to a house in the Rue de la Tannerie. . . ."

Oneself, coming down that gray street in the dawn long ago, had seen a woman, hooded, cloaked and very beautiful. A lost child, hurrying already toward the dark. Françoise was silent, hands clasped in her lap. She must listen, and say nothing. Enough had been told.

"The other time was at a house near Montlhéry, this time well out of town. I had already taken some note of her, you see. It behooved her to be circumspect."

Suddenly, uncontrollably, the muscles at one side of his mouth began to twitch. It was not laughter nor the ghost of laughter.

"All her hate," he said, "was for Louise de la Vallière. You saw Louise; she wouldn't have harmed a soul. The strength of that woman's hatred was astonishing. She had pigeons' hearts offered up, in the church of Saint-Sévérin. And the death of Louise was applied for on human bones."

He talked on, relieving himself of details revolting to his mind; surprising himself with his own insistence. Was this himself, Louis of France, who had hitherto said of a distasteful thing only, "I will see!" and left it at that, not sullying the understanding that was so fastidious, so royal, with mud scraped from the gutters of the streets? But now the things of which he unburdened himself would have turned the stomachs of brothel-keepers.

Yet this woman, his friend, listened. She did not protest or swoon.

"Certain extremes have not come to pass."

Her voice, dry, even with humor, answered so his description of the terrible oath incumbent on Athénaïs, as suppliant, in the Black Mass. "The Queen was *not* barren. Your son has lived. *His* son is healthy. You should thank God for many things. All this will pass. Believe me. I *know* it will be so."

She went to him. He had begun to shake like a man with ague and she cloaked her mind and speech with that deliberate dryness, sustaining him.

"Your Majesty."

Her fingers were beneath his arm, to steady him. He turned suddenly and grasped her hand, as though for protection. In their proximity they breathed as one; she felt the tension in him communicate itself to her.

"That woman La Voisin I saw once, at Saint-Germain. Her appearance was so extraordinary I asked who she was. A great gross pouting-faced woman, dressed *à la Turque.* They say she makes lovers of priests who have forsaken their calling." His voice rose uncontrollably. "More than two thousand corpses of babies were found in the garden of her house at Villeneuve. She would hold lantern-fêtes, carouses, there." He shuddered. "The woman's own daughter had a child once. She had to smuggle it unacknowledged out of the house in case it would be used for—for— Ah, *mon Dieu,* they would cut the babies' throats and use the blood, as it dripped, still warm in the chalice for the devil!"

"Hush," she said. "Hush, Louis." She allowed him to cling to her. Never before in her experience of him had he spoken so, without reticence, without a vestige of *hauteur;* this man who had been stripped naked, ridiculed to his inmost self before the eyes of his *commissaires de police;* in his own eyes deprived not only of manhood but of kingship itself. After thirteen years of being the woman's lover, of fathering her children, he had found out this. . . .

It was as if he read her thoughts.

"What is there for me now?" he said, with a curious considering humbleness, alien to him. "Everywhere I go there will be laughter. I have always loathed the thought of that kind of laughter."

He stared at the empty wall. "Everything I have loved was half her flesh," he said. "Cannot you see what will happen? Day by day, year by year, as the whispers grow, they will say 'Ah, he was a great king except in the one instance! Once a harlot bought him through trafficking for drugs with a gross old *procureuse* in the Quartier Saint-Denis.' And they will laugh."

She strove with him, and with the pity in her mind that denied the heralding of a great light. "Wretches under torture make strange confessions," she said.

Louis shrugged, laughed, dropped her hands. "How much pity there is in you! No, I've proof within myself—within *me*—nourished as I've apparently been on bats' blood, cantharides, toad-muck, vile and nameless things. The very cupbearer was in her pay, she cozened him and he brought me—that—in my food."

He turned to her; his eyes were dark. "Blood, bone, marrow are made of it! I can't be rid of that vileness if I live a hundred years . . . the very fact of it . . . a part of *me* . . . do you remember, Madame, how I had headaches, and how I blamed the essences some women wore? It was not that, it was—it was—ah, that damnation!"

He began to move up and down the room, as though movement could shed the pollution from him more rapidly. Accusations, some of them against the Marquise, came from his lips. Athénaïs had sent, he swore, a poisoned letter to Fontainebleau on a day when he was to be there to hear supplications. She had caused other poison to be impregnated into Angélique de Fontanges' glove. Françoise reasoned with him. "Why terminate Your Majesty's life, when her power would have ended with you? And the Duchesse de Fontanges has a rot of the lungs."

As she said that, she was aware of suspicion. Could any consumption waste one so? The withered old woman, driving in the pumpkin-coach with her hair still of bright bronze-gold. . . .

"The will of God may be found in all this."

She heard her own voice, trite and dry still with the proverbial astringency of the governess. Helpless pity wrung her for the man who was King of France. No matter how the soul might be cleansed with repentance, prayer and fasting, there would always be that inner shrinking of remembrance of a time when the very intimacy of the flesh had been derided.

She recalled other things. Louis, bewitched in middle age by Fontanges and the rest; going out in half awareness of wrongdoing to perform it more widely and less discriminately. The evil done to the soul through the body had bitten deep. She remembered her own long hours of prayer for him, seeming unheard in their constant repetition. But perhaps after all they had not been.

"You are crying," said Louis.

Suddenly he moved toward her again and with great gentleness took her face between his hands and kissed her; her mouth, her cheeks and eyelids, then her hair. In the swiftness of change that had come over both of them she heard his voice altered, like a man's who is alive again having once died. "You are all I have," he said. "You are everything to me."

Françoise opened her eyes and saw his ravaged face. He was like a man who in the space of the last hour has heard of the death of an army. The color of his skin was ashen and the lines about his mouth and eyes seemed to follow the pattern of a skull. The eyes beseeched her.

The years fell back and she remembered Villarceaux.

She had been young then, and that fire she had thought died with youth. But how much greater the temptation seemed now! A fire lit in autumn, now that both of them grew old. A kindling of dry sticks to flame.

Such things were taught as pertaining to the devil. Had she not found that God, against her own will, always guided her? And to let the King be her lover now would not be the will of God.

287

"The Church says . . ." Somewhere, from the deeps that lay in her mind, that phrase stirred. She had found it a wall of stone against which argument failed, but one could lean thereon with reliance. In it was a gate to peer through and see the white-winged angels of God and breathe their content, a little. One did not pray, always, on a cushion before a crucifix, or on the steps which mounted to one's bed.

She saw his hurt as she withdrew. Dear God, must she wound him further? To put her arms round him would be what she most desired, and later nurse his head in her lap, as she had done so often with Louis-Auguste when the world laughed because he was lame.

"My poor little Louis. My own dearest boy."

She could not say it, even now, in the moment's resemblance he bore to the child she loved. She had said nothing; only withdrawing from him a little way, so that a square or two of the great baroque carpet lay between them. She knew how she would presently seem to him, after that denial; only, again, Maine's black-clad preceptress, whom he had for an instant desired out of a need for comfort rather than passion. She prayed that when she left him now he would not go from the room to a Soubise or Grammont, sidling by window-curtains or behind clipped trees in the garden. There was so much of that easy assuaging for him, with ashes afterward.

"I beg that Your Majesty will listen to me."

He had not moved again, only stood there where she had left him. "Do we need more words?" he said. "Surely you *know*—now! You're a woman; one whom I trust and need. You know of my hurt. There's no one else I could tell of it. Will you deny me, now, the comfort only yourself can give? You—who have seen how dearly I have paid for folly?"

His voice rose; he was, she saw, almost in anger. He had risen from that crushed shadow of himself to the likeness of a man who has been denied something he covets, which he thinks is his by rights. She rejoiced in this change in him, knowing that it would help him more easily to bear what she would have to say, later; what she must say now.

"It is no remedy for folly to embroil oneself further in it. As for hurt, it can be borne. I myself have borne it. The world goes on, and does not remember even kings for very long, in its pursuits. What has happened to Your Majesty need alter nothing, except to make for greater watchfulness. It has been known for long that *that* liaison must cease, as unworthy of you. What difference do these findings make—to that? For myself, I see none."

"For yourself!" he said. He was regarding her strangely. "You do not pretend amazement at my regard for you. You're not coy, thank God, like most women. Yes, I'll cease traffic with Madame la Marquise—I have done so for long. And then?" He smiled. "Let us not hedge regarding it. I have a higher opinion of yourself than of any woman I know. This faith is with the mind; I would wish to include in it the body also. Is that so desperate a matter? Yet you deny me."

"It is desperate indeed when the King of France goes from one adultery to another, forgetting his responsibilities in the lusts of his own flesh."

For an instant he recoiled, and his face became the cold-eyed mask she dreaded, knowing it for what it was, a protection against meddlesome fools. Had she gone too far, presuming overmuch on her influence with him? She waited, while a clock struck somewhere. The room felt cold.

Louis turned, and deliberately going toward a timepiece on the mantel, wound it. The little rasping sound broke the silence. The clock was tall and gilded, with weights in the form of sun and moon.

"You know how I am placed," he said. Carefully, his long fingers adjusted the pendulum. The steady ticking started, once again; he closed the case. She heard her own voice, clear and crisp as ice.

"Your Majesty is placed in a state so high that every least action of yours is reflected in all corners of Europe. When it pleased God to call you to the throne there was chastity and some fidelity among the people. Now in your own realm every young man beds with his neighbor's wife. Elsewhere in little courts where dukes lived simply, contentedly with their wives and children, there is now corruption. Each has his gilded coach, his *maison de joie,* in which

289

to parade his Montespan. I am aware that I shock Your Majesty. Possibly no one else in your realm would speak so. May I continue?"

He gestured with his hand. His face was turned from her, looking into the fire.

"You are the arbiter of Europe," she said. "Had you displayed the virtues that matched your magnificence, all the world would have followed suit. You have seen what befell instead of that. What then is said—" her voice trembled— "when the King of France, ending one double adultery, proposes to set up afresh, this time with the governess of his discarded mistress's children?"

"You are not—" he began. She silenced him.

"What will the world say, Your Majesty? What will it do? Do you think it will not laugh, because you dislike laughter? It will sin again, as Your Majesty shows no aversion to sinning. Ah, don't speak to me, or say I presume! It has been your fortune to occupy a place in the world whose influence in worldly things is so many times that which belonged to the Carpenter of Nazareth, that your failure is the greater disgrace."

She was erect, flushed, challenging him; seeing her, he was amazed. The meek widow Scarron! The comforter— this woman!

"You are like an angel of God," he said; his face was white. He spread out his hands, quite simply. "What would you have me do?"

She did not hesitate. "Go back to your wife, and make up in part for the years of unhappy neglect you have caused her."

He stared. The conception she presented was so alien to his long accustoming that his first thought, even now, was of repulsion. Some would say that Bossuet had prepared in her this speech, using his superb oratory through her gestures, her mouth. Others would assume a cruder reckoning and sneer behind raised hands. *Ménage à trois,* they would say, as Henri II and Catherine de Médicis had lived to the ordering of Diane de Poitiers. They would point to this woman as his *maîtresse en titre,* his black-robed whore in the sight of all heaven. There was nothing they would not say if this came about. "To curry favor," they would put it, "through the Queen!"

"But God will account it to Your Majesty," said Françoise softly. "Do you believe that you will regret?"

He shook his head, unable to find words. As though the racked emotions of the past hour had drained the strength of both of them, they moved with one volition and seated themselves, he assisting her gently, on the sofa. There was no need now to fear the onset of passion or to recoil at its swift denial. From then on they talked, in low voices, of many things; a middle-aged man, a middle-aged woman, seated side by side, not touching one another; only their hands lay near.

XII

Louvois by much pressure arranged an interview between the King and Madame la Marquise. Louis insisted that Françoise should also be present. She would not repeat anything of that degrading interview, in which Louis and herself had been insulted in every imaginable term, Louis particularly in the way in which he was vulnerable, owing to the remembrance of intimacy. Whatever else befell he would never forget that, or the things which had been said, or the manner of their saying. She herself had had the everlasting taunt of age, the usual names hurled.

She had stood with Louis later in the evening sunlight. Long shadows were beginning to lie on the terraces from the stiff ornamental trees. It was August and the dust outside made everything weary, scarcely enough water being found in all France to wash the pores of the jaded leaves.

The man beside her, who had been subjected to every conceivable coarseness of speech the hour before, did not turn or move.

"She told me," said Louis at last, quietly, "that my breath stank. If that is so I ask the pardon of those I have incommoded. One is not always aware of these things."

"One is not," she said practically, "and they make neither the beginning of this world nor its end. If Your Majesty is in any discomfort regarding it, a little box of cinnamon lozenges carried and taken from time to time will serve." She remembered Paul, whose teeth had blackened with his disease, being glad of them.

Louis turned to her on a gasping note of laughter that was more than half tears.

"How little vanity is left me," he said, "and how I thank my God for you!"

XIII

"I loathe death," said Louis.

Fontanges lay dead in Port-Royal at last. There was talk of poison. All his days Louis would hear that whisper for dead youth, accompanying the whispers already current for beautiful English Madame. Then, as now, it had been, "She could not have been ill enough to die; she was so young." Athénaïs, they said, had put poison in Fontanges' wine, steeped her glove in poison so that it entered through the skin at the base of the nails. She had engendered this slow rot, which killed slowly. They would say anything now of Athénaïs.

"I do not believe that," said Louis in his slow way. He had been unwilling to visit Angélique. He had gone, at last, returning filled with the disgust of death that had been with him from the time his mother, Anne of Austria, died. He began suddenly to talk of that now while the dark-red curtains of the traverse swung, swung. Hour by hour he would sit in it and talk thus, while Françoise listened, and outside the Court whispered about the length of their conversations. The *maîtresse en titre,* they called her now; yet they knew that Louis had gone back to the Queen. They were unable to tell, from the unemotional mask of the King's face, what he felt. Only Françoise knew. It had been purgatory to Louis to visit Angélique before she died, to order the carving open of the white skin after death, to keep hidden what had emerged from the mélange of blood and entrails; all findings locked away, unspoken of. The mother of his children should not know shame by even the voicing of suspicion; but he, who had been so enthralled by beauty and the world's glory, was faced now with the aspect of himself, nauseated by his body's recollection.

"Think of your own death," she had said to him, when he was unwilling even to visit Angélique. "She is dying; she has pleaded to see you." It was the same, she thought, in the shadows of the Queen's boudoir; with neither comfort nor solace except in one's own soul.

He had looked at her strangely. "In the hour of my death," he said, "I pray that you will be near me. I ask no more than that of God."

"She is dead," said the Court, and forgot.

"She is dead," said Athénaïs, and laughed to show that she had no care in this, that she would show her face in the world. The Duchesse de Fontanges had expired at half-past three in the afternoon. At the same hour on that day the first corner-stone had been laid of the convent built by Madame de Montespan for the Sisters of Saint-Joseph in the Faubourg Saint-Germain. Did not mesdames think that a singular coincidence? If others were *dévoué,* so would she be. Had she not always weighed her bread very carefully during Passion Week?

The legend of her new devotion ran about Paris. It was

assumed in many quarters that she, like La Vallière, would decide to take the veil. "How wrong they are!" said Athénaïs smoothly. Her blue eyes gleamed in anticipation. She would have a closet with glass doors facing the high altar. The great bell would ring out over Paris whenever she, the foundress, approached the building. Such a token of esteem gave one satisfaction. It was true that such as Madame de Maintenon would abjure this and similar innocent ambitions, dismissing them under the name of pride.

"But there are others to which she has attained, *sans doute,* which are less widely venerated." Madame la Marquise smiled, looking in her mirror. Her beauty was undiminished. She would win Louis again. How repulsed he had been by that death-bed! It had been mistaken of Madame to be so insistent on his attending it, as if visibly to triumph over her rival. Poor Fontanges, only remembered now as a manner of doing one's hair, in the way she had once tied it back, as a makeshift measure, while hunting, and Louis had asked her to wear it so always! Well, styles of hairdressing, and hair itself, were useless to Fontanges where she was now. How wise she had been to take so little notice of the King's lapse! Every man in middle age had one or two.

The King was so fond of little Toulouse. He would do anything for him. Surely Toulouse's mother would not be forgotten.

But the invitations for the Court progress into Flanders were issued, and Madame's name was not among them.

Appearances were preserved. The Queen was happy. Since her marriage she had not, she told everyone, had so much unfailing kindness from the King. "He came to me last night!" she would announce, like a child, rejoicing over cups of her interminable chocolate. The Court laughed and shrugged, turning to another domestic *dénouement;* the rupture of the Mademoiselle-Lauzun affair. The little man had grown in heedlessness and impertinence since his release. One day, returning from hunting covered with mud, he had flung himself down by the fire in Mademoiselle's *salon.*

"Louise de Bourbon, pull off my boots!" he demanded, and Mademoiselle, who had had a great deal else to put up with, rose suddenly to her great height and ordered him out of her presence.

XIV

THE COURT was changing. It was not a matter of one day, or even one year to the next. It would not have been possible for a traveler one season to describe Versailles as an access of bare perfumed flesh, transparencies, light satins, much paint and frizzed uncovered hair; and the next to see all in a darker tonality of plain gowns, heads covered with the discreet commode; a little book in the hand where before there had lain a spaniel, and a single jeweled crucifix worn instead of pearls. The *maintenon* was in vogue, the *fontanges* forgotten. One attended Mass, because the King did so.

He was increasingly regular in devotion. He was, as one knew, half Hapsburg, of that blood which had darkened and thinned into fanatical piety over generations of inbreeding from its source. Always by nature religious, he returned now to organized faith. The lapses with Montespan, the sporadic returns to the Church when he and she had parted company for Lent or the religious jubilee, flayed by the powerful oratory of the Archbishop of Meaux into a repentance that was temporary only, were over. Watching this quiet man, the distinction of whose sober dress so well became him, it became possible to sense the change which his spiritual reawakening had wrought in the very flesh. The face Françoise had once seen as a thought overlaid and gross was etched, now, almost invisibly until he laughed, with little lines. The features were fine-drawn, with the brows' high arch commanding. In any company, in any age, he would have been singled out as uncommon; would have dominated any assembly; would have graced, even, any stage.

He was the aristocrat *par excellence*. Years later, Françoise was to see him die. Before that she was to stand by him while surgeons made an incision into his bowel. Her memories of the final stench of gangrened limbs would be bound up with the remembered sight of the blood gouting, in little scarlet points, onto the whiteness of the towels she held. On both occasions Louis was fully conscious. On neither did he show any emotion other than disdain regarding his ordeal. He had once bared his heart to her, at a time when the foundations of his esteem crumbled. It was not necessary to do so a second time.

XV

OF THAT JOURNEY into Flanders she recalled many things, among them the puling of Madame la Dauphine, delivered recently of a second son and inclining, over-increasingly, to the solitude of the grave. To one of such expressed opinion it must have been doubly hard to be bundled into a State coach and exhibited at the various towns they passed through, "like a relic," she complained, "or a horse at a fair."

Her dark face settled into lines of discontent and she made to draw the blind across the window of the carriage. The *dame d'atour,* who rode opposite, prevented her.

"Let them see you," she said. "It's the only chance many of them will have."

"Why should they want to see me?" said the Dauphine fretfully.

"Because you are the mother of the heir to the throne. Remember the rejoicings when the Duc de Bourgogne was born."

Marie-Anne-Christine-Victoire shuddered. The noise of the crowds then had been abominable, and the bonfires they lit outside had made her start in her bed, thinking the Palace was on fire. "Thank Providence," had said her pig of a husband, "that this does not happen often. I could not endure it."

"*You* could not!" retorted Marie-Anne.

She turned her face away and thought how she detested all of them separately. But the King had dragged her on this interminable summer journey, to expose herself to the curiosity of the *canaille* inside a hot stuffy coach. And the purpose? Nothing but his own gratification. "He has no right to the towns of Flanders, in any case," thought Marie-Anne.

Then there was her husband, who increasingly resembled a toad. How she detested him! At least, with the passing of time, he had begun to leave her alone. He had attached himself to a fat pale devoted girl called Emily Choin, who had very bad breath. They lived together in undisturbed comfort at Meudon. But Monseigneur had been dragged on this journey too.

No one had wanted to come. Even that woman who sat in the coach, the *dame d'atour,* whom one detested also, had not wanted to come. All she wanted was to be at Maintenon, or to sit in a padded chair away from drafts.

"How hot it is!" said Marie-Thérèse.

Her face glowed and shone with heat so that the paint melted in runnels. The superb weather had continued till they reached Dunkirk. Everyone sat in barques and watched the glassy water disturbed by a sham fight between two frigates whose outlines were blurred with mist till they seemed like sea-phantoms. The heat was oppressive; the thunder of mock shells fired to play at war tore through the haze, and everyone expected a deluge.

Marie-Thérèse beamed at the *dame d'atour,* who sat near by, and then looked past her to where, in the distance, one could see a scarlet-clad back. The King and his gentlemen were in their own barque; from here, one could make out an array of periwigs. These closed together, almost merged with heat, wavered and fell apart. The water became a series of deep ripples. His Majesty was about to board the man-of-war. A twittering like that of many doves rose from the ladies' barque, and they perpared to follow.

Françoise sat motionless, feeling the pull of the boat. The heavy day had made her lethargic; she seemed to have been journeying all her life. Flanders, Alsace, land and water; Ambleteuse, Calais, Dunkirk, Sedan, Trèves. There had been feasting and military maneuverings and excursions and picnics. She went through it all placidly, a handsome middle-aged woman in a head-dress of black lace. She knew they pointed her out; that the crowds, regarding the Dauphine's lackadaisical face and the puffy one of the Queen, saw her also, and whispered. About that also she had acquired philosophy. She disliked these journeyings, but it was possible to carry oneself wherever one went. She disliked rumor, but was beyond it now. Whereas she had once been necessary to the King's children, so now she was necessary to the King.

He consulted her on everything. Before her eyes now she could see Louvois' face, with distrust written on it. Interfering, spying old woman, he called her, thinking of the beauty of Montespan, whom he adored, and of how it was seen no more.

Louvois suspected Françoise of wishing to direct affairs of State, but it was not so. She had obtained Charles his governorship long ago; she had placed an Abbé, a bishop, four nuns in responsible positions. More than that she had not done, and when Louis would turn to where she sat at her tapestry frame and ask, as he so often did, "And what does Your Solidity think?" she would say nothing of any value unless pressed for it.

But none of that would alter rumor, or prevent foregone conclusions.

The sound of dipping oars ceased. Strong arms assisted her, with all of them, up the ship's ladder and onto the deck.

The smell of tar mingled with the heat and the strong salt air. Men with lank pigtailed hair stood gaping at the ceremonies of Versailles. His Most Christian Majesty, Louis XIV, seating himself with his Court in precedence behind him, received representatives from England and Spain. Among these foreigners Françoise noted one man in particular; his great height singled him out, and also, covering his shoulders, the splendid luster of his own bright hair. His eyes were blue, set rather too close together, and she saw them rest for an instant on herself. She inquired who he was, when she could do so conveniently.

"Marlborough," came the reply. Françoise watched him, smiling and urbane above the King's hand. Something about the Englishman was too sleek; she did not trust him. Long afterward she was to remember clearly the impression gained on that day; but there was then no evidence that the sky had darkened, or the sound of the sea grown mournful.

The King gave a great fête on one journey. Fireworks shot and glittered into the night air as they had often done at Versailles. During the day they had all watched the red coats of Louis' army march, form, circle, present arms and disperse. Marie-Thérèse complained of the odor of gunpowder and of the released fireworks, which she said made her head ache. In front of her eyes were blobs of scarlet, marching.

How often she had watched the King's soldiers! Once she had seen them march through her land. It was true that the Low Countries were no longer strictly hers, because she had signed them away when it was arranged that she should marry Louis. But since then Louis had said that she should again possess them, and accordingly had marched his armies through. Marie-Thérèse did not care very much. If it pleased Louis, he could have the lands. She would rather he had them than Carlos, whom she could scarcely remember. Lands, armies; what did it all matter? The tramp of marching hurt her head; the blood beat against the top of her skull, like waves in a dome.

"They may take the lands," she thought, "if only we can go home," and somehow home seemed no longer Versailles, as it had been for so many years; but far across the southern peaks that jutted into the sky, that she had crossed that day to her wedding with the most splendid king in the world. Back, back; always forgetting, so that the kind arms of Molina, the soothing voice of Madame de Maintenon, the gleam of her own portrait on Madame's breast, faded, and she was small again, playing in the high-walled gardens of the Escurial, too small to do anything but tumble if she tried to run, so that someone, the voice of her stepmother Doña Mariana, scolded and said that it was not dignified.

Dignity; princesses. She was an Infanta of Spain. Infantas must live and die with dignity, must never cry in public, must never show their feelings; stiff, as though they were masks; painted, as though they were dolls. To live and die so; to live . . . and die.

"Versailles," said someone. "She should be got back to Versailles."

Madame, it was, speaking. Madame de Maintenon, the dark woman who had been so kind. Through the bounding pain of her head and her dry throat Marie-Thérèse sensed her presence; reliable, cool, efficient, making no fuss. She was glad Madame was here. Where was Louis?

Louis also had been very kind. She was so stupid. . . .

"*Querido*," she whispered. What was it she wanted to say? There had been so little time to say anything, and she was unable, in any case, to think of what it ought to have been. She felt the hands and heard the voices, passively; they seemed beyond her, as though the pain lowered a curtain between them and herself. She was hot, with a raging heat as though the sun were too near her. It burned her to the heart, this pitiless sun. The blood in her was boiling, leaping. There was no coolness anywhere. Always the yellow dusty roads were seen beyond the windows, as they had been ever since that journey long ago. What was it someone had said then, a man, a great Cardinal in his red robes, who had made

300

her marriage? His smile was like a cat's; she saw him against the jagged barren peaks that pierced the sky.

"There are no more Pyrenees," she heard him say.

"Thank God you saw how it was with her," said the King.

Versailles was about them. In its formal rooms, the final formality of royal death would come. On the bed lay the Queen, her face beaded with sweat. They had undressed her and the physician, Fagon, prepared to let blood from her arm. The faculty had shaken its head.

"If blooding will relieve the pain, for God's sake let blood," said Louis. He was white about the mouth and shaking, as always at the sight of infirmity. Fagon had curious ideas, it was whispered, about blood; he said it circulated through the heart and lungs.

"A botanist by trade," sneered Louvois. "He had better confine himself to herbs."

The room was crowded for the ceremony of the blooding of the Queen's arm. Courtiers elbowed one another; it was difficult to breathe in the close air. The sunlight was excluded by heavy blinds. On the bed the little, flax-headed woman moaned. Those who were unable to see, for the press, could hear.

"An abscess has formed under the arm." The news passed from Fagon to Madame de Maintenon, to the King, to the bystanders. Details were whispered and grew in importance until they bore no resemblance to themselves.

Fagon received the blood in a silver basin. It was dark and thin as wine; its letting seemed to give the patient some relief. The physician raised a harassed face that shone with heat under his curled perruque. "An hour will tell," he said. The Queen seemed to sleep.

Presently she opened her eyes and called for Françoise. "Madame, Madame."

"I am here," said Françoise.

"You are so good," said Marie-Thérèse. She struggled to speak. Gradually the things she had intended to say seemed less important, and the bed which contained her short body made up the whole of her world. Shapes came to her, both dark and bright; the voice of the priest, bringing the viaticum; the weakness of her own voice, making confession. The dry wafer of God lay between her lips and tongue. She was not in pain now, and for that she was glad. There was something, only something, she had to say. . . .

"Fix your thoughts on God," said the priest. She heard him, with a faint irritation. How could she do so, till she had done with the things of the earth? A dark shadow moved, against the color of the curtains.

"Madame—Madame—"

A voice answered; she could no longer hear the words. A mist was about her, blurring all features, all details; steadily deepening, like the falling of night. The thing she had to say was so important it must be shouted aloud, or no one would hear. Summoning all her strength, she called a name.

"The King!"

There was a ring on her finger. The removing of it took all her strength. She took it off, held it forth into the darkness.

"Madame . . ."

Someone answered; there were arms supporting her, tears falling on her face. A pleasant drowsiness overcame her; she had no limbs any more, no body. In herself she knew, without any fear, that she was dying; and presently they would carry her, with candles, into a great black-hung hall. Bells would toll for her, as they had done for dead Madame of England; only with longer sounding, as it should be, for a Queen. And presently the voice of Bossuet, the great Archbishop, would be raised for her, preaching to tiered row on row of listening courtiers. Seemly and eloquent, the funerals of Queens; pleasant to the waiting shades of one's forebears, the Kings of Spain, who stood about one now, the light shining on the odd apricot color of their hair.

"This is the first sorrow she has caused me through twenty years," said Louis. He had wept at the death and at the lying-in-state, but the day of the funeral he spent the evening hunting. Monseigneur the Dauphin passed the time in watching a circus horse. Madame la Dauphine went to bed, and Madame Liselotte wrote letters. Madame de Maintenon stared reflectively in front of her at the candles she had lit for the Queen's soul. The light from them flared on a diamond ring, and its clear blaze disturbed her thoughts, which were melancholy.

XVI

"WITHOUT YOU, where will he be?" said the Abbé's voice. "To whom will he go? To what woman? There has always been a woman; that is necessary to him. If he chooses a mistress, he will revert to a state of sin. That is understood; then he must re-marry, Madame, but where? Can he not follow his inclinations? The succession is assured. In all Europe it would be hard, at this present time, to find a princess suitable, even did the King desire it, which he does not. The King inclines to yourself, Madame. Is it for you to refuse God's task?"

The voice carped on, bringing with it a vision of lowered eyes behind spectacles. Françoise felt herself swamped, bedded in virtue. Was she to have no free choice?

Maintenon. Once she had considered that her dream, her life's fulfillment. Now—

"He will build you schools," said the Abbé's voice in her mind. With it there wrestled the voice of her own conscience, borne up, oddly, by the long-forgotten humor of Paul. She could almost hear him now, gibing at her. "Build schools? *Nom d'un nom d'un nom d'un chien,* why marry a man for such a reason as that?"

*　　*　　*

303

Madame de Montchevreuil, the wife of the King's confidant, was in the way of rising early in the morning before the sun had grown too hot. In this manner she looked forward to a cool walk in the woods, undisturbed by other company than that of the birds who sang so delightfully. Most of her own sex, she knew, were not due to be called for an hour or more with the indispensable morning chocolate; and about the other she troubled very little, having arrived at too many years of discretion for its members to trouble her.

Therefore she was surprised, when walking along the paths, to see on this particular morning a female figure, exercising itself among the trees. The woman was not, Madame felt sure, a lady of quality; she wore a plain hood tied over her head, and her skirts were of dark stuff. Nevertheless the peculiarity of her conduct intrigued Madame, who accordingly went toward her.

"You are in trouble—Madame?" The woman had, one saw, her face upturned to the sky; her hands outspread, as if to receive their benison. She was like a gipsy woman, who makes her life in the open; she seemed to have a oneness with the earth and the trees.

Then she turned, with a quick movement of her dark skirts, and one saw—with astonishment—Madame de Maintenon! What in God's name could she be doing here, at this hour? Madame—the all-powerful, whom one no longer mentioned except in whispers in very, very discreet company . . . who was said to be . . . *Mère de Dieu,* oneself had known her, a little, when she was Madame Scarron, and had a nodding acquaintance since, but now, this instant, what was one to do?

Yet there was no need to do anything—Madame de Maintenon, restored to sanity, came forward with her pleasant smile and her *"Bon jour, Madame!"*—as if there were nothing extraordinary. Well, she supposed there was not . . . for herself. But for *her,* who was never seen without a high *collet* and her hair covered with a hood, although, one now saw, she had very beautiful black hair still, and a beautiful white throat, which the wrapper she wore did not serve to conceal.

Madame de Montchevreuil chided herself for staring, and replied to Madame's *bon jour*.

"It was a surprise," she said, "to see Madame. I generally walk here by myself. The young ones, without doubt, are all asleep, and it is one time of the day when one has peace, to collect one's thoughts."

"Ah—peace! How much I desire it!"

One saw that Madame's head was turned away. From her, with the turn of the neck and shoulder, she seemed like a young girl. Had there not been some tale of when she *was* a young girl, running free in a Huguenot field in . . . Dauphiné, was it? Languedoc?

"Poor soul," thought Madame de Montchevreuil, who had a kind heart. She began to talk lightly and easily to Madame de Maintenon. Whatever heights she might have attained, or planned to attain, there was no doubt that troubles came too. And there was nothing, Madame knew, like company in trouble. She talked soothingly, lightly, of unimportant things. The sun rose and sent a golden radiance through the leaves.

"Listen to that bird!" said Madame de Maintenon.

She suddenly turned and, with an impulsive movement, laid her hand on the other woman's arm.

"Let me walk with you again tomorrow," she said. "In the early day."

XVII

So OFTEN she had risen, as now, and dressed herself to the light of candles, making ready to receive God before night turned to day. The movements of her fingers achieved from habit a certainty in the fastenings of laces and hooks; the freshly laundered linen fell, with a crumpled sound, over her head and shoulders as Nanon flung it, expertly and without disarranging her hair. Everything was familiar, and yet not so; this night was as other nights and yet so different as never to have been lived through before, nor ever to be so again. Outside a storm was blowing, as it had been on the night when Maine was born.

"How cold it is," said Nanon, and shivered. "Madame must guard herself against chill later, traveling to Maintenon in this snow." She drew aside the curtain a fraction and revealed the drifts, white and steadily thickening against the windows.

Françoise made a little peremptory movement of her hand. Drop the curtain, it said, we may be seen. She made a last adjustment of the lawn veil about her head; seeing, in the dim glass, the bride of Louis. She smiled; she was not so ugly.

> *Je ne suis pas si vilaine*
> *Avec mes sabots;*
> *Car le fils du roi m'aime . . ."*

Irresponsibly, the old song ran in her mind. For a moment she was Bignette again, running across the turkey-field to where Marie waited, her sabots making a clattering noise. There would be no more running and freedom again; no clear skies except in the spirit. Murcy was gone, and Maintenon. A princess spinning gold from straw. . . . Her realm would be in shadows. Never any more would she be alone.

"Madame, it is twenty-seven minutes past twelve." Nanon's voice. The schedule was appointed, the ceremony about to begin. One must not be late for a wedding with the King of France.

"I am ready."

The woman put her missal into her hand. It was elegantly bound with velvet, tooled and impressed heavily on a ground of golden silk. Her gown was likewise gold, with a stately pattern of twining leaves in the fabric. The linen which showed at throat and wrists was lawn-fine, plain and delicate. The head-veil of golden transparent stuff covered her hair. Her cloak was blue.

"Madame is beautiful," breathed Nanon. She saw again the little Françoise, with the white intelligent brow surmounted by a peak of soft hair. As Françoise moved to the door she felt the dragging of the heavy gown. Marie-Thérèse when she married Louis had had a train of silver so weighty that it had taken three attendants to bear it up. She herself was not so trammeled. She made her way to the place arranged.

The King came through the far door as she approached through the nearer one and she saw with relief that she had not kept him waiting. He was paler than usual, but calm; he smiled at sight of her, and bowed slightly. With him were Père La Chaise and the Marquis de Montchevreuil. Louis came over and placed her hand on his arm.

"Harlay is robing," he murmured. "Before he comes—"

He gestured, and there was brought to her a cloak the color of her own. Edging the sapphire-blue velvet was the royal ermine. "Only for tonight!" said Louis. They put it on her shoulders.

Now she was appareled like a queen. The door opened again and the Archbishop of Paris entered. Françoise saw the glint in his green vestments from the candle his almoner carried. The scene had taken on again the quality of a dream. The fine stuff of Louis' coat was the only reality, felt beneath her fingers. His arm beneath was steady and firm. They walked on, as it seemed unendingly, through the unlit corridors. Their branched candles flared for an instant across capitals and walls and then left them, again, in darkness; their footsteps on the thickly carpeted floors made no sound. A procession of ghosts, she thought. "A goose walked over my grave. . . ."

The remembered voice came, light and childish, heedless in spite of that moment's fear. The fair flesh, the golden hair, were before her, as if the candlelight conjured them. Athénaïs, alone and forsaken, the prey of terrors by night and partaker of ashes by day, that woman dead while yet living, why did she recall her in this hour? What did she think of, alone in her great bed at Clagny, at Bourbon, in her house in

Paris that had cost four million écus to build? Did she think of *her* on this night? Did she pray?

Tears filled Françoise' eyes. She would never be free of memory. No matter whether or not they ever met again, each would remain in that of the other.

The chapel glimmered with lit candles. Spread on the altar was a snowy cloth, with grapes interwoven for the true vine. Françoise fixed her eyes on the altar as they made toward it. Last time—last time, it had been Paul who waited for her, sensitive to ridicule so that he made the priest say their Mass in his own little oratory rather than in the public church. The room then had been thronged. It was not so now. A few invited figures were grouped about the altar. Louvois, her enemy, was there. She saw his opaque eyes fasten on her face. Nanon and Montchevreuil's wife were the only women. Chamarante, the King's confidant, and Bontems, his valet, and the three priests made up the rest.

She knelt with the King before the altar. The watching faces faded. The murmur of the voice of Père La Chaise, beginning Mass, grew louder and more distinct. Last time she, a very new convert, had hardly known the variations and what they meant.

"Accendat in nobis Dominus ignem sui amoris, et flam-mam aeterne caritatis . . . pleni sunt coeli et terra gloria tua. Take, and eat ye all of this . . . may the author of sin have no share in any of her actions."

She heard them all; the prayers for fruitfulness, when she knew bitterly, as before, there would be none. She received the Body of God by the side of Louis; they exchanged their rings. She forgot the others, the hatred in the heart of Louvois so that he had only consented to be present at this marriage provided it was never made public; the mockery and laughter there would be on the morrow, when the world heard. More and more the presence of God seemed the only reality, and His will the only mystery in the making of Louis and herself one flesh. What the purpose of it all might be she did not know. Later, remembering, it seemed that that one prayer sounded more strongly than all the others, and that the candles shone brightly behind the white head of M. de Paris then, investing it with a kindly and benevolent light.

"And mayest thou see thy children's children; peace upon Israel . . . even unto the third and fourth generation; and arrive at their desired old age."

"The King of France is the husband of the widow of Scarron!"

Versailles chattered of it; the bells of Paris rang with it. The secret that was no secret would be known everywhere by word of mouth. There was much laughter, as she had foreseen, and the launching of scurrilous verse. One cartoon showed the meeting of Paul and Louis at the gate of the infernal regions. Nothing was left unuttered by the tongues which had given her no peace.

They would talk, as she knew, for the rest of her life; most of all those who were too young to remember. Ah, the widow Scarron had done well enough! To have come from a prison, where she was born, through a life of light virtue, through marriage to a buffoon, through the feeding of oats to the horses in the stable of M. d'Albret, to the King's bed!

"There is no compensation," she was to write later, "for the loss of liberty." But now, in the firelit room of the Château de Maintenon, it was not time to remember such things. Those who laughed callously were many, vying with those who said that, after all, this was no new matter, one favorite replaced another; "Maintenaint" had been the King's mistress for years.

Only she knew, and he, what passed; the truth in both their minds was clear. Later, remembering that night, she recalled gratefully that he had used her with great gentleness and courtesy, his aging bride. Often in earlier days, it had been she who, as the elder, had thought of him as a boy; almost as Louis-Auguste whom she could protect and nurse tenderly. Then again he had been the King whose will she, as so many others, dared not oppose. But now it was neither of these, and they were to one another as she described it, later, in the darkness of the curtained bed beyond which, dimly heard, the storm still raged on the road between Maintenon and Versailles.

"Only a man and his wife, Louis. Both of us growing old. Is there any other end to which we must come, after all?"

He smiled in the darkness. "We are not yet so old that I cannot love you. And so I do, I have done—ah, for long, my dear!"

He must not forget, he told himself, her physical delicacy in his own robust strength; her inexperience, despite her age and great learning in almost every other matter. With the humility grief had brought him he saw himself, not as the sultan of a score of pampered women, but a man, naked as he would be before God, to this woman who looked first at the soul. To his doubt as to whether he could ever bring her bodily pleasure was added remembrance, like and unlike hers; the memory of the Spanish marriage, the prudish resistance of the little overbred, nunlike Infanta Queen; driving him to the Grammonts, the Montespans, the Fontanges of the world, until through the flesh his very self had been imperiled.

What wretchedness there had been! But now there was a glow in his heart. He was aware of the presence of his wife, calm and fulfilled in the darkness; he heard her quiet breathing and spoke softly in case she were already asleep.

She answered him swiftly, however; turning, he could see within the curtains' dimness the bird-bright quality of her eyes. He watched, quietly happy, the light spread and grow through the joints in the shuttered windows.

EPILOGUE

Saint-Cyr, 1717

THE WOOD-ASH FELL in the grate with a soft crumble; the tiny sound recalled the old woman in the bed. She stirred, smiled faintly, and moved her fingers as if to test their stiffness. There had been voices, sounding lately in her ears; how near they had seemed! "It is almost as if I were already dead, and again with them."

But she had not that burden typical of the very old, the clouded mind that confuses past with present. The owners of the voices were dead, and she knew it. She had outlived them all. The actors in her early story, shadows in the night; Villarceaux, Paul, the thousand clowns of laughter; Ninon, dead in sorrow for the death of her son. Ninon, whose magic had destroyed three generations' happiness, who had lived to be very old. Why should she come to mind so clearly? Their paths had crossed, true, but then they had divided; neither wanted the same things from the world. But once when Ninon was greatly aged, she had come to her, Françoise, secretly at Marly. There, among the tasteless magnificence that Louis had raised out of a valley cleft between arid rocks, she had heard the old woman's cackle over matters that were unmentioned now.

"So your own foundation of Saint-Cyr bought the portrait of you, *chérie,* that Villarceaux painted to console himself, as naked as the day you were born; and have destroyed it, or hidden it in a cellar, or painted a Superioress's robe over the top." And she had laughed, with her high cracked silvery laughter, and tapped her stick on the ground, and made idle remarks about her *chambre jaune,* and soon after taken her leave. One would never know if it were true about the son who had slain himself for love of her, half-crazed with shock when he found she was his mother. One would never know so many things.

A Superioress? Was she so? She remembered Ninon's gibe. It was true that, when Saint-Cyr had first been built, Françoise had not meant it for a cloister. Louis would not have had it so. Louis had insisted that the instructresses should not be nuns; that the pupils should wear brown tammy gowns with lace cuffs and collars and aprons, never black. "I detest black. . . ."

Well . . . Saint-Cyr was a convent now. Such a change had been found necessary, not only on account of that theatrical production of Racine's which everyone talked about and which had put frivolity into the girls' heads even though its subject had been chosen to be so innocuous.

Esther. She grimaced a little into the darkness, recalling the excitements of the time. It had been the year after the revolution in England and James II and his queen, that Modena princess who had once been involved in the affair of Agrippina's crown, had come to one performance. It had been a diversion for them in their exile, as well as being a pivot of speculation for all the Court.

Esther! How many tongues had wagged round that subject of Racine's, saying that it was all an allegory chosen by Françoise, herself, she being the virtuous Esther who married King Ahasuerus after his displeasure in banishing haughty Vashti, who was of course Athénaïs. And somehow during the presentation of Racine's lines by the pretty young girls who were attired, for the occasion, in jewels once worn by Louis himself when he had danced in the Apollo ballets—and with such success that Racine, when called for, had been found on his knees in the oratory, terrified of falling again into his besetting sin of pride— somehow, during all that, Françoise had thought of Athénaïs, the disgraced and banished Vashti, and had not been able to get her out of her mind.

They said Athénaïs had grown very devout, giving away all she had in alms to the poor and sleeping always with candles lit by night in terror of the devil, with a metal belt about her that pierced her flesh.

"She continued on into old age still as beautiful as the day."

So they said, so the Marquise's kinsman, the little, hyper-critical Duc de Saint-Simon said, hating the supplanter who was herself. He could never credit in her any good intent, could not believe that, when she heard of that lonely death and sought for privacy to weep alone, her tears were genuine.

"How can she presume to show grief for Madame de Montespan?" came his voice. "What a hypocrite she is—that old witch!"

Always he had called her so. He and Charlotte-Elizabeth of Orléans had vied with one another in the foulness they spread, both in France and abroad, concerning her. Long ago when Louis was alive his officers had intercepted a letter of Madame Liselotte's. Françoise had faced her with it quietly, leaving the woman terrified and weeping. But now Louis was dead the letters would again be scudding across Europe toward Hanover and England, carrying lies about her to the sound of the courier's hooves.

Yes, since the English Revolution there had been a focus for resentment against Louis' action in revoking the Edict of Nantes.

They blamed her for that. It was convenient now to do so; to gloss over the fact that the Revolution had been a step long expected, not dictated suddenly by force of altered circumstances, or a sudden intensity of hatred flaming out of the old feud. She could no more have hastened or prevented it than she could have stopped the tides from running. She had prayed for the Huguenots in her little gilded gallery in the Chapel of Versailles and tried to see that the matter might, eventually, come to good. More she could not do.

Had hers not been a forced conversion? Where would she have been, now, what could she have done, if she had continued to hold out against the forces that drew her against her will, toward the center? There would have been no Saint-Cyr, no Noisy and Ruel even, no Maintenon, where so many penniless girls had learned to lead happy, useful lives.

That had been her achievement . . . and the child whom

she had taken from a starving mother's arms by the roadside and brought up as her own, and the little daughter of Charles who had been neglected and ill-treated by her parents, and even the small Mademoiselle de la Tour she would have brought sometimes to her now, here, in her chamber, would have been homeless, hopeless, as so many others.

She had had to suffer to be able to understand.

"If in my Lord's sight I have betrayed my own conscience; if I have broken faith for my own advancement; if I have done the things I ought not to have done, and left the things I should, then may God punish me."

Strange that, in the darkness of the night as now, she should sometimes in her own heart go back still to the impromptu Huguenot prayers.

But now there were others with which to pass the darkest hours. Silently, and with the laboriousness which she always attached to it, she said over the silver beads of her Rosary; three times over the joyful, the sorrowful, the glorious mysteries. With every bead a picture grew in her mind; Christ incarnate; Christ wounded; Christ risen, and ascended into Heaven.

"So may He take me to Himself, as I pray. So may I rejoin all my dear ones."

How beloved she had been! Not as many women are; not by children of her own body. Not, in the end, for that body at all, in spite of beauty; not for youth. But of the love that comes with giving, found in odd corners and hidden ways, she had had her abundant share.

She crossed herself devoutly in the dark. Very soon, in the nature of things, she would die. She felt the approach of death as a gradual severing of ties, an acceptance of its nearness as no longer strange. It might come tonight; she knew no fear and small curiosity. God, Who provided for all contingencies, would provide for that. If she lived till tomorrow she would again receive His body. If she died tonight she would see Him with her eyes.

"And so we go on, and this is only a beginning."

Marie d'Aumale, stealing in a little time later, saw the stilled hands and breathed a prayer of thankfulness that after all the excitements of the day *la mère* was peacefully asleep.